HALF A REVOLUTION

Half a

CONTEMPORARY FICTION
BY RUSSIAN WOMEN

Revolution

edited and translated by MASHA GESSEN

with a preface by OLGA LIPOVSKAYA

CLEIS
PRESS

Published in the United States by Cleis Press Inc., P.O. Box 8933,
Pittsburgh, Pennsylvania 15221, and P.O. Box 14684, San Francisco,
California 94114.

Book design and production: Peter Ivey
Cleis logo art: Juana Alicia
Printed in the United States of America
First Edition
10 9 8 7 6 5 4 3 2 1

Library of Congress Cataloging-in-Publication Data:

Half a revolution : contemporary Russian women's short fiction /
    edited and translated by Masha Gessen ; with a preface by Olga
    Lipovskaya. — 1st ed.
        p.   cm.
    ISBN 1-57344-007-8. — ISBN 1-57344-006-X (paper)
    1. Short stories, Russian—Women authors—Translations into
English. 2. Russian Fiction—20th century—Translations into
English. I. Gessen, Masha.
PG3286.H35 1995
891. 73'01089287—dc20   94-40988
                                                              CIP

Contents

Acknowledgments

This project was inspired by the work of my mother, Yelena Gessen, a writer, translator, and scholar of Russian women's fiction. My mother, who taught me most of what I know about writing and literature and everything I know about translation, died of breast cancer in August 1992, a week before her fiftieth birthday. She never knew I would work on this project, but I have her to thank for inspiration and wisdom.

Many thanks to the people who took the time to read and comment on parts of this manuscript: Lisa Frank at Cleis Press, Keith Gessen, Mimi McGurl, Sara Miles, and Katrin Sieg.

Many thanks to the writers who took the time to work, talk, and become friends with me in the process of working on this anthology: Nina Gorlanova, Marina Paley, Natalia Shulga and her husband Denis Klimanov, Nina Sadur, and especially Svetlana Vasilenko, without whom this book would not have been possible.

A Note on the Translation and Transliteration

I have attempted to create texts that are seamless and idiomatic in American English without introducing cultural references that are not in the original text. Thus, any obvious English-language references or quotes come from the original (for example, the T.S. Eliot quotation in Natalia Shulga's "Mashka and Asiunia").

The names of books or periodicals mentioned in the stories appear in translation unless the Russian name is used because it is extremely well-known in the West—for example, *Pravda*.

I have chosen transliteration conventions used by most U.S. English periodicals as being most likely to be familiar to the reader. These are used in transliterating all Russian names and other words unless an American spelling of a particular name is firmly established (e.g., Tchaikovsky) or the transliteration might cause confusion (e.g., a name is transliterated as *Asya* rather than *Asia* to avoid confusion between a girl and a continent).

Names

Every effort has been made to make references by name consistent within stories. Still, a brief explanation of the Russian system of address might help alleviate confusion.

Russian operates in last names, names-and-patronymic combinations, and first names and their diminutives. In marriage, the wife usually (though not always) takes the husband's last name by adding a feminine—an *a* or a *ya*—ending to it (with the exception of some non-Russian last names). The last name of a character in Irina Polianskaya's "The Clean Zone" is Tisyn. His wife's last name is Tisyna.

The polite way to address an adult in Russian is by using her name and patronymic. The patronymic is formed from the father's first name. For example, Tisyn is addressed as Anatoly Vikentyevich—Anatoly, son of Vikenty.

The full forms of first names—such as Maria, Natalia, or Yelena—are rarely used alone (without a patronymic). People who know each other well use the diminutives of each other's first names. Often, a diminutive is formed by replacing the last syllable of the full first name with the sound *sha*: the diminutives of Maria and Natalia are Masha and Natasha, respectively. In other cases, a name is shortened: Yevgenia becomes Genia, Yelena becomes Lena, and Svetlana turns into Sveta. Other diminutives "soften" a name to the Russian ear—as with Anna, which turns into Ania or Asya.

The formation of diminutives doesn't end there. Endless combinations of suffixes and endings are available to create modified forms of diminutives. The most important of these is the suffix k, which is used to refer to someone in a more familiar, slightly dismissive and borderline rude way. An example is Mashka, the form of the name Masha used in Natalia Shulga's story "Mashka and Asiunia." Children use the -ka diminutives more often than adults. Other suffixes serve to create more affectionate forms of address. Asiunia, for example, is an affectionate form of Asya, which is a diminutive of Anna.

Some terms that appear frequently in this book

The Komsomol (The Communist Youth League): the Communist Party organization for fourteen-to-twenty-eight-year-olds (membership was virtually mandatory).

NKVD (Narodny Komitet Vnutrennikh Del): The People's Committee for Internal Affairs, as the secret police was once known.

The Oktiabrists: The Communist Party organization for school children between the ages of eight and ten (membership mandatory).

The Young Pioneers: The Communist Party organization for schoolchildren between the ages of ten and fourteen (membership mandatory).

Preface

OLGA LIPOVSKAYA

Re-vision—the act of looking back, of seeing with fresh eyes, of entering an old text from a new critical direction—is for women more than a chapter in cultural history: it is an act of survival.
—Adrienne Rich, "When We Dead Awaken: Writing as Re-Vision"

Women's literature in Russia, from the time of Katherine the Great to the present, barely exists outside our imaginations. It does not exist as a separate entity because what exists is Great Russian Literature, undivided by gender. Yet if an average Western reader were to name three or four Russian writers, all of them would without a doubt be male: Tolstoi, Dostoyevski, Solzhenitsyn, and, maybe, Pushkin. If a woman writer wanted to assert herself as one, she was welcome to "ladies'" lit—and male writers would oblige by kissing her hand and providing paternalistic support. Most ladies did not take this option. The stereotypical Russian perception holds the feminine to be secondary, meek, like vignettes or miniature landscape paintings—the minor weaknesses and avocations of bored pretty ladies. Even self-confident women writers like Anna Akhmatova, Marina Tsvetayeva, and our contemporary Tatiana Tolstaya, avoid the "ladies" definition like the plague and insist on using the masculine form of the words *poet* and *writer* to refer to themselves.

Against the backdrop of an apparent and ideologically sanctioned equality of the sexes—reflected in many of the best examples of the Socialist Realist school of writing—the Russian and Soviet everyperson's consciousness continued to hold the male to be primary and the female secondary. While the works of Soviet writers always featured a female colleague, a faithful companion, or a leading female tractor driver alongside the male hero, in the real live writers' world, their female colleagues remained secondary players—always the second secretaries of the party committee, real or fictional.

The transformation of the Soviet regime beginning in the mid 1980s created new conditions for the development of literature. Frames widened and floodgates opened. New kinds of literature emerged with uncanny speed from the Russian underground and diaspora. Literature of the Socialist Realist variety was slowly but surely pushed aside by the emerging works (though I want to believe that the former will not become history but remain as just one of many literary movements).

Thanks to these changes, a Russian women's literature began to take shape and gather strength. Political and economic transformations along with a revision of the goals and meaning of the creative process compelled writers to unite into groups that would help them to survive culturally, socially, and economically.

Politics divided writers into the "left" and the "right" (I am using quotation marks to denote the purely semantic value of these categories to a Western reader), "Westerners" and "Slavophiles." As the underground culture made its way to the surface, divisions among literary schools and movements began to emerge: conceptualists claimed their place, as did avant-garde writers, writers of the "literature of evil," necrorealists, and even classical realists. Living conditions demanded a division between men and women. The articulation of gender divisions on the literary scene took place against the background of a shift in gender relations in society, whereby women were forced out of the political arena, economic structures, and the cultural elite. Women, who had held a third of the seats in the Supreme Soviet under the Soviet quota system, hold barely over five percent of the seats in the current parliament; among the growing number of unemployed, seventy percent are women. Meanwhile, the mass media spare no effort in pushing the image of the traditional bourgeois family, in which the husband makes money while the wife is a happy homemaker and mother.

Women had to fight for the right to speak in the new conditions of market competition in the publishing field. The power in the literary establishment continues to belong entirely to men, as it always has. A collective effort on the part of women writers was necessary to obtain the means of and access to publication. It was in this almost accidental way that contemporary women's literature emerged. A conscious unity would come later. It is no accident, in my opinion, that the titles of collections of women's writing have evolved from *Women's Logic* and *A Clean Little Life* in 1989 to *The New Amazons* and *The Abstinent Females* in 1991 and, most recently, in 1993, *What Does Woman Want*, a collection of winning entries in a women's fiction competition that even included a prize for the "best feminist story."

The names of authors are different from book to book, and newer collections boast a wider age range, stronger voices, and a variety of new young names. Only in the last four years have Marina Paley and Valeriya Narbikova been publishing their work; each has asserted an independent and entirely new voice in contemporary writing (although, strange as this might seem, this fact has gone almost entirely unnoticed in the numerous works of contemporary literary criticism). By and large, Russian critics do not focus on women's writing; gender analysis in literary criticism is almost entirely absent, and the works of women writers are mentioned far less frequently than the latest creations of male writers.

Meanwhile, there are significant differences in the works of male and female writers, which could make for some interesting analysis. Briefly, as the realities of men's and women's lives have diverged in the last five to seven years, so has the distinction between male and female writing become more apparent in purely formal, external characteristics. With the advent of "freedom of speech," stereotypically masculine traits in men's writing have become more vivid and pointed; much is written about war, violence, the military, prisons—and this picture is colored, too, by the publication of older authors' writings about the horrors of the Gulag; sexuality is discussed in more explicit and crude ways, as though Communist censorship had forced authors to portray romantic love in place of real biological instincts, and, relieved of its burden, the Soviet male has started hollering full-voice about his previously suppressed sexual needs. Add to this all sorts of off-color subject matter, which has become profitable. Male writers of the older generation—shaped in the Writers Union— are able to stake out the more marketable literary areas, an ability that is perhaps directly traceable to the Socialist Realist past, when the province of women writers was love and domestic drama (distinctly less significant topics, from the viewpoint of ideology). In this environment, honor and respect were reserved for writing concerned with pressing sociopolitical issues—the province of men.

Women's writing has tended toward what might be called universal human subjects: interpersonal relationships, helping one's loved ones, love and survival. It seems that women have claimed these themes from classic Russian literature, with Ludmila Petrushevskaya and Marina Paley picking up the great tradition where Tolstoi and Dostoevski left off. Conditions in which Russian writers—and readers— live and work grow more cruel every day. But while most work by male writers reflects and amplifies this cruelty, the stories of women writers clearly (again, in keeping with the traditions of Russian classics) evidence the search for a way out; through compassion, the belief in goodness, a conscious resistance to evil, and a struggle for survival. Women's consciousness as it is reflected in women's literature refuses to submit to *temporary* evil such as war, violence, or a people's court (as in Vladimir Makanin's "A Table Covered with Cloth," a vivid example of contemporary Russian dystopian fiction). Women cannot afford to believe in a transcendent evil, for that would destroy our hopes for our children's future. Not coincidentally, more attention is paid to children in Russian women's literature than in Western women's writing—and this, in my opinion, also reflects reality. We spend more time talking about our children than is customary among my friends in the United States, Britain, or Germany. We don't just talk about them; we are sick at heart for them, as Nina Gorlanova describes.

Finally, a few words about the translation. Translation is always an approximation, always a tightrope-walking act. Often the most common of words and the most everyday of details are distorted for lack of cultural equivalence. Mastery of the language, no matter how great, is insufficient for finding those bridges and tie-ins that will allow a curious American reader to reach an understanding of the conditions of our lives, the makeup of the air in Perm, or the atmosphere in the bohemian cellars of Moscow. Masha Gessen has met this challenge, and the result will be another set of bridges and passageways between our two cultures. I happen to believe that women's writing is better suited for this purpose of cross-cultural communication than men's writing. For me—as, I believe, most women—language is a tool for expressing empathy, whereas in the male culture it is more often an instrument of control, power, and manipulation (this is, of course, merely a hypothesis). In addition, the works chosen for translation by Masha Gessen and the mastery of the translation prove once again that in the verbal sphere women are more highly evolved than men.

This collection includes almost no writers of the youngest generation, but I hope that if this publication is successful, it will serve as only one of the first steps in acquainting Western readers with the richness and diversity of contemporary Russian women's writing.

Olga Lipovskaya
St. Petersburg, Fall 1993

Olga Lipovskaya is the founder and editor of Zhenskoye Chteniye *(Women's Reading), a formerly underground journal that introduced many classic Western feminist texts (most of them in Lipovskaya's translation) as well as the writing of then-unpublished Russian women to the Russian reader. She is the founder and director of the Gender Issues Center, a research and education group in St. Petersburg.*

Introduction

After sketching out this introduction—a few paragraphs explaining that women's fiction in Russia has just started to emerge, that a critical discussion of it has barely begun—I went looking for details to flesh out these statements. I surrounded myself with about five years' worth of back issues of the so-called "thick journals"—the half dozen literary monthlies that traditionally serve as harbingers of trends and names in contemporary writing and criticism. I was operating on the assumption that work by writers I think of as new would have appeared in these journals for a few years before they became "names" on the literary scene, and that a discussion of women's writing would have been simmering for a while before it seemed to reach a boiling point in 1990. I was wrong.

Hours of scanning the tables of contents of the journals yielded nothing aside from a couple of stories that were also included in anthologies of women's writing: no earlier works, no indication that a trend was taking shape. What I had thought was a heuristic oversimplification proved entirely, absurdly true: women's fiction—which is to say, fiction by women who believe that being women is not incidental to their writing—is a new, almost totally unexamined phenomenon in Russian literature, and, unlike other literary trends in recent years, it emerged from outside the literary establishment. It is a phenomenon that announced its existence in 1989, with the publication of three anthologies: *Women's Logic*, *A Clean Little Life*, and *She Who Bears No Ill*. As the critic Pavel Basinsky wrote in *The Literary Gazette* in 1991, "The sound of the explosion was deafening."

This sardonic statement served as the opening shot in a debate on the subject of the very existence of women's fiction as a literary entity. Writing about the anthology *She Who Bears No Ill*, Basinsky said, "Whether the authors intended this or not, what happened was an action that is immodest, a challenge: they have declared the existence of a certain new entity in contemporary literature, and they are the only ones who can be held responsible for assessing its true scale."

A subsequent issue of the newspaper carried a reply by the critic Yelena Gessen, which introduced the term *male chauvinism* to Russian mass media. Still, in response to the above quote, Gessen wrote, "That is, basically, a fair statement. This is the first time we have talked about women's fiction that identifies as such, that declares itself as such, and that defends its right to be considered a genre."

Most of the stories in this collection come from two of the five anthologies of women's fiction that have been published in Russia in the last four years—the two that were edited by women. This distinction has far more than a symbolic significance. Against the background of the discourse on the existence of women's fiction, these two anthologies were compiled by editors who themselves identify strongly as women writers. These editors—Larisa Vaneyeva, who put together the 1990 anthology *She Who Bears no Ill* (the title story from which is included in this volume), and Svetlana Vasilenko, who compiled the 1991 *New Amazons*, have been primarily responsible for asserting and maintaining a collective women's voice in post-perestroika Russian literature. I owe a debt of gratitude to Vasilenko, who helped me immeasurably with contacts, advice, and, generally, her deep commitment to seeing that the work of the loose and ever-expanding group of women to whom she refers as "the girls" finds an audience.

Only one piece in this volume is not in one of the anthologies that have already been published. It is Natalia Shulga's "Mashka and Asiunia." Shulga's story is different from the others in two additional ways: its theme—lesbian—and the age of its author—twenty-three. The piece was recommended to me by Vasilenko, who had selected it for her next volume (and who was the only person in the literary community to respond to my desperate calls for lesbian-themed short writing—a search that yielded little else). Vasilenko's next anthology, which adds several new and younger voices to the ones featured in the previous two books, has been languishing in search of a publisher for over a year. Moskovsky Rabochy, the large Moscow house that put out the first two books, has switched entirely to the more commercially viable mystery and romance genres. Vasilenko's efforts to self-publish the book have so far met with a cold response from virtually everyone, including potential printers.

The difficulty of selling newly commercial publishers on serious work is not unique to women writers, of course. But women writers cannot lean on the support structures enjoyed by men, be those the old establishment with its roots in the Writers Union or the new establishment with its roots in the old underground. As Olga Lipovskaya describes in her preface, the old establishment is stolidly male-dominated, as was the underground, whose legacy is dozens of "typewritten journals." In 1986, when Lipovskaya declared her intention to start a journal dedicated to women's issues, her choice of subject matter was roundly ridiculed by members of Leningrad's Club 81, an association of underground publishers. In a time when writers, allowed a brief period of heady free-for-all exchange under glasnost, are facing new challenges in the battle to be heard, women writers are silenced twice: by a lack of interest on the part of publishers and a lack of support on the part of "serious" literary structures.

All of the pieces in this anthology are, in a sense, about silence. It is not coincidental that the majority of writers whose names have become associated with women's fiction—and the majority of writers in this anthology—belong to what the writer and critic Andrey Bitov has termed "the mute generation." Until the late 1980s, the generation that came of age under Brezhnev, having missed the relative freedom of exchange allowed during Khrushev's "Thaw," was virtually unrepresented in Russian literature. "Resigned, we never stuck our necks out, living through twenty years of winter," sang Russian singer-songwriter Katia Yarovaya about this generation at the dawn of glasnost. "And no longer does anyone wait to hear what our generation has to say—when now is precisely the time when we should be in our glory." So when this generation of thirtysomethings finally asserted itself in the latter years of perestroika, much of what its representatives—especially its female representatives—wrote about was silence itself.

Some, like Nina Gorlanova in "Confessional Days at the End of the World" and Irina Polianskaya in "The Clean Zone," dig for the roots of the silence: Gorlanova deals with the relationship between the writer and the censorious state while Polianskaya, whose story is set in a nameless nuclear-research town, chooses characters whose lives were shaped by forbidden subjects. Galina Volodina, Tatiana Tayganova, and Shulga also choose characters who have been denied the right to speak: the group of tenants in "Election Day"; the peasant woman in "Speak, Maria!"; and the young girl who is in love with her best friend in "Mashka and Asiunia." Other stories in this collection represent demonstrative violations of the rules of socialist realism. Yelena Tarasova's graphic journey into a mysteriously diseased body is an affront to the disembodied tradition of Soviet literature (the story itself was received as a personal affront by a number of literary critics). Nina Sadur's set of short shorts dedicated to the world of supernatural phenomena, "Touched," is a playful answer to censors who banned her work for years for being "mystical." Valeriya Narbikova's "In the Here and There," packed full of literary, pop-cultural, and political references, seems to laugh at the critics who have thrown up their pens at Narbikova's hallmark absence of narrative:

the ultimate insult to a system that has demanded that every story have the *right* beginning, middle, and end.

The publication of these stories in recent years in Russian—and, now, in English—is hardly the "deafening explosion" heard by Basinsky; still, the fact of their appearance is revolutionary. In Russian a hot-blooded person, like a fast car, is said to "start at half a revolution." That saying could well be applied to the speed with which women's fiction became a literary phenomenon in Russia. But with all the obstacles facing these writers, theirs is in danger of remaining merely half a revolution. We can only hope that the work done by Vasilenko, Vaneyeva, and other women writers will form the foundations of women's literary presence in the new world of Russian literature that is just starting to take shape. We can only hope that the publication of these anthologies in both Russian and English is not an isolated blip on the historical radar screen but rather the opening phrases in a long conversation between Russian women writers and both Russian and American readers.

Masha Gessen
New York and San Francisco, January 1994

I. Realities

Confessional Days: In Anticipation of the End of the World

NINA GORLANOVA

"We were born to turn the fairy tale into reality," declared an early Russian Communist youth song. As it happens, the Russian word for fairy tale (skaska) rhymes with Kafka. Hence a parody: "We were born to turn Kafka into reality." Perhaps no one conveys this sentiment more clearly than Nina Gorlanova, whose largely autobiographical short stories have been gathered into two collections, A Rainbow Every Day *(1987) and* Loved Ones *(1990).*

Details of Gorlanova's life are woven tightly into her work, including "Confessional Days": She was born in 1950 in a village near Perm, a city in the Urals, where she now lives with her husband (also a writer) and five children. The terrain of her writing—the day-to-day travails of the mother in a large (giant, by Russian standards) family; the life of the academic and literary intelligentsia; the struggles of "undesirable" writers—is familiar to her. Educated as a philologist, Gorlanova started writing fiction when she and a colleague were traveling in rural Russia researching their dissertations and decided to write a novel together. When her dissertation was finished and her defense scheduled, she quit graduate school and went to work in a library to have more time to write. Her first work of fiction was published in 1980 and was well-received. That first publication turned out to be a fluke, however: soon, Gorlanova found it was difficult to get published because her work was not considered ideologically sound. Like many writers of her generation, she has gained access to publishing only since the advent of glasnost. In addition to her two books of short stories, her work has appeared in several anthologies. Two of her novels and a novella she cowrote with her husband, The Hebrew Teacher, *were accepted for simultaneous publication in Moscow in 1993.*

This piece, written in 1989, appears first in this anthology because I believe that it does a better job of setting the context for the rest of the work in this volume than any number of introductions and editorial notes could. The experience an American might have reading it is not entirely

21

dissimilar from what many Russians experienced in the late 1980s. It was a time when most of the reading and television-watching public seemed to experience information overload. A flood of confusing historical information and current news broke through in a tidal wave of confessions and testimonials of a nation, but much of the information that was necessary to make sense of it was still lacking.

In the fall of 1989, for the first time in Soviet history, a meeting of the Congress of People's Deputies was opened to public scrutiny via live television broadcast. Nearly ninety percent of Russia's television-owning households (which account for more than ninety percent of the population) tuned in to the unprecedented spectacle. Documentaries and articles began to show other current and recent news events that would have been suppressed in the past—be they the 1986 Chernobyl disaster, the deadly 1989 earthquake in Armenia, or the 1989 train fire near Ufa. Contributing to the apocalyptic flavor of the new media were periodicals—especially the magazine Ogonyok, *a flagship of glasnost—filled with stories of atrocities committed by Soviet authorities. Life stories of the victims of repression appeared side-by-side with stories of their demise. One such story mentioned in "Confessional Days" is that of Vavilov, a world-renowned biologist whose executioner's name was made public.*

*Many of the references in this piece are to writing that was allowed to see light for the first time during this period. The book referred to throughout the story—*The Accursed Days*—had just been released simultaneously by several publishing houses. Banned in the Soviet Union for seven decades, it contains émigré writer Ivan Bunin's memoirs of life in Russia right after the revolution—the beginning days of the period for which the country was now confessing. On the other end of the timeline, the pointedly unhopeful writing of fiction author and playwright Ludmila Petrushevskaya also broke out of the samizdat and onto the printed page and the "legitimate" stage. The work of two other suppressed writers—the poet Nikolai Gumilev, a White Army officer executed by the Bolsheviks, and his son, the ethnographer Lev Gumilev, who spent years in Stalinist camps— was also published (along with writing about the life of the elder Gumilev, which the narrator is clearly also reading).*

The work of the younger Gumilev briefly captured the attention of a country caught up in a fitful search for new idols, ideals, and totalizing theories to replace the ones rapidly being discredited. Gumilev's heritage was partly responsible for this: he was the son of Nikolai Gumilev and the great poet Anna Akhmatova. But in this time of televised hypnotists and psychics, his biologically determinist ethnographic theories were especially compelling for another reason as well: his authoritative affirmation of the

NINA GORLANOVA

well-established Russian habit of categorizing people by membership in ethnic groups, and the anti-Semitic undertones of his writing. He claimed to have spent months in labor camps puzzling over the question of why Jews tended to be at the forefront of social movements (including the Russian revolution) and concluded that the key was what he called "passionate ethnos."

Any number of rationalizations were used to pump up the volume of hateful rhetoric in literary circles. The newly formed Russian nationalist organization Pamiat (Memory) counted among its members and sympathizers several prominent writers, including Valentin Rasputin and Stanislav Kuniayev. Large journals and newspapers, including The Young Guard and Our Contemporary turned openly nationalist while continuing to receive state funding. The public flogging of the Communist Party resulted in an inevitable backlash, with some people (including Rasputin) joining the party for the first time. A woman by the name of Nina Andreyeva rose to instant fame by writing a letter to the newspaper Soviet Russia defending the party. She joined others, like the writer Prokhanov, in becoming a leading conservative spokesperson.

At the same time, grass-roots pro-democracy groups began organizing around the country. One such organization in Perm, called Dialogue, included most of the city's intellectual elite and was founded on the belief that intellectuals—and especially writers—had to act as the country's conscience. For writers of Gorlanova's generation, this heady talk fought for attention with the growing hardships and uncertainty of middle-aged family life. Generation gaps appeared and grew wider between the older generation (often frightened by and opposed to change) and Gorlanova's generation (which was largely responsible for change), as well as between the children who were becoming cognizant as the world around them was changing and adults who had been shaped by the regime they were now attempting to dismantle. In a country where trust had always been a rarity, antagonism grew along all sorts of group divisions: generational, class, and ethnic.

—M. G.

"Mommy, will you buy me a ducky?" Agnia is begging again.

She is turning five soon, and she is apparently hinting that she wants a duck for her birthday. But we already have a cat, which at the moment has four kittens. Nikolai Gumilev had squirrels, birds, white mice, and guinea pigs—all at once—when he was little, while all my children have is a cat. I promise to buy the ducky.

"Hooray! I'll fill the ducky with air and then I'll swim to save my life on the 'sixty-second.' Right?"

Gods! She meant a rubber ducky! We are expecting a cataclysm in Perm in the form of an earthquake followed by a flood (the dam will break). Apparently, panic has even reached the nursery school set. They say the stores are sold out of flotation devices: life vests, air mattresses, inflatable toys.

"Even among rats there are people who sacrifice themselves for the sake of the rest. And look at us…" I light a cigarette. (Lyuda Ch. has suggested that we get together to send a telegram to Gorbachev: "If you don't purchase disposable syringes, we will curse you." We sent a telegram once before—in support of Sakharov—but this wording is making me nervous.)

In the kitchen, two visiting geniuses are grousing as they open a bottle of vodka:

"Disposable syringes aren't the best defense against AIDS…"

"Listen, you have no goblets—just tumblers!"

"Drink vodka by the tumbler in this heat? With pleasure!"

My husband, enraged: "Everyone's smoked so much that smoke is coming out of every pore."

Too bad that people who sacrifice themselves for the sake of the rest are found only among rats. Galia K. came by and told me in confidence that there is meat from Chernobyl for sale in Perm stores. The level of radiation is horrifying. But none of the authorities would take on the task of saving the rest of the Perm population.

Then again, the first secretary of the regional party committee hasn't even moved his family here. He doesn't consider himself a Permian, so he's got nothing to be afraid of.

"From the Ruins" is the name of a special television report.

"When the earth shook in Armenia, the entire world shook from the tragedy. The initial shock of that event has yet to pass. We have visited the current epicenter of reconstruction: Spitak, Leninakan, the village of Djajur…The cities—especially Spitak—have turned into a series of dug-up vacant lots. Only the roads, now lined with trailers and pits where there were once foundations, suggest that residential buildings once stood here. Most of the debris has been removed, but the roar of excavators can still be heard here and there, ripping into the steel jumble of reinforcement and loading the concrete remains onto trucks."

Turns out that real people can be found not only among rats. Two sev-

NINA GORLANOVA

enteen-year-old girls ripped down a flag on a KGB building. The girls were arrested. But what did THEY think—that they can print the truth about torture at the hands of the KGB every day without a word of remorse from anyone in the KGB, and people will stand for this? Of course not. Certainly, young people won't: they aren't disabled by fear like we are.

I propose taking to the streets with posters, but the girls' parents don't believe in the reality of democracy. They want to go to Moscow, where they have influential relatives.

My husband says, "You start feeling sort of elitist. Turns out that only a select few, like Sakharov, retained a sense of morality through the years of totalitarianism. The majority were indifferent or were torturing people or broke down at interrogations or wrote reports."

Two visitors (the geniuses): "When we told you that before, you'd get all huffy, saying that the people were the guardians of morality."

Our district doctor shows up unexpectedly. "Nina Viktorovna, I'm here to see you. I haven't seen you in a while, and it must be time to check your blood pressure."

It's true about the blood pressure, what with my kidneys. But I am shocked by her solicitude. Who's ever heard of an overworked Soviet doctor taking the time to visit a sick patient without being asked? The shock even makes my blood pressure fall. But I figure I'll make use of her visit by getting a prescription for a syringe, since the neighbors broke my old one.

"Of course. All you have to do is come by for an appointment and I'll give you a prescription for a syringe. Also—tell me, Nina Viktorovna, what do you think about all this earthquake talk?"

Now I get it. She came by to find out about the anticipated Perm cataclysm from me, an intelligent woman (in her opinion). I try to calm the doctor down as best I can. I tell her that they've already started draining our reservoir because the crack under the dam had gotten pretty wide.

The girls are fined and released. Turns out they testified in court that they'd planned to place the flag at the top of the Yermak mountain because they are mountaineers and such. And THEY believed them. Or decided to pretend that they believed them. The parents still can't get over their surprise at such resourcefulness; they are suffering from insomnia. Looks like the younger generation of Permians will be more flexible than ours.

"Spitak children's drawings of stacks of coffins. The exhibition is sponsored by activists from the Lenin Children's Foundation in Armenia."

Some acquaintances of mine call up the regional party newspaper to ask about earthquake forecasts. They are told no one knows anything.

My husband says that even if there is going to be a cataclysm and we are doomed, our thoughts have already been written—imprinted—in the noösphere, which, unlike bodies, does not die.

I decide to call a friend at a publishing house in Moscow. I figure they are better-informed.

"You know who benefits by such rumors, Nina? Thieves. Because a lot of people will leave town for those days, and there will be robberies."

"Good work today, good writing, doing my part for the noösphere." I take a newspaper and lie down on the couch resolutely, planning to rest.

"Nina?" A neighbor friend has come by. "Would you give me five injections in an hour?"

She is pregnant, and the injections will make her abort.

"Listen, I can't do anything immoral! I know myself too well. I don't have the right to decide the fate of your baby."

The neighbor looks at me plaintively, and I start calculating in my head: one, I'm constantly borrowing money from them; two, I frequently come by to get some salt/baking soda/medicine; three, I use their phone to call Moscow…I take a nail file and cut into the capsule. One down. I break it off and cut my hand. Blood starts to gush, the neighbor goes pale, and I explain, "You see, I can't do these things. I have too close a relationship to the noösphere." I point up with my finger.

Oh, yeah? Then ask your noösphere: Is there going to be an earthquake or not?

Andrei, a friend who works for a cooperative, got his pay—a thousand rubles—and brought gifts: a luxurious bouquet of gladioli, a smoked sausage, two cases of beer, a radio that costs over a hundred rubles, and sixty rubles cash. My first thought, at the sight of all this, is, *He lives well, so the cataclysm is more threatening for him.*

After I've bought Lev Gumilev's book, a friend brings Nikolai Gumilev's book over. I put them next to each other. Father meets son.

"Now I know why Chukchi people are so kind and trusting: It's their ancient ethnos," says my husband, brandishing Lev's book on ethnology (he's been reading it constantly and is completely gumilev-ed).

An acquaintance has returned (after discharge) from the Chinese border. He says students are crossing the border by the hundreds every day. No one is stopping them on either side. What does this mean? Most likely that there is an agreement with Gorbachev, who has ordered that the Chinese students be shipped back quietly by bus.
"And the West believes that Gorbachev is a democrat!"
"The West is like the Chukchi: an ancient ethnos, trusting and kind."

"Human potential! Has anyone ever measured it? Take the train fires near Ufa—did you read about them? This soldier was tossing children out the window, saving them. Saved a whole bunch. Then he crawled out himself, and when they saw him, no one could figure out how he'd been standing, because all he had left were charred bones in place of legs. And he just kept standing there tossing the children out!"
That's drunken visitors admiring the bravery and heroism of the Soviet man. If there is a cataclysm in Perm, there will be endless possibilities for heroic acts.

I dislocated my arm indignantly putting out a cigarette. It's all because of this congress! Today is the last day. A group of one hundred thirty delegates proposed the immediate adoption of their program for aid to the disadvantaged. Gorbachev rejected all that. Meanwhile, Dasha is bawling, demanding cherries (she saw them in a neighbor's kitchen). But there is no money. And I'm close to tears myself because of the mean congress that didn't aid the disadvantaged. I long for the cherry of democracy.
"Just a little!" Dasha is begging. (She is six years old, and she doesn't know how to wait.)
"I want just a little, too," I say.
"I want it now!" she repeats.
"And I want it now, too!" I'm almost crying, understanding full well why children cannot be satisfied with "later."
My husband: "Your screaming at the congress doesn't enrich the noösphere but drains it instead, because it is forced to expend energy on supporting you—and you self-destruct little by little as you scream."

I run into an acquaintance. The conversation, of course, turns to the cataclysm.

"I got all my gold together and am carrying it with me: a necklace, earrings, rings. If it starts and I survive, there will always be greedy people who'll buy from me. And I'll be able to live off that money at first."

The director of the store where my husband works is holding on to two books by Brezhnev.

"What do you need them for?"

"What if they start honoring him again?"

"Not a chance. He was a criminal who managed to evade punishment. And all his speeches are addressed to criminals."

The director turns away, skeptical. Like she is going to listen to some grocery loader!

Before taking a book of Andrei Voznesensky's poetry to the used-book buyer, I reread a few things. Pasternak wrote to him: "the ancient continuity of happiness is what we call art." One good shakeup—and no more continuity...

Only the Lithuanian edition of *Soviet Youth* prints the details about the reforms in Poland and Hungary. Our central newspapers are writing something inarticulate through clenched teeth.

"Bush believed that Jaruzelsky is a democrat! Can you believe it?"

"The Chukchi. The ancient ethnos," is all we can say.

Everyone we know is receiving treatment via the television from Chumak, a psychic. Many are helped. They want to die healthy—never has that phrase rung as true as it does now.

Seems that a few dozen trailers have become the center of activity among the piles of broken rock in Spitak. They house the regional committees of the party and the Komsomol, city offices, and institutions. The sign on one of the trailers says, The Office of Political Education. Numerous posters warn against promiscuity.

Indeed, one shouldn't be promiscuous among the ruins after an earthquake! It's 1989 in the land of socialism. Here are some lines from Bunin's *The Accursed Days:*

April 20 (Odessa, 1919)
Aniuta says it's been two days already since they stopped hand-

NINA GORLANOVA

ing out the awful pea bread that made everyone in the building holler with indigestion. And who's been deprived of bread? The very proletariat they were trying so hard to entertain day before yesterday. The signs on the walls urge, "Citizens! May everyone become involved in athletics!" Absolutely incredible, but true. Why athletics? How did athletics get into these hateful skulls?

The only difference is that Bunin wrote "absolutely incredible," which we don't. We're used to it.

I run into a friend. Her first question is, "Are you a good swimmer?"
"Not so good."
"I can't swim at all. What am I going to do?"

R. comes by. His grandson has died at the age of three days. The mother became infected with hepatitis in the hospital, and they broke the baby's spine during birth. One of those two things would have been enough, but here they like to do all two hundred percent of the possible harm. R. wants me to distract his son and daughter-in-law somehow, but one look is enough to make you stop fearing the cataclysm—you just don't want to go on living. How am I supposed to entertain them?

The structure of the everyday: passing a hardware store, I see a red flag lying on the ground. Why? Because I need to write something about those girls who took the flag. This is a reminder, the voice of a higher power.

The kitten is beautiful—like the book cover for *1,001 Nights*—with such an intricate design on its back, which is shivering. Kristina asks, "Auntie Nina, what are you gonna do with Mirza's kittens? 'Cause Mama brought this kitten from work; she felt sorry for it 'cause the men there toss them into the furnace." (They are steelworkers.)
Natasha: "It's so pretty—how could they throw it in the furnace?"
"Would it be all right to throw an ugly one in?" I ask, admiring the kitten, which is shivering in its sleep—dreaming of the furnace, maybe?
"Right into the furnace," Kristina repeats, confused.
This is our Soviet brand of humanity.

R. can see that I'm depressed.
"Let's go see the Gypsies. I've got a thing going with one of them.

You should see how a Gypsy woman trusts the earth when she sits down on it—"

"What's wrong with you? Don't you know there was a Gypsy pogrom recently and they all got beaten up and went into hiding?"

"I heard about the pogrom at the marketplace and all the southern traders getting beaten—but I haven't heard anything about the Gypsies."

Perm television airs a program—a refutation, that is—on the earthquake and the flood. Nauseatingly helpful, done in the Would You Be So Kind as to Shove It school. Supposedly they even called Vanga the Prophet, and she assured them that she'd prophesied nothing of the sort. They checked with every source with the possible exception of aliens from the planet of Kisherti, and everyone said, Not to worry. Nothing's going to happen.

Panic grows following the program. That's how we're used to thinking: if the authorities refute it, that means it's definitely going to happen.

N. comes back from Leningrad. She says people there are resigning from the party *en masse*.

Dasha: "I had a dream that Marina from downstairs became a queen and invited us into a garden where there were magical apples and the branches were bent and spoke in human voices: 'Climb on up!' There were these little nests up there, and we climbed in and ate apples— as many as we wanted..."

All of my children's longing for fruit is in this dream. Of course people should be resigning from the kind of party that can't even give fruit to the children. But my husband Slava resigned in protest three years ago already. It's someone else's turn.

We are standing in a food line for families with many children. I'm complaining that they have no buckwheat again. Slava is trying to distract me: where would they get buckwheat, no one's been growing it, the only place that may still have a buckwheat plot is the Kremlin, where they grow buckwheat for Politburo members...so this line of slaves immediately starts judging us.

"You are young. You could be growing it yourself," says a little old woman.

"True, we could, but we don't know where to start: grow buckwheat, make sausage, or cook soap?" I reply.

NINA GORLANOVA

Unfettered, the woman relates: "Why not? I've cooked soap—not soap but detergent. Find a dead dog, boil the intestines, and you've got yourself detergent. You can use it for washing. It stinks, of course, but we didn't have soap then—"

All the USSR is a stage, and the play is by Ludmila Petrushevskaya...

"Children who lost only their fathers or only their mothers or lost neither of their parents do not qualify for tickets to resorts...But many of them spent three or four days in the rubble, fighting for their lives."

It's the summer after the earthquake. Bunin, bless his heart, would have poured out so much bile at this! But these days, journalists aren't surprised at anything.

"Mama, they are saying there won't be any matches, so I bought a hundred boxes just in case." Anton places a pile of matchboxes on the wardrobe.

T.T., who is visiting, is making fun of this: "Oh, sure, matches will come in real handy during the flood—we could put together a little raft or scrape off the sulfur and make fireworks to let rescuers know where we are..."

"You aren't stocking up on anything? Honest?"

T.T.: "Being a civilized human being, I am not susceptible to the panic. So instead of getting ten packages of salt, I bought only two. I wanted to get three but couldn't get rid of the last vestiges of civilization in myself."

Exactly one week to cataclysm.

A banging noise wakes me up in the middle of the night. Has it started? What am I supposed to do first? I jump up and see what the noise is: the cat has knocked our hundred matchboxes off the wardrobe. She is always roving in search of a place high up where she can hide her kittens; it's in her genes.

What about us Soviet mothers? Where are we supposed to hide our children to save them? I light a cigarette in the kitchen, checking our salt supply first just in case.

T.T. is visiting again.

"I am proud that in ten years of working at the university I've gotten twenty rubles' worth of raises, so that I'm now making one hundred eighty-five rubles, but my son says, 'Mama, you work so much for so little!' He is always indignant: 'Darned city—no places to go! Darned country—there are no children's books in the stores.' It's odd to me; I'd want him to be indignant that we have no freedom, but he is only concerned with consuming."

Her son is ten years old.

"But we ourselves have come to understand that freedom takes root in consumption," she continues. "Turns out it's all connected, but from childhood, we've been taught: don't consume, the most important values are spiritual."

My son brings in the mail, including the journal *Issues in History*. The ad on the back cover announces in bold black letters: THE GREAT OCTOBER. 70 YEARS. SCIENTIFIC, TECHNICAL, AND SOCIAL PROGRESS. 3 RUBLES 90 KOPECKS.

T.T. is close to tears: "Progress...sure. Students are so different now. I'm tired. I want to quit. Plus, I've been reading Orwell. I was administering exams, and the students were so dumb, like Orwellian characters, that I wanted to hang myself right in the auditorium; I would have administered the last exam standing on a stool already and soaping the rope—but then I remembered that there's no soap."

She also says, "A long time ago Asya came back from a trip to Poland with the news that they had no sugar. I thought, 'How is that possible?' Now I think, 'How is it possible that we ever had sugar? As much as our hearts desired? No, it was always rationed.' Let there always be rations! That's how quickly our consciousness has been reformed."

"It's the age of reforms."

Dasha and I are on our way to the store. Suddenly, she stops underneath a lamppost.

"Mama, that apple tree was this tall!" She means the magical apple tree from her dream; this means she is constantly thinking about fruit.

During a meeting with the People's Deputies, a lady from the regional party committee brings some sort of accusation against Vinichenko, the head of Dialogue. She is immediately booed and forced off the podium. And suddenly she screams back, "That's just how Sakharov was forced off the podium!"

Bunin, where are you?

NINA GORLANOVA

Apparently, a certain deputy, K., has joined the progressive bloc in Congress. O. and N. start calling the regional party committee right away to complain about the head of Dialogue: Vinichenko's got all these demands, and they just want to be like everybody else, and they just want to retain their individuality. They are outstripping the lady who compared herself to Sakharov. Bu...

Recently I discovered that this was not an isolated incident; this is a phenomenon! Writing in the magazine *Ogonyok*, Rassadin, a critic, condemns Kuniayev for his anti-Semitism—and Kuniayev goes to *The Moscow Literary* and threatens to *slap* Rassadin if he doesn't apologize. So there it is: everyone wants to be like Sakharov. Sakharov slapped someone who'd slandered his wife for the whole country to hear. Kuniayev, on the other hand, wants to be like Sakharov but without the consequences. It's not like he started out by speaking out—alone—against the war in Afghanistan, or being exiled, etc. To be like Sakharov, one would have to be Sakharov.

It's time to face the fact that Bunin is not going to show up to help me; I have to rely on my own abilities, even if they have been weakened by the Soviet powers. But the Soviets never had any power! That's right. And if there were no Soviets, then no one was anti-Soviet...

Mila Kh. got tired of the congressional catch phrase "as a rule"—as in "As a rule, deputies can work in the Supreme Soviet." What that means, in reality, is rarely.
POWER TO THE SOVIETS, AS A RULE!
That's a poster she made for this rally. Even the policemen laughed. But all Mila had done was take the logic from one realm into another—a more spacious one.

I'm having one attack after another. It's my kidneys. We have no television and no money for one, so I can't get help from Chumak the psychic. The drugstores are empty.
"Tolya, do I have to come to your house to get treatment via television?"
"From Chumak? You think he can heal? He is infecting the whole country with love for Gorbachev while everyone believes that he heals. Blessed naïveté!"

The benefit of selling my books is that before taking them to the reseller I reread them. It was Gerzen's turn. Here was this duke being exiled from Perm to Verkhoturiye (he'd misbehaved). He calls all his functionaries together for a farewell dinner, promising an unbelievable pie. Unable to resist, the functionaries come to find a pie that is truly heavenly. When it has been eaten, the duke announces with pathos, "It will never be said that I held back when it was time to say good-bye to you. Yesterday, I ordered that my dog Gardi be killed for the pie." He then orders that Gardi's coat be brought in (his insides are in Permian stomachs).

"Half the city became ill with horror," Gerzen wrote.

Those were the czar's functionaries. They were overthrown. So now what? During the recent Perm elections, the first secretary of the regional committee of the party was kicked out of office, but he not only did not become ill with embarrassment but got on TV and said, Too bad you didn't elect me, because if I were in the Supreme Soviet, I'd be able to do more for the city, and now I won't be able to.

"She is a department head in the area party committee. She has this fear that they'll be doused with gasoline and set on fire, like in Uzbekistan, because there they burned the area committee members for some reason."

I shudder. These people were raised to be intolerant of difference—and now, when the people have no energy left to tolerate *them*, it's the same intolerance again, the same hunger for blood and more blood. And what's all this going to come to? A vicious circle.

I value Bunin's *Accursed Days* highly: it's a very great and truthful book. But there is so much personal hatred in it: " 'They don't make revolutions in kid gloves'—so is it any wonder that counterrevolutions are made by iron fists?"

But shouldn't the bloody circle break somewhere?

I'm standing in line for chickens. I'm on my second hour. The line is angrier than a hundred Bunins put together.

"Look what we've come to—there has been no chicken in this city for three weeks! There is nothing except for twenty-five grams of sausage a day, rationed…And there is nothing else in the stores…"

Three days to cataclysm.

Radio Free Europe broadcasts an interview with Nina Andreyeva by a correspondent of the *Washington Post*. First she talks about the principles her generation once held and how they should not be abandoned. Then she says that she wrote the newly famous letter to *Soviet Russia* on her own, albeit under the influence of Prokhanov's articles. The editors did add a few quotes, but those only clarified her meaning.

Then Nina Andreyeva feeds her guest dinner. As the American journalist notes, Russian conservatives, as a rule, are good cooks. Judging from the poverty of Leningrad stores, the food didn't come from there. (Then where? I want to know who feeds Nina Andreyeva.)

Then Nina Andreyeva and her husband walk their guest down the street. She says that before the letter was published, the newspaper had given it not only to Yegor Ligachev but to Mikhail Gorbachev to read, and neither had had any objections.

My son and I nearly fall over. Once a friend was at our house trashing Ligachev, contrasting him with none other than Gorbachev. And my husband claimed that they'd simply made a deal that Ligachev will play the conservative and Gorbachev the liberal, to make like pluralism.

At this point my friend seriously took offense on Gorbachev's behalf. And what do you know? Here we were thinking that Nina Andreyeva's letter was an attack on Gorbachev. And we weren't the only ones: they said during the congress that things like this are always happening in Gorbachev's absence.

All the newspapers are writing about aliens and flying saucers in the Perm region—near Kungur, where there used to be many camps that held political prisoners. Why there?

"It's a well-known fact that aliens like to fly over places with a high concentration of morally pure people."

Andrei the cooperative worker gets paid again and gives us two ten-ruble bills—new, like starched.

"Just some of our depreciating currency. The bank is always giving out new bills. The printing press must be running constantly. There isn't an old bill in the entire bank."

I was throwing out some old newspapers. Found an article by Kariakin about how Sakharov was beaten by the KGB. "They beat an old man!" Kariakin is indignant. But the amazing thing is not a single letter to the paper followed with questions like "Who exactly did the beating?" or "What's the name?" We know the name of the one who beat Vavilov, you see; it's Khvat. We even know from watching the meetings of the Supreme Soviet that Khvat's son is very well-positioned in the highest echelons of power. Meanwhile, recently—during all our lifetimes—Sakharov was beaten, and no one is demanding the name.

And then I thought about how Lyuba, with whom I once shared a kitchen, used to beat me. She'd throw the frying pan at me and the coffeepot, or just kick me. Who in the Soviet Union hasn't been beaten? Show me that person!

I was throwing out an issue of *The Young Guard* and saw an interview with Kuniayev. A local writer named Tiulenev took a trip to interview him. As well he should: there is a demand for Kuniayev's wisdom. The wisdom boils down to the fact that the Masons and the Jews are to blame for everything. Oh, and rock music, too. If you take two people and one of them likes rock music and the other gets a heartache from the sound of the folk song "The Volga River Flows Between the Steep Banks," then whom would Kuniayev pick to oversee, say, the cleanup of the great Russian river the Volga? The one with the heartache, of course.

I sat down at the typewriter and wrote: "Are there any statistics as to how many devotees of Russian folk music worked in the Ministry of Water Resources that ruined the Volga? What about among the administrators of the Chernobyl nuclear power plant? And rumor has it that the Gulag administration didn't have a single person who liked rock, and still that didn't save us..."

My husband grumbled that they wouldn't publish my letter because I have a reputation. So I signed it "Ilyichev, a locksmith."

The Young Guard arrives with my letter in it...

I run into my district doctor.

"So are you ever going to get out our way to pick up the prescription, Nina Viktorovna?"

"What's the big deal? You're right nearby."

"Don't you know? We were flooded. On Friday night they opened up the roof for repairs, and on Saturday it rained heavily. The floors have all buckled, the wallpaper has slid off, all the equipment is trashed. We've moved to Yubileiny. The reconstruction is going to take about two years."

Who needs the Masons when we can ruin ourselves?

We are buying Dasha's school uniform for first grade. My husband is complaining: "I keep thinking that Dasha will be inducted into the

Oktiabrists and that she'll have to sing, 'There is a reason that we have this name: In the month October revolution came.' "

Dasha says, "Daddy, I'm not going to sing; I'll just open my mouth."

A friend who is a Zen Buddhist is visiting. He is calm. The failure of perestroika should not stand in the way of happiness. One's karma can and should be improved. One should choose a love object, such as children, work, etc. The stronger the ties between you and this object, the better.

"That's all fine and good, but what about the two thousand people who died in the explosion near Ufa? They were riding the trains in peace, loving someone somewhere, bettering their karma. And then—*bang!*—death! A gas explosion. You know, karma in the USSR—"

"But remember—that's not the end. Their souls will begin a new cycle, and what these people thought in their last moments will be taken into consideration. Everything counts."

Really, it's time to convert to Zen Buddhism.

My husband took the last of our money and left for his father's funeral. I tried to buy medication from some resellers, but I don't have that kind of money. I'm lying with my hands on my kidneys to get at least a little relief. A friend comes by. She says she and hers just came back from Finland. They have special seats in their Parliament hall for visitors. We are getting high off the fact that they are showing the Supreme Soviet—our parliament—on TV: Check out this glasnost thing! It's the limit! Meanwhile, in Finland, anyone can come in off the street and watch. So, at the present, they have two issues on the agenda: how productivity can be lowered and whether people should be guaranteed a minimum living wage starting at the age of seventeen or eighteen.

"What I think is most outrageous," my friend exclaims, "is that no one's asking us what kind of regime we want!"

"Look, in the Polish elections they kicked out the Communists. They voted for—Ss—"

"What's wrong? What's happening? Is it your kidneys? Is it Slava's father's death?"

What was happening was a hysterical fit. Brought on not by Slava's father's death but by the death of my illusions.

The friend leaves, someone else comes, then someone else, and no one can stop the hysteria. I start having chest pains, and there is nothing for the heart at the drug store. We could call an ambulance, but I have no disposable syringe and their syringes are dangerously dirty...Fortunately, I get some relief from a cigarette offered by a neighbor.

I read in *Soviet Youth* that Pamiat held a rally in Moscow, at the monument to Yakov Sverdlov the revolutionary. They placed a wreath of barbed wire on him and said Jews were to blame for everything. Things must be bad if they are using Pamiat to distract the people from their problems and sick them onto "others." It's a well-known fact that the government pays for Pamiat's publications, *Our Contemporary* and *The Young Guard*.

I'm walking down Komsomolsky Prospect toward the post office. Black clouds are coming out of chimneys, and on the left, past the Chkalov Station, there seems to be another fire, and fire engines are swarming. Bunin was so much more fortunate than we! He had mother nature as a counterpoint to all the blood, blood, blood, and idiocy of the revolution: in every entry he's got either azure skies or clean clouds. We, on the other hand, live in a state of harmony: our society is rotten, and our environment is ruined.

In the midst of the familiar thoughts flowing parallel to Bunin's *Accursed Days*, suddenly I see that Pamiat is marching toward the Sverdlov monument (it's by the Sverdlov factory, behind me). There are about thirty of them, all in black—in broad daylight, right in the middle of Komsomolsky Prospect! All of them are carrying posters. Someone in front is waving her arms, demonstration-style. Plus, they are carrying two brooms—I conclude that they go with a banner that says SWEEP THE JEWS OUT OF THE USSR.

Feverishly, I try to think: Should I hide in the bushes and throw mud on them—fortunately, there is plenty of it around—or should I run up to them and scream something confrontational, like that if we kick out all the Jews there won't be any Nobel laureates left. We should be grateful that they have such good genes, such a talented people we can mix with...

Meanwhile, I'm running toward them, but they are no longer standing in place. Suddenly, I see that it's a building manager leading a group of street cleaners somewhere with their scrapers because apparently something needs to be cleaned on an emergency basis— probably the summer vegetable market which has been trashed over the winter. The street cleaners don't want to go. The building manager is waving her arms, trying to convince them. They are all wearing black robes like they are supposed to. And they've got two brooms, too. Damned smoke from the fire! What if I had hidden in the bushes and thrown mud at them? In the morning the regional paper would announce, "Crime is on the rise. Yesterday, writer Gorlanova, whose extremist views are well-known, threw mud from the bushes at street cleaners who were peacefully walking to take care of their cleaning business."

Two days to cataclysm.

There is no chicken. The deli has some stuffed cabbage, but it's forty rubles apiece. That's too expensive for my family. But there is nothing I can do, and I buy six—one for each of us. I put them in the refrigerator and lie down; my kidneys are hurting. Sonia comes in. I say that I got some stuffed cabbage, which needs to be fried. Convenience food...

"Really? It needs to be fried? I just ate one as it was; I really wanted some meat."

Galia K. comes by and says that what is going to happen is not a natural disaster but a pogrom. A Jewish one. Well, if we've already had a Gypsy one and a pogrom of the southern traders at the marketplace, then the next one has to be Jewish. Even if this is just a rumor, what a horrible thing it is to do to Jews.

"If a mêlée starts, we've gotta beat it," says my husband, a Hebrew teacher.

I drop my piece of bread and butter—buttered side down, of course. My husband starts up, imitating a Pamiat member: "Za law of za buttered bread. Ze Jews discovered it. Ant vot does it mean, eh? Zet zey alveys have bread and butter, which they throw around to boot!"

All our acquaintances have split up into two groups: normal people and anti-Semites. This means endless arguments.

"Nina Viktorovna, Dzerzhinsky's got blood on his hands!" says Olya G.

"And Stalin doesn't? And Beria? Still, they are not Jewish."

My husband mutters that secret police founder Felix Dzerzhinsky, incidentally, wasn't a Jew either but a Pole, and gentry at that.

Say you've slaughtered all the Jews—then whom? Oh, the Moldovans! They are the only ones who are given the lighter courses in schools, because they can't handle the regular course work. My husband, who is half Moldovan, thinks the reason is the Cyrillic alphabet was imposed on the Moldovan language, introduced by force…When you are finished with the Moldovans, who are you going to start on, who are you going to take it out on? On fat people? And then? Short people? And then? Then every other person.

This is what I mumble as I walk to the store. Something must not be quite right with me, because out of the corner of my eye I see Vasily Belov fly across the sky on a wooden plow. And I thought he was a writer.

He and Valentin Rasputin are two of a kind. They are writers of the heart rather than writers of the mind. Vladimir Makanin, on the other hand, is a writer of the mind. My husband used to say that he'd never turn into an anti-Semite. Why not? Because there comes a time to use your mind. Like in that prayer—"God, grant me the strength to accept that which I cannot change, the strength to change that which I can, and the wisdom to know the difference."

They didn't get a mind to tell the difference? Or maybe it works in someone's favor for the people to be distracted from the real problems? Is someone fishing in these muddy waters?

In the stores everyone is talking about the pogroms. Women tend to be in favor.

"Wherever you look, it's all non-Russians."

"Maybe the redheads are to blame for everything," one man tries to crack a joke.

The joke doesn't work. Though then someone tells a joke that's a very subtle parody of reports about Gorbachev's trips.

Here it is:

" 'How is life?' Mikhail Sergeyevich asked the laborers.

'Good,' the laborers answered in unison.

'It will get even better!' joked Mikhail Sergeyevich."

Olia Merlina is visiting. She is talking about a famous surgeon, a bone oncologist. His son was harassed—called a kike—in first grade, and the father wanted to go beat up the perpetrator. But his wife begged him not to do it and settled everything through peaceful negotiations. Ten years pass. A young man comes to see the bone oncologist; his arm is twisted behind his back in such a way that even the professor has never seen anything like it before. He starts treating the young man, going so far as to bring him fruit that's been worked over by a psychotherapist friend. At home, he is constantly talking about the poor guy's pain—until his wife can't take it anymore and asks why he is knocking himself out for this lowlife, who once harassed their son, calling him a kike, and stopped only after she gave his parents ten rubles. The professor listens, nodding, and then says that, yes, he recalls something like that—but now he is the most severely ill person on the ward and must be cured.

"This doctor is one of the people we want to call enemies!" I'm getting started, running around the room.

"That's nothing," says Olia. "Recently, his wife talked the surgeon into going to the housewares store to pick up something for the kitchen. There he spotted some gilded spoons. He said they should get them for the children who've been in the hospital for so long they really need something to lift their spirits. They bought twenty spoons, fourteen rubles apiece. Three days later, the wife came by his work for some reason, and saw that there were no spoons there. Where were they? Well, the professor shrugged his shoulders, they must be in the kitchen, being washed. Meanwhile, the employees had long since stolen them. There was nothing that the patients, who are bedridden, could do."

Some Jewish friends of my husband called the Perm office of the Ministry of the Interior to ask whether they were prepared to protect the city's residents against pogroms.

"We've had no indication that will happen," was the answer they got.

"What if we go to the summerhouse?" asks Liusia G., who is married to a Jew. "Maybe we could sit it out?"

"That would be even worse: no phone and no hospital," I say. "I'm planning to call our Jewish friends and invite them to spend that deadly night here. Maybe we could fight them off all together."

"What annoys me about Jews is their ability to use any little tiny talent to the fullest," says a journalist friend of mine. "A Russian wouldn't even think of realizing something like that."

My husband makes a face.

"Have you read Lev Gumilev? All that is, is passionate ethnos."

"What makes some Mongol worse than them?" the friend refuses to give up.

"Not worse, it's just that they have already completed their passionate stage—when they were marching upon us by the thousands they heated up quickly and then burned out. The Jews, on the other hand, use their energy resources economically, and will continue to be active for a long time."

I just can't stand this kind of abstract argument when there are perfectly real ones to be made. Take our Perm writers union, for example. Everyone has just a sprinkling of talent—barely noticeable. Exceptions number one or two. How much talent does T. have, for example? .0001 percent, maybe. But they are all Russians. And they all use their .0001 percent as though they had a hundred percent. Everyone's joined the union, everyone lives off of writing fees, and so on. And they are all Russians! How can Vasia explain that?

Vasia is quiet. Nothing to say. It's true, he says, some don't even have that fraction of a percent of talent, some have nothing at all, but they've made a livelihood out of it.

"These are some sort of super Jews," I yell, getting started and waving my arms and knocking over a vase with flowers.

T. has applied to join the party.

He's hung up a huge poster advertising the Fellowship of Russian Artists in the Writers Union building. They gather under the auspices of the Interior Ministry. It says so right on the poster. Here people are fighting against the Ministry of Culture as an institution, against the Writers Union with its military regime. Meanwhile, they are trying to get the military to adopt them! The Ministry of the Interior as a muse! Only a Pamiat member could have come up with this one. There is a field of vileness surrounding this mixture of the Interior Ministry, Pamiat, and the Russian soul.

"Why are you joining the party when everyone else is jumping like rats off a sinking ship?" T. is asked at the city party committee.

"Because Rasputin joined."

I'm reading singer Galina Vishnevskaya's memoirs about her husband, exiled cellist Mstislav Rostropovich, aloud to the younger children. Sonia comes in, turns on the iron, starts ironing, and listens also. At the point where Vishnevskaya says good-bye to the Bolshoi stage, we all burst into tears. Agnia even falls asleep from overexcitement. But Dasha keeps urging me on: "Keep reading! Keep reading!" We read to the end. Then I ask, What did they remember most of all? Dasha says the part about how she said good-bye to the stage. Then Agnia wakes up and gets ready to go for a walk—and suddenly they are fighting over the raincoat.

"Dasha, Rostropovich gave Solzhenitsyn his summerhouse—he held nothing back, even though they got kicked out of the country for this—and you are too greedy to let your own sister wear the raincoat!"

NINA GORLANOVA

Do you think this had an effect on my six-year-old daughter? None. Her face got an expression that said roughly the following: Solzhenitsyn is one thing—he is practically god—one could even part with a motherland for someone like him, but as for Agnia—it's my raincoat, why should I have to sacrifice?

"I see I read all this to you in vain. I won't read anymore."

That gets to her. She gives Agnia the raincoat.

How to Become an Anti-Semite: A Story in the Form of an Algorithm. Pass by signs saying NO SEATS; NO BEER; NO SUGAR; NO NOTEBOOKS. Enter your apartment to discover that there is no water either. Forgetting to turn off the faucet in the bathroom, go down to the bakery to find that there is no bread anymore today, go to another one and then a third, and come back to find that now there is water. And there is also a bill from the downstairs neighbors, who've been flooded. And their last name is Jewish. Their lawyer's last name is Russian but his face is definitely Jewish. The second lawyer has a Russian last name and a Russian face but a Jewish way of pronouncing the letter "r."

Who is to blame?

1. The devil.
2. Imperialism.
3. Aliens.
4. Jews.
5. Psychics.
6. The Mafia.
7. Bureaucrats.
8. Bohemians.
9. Cooperatives.
10. Glasnost.
11. Historical factors.

Vitaly K. is visiting. A genius is a genius. He says that he approached T. and said that if it is confirmed that T. had something to do with the pogrom rumors, K. would borrow his grandfather's double-barrel shotgun and personally blow the anti-Semite's skull into pieces. You've got to have courage even to say something like this. Suddenly I realize that once the circle of revenge starts, that won't lead to any good either.

Two alcoholic geniuses are visiting. They've brought vodka. They are amazed that we have any worries when we've got a family and mutual understanding (their wives have long since left them).

"What are you talking about—in this heat," my husband mutters in embarrassment.

"We are all sweaty," I respond, equally embarrassed, just to say something as I hand the guests their tumblers.

"Warm vodka by the tumbler in this heat—with pleasure! Sweaty women in this heat, in the summer—with pleasure."

"My kidney hurts constantly," I change the subject.

"That, my dear, is your own fault. Moral people have no pains. Somewhere along the way you committed an offense before—" He gestures upward.

Everything has coincided: the call of the (totalitarian) state to (totalitarian) confession and the contempt of two philosopher friends. This is the beginning of three hours of nonstop confessions.

"Sonia, get the potatoes from the box that I stole from the milk factory," says my husband.

"I never did get the sea-buckthorn oil, the medicinal stuff," I relate.

There was a letter about the oil in *Soviet Youth*. There is a woman who's been paralyzed for two years and screams like she is being slaughtered when she is turned over: bedsores. And there is no oil. I decided I had to get some. I sent Anton, the letter in hand, to the administrator of the drugstore. The answer was no. The next day I sent a package with baby oil. I enclosed a book, too, a nice edition of Manon Lesko—maybe whoever is taking care of the woman will take it as compensation.

The next day I went to the city health office to see the director. He was a man with a wide-screen, well-worn rear end. I knew right away that I may as well not try with someone like that; it would be useless. But the woman screams in pain. So I tried to appeal to his empathy— here is the letter, she needs help.

"We'd have to ask the drugstore directorate anyway."

"But it's not like you and I are paralyzed! Besides, I'm the kind of person who will get the oil anyway. Whether I have to mobilize all the journalists in the city or make a statement to the Dialogue club or organize a demonstration, this woman is going to get her oil!"

"Go see S. at the drugstore directorate."

"Maybe you'll call her first? It's one thing if I just show up, and it's another thing—"

"I told you, I have to ask them myself—I just called them today—"

"So call again."

"I have no right."

"What kind of a fascist country is this," I say emphatically and go to see S.

She is not there, and my kidney hurts, so I can't wait. So I tell her secretary, telling again about the demonstration I'm going to organize, but...Anyway, I leave the paper, take down S.'s phone number and start calling every half hour (from home). The secretary tells me that S. is in her boss's office. I know already that she is hiding from me, but the next day I go to N.'s house and call again from there. S. isn't there. Oh, well. Before leaving the clipping from the paper, I asked the secretary, "This S.—has she ever heard the word *mercy*?" And the secretary said, "Yeah, she's no worse than anyone else."

That's true: she isn't.

I borrowed ten rubles from Liuda Ch. to subscribe to *The Young Guard.* As a supplement to the local youth paper, I got a two-volume edition of Pikul, the historical-romance writer. I need Pikul like a hole in the head, but I can exchange him for science fiction. Fool's currency. I go to the post office and see that some private peddlers are selling...sea-buckthorn oil. How can I tell it's not fake, though? The seller is a man of about seventy-five. I think: *He went through collectivization, repressions (if he didn't go through it himself, he lived through the period), then war, then more repressions. How can a person like that have a conscience?* Everything comes down to the conscience of an ordinary Soviet citizen. Soviet humanity, do you hear me? No answer.

I bought a small vial for six rubles, packaged it with a beautiful edition of Lermontov, and sent it off. But what kind of help is that? What I should have done is bribed the head nurse at any hospital and bought real medical oil. I confess I didn't manage to borrow the money. No place to get it now. But I should send a package with other necessary things that are hard to get: I throw in a box of imported laundry detergent, Indian soap, toothpaste, sugar—everything I have in the house. But I don't feel any better.

In *The Accursed Days*, Bunin writes with outrage about Katayev,* then a young writer, saying that he would be willing to kill a person for a thou-

---

Author's Note: Valentin Katayev was a writer who, after the revolution, put a great deal of effort into creating the so-called Literature of the Proletariat. He was acquainted with Bunin and, taking advantage of the opportunity to say the definitive word on his relationship with the writer, wrote a book about him in which he claimed to have been a close friend of Bunin's. Not until *The Accursed Days* was published did it become known that Bunin despised Katayev.

sand rubles because he wanted to be able to dress well and wear a hat.

Now, the people at the head of Pamiat are all writers, poets, and critics—and they are willing to kill all the Jews in our country absolutely free of charge. That's the kind of progress that seventy years of Soviet rule has brought us.

And they are all members of the Communist Party, and those who aren't, are joining post-haste, like T.

At the Factory of the Great October Revolution, they've hung a poster that says, PERESTROIKA CONTINUES THE WORK OF OCTOBER! What a thing to write. Tolia K.: "I wish they'd at least find another name— like *plurarule* or something." For most thinking people, perestroika may be continuing the work of the democratic February revolution, but never the October Bolshevik takeover.

The confessions continue. My typist comes over in the evening and says, "You know, Nina Viktorovna, my husband went to Georgia April 8 because he's transferred to Special Assignment. And all the military commanders in Perm assured the whole area that no one from here went!"

So they lied and they keep lying—that wouldn't surprise anyone here. But what am I supposed to tell the typist? She is being tormented by a guilty conscience, and her husband—what is he: not quite slime yet but pre-slime? I can't find anything to say. If I have to talk about pre-slime, then I would say that he should resign from Special Assignment—but what if the typist takes offense and asks me for the fifty rubles I owe her?

She leaves and I start tormenting myself: because of fifty rubles, I didn't have the guts to tell her what I thought. But what am I supposed to do if I have no money?

Confession is a bottomless pit...

The most unexpected confession yet! N. N. comes by. Very matter-of-factly, he lays a piece of paper on my desk: "This might be useful in your work. It's a rough draft—of mine."

I unfold it and can't believe my eyes. It's a report on a mutual friend. Regarding anti-Soviet speech. To the KGB. Dated June 1984. The writing is remarkable: "Whereupon he began speaking about the violations of human rights in the Soviet Union with all the passion of the radio commentaries by foreign slanderers. Meanwhile, he recently got married, was given an apartment—one would think that he'd want to enjoy life..."

　　　　　　　　　　NINA GORLANOVA

In order to write about the "passion of foreign slanderers," one would have to have heard them oneself at least once, wouldn't one? He gave himself away...Well, well, well! How am I supposed to react to this?

"Did you send the final draft off?"

"No."

Somehow, I'm not so sure. I ask, "Why? Why didn't you send it?"

"I don't know...I guess it's not really compatible with my lifestyle."

Tania K.: "I finally bought Volume twenty-five of the Dostoevski collection—the one where he is against Jews. You know, the Jews have been buying it up and burning it."

"How'd you figure that?"

"Because you can't find it anywhere!"

"There is a lot you can't find. Not to mention that I've never seen the rest of the Dostoevski books for sale either."

"But I tell you: sometimes, at least, you can find one of the other ones, but the twenty-fifth—almost never."

"Maybe that's because ardent anti-Semites like you keep them at home instead of selling them."

My husband is muttering that we shouldn't use the word *anti-Semite* and say directly: *racist*.

As for Dostoevski, he simply confused the Jews with the bourgeoisie. That there is always a Jew that will give a Russian a drink means only that the bourgeois was frequently assisted by Jews. Besides, after the fascist concentration camps, even Dostoevski would not have been writing on such dangerous topics—he just didn't know what anti-Semitism could lead to. Himself, he favored assimilation, mixing of the Jews with other peoples through marriage. He wasn't in favor of pogroms, like you...Soviet racists.

One day to cataclysm. What about the night? Is it going to start at night?

Nuriya, a little girl, the daughter of a friend: "Auntie Nina, there is a new group in town—they hunt Jews." That's what she said: *hunt*.

Sh.: "The thing is, those people think they are too smart. That's why they strive for world rule."

"I have lots of Jewish friends, and none of them wants to rule the world."

"That's just camouflage."

Very good camouflage, apparently. A Jewish friend of mine, a tremendously intelligent woman, still hadn't defended her doctoral dissertation at the age of forty-five because she was told to portray Soms in *The Forsythe Saga* as a bigger scoundrel, because, supposedly, she hadn't condemned the damned capitalist properly. She refused to compromise her beliefs. Now she works half-time—a fact for which her director is harassing her, but my friend doesn't know how to respond rudely enough. Turns out this is just camouflage, though—and behind the camouflage, my friend is rapidly approaching world rule.

There was Stalin, Mao, Napoleon, and so on—so many people who wanted to rule the world (starting with the Tartar Mongols), and not one of them was Jewish.

In the morning, Natasha brings over some water that's been "blessed" by Chumak. It starts to help right away. An hour later, neither of my kidneys hurts! That makes the prospect of death even scarier.

Andrei comes second. He relates that his mother has been released from the nuthouse. In the street she ran into an acquaintance who started talking nonstop: "You know, we used to laugh at people like you, but now they are on television every day—psychics treating people...Would you give a consultation regarding a sick child?"

Andrei's mother: "You didn't just laugh at me—you had me committed. Now I don't do consultations. I've been cured."

Next are two geniuses bearing hair fixative. They are drinking it in the kitchen. For some reason, they are talking about the television quiz show, "The Fun-Loving and Resourceful Club."

"The worst is the Institute of International Relations team, of course. And the ones from Kharkov are the best—"

"Is International Relations really the worst?"

"Well, they bear a distant resemblance to human beings, but they are nothing compared with normal Kharkovans. I mean, the students there are all children of the nomenklatura—and the nomenklatura isn't capable of producing anything, much less normal children."

"But those are the kids that will be safe in any cataclysm."

"If the AC allows."

What AC? Oh, the alien civilization! Here we go again: we used to believe in god, then in communism—and now, with the aliens, we'll get ahead of the rest of the world again.

NINA GORLANOVA

My daughters are home from daycare: "Mama! Mama! Did you read in the paper that there were aliens at the pioneer camp? The counselors saw them, too!"

Turns out there have been scattered sightings of aliens in the Perm region for a week already. I go over to the neighbor's to borrow some newspapers and learn a slew of new things. One child threw a rock at an alien, who responded by threatening him ("aiming at him") with something akin to a comb. The child experienced fear and ran away, but the grass under his feet was on fire...

That is the scariest part.
  Why?
  Because in ancient Rome, just before the start of the civil war (between supporters and opponents of Caesar), thousands of people saw corpses walking the streets.
  My husband explains: "In a tense social atmosphere, any event in nature can serve to release the tension. There is no doubt that some sort of natural irregularity is occurring in Perm at the moment—and it will serve as the trigger."
  "You mean the counselors and children didn't really see aliens? What did they see, then?"
  "They saw what they wanted to see. Or, according to Freud, what they fear..."

Midnight. My husband is not home. He went to the Brushteins' to discuss self-defense. I hear footsteps in the stairway—many men. Then I hear them running back down from our floor. Why are they running? Because they've placed a bomb and are in a hurry to get away from the explosion. I guess it's started. Shaking, I step out into the hallway, turn on all the lights (including the kitchen light, for some reason), and reach for the lock. I'm scared. But I have to open the door as quickly as possible and throw the bomb down onto the heads of the people who are about to run out the building door—the ones who put it there. I jump out into the hall—and see nothing. I go up to the attic and discover a puddle of urine. Oh, so it was just some anonymous alcoholics stopping by to do their private business. And look at me...Right about then my husband comes home. I tell him. He looks stricken.
  "Better to die once in a pogrom than many times over in your thoughts. Go to sleep."

I dream that we've already moved to the Solovskiys' apartment, which we've been promised.* There is a door from the hallway into the office, and we've closed it up with bookcases, as though it was never there, to hide all our Jewish friends and my children. When they come from Pamiat (all people I know), they walk by the bookcase door when Agnia's laughter sounds from inside...I wake up.

I cry in the bathroom so that I won't wake anyone. Smoke a cigarette and lie back down. In the morning, I take the little ones to daycare and get in line for tomatoes at the Products of the Rural Economy store. Suddenly an awful crash explodes in my ears. But over it, I hear the screams of the women standing in line. What an awful scream.

Turns out, some drunken loaders dropped a case of clarified butter in glass jars. And look at us...But today is the day: "The sixty-second"!

Both packages to the hospital in Frunze come back marked "Addressee deceased." Too late...

Nothing else happens all day. Some time passes. I've calmed down some, but not too much: every day there is something in the papers about an explosion on a nuclear submarine or a train transporting chemicals, or...Plus those aliens are being spotted more and more often; there was an expedition working in the Perm region that supposedly had contact with them. This is reported in—*Soviet Youth!* Where else would Perm residents get their news? In the Lithuanian media, of course!

And then, on August 18, I open *Komsomolskaya Pravda*.

"One April morning, Perm region residents were awakened by a vague, menacing rumble...This was the sound of an earthquake rated six on the Richter scale. One in a series of natural disasters would have been lost in the long line of calamities that have plagued us if it weren't for the fact that in the affected region, within one hundred kilometers of each other, two nuclear power plants were being constructed..."

Isn't it over yet?

---

*Families that had applied for exit visas to emigrate often "bequeathed" their apartments to people staying behind.

NINA GORLANOVA

Election Day

GALINA VOLODINA

"Muscovites aren't a bad lot, but they've gone nuts over the apartment issue," pronounces the devil in Mikhail Bulgakov's classic novel The Master and Margarita. *In the nearly six decades between the time Bulgakov wrote those words and Galina Volodina wrote "Election Day," the specifics of the apartment situation in Moscow changed, but its role as powerful motivator and indicator of the relationship between the state and the individual became only more entrenched. Volodina contrasts what are arguably the two most powerful forces behind any sort of mass mentality in Moscow and many other places in Russia: the apartment issue on the one hand and fear of the authorities on the other. In this story, both are shown to have long histories. The apartment issue goes back to the time right after the revolution when the warehouse in this story was converted to apartments, and the fear dates back to 1937, a year of some of the best-known and most brutal Stalinist purges. The outcome in Volodina's narrative is utterly and depressingly predictable: the characters will vacillate, temporary alliances will be formed, but ultimately fear and the state will prevail. The story ends on the fatalistic note characteristic of Russian literature of this century and earlier: things will happen when they happen, and life will go on as it has before, and neither individuals nor groups have a role to play in determining what will happen or when.*

Like several other pieces in this collection, this story was created during what is now known as "the period of stagnation"—Brezhnev's reign of 1964–1982—by a writer who came of age during this period. Volodina had completed a collection of short stories soon after graduating from Moscow's Literary Institute in 1980. The collection was circulated widely in Moscow's writing circles and gained wide acclaim but was never published. Three of the stories from the collection, including "Election Day," saw print for the first time in 1990, in the anthology of women's writing entitled She Who Bears no Ill. *—M. G.*

The building on the hill never bothered anyone. It stood adjacent to a factory fence. Behind the fence, there were peeling red structures. The building looked like it belonged with them. Before the revolution, it had. It had been a warehouse, but in the thirties it was subdivided into cubicles—one window each—given a new spackle job, and stuffed full of people. Demand for shelter was high: each of the building's communal apartments, with its long hallway and a single kitchen, had about ten families in it. Fallen bricks had left the building pock-marked, but it remained firmly planted on the hill. Old-timers said that during the war, when the Germans were bombing Moscow, a new building collapsed when a bomb landed nearby while this one just kept standing.

Across the street, buildings were being demolished; people moved out, leaving unwanted things behind. Kids poked around the empty apartments and brought home the loot: junk of all kinds, some useful, some not. Adults didn't look down on this activity either: there were often tubs left in the buildings, and these would be placed about the attic, because the roof always leaked. Floorboards and old furniture made good firewood—the building was heated with wood stoves.

The building had been slated for demolition before the war, but it never came down. Every time a section of wall caved in—which was most likely to happen in the spring—some of the younger residents would get active writing letters to various authorities, the district executive committee*, and the papers. The letters always got responses from the executive committee or the residential authority saying that the building would be demolished and even specifying the date when that would happen. The residents waited patiently, but when the date came and went, they resumed their lobbying.

The old-timers viewed all this activity as a waste of time, but the children living in the small, dark rooms with moldy walls kept getting sick. During inspections the building was invariably declared uninhabitable.

"Fungus," Petechka would say, puffing on a cigarette on the front porch after yet another inspection. "It knows how to do its job right: it will eat the building for sure."

"Yeah," Vania would add philosophically. "We'll all end up that way."

"Of course, they'll demolish it—but when? That is the question!" Volodia, who had recently moved to the building, would make his contribution.

"What did you think—you are gonna live here a year and then you qualify for an apartment?"

"What's this got to do with Volodia? His wife was born and raised in

---

*The executive branches of the governments of any of Moscow's twenty-nine districts.

this building, since she was this big. What are you yapping about, Petechka?" Vania would stand up for his neighbor.

"You're the one yapping," Petechka would grumble in response.

"Check out that babe," old man Klochkov would say, in keeping with his custom of not taking part in conversations about the building. He would nudge Petechka, raising one of his gray eyebrows and pointing with his eyes to a woman passerby.

"Yeah, that's one hell of a broad! That's all right—her man'll give it to her," Petechka would grunt.

"He'll try, that's for sure, ha-ha," Klochkov would laugh, pleased that his attempt at distraction had succeeded.

Then the men, out on the porch for their morning smoke, would follow the "babe" with their eyes until she disappeared around the corner.

"Time to chop down your lilac tree, Petechka. It's blocking all the light from my window," Volodia would say, to continue the conversation.

"Like hell I'm gonna chop it down," Petechka would say and disappear into his room to escape the unpleasant conversation.

"Vania, did you see the inspection yesterday?"

"Yesterday? Sure. They went into my room and shot right out of there. Went out on the porch to get some air, like we are now—the air in my room is a little—"

"What's with all the inspections? Your Lenka must be wasting paper again," Klochkov would say, unable to contain himself any longer.

"Why shouldn't she write? It's all true!"

"Let her speak for herself. I, for one, don't need a new apartment. They'll put me in the middle of nowhere. Meanwhile, here I've got a cellar, my own cabbage and potatoes."

"Yeah, gramps, if you'd just get a pig, too, you'd have yourself a meal."

"I would, too, if the police'd let me."

"I bet you we'll live here another five years at least. Then we'll see. So, Klochkov, you've still got time left to eat your cabbage," Vania would sum up.

The old women were glad the building would be standing for a while still and would say to the young women, "What's with you, you fools? There's a lot of years still left in this building. Look—the walls are a meter deep. They don't build them like this anymore."

But every year, the building, which had no foundation, sank deeper into the ground, slowly settling. And even though some tireless owners of private gardens had planted trees on the hillside leading down to the road, the building seemed to be giving at the seams, swelling up as though the walls could not contain the abundance of people living on the two floors of long dark hallways. The cracks in the corners of the rooms and the kitchens grew gradually deeper, and since the building continued to straddle the line between life and death, inspectors kept coming to give their verdict: it should be demolished. The residents grew used to this and no longer drew hope from it. Life in the building continued at the bustling pace of a large anthill.

Old women would gather on the bench in front of the building and agree that the young ones could move if they wanted to so bad—but the old people would do just fine in this old place. They recalled instances when single women had died in their own apartments with no one to bring them a drink of water. They remembered neighbors who'd tried to force them out, spitting in their pots and making all kinds of trouble.

The younger residents, on the other hand, grew more and more restless and vocal. They didn't want to grow old in a building they hated. Construction on a high-rise began nearby. The more stories it acquired, the more agitated the building's residents became. By spring ceilings in the building had sprung leaks and started caving in. Temporary supports were constructed in the kitchens. Still there was no reliable information about the demolition.

Festive bright lights lit up the door of the dormitory across the street. Illuminated signs proclaimed CAMPAIGN OFFICE and EVERYONE VOTE. Some more inspectors came by to check out the holes in the ceilings, test the supports, estimate the cost of repairs, and tell the residents that in due time the building would definitely be demolished, and in the meantime, if they felt crowded, some people could move into newly vacant rooms in some older buildings. This option satisfied a few people, who moved out much to the satisfaction of neighbors who took over their rooms.

A depressing and distressing event that occurred a couple of weeks before the elections affected not one but all the residents of the building. The month was March but the weather was frigid; there were still barrels of sauerkraut and a decent supply of firewood left in the sheds. The sheds—havens for pigeon lovers and all manner of riff-raff—caught on fire at night, and before the fire trucks arrived almost everything had burned. Not only did the firewood burn, but the animals—Uncle Vasia's hunting dogs—were barely saved, and then only because they were in the last shed.

Having watched the fire and cried over the lost goods and the prospect of freezing, the residents returned to their apartments, where they continued to discuss these topics—which is to say, the night was restless. In the morning, many of them went to check out the site of the fire again and look for things that could be salvaged. Petechka alone had luck: he managed to dig a barrel of sauerkraut out of a cellar deep under the former shed, though this barrel immediately became the subject of a dispute between Petechka and his neighbor Vania.

Rumors that one of the residents had started the fire to speed up the resettlement spread through the building. The old women cursed the young residents and confronted each of them with the question "Are you the one who set fire to the sheds?"

A flurry of visits to people's deputies and the executive committee followed, resulting in some trucks dumping a load of fresh lumber by the building. Nearby owners of summerhouses circled the lumber looking indifferent, but since carpenters arrived on the heels of the trucks there wasn't time to steal the lumber. In just three days of cracking jokes and smoking cigarettes, the carpenters put together sheds that were not only closer to the building but better than the old ones: each had its own wooden floor instead of the dirt floors the old sheds had had.

For the old women, the event served as proof positive that the building was fated to live forever. They started recalling how way back before the war some big boss had come by, all polite and considerate, and how he had allowed the building to be repaired instead of demolished, which the authorities already wanted to do then—but, thanks to all the repair work, it was now still standing. And, thank god they lived in the building rather than the resettlement barracks where they would have had to go.

The atmosphere in the kitchens grew tense and adversarial. A young mother would come out into the kitchen to hang swaddling clothes on the line and dream aloud of having running hot water in a new apartment. If an old woman happened to be in the kitchen at the same moment, she muttered, " 'Partments, 'partments—you'll sit your ass off in that 'partment with no one to talk to. What don't you like about this place, where someone'll watch your soup for you or keep an eye on your fire? You live like some sort of lady and don't even see the benefit, bitch."

Lenka got it the worst from the old women because all the complaints and appeals had been written in her room.

While they were waiting for the new sheds to be built, the building's residents raided all the stores in the vicinity for empty wooden boxes, which they used for heating. Lines of people carrying boxes snaked toward the building, but soon the stores started guarding their boxes. Then the residents started stealing boxes at night and brazenly breaking them up during the day on the front porch, angrily stomping on the resistant boxes to crack them.

In anticipation of the elections, the feverish residents discussed their problems once more and decided not to vote: maybe then they'd get someone to pay attention; maybe then they'd see some action.

On the night before the election, the building was filled with a special kind of excitement, which manifested in polite knocks on the door announcing frequent visits of one neighbor to another, in the fact that the old women gathered in the room of the most ancient of them, Chulanikha, and even in the fact that a woman given to eavesdropping by the door, when caught in the act, did not pick a fight with her neighbor but straightened up proudly and marched down the hall with dignity to disappear into her room.

The men gathered at Petechka the bachelor's. Someone ran out and got wine. Finishing off yet another bottle in a cloud of cigarette smoke, the men bragged that no force in the world would drag them into the voting booth.

"Why should we fear the authorities? They are a joke," Zhenka announced to everyone's delight. Around the building he enjoyed a reputation for being young and feisty. "One day I was leaving early. The boss, he's got me confused with someone else." Like many of the building's residents, Zhenka worked at the fur factory. "He got into the habit of standing in the door with the guard, so he's screaming all sorts of things about how I'm irresponsible. Got so heated up he got all red. I'm just standing there quietly, watching him lose it. He's checking my toolbox, emptying everything out onto the floor. He stops screaming finally 'cause he's out of breath. So then I say all calm, 'Is that all? Now, zip up your fly. You can see the mink in there.' That's where he'd hidden the fur, the greedy bastard. He's been afraid of me since. He knows he's been caught red-handed."

"Hey, you know, Zhenka, Valka had some furs that burned up in the shed."

"Shut up about that."

"Sure, I understand—a heartfelt attachment to little fur things."

"Shut up if you're so understanding."

"It's true that there is no reason to fear the authorities." Petechka,

GALINA VOLODINA

the host and an electrician by vocation, entered the discussion. "What are they—some kind of beast or something? They are people just like us. There was one had me over to his house. So I was fixing this stationary hairdryer for them. I'm thinking, *What hair salon did you steal this from?* But he poured me some cognac, we had a good talk. My job's to keep quiet."

"Yeah, not all bosses are the same. There are some that don't steal."

"Enough talk about the authorities already. Say, what's it gonna accomplish if we don't vote? Maybe we aren't doing the right thing."

"No, since we all decided, we aren't voting."

The next morning, the old women were the first to vote. When election workers started making the rounds of the rooms, a trickle formed from the building to the polling place. Some resisted, but their wives dragged them to the polling place, shaming them for all to see and loudly recalling the year 1937, when half the building's population went to jail. The heroes of the day before were faced with a family situation that had turned nightmarish overnight. There were some who'd had a drink to get up the nerve and voted early in the morning and then spent the rest of the day watching others. Some left the building altogether and weren't heard from all day. By three o'clock everyone had voted except for one young couple, who stubbornly refused to perform their civic duty.

She was breast-feeding the baby when the election workers came around for the third time. An entire procession squeezed into the room: a young district party committee worker, several members of the election commission, and her husband's boss, who'd been fetched by the election office. Crowding into the doorway, all of them surveyed the dark room. The commission chairman knew right away that this stubborn woman would not budge.

"There is something odd going on with this building," he whispered to the district party committee man. "It's supposed to be demolished this year, but it's not on any of the lists."

"Aleksei Borisovich, why don't you and the comrades go out for a bit while we have a talk in here," responded the party committee worker, hanging his coat over the chair. The gold frames of his eyeglasses sparkled; his suit and everything else he was wearing were high-quality and fit well. Cautiously, he sat down on the couch and looked at the young woman with sympathy. "You and I are both young," he said. "I think we'll be able to find a common language. No one's going to let you go without voting. You have to do it. And why are you resisting, anyway?"

"My child is sick," she was saying. "It's damp here. You can see for yourself how we live. And all we get is promises. By the time they move us, the children will be sick for life."

"If I were you, I wouldn't have had a child in a building like this. You have to have the right conditions before starting a family."

"So you make babies according to plan?"

"Personally, I don't have any children. But if I lived in such conditions, I wouldn't allow myself to have a child. You, on the other hand, are trying to use your child to get something. Meanwhile, you have no one but yourself to blame."

"For what?"

"There are thousands of buildings being constructed. But we can't give everyone an apartment at once. We've still got native Muscovites living in cellars, and here you are—"

"I was born in this building myself. Here, look." She handed him a folder, fat with responses to her letters. "Our building was placed at the top of the list five years ago already. I voted for him—for Likhanov—and went to see him even—and what did that do? Why should I vote for him again when he doesn't even want to hear about our building? He's doing just fine, but he lies to us."

"Well, in that case, I can't tell you anything good is going to happen to you. By the way, are you planning to go to school?"

"Of course."

"Then you should know that you will not be accepted by any college. We'll take care of that. And you'll never get a decent job—not in this area, anyway. Think about that. And then I suggest that you vote."

At the same time, Lena's husband Volodia was talking with his boss in the kitchen.

"Just go and vote already. Why are you asking for trouble? They'll demolish this building anyway. Look—they are putting up buildings all around here."

"Yeah, I know."

"Well, if you know, then go and vote. Or you'll lose your job."

When the delegation departed, the young woman sat down by the window. Through her tears she could barely make out the sign: EVERYONE VOTE!

"Hey, Lena," she heard her husband's guilty voice behind her. "It didn't work anyway. The whole building voted. I'm gonna go, eh? Let's go together—stop being so obstinate?"

She said nothing. When her husband left, she swaddled the baby hastily and ran out after him. She caught up with him at the polling place and put herself across the door.

"Don't go!"

A poll worker with a red armband looked questioningly at the cop assigned to the polling place. The young cop shifted from one foot to the other. Volodia pushed his wife out of the way, and the cop kept her from getting back to the door.

She came home tired and empty. It was a while before her husband returned. She heard him in the kitchen saying that the cafeteria was selling beer and red caviar.

She sat quietly, holding the baby in her arms. The baby, happy about something, was babbling and trying to stick his foot in his mouth. When he fell asleep, she went up to the attic, where the swaddles hung drying. She stood in the semidarkness, looking out on the huge city through the attic window. On a clear day, you could see the Kremlin from the attic, where, now, she burst into hurt and angry tears.

By evening, the building's residents were baking and frying food for their holiday meals. The wives were talking in the kitchen.

"My guy didn't want to go but I made him because you never know. Next thing he could get arrested."

"Why would anyone want to arrest your Semion? Times have changed."

"Have they? If you say so. But you never know—they could just come, arrest him, and send him to prison. And later they'll tell you what for."

"What for? They don't arrest you for a reason. They arrest you for no reason. Look at Tatiana and Danila. They came back from exile all old and quiet. That's not what they used to be like. Motka had turned them in—and all they ever found in their room were some wrappers from tea packages, you know, silver ones. So they did fifteen years for the wrappers. Now they are wasted, no strength or health left."

"I had to give my husband a half liter. Barely talked him into it."

Maria Pavlovna from room seven, whose husband was on a business trip abroad and who generally didn't talk with the neighbors because she considered them beneath her, put in a word of outrage: "Enough babbling already. Can't you stop talking nonsense! If the NKVD could hear you now!" She walked away from her embarrassed neighbors, her silk robe rustling.

Only once the door to Maria Pavolvna's room had shut did the feisty

Katerina Veretenova march across the kitchen with her butt stuck out demonstratively and say, "Some lady! From rags to riches—and now she thinks she can threaten us. Like we don't know the truth."

By the truth Katerina meant that Maria Pavlovna's husband got rich during the war because he was in charge of a gold warehouse. Everyone remembered, too, that she got married with one dress to her name, and he'd given her everything and made a person out of her.

In the hallway, Nikolai Chuprin, who was drunk, was talking to San Sanych, a man of about fifty who had gray hair, a huge nose, and bug eyes. Chuprin was poking him in the chest for emphasis.

"I didn't get caught up in their thing! I voted at six. No one's gonna make an enemy of the people out of me. I know what's what. Get it?" He pushed San Sanych up against the wall and started whispering passionately, "Tomorrow they are gonna take them all away! Then there'll be lots of empty rooms."

"Come on! You shouldn't talk like that."

"I'm telling you—they'll arrest them all."

"Idiot," spat San Sanych and, pushing Chuprin out of the way, stepped toward Dora Dmitriyevna, who was walking by wearing a colorful Chinese robe. He pushed her into the corner. "For old times' sake, neighbor," he said, smacking his lips loudly on her cheek. When he let her go, he added admiringly: "Look, the broad's pushing fifty, and still looks like a young girl."

In room number seventeen, two tipsy couples sat at a table crowded with marinated mushrooms and other treats. A burly woman with ruddy cheeks draped her arms around the neck of the head of a large family—which, at that moment, was running up and down the hallway or hanging out in the yard. He lived in a sixteen-square-meter room with his wife and six kids—the burly woman's godchild included.

"You know, buddy, you've got your whole life ahead of you."

"Sure, sure, the hell with them all," he said and then whined the words of a song: "We'll go drinking and we'll go partying, and when death comes to get us, we'll go dying."

"When death comes to get me, I won't be home," added the woman.

"There, there." His wife had secretly been observing the pair. "You'll get it at work tomorrow—we'll see how you'll be singing then."

And he hastily freed his neck from the woman's arms.

In the hallway, where the wood stove crackled, Uncle Andrei sat in the dim light, softly playing the "The Waves of the Amur" waltz on his accordion.

GALINA VOLODINA

"Andrei, someone's here to see you!"

He stopped playing and as he was taking his accordion off, he felt a pang in his heart: he remembered how they came for his friend Ilya, taking him from his own wedding: someone had screamed that someone was here to see Ilya—and now he still hadn't come back. That's when Andrei got the accordion—before the war still. But this time, it turned out to be a false alarm: it was just a relative who'd come to the city and was looking for a place to stay.

The room where Lenka, who hadn't voted, lived with her husband was the only one that had had no visitors. They sat quietly, feeling hostile toward each other. Volodia was thinking that his wife was a good woman but reckless, which made it hard to live with her, and that it would be better if she were simpler, like everyone else. She, meanwhile, decided that she would be making the move to the new building without Volodia.

A year later, nothing was left of the building. The factory was moved to Rostokino. The hillock had grown over by daisies and fireweed a half meter tall. At regular intervals, the election headquarters in the dormitory across the way still hung out the same fading banner: EVERYONE VOTE!

The Day of the Poplar Flakes

MARINA PALEY

"It was never my intention to scare my reader with descriptions of the horrible horrors of the Soviet health-care system," writes Marina Paley (pronounced Pah-LAY). "Journalism is a more expressive tool for illuminating this depressing issue; statistics would be more articulate than fiction.:.I just wanted to show the outstanding separateness of the transitional place called a hospital, which is where a person comes into this world and, most often, leaves it as well. The existential nature of this institution, which exposes the bases of life and death with shocking ease, is similar to the nature of military barracks, jail cells, space ships, concentration camp barracks...The list goes on."

The list does indeed go on, but the difference between hospitals and the rest of the institutions Paley mentions (all of which, with the possible exception of space ships, have spawned mini-canons in postwar Russian literature), is that the Soviet hospital is traditionally a feminine domain. Medicine is a nonprestigious, "feminine" profession, like teaching. In this story the stark realities of medicine are interwoven with another "feminine" motif: young love. The days of early June, when the sun never sets in St. Petersburg and poplar trees (relatives of the American cottonwood tree) blanket the city with their cottony seeds, are endowed with a special romantic significance. Fittingly, the female protagonist—apparently a medical student starting her summer internship—is both in love and in medicine.

The author is a 1980 graduate of the Leningrad Medical Institute. She worked as a doctor until 1985, when, drained to the point of paralysis, she quit and found a job as a security guard—the classic vocation of Soviet intellectuals in the Brezhnev years. She began writing—first, poetry, then literary criticism and, finally, fiction—and found acceptance and even acclaim with apparent ease. She was accepted to the Literary Institute in Moscow in 1986 and published a book of short stories entitled The Ward of the Doomed *in 1991, the year of her graduation. Her 1992 novel,* Yevgesha and Avgusha, *was nominated for the Booker Prize.*

In many ways, Paley's personal story is the story of women's fiction in Russia: She stepped off traditionally feminine terrain into a historically masculine field at the dawn of glasnost with a voice that seemed instantly strong and definitive. Her subject matter—the "horrible horrors" witnessed

and experienced by the women in her fiction—is the unseen, unheard
woman's experience of Soviet reality (a fact that sets this story far apart
from the mainstream of Russian "hospital lit" in the tradition of Solzhen-
itsyn's Cancer Ward). Finally, like women's fiction itself, Marina Paley—
a single mother with retired parents who has been pronounced one of the
leading voices of her generation—is engaged in a daily struggle for eco-
nomic survival. —M. G.

A woman lies on the bed with her head to the window. Above her, the gaps in the window frames slowly fill up with something resembling the cotton stuffed into the window frames in the winter for insulation. But the woman cannot see the window. Nor can she see that under her bed, the floor around the enamel bedpan with the red words, "Intensive Care," is covered with a grayish layer of the same stuff, which could be cotton or moon dust. "Damned mess!" says an elaborately made-up nurse as she walks by. "It's all over the place again." She says it as though she blamed the woman who is lying there with her head to the window.

The Intensive Care attendant has been getting called out to the reception area all day long. She runs out full of hope every time, but again and again it's some relative of a patient she knows nothing about shifting uncomfortably from one foot to the other. She explains that the patient is no longer in Intensive Care, that they've probably been moved up to the ward and that it's her first day here anyway, but shaky hands shove apples, oranges, candy, and some kind of home-made piroshki at her, and she pushes it all away, the way a child pushes away a spoon. But the worst part is the embarrassed, sneaky gesture with which they keep trying to shove balled-up green bills into the breast and side pockets of her coat, the way a cheat-sheet is handed over during a test. The relatives don't believe—or don't want to understand, because she is the only attendant in the building—that she has no connection to their loved ones. They nod obediently in response to her explanation, smile solicitously, and ask her to *look again, a little closer.* "Don't worry, you'll get into the swing of things," the surgeon on duty reassures her. "And don't take the three-ruble bills, of course. In fact," he says, raising his voice to make sure that the beautifully made-up nurse can hear him, "tell them to go ahead and hand over three hundred!" He puts his hands together and extends them, palms pressed against each other, forward and upward, as though begging the skies for the three hundred rubles, then suddenly claps his hands and presents them to the nurse triumphantly. "Did you score a mosquito, oh fearless leader?" she inquires in an angelic voice. "What the hell would I need a mosquito for when I'm expecting that letter tomorrow?" says the surgeon meaningfully. A poplar flake—a white wisp with a seed in it—slowly floats up from his hands.

"Miss," whispers the woman with her head to the window, smiling guiltily, "give me some water—Please—"
  "You aren't allowed to have water. The doctor told me—"
  "Just one drop—I can have a drop—"
  "I can't, don't you understand?"
  "The doctor won't find out—Just one sip—"
  "It would only make it worse, believe me. Try to be patient until tomorrow. Let me moisten your lips—but I can't do anything more, so don't ask anymore, all right?" The attendant winds a strand of cotton onto a pair of tweezers, which she dips in a white mug with a spout. The convulsive greed with which the woman's lips grab the pathetic tampon is unbearable to watch. She sucks from it loudly, then help-lessly reaches her yellow-coated tongue in a silent plea to have it wetted again. The attendant dips the cotton in the mug again. "Thank you," the woman whispers. Revitalized by a drop of water, her mouth is capable of producing a slightly more distinguishable rustle. "May God keep you healthy, dear." The attendant is unbearably ashamed that the woman is lying there with a guilty face, pitifully thanking her for nothing. But the hardest part is that the woman will most likely keep asking for water all day long. She'll keep asking like a defense-less animal, and the attendant will never get permission to give it to her. "Do you want a wet towel?" Not waiting for an answer, the atten-dant rushes out to the dressing room, where she stays a long time, holding a thin cotton towel, with the stamp "Intensive Care," under a strong stream of water. The water gets colder and colder. Thank God the sick woman cannot hear the coveted splashes and probably does not realize that the attendant came in here on purpose even though there is a faucet in the room where the woman lies as well. She goes back and runs the towel over the woman's face very quickly, trying not to tempt her tense lips; then she goes over her neck, her chest, and her hands. She wets the towel again, wrings it out hard, and places it on the woman's forehead. The woman tries to give her a cheerful smile, at least to thank the attendant with her eyes—but her eyes are still pleading for *just a sip*...

MARINA PALEY

The air has been growing dully, oppressively stuffy since this morning both here on the ward and out in the street. Opening the windows wouldn't help and might even be dangerous because every so often the dense outside air bursts in like a wide blade of humid wind bearing not relief but the insistent poplar flakes that wedge themselves into cracks in space. A few days ago, the flakes were flying around happily, falling onto the pavement and sticking together into airy white bubbles, sparkling like white foam in the bushes, shimmering like a snow-white bedspread on young grass. Boys set fire to them. The flakes never paused for long; they flew and flew without stopping—free, high up, as though surveying the area for new destinations for their carefree journey. Suddenly, today, the flakes pouted and turned to fuzzy dust, forced down in a gray and immobile mass by the dull humid air. Just yesterday the flakes were playful; today they are like the refuse left after a game—eliciting boundless disgust in the exhausted body.

"Someone's here to see you, you know," says the nurse matter-of-factly.

The attendant makes her back very straight and slowly floats out into the hallway, where she looks back over her shoulder quickly and then bursts out into the reception area. But there is no one there. She runs out into the yard. No one. The lethal air has even put a stop to the innocent fuss of pajamas on the hospital benches. She returns to the building agitated. Beneath the stairway that leads up to surgery, a black hole beckons her to the basement, which houses the employee cloak room. Cautiously, she steps down the stone stairs.

"Is everyone here as pretty as you?" the visitor's toothy smile greets her. He is holding a bouquet of tulips as though it were a broom. Flakes cling to his tight black tee-shirt, so he looks covered in cotton; a dark curly beard frames his juicy, very red mouth—and the beard, too, is speckled with white flakes, as if he had been eating live chickens.

Later she walks him to the hospital gates. Puddles left from a rainstorm that struck a week ago now look like foggy mirrors grown over with centuries-old dust. They are covered with a thick, impenetrable layer of flakes, but the slightest breeze causes a few of the top ones to fly off in a compulsive last attempt to change something. The flakes latch on to eyelashes, fly into eyes, eat their way into hair, stick to the aching, sweaty body, uncaringly stuff themselves into ears, noses, throats, oblivious to where they plant their seeds—in the earth, in a person, or in a rock—as long as they can sprout fresh stems that will give life to new airborne seeds.

When she comes back to Intensive Care, she sees that the woman with her head to the window has closed her eyes. There are two thin tubes coming out of her nostrils; they branch off a thicker, clear oxygen line, which stretches above the bed and along the entire wall. It's probably easier for her to breathe now, in this unimaginable humidity.

In the dressing room, the attendant takes an empty glucose bottle, fills it with water, wraps it in wax paper, and places the tulips in it. Back in the room, she softly puts the flowers on the night stand next to the woman's bed. "I'll just leave them here," she says, trying to get ahead of the guilty smile that appears as the woman slowly opens her eyes. "These are mine. I'll just leave them here until morning, all right?" The woman tries to pull her lips apart; their awkward motion means *You shouldn't have*. One of the tubes falls out of her nostril and trembles over her upper lip. The attendant carefully replaces it, noting with surprise how loosely it is attached.

There are only two beds in the small Intensive Care room. The woman with the tubes is in one of them; the bed on the other side of the room divider is vacant. But there is plenty of work for the attendant: this is her first day on duty, and before she got through the door, she had declared that she was willing to do anything and everything except please don't make her deal with the corpses. At first the made-up nurse couldn't even understand what she was talking about: "Oh, you mean the shuteyes? That's just where you don't have to do much—just sign off on one foot with iodine: here is the jar and here is the stick. I'm not gonna send you to the morgue alone, of course— you wouldn't make it—but I've always got alcohol ready to drink for the attendants they send over themselves." But the attendant shook her head so desperately during this monologue that the nurse gave her an "It's your loss" look, throwing, "That's just fine with me," over her shoulder as she went about her business. But she registered both the plea and the promise to do anything and everything else.

"Miss," the woman with the tubes in her nose calls for her softly. "Would you cover my feet, dear? Please—I don't know why, but they are cold—" The woman's head has slipped down off the pillow, and the yellow soles of her feet are now pressing against the metal bed-posts. The attendant helps the woman arrange herself more comfortably, then folds a flannel blanket twice and places it over her feet, tucking it in on all sides. "They are still cold," rustles the woman. She is oddly agitated; her guilty smile is gone. "Would you rub them, dear?

Make them warm—please—" It's odd that they are cold in this heat, but the woman's feet face the door, and the attendant figures there is a draft making her feet cold. She starts rubbing the dry, flaking soles as hard as she can. "What are you doing?" the nurse raises her plucked eyebrows as she passes by. "What a waste of time!" The woman's eyes are closed, and she probably can't hear very well—but most important, she cannot see that the attendant, who continues to rub her soles, is flustered. "I'll be right back, just a second," she says to the woman, in the pseudo-confident, reassuring tone of voice doctors use.

"Why did you say that I was wasting my time?" she asks as firmly as she can when she approaches the nurses' station, trying her best to hide her embarrassment.

"What were you doing?" the nurse repeats irritably. "Can't you see she is going?"

"What do you mean?" asks the attendant.

"Does everyone at your school have a screw loose like you?" the nurse asks in utter amazement. "And they are studying to be doctors! Go take the trash out instead. After that you'll be marking the test jars—"

The attendant walks out into the hospital yard, carrying an enamel bucket stuffed with empty medication boxes mixed with bloody gauze, broken vials, and strong-smelling cotton batting. Despite the endless daylight, it must be evening, because the merciless humidity has congealed into a gigantic air clot that reaches from the ground to the sky and it seems that if it is not moved, if it is not pushed through, it will suffocate anything that is alive. Inside this immovable haze, inside this slab of melting glass, thawed patches of air are still shivering thinly in places, pulsating nervously in early gusts of wind, causing the poplar flakes to soar upward convulsively, rushing away through the air tunnels, which widen in an attempt to break the deadened mass from within. The gusts are getting stronger—the storm will start soon—and the poplar flakes fly and fly in their blind hunger for multiplication. They greedily latch on to any opportunity to prolong their lives; they fill up any space, whether or not it is suitable, even if it is the kind of place where no seed will ever take root and sprout. The flakes fly and fly, stuffing themselves into cold stone cellars, collecting in attics full of junk, spreading like loose ash over people's homes, latching on to clothes, flowers, and tree leaves—and take to the air again and fly, splashing in their blind and pathetic righteousness like a generous stream of dry, hot summer semen.

Back in Intensive Care, the attendant sees that both tubes have popped out of the woman's nostrils. She should secure them in place with tape but she doesn't dare approach the nurse, so instead she quietly goes off in search of the surgeon on duty. The surgeon comes into the room with his hands in his pockets and addresses the woman in an unnaturally loud voice: "Well?! How are we doing here?! What would we like?!" Without opening her eyes, the woman responds with unexpected clarity: "Cold tea—with lemon—" The surgeon looks aside and says to no one in particular, "Oh! We have exotic desires indeed, don't we?" He instructs the nurse to secure the straws with tape. "Do you have any wishes that are more realistic? Are you comfortable?" the surgeon continues.

The woman does not respond. The surgeon looks into her face with a special sort of attention, then starts rocking from heel to toe and lecturing the attendant: "Well, what have we here? Thirty-six years old. Cancer of the liver. We cut in—and the tumors were this big," he says, pulling his large fists out of his pockets and raising them to the attendant's face. "We sewed her up—" The attendant nods anxiously, glancing over at the woman in apprehension: What makes the surgeon so sure she can't hear anything? Suddenly, the woman mumbles something unintelligible; in the mess of words, one can make out "take me out in the fresh air...fresh air..."

"Soon! They'll carry you out!" the surgeon says with surprising rancor and in a suddenly forceful and bitter gesture hits his index fingers against each other, making a momentary cross over the woman's face.

And he leaves without looking at the elaborately pretty nurse.

And the attendant keeps running errands, but now she tries not to look in the direction of the window. At night she bumps into the coat-check lady and the elevator attendant at the door to the room. Barely disguising their curiosity, they are staring through the door at what is now lying with its feet to the door.

The onlookers are chased away by two operating-room nurses who wheel a very heavy old woman into the room and flip her onto the vacant bed on the other side of the room divider. She is just coming out of anesthesia; she is shaking her head on the pillow very fast and without stopping, and screaming bloody murder: "Ooooh! My head is rolling off! Hold on to my head!" She must be horribly dizzy. The attendant presses on the woman's temples forcefully, pushing her head down on the pillow. "Calm down," she says as though she were talking to a child. "Calm down, please. They already operated on you," she is stretching her words, trying to lull the old woman. "They already did it, do you hear me? Please, granny!" But this is an extraordinarily strong old woman. She keeps trying to get away so that she can start rolling her head again. The attendant presses on her again, using all of her skinny body to help her hands. She likes the old woman's surprising strength.

The old woman had an emergency operation because of an acute intestinal blockage. Liquid stool now starts gushing out of her. Her energy doubled, the attendant starts pulling dirty linen out from under the old woman, washing her with warm water, wiping the plastic sheet underneath, and putting down fresh linen. She repeats this routine over and over, but the stool keeps gushing—and it gushes out at the most unpredictable moments, making any sort of bedpan useless. But the attendant makes the heavy old woman's bed over and over again cheerfully, urging her on in her head: *Go on, granny, go on, dear.* She is no longer paying attention to the nurse's apparent annoyance at the way she is wasting linen; she is no longer noticing the weight of the body she keeps having to lift; she is laughing at the old woman's folksy cussing, and she is not disgusted by the dense and heavy stench of warm human waste because this is a smell of life, and she would so much rather inhale that than think about the object that now lies on the other side of the room divider, still, quiet, clean, and so far devoid of any smell.

In the morning the bed behind the room divider is empty.

The attendant wipes the plastic sheet on it down with Lysol. She washes the floor. The Lysol smells nauseatingly like rancid sausage, and it is making her hands numb. Still, this is wonderful, because, as the girl already knows, the sensation in her fingers will return. She leaves the tulips on the night stand. After what the flowers have seen, they have no place among the living.

Out on the street, there are no more poplar flakes. It rained all night, and the rain plastered the flakes against the pavement, and the ones that stuffed themselves into nooks and crannies in an attempt to save themselves were easily plucked by a light breeze and then also destroyed by the rain.

II. Transitions

The Clean Zone

IRINA POLIANSKAYA

The hero of Nikolai Gogol's short story "The Overcoat," Akaky Akakiyevich Bashmachkin, is the original "little man" of Russian literature, not only poor and downtrodden but pointedly mediocre. The plot of the story revolves around Bashmachkin's acquisition and subsequent loss of a new overcoat—a symbol of higher ambitions and greater possibilities for the shy, docile clerk. Robbed of his new overcoat and ignored by authorities to whom he appeals for help, the heartbroken Bashmachkin dies. After his death, the authorities and residents of St. Petersburg are punished for their indifference by a rash of violent overcoat robberies. While "The Overcoat" is considered the work that launched Russian realism (Dostoevski is said to have remarked that all Russian writers "come out from under Gogol's Overcoat"), the story of the "little woman" has been a long time in coming; indeed, Irina Polianskaya's "The Clean Zone," which is full of more and less obvious references to "The Overcoat," is one of the first of this kind.

Polianskaya writes that the goal of her writing is to transcend mundane existence. "From the beginning, each of us knows right from wrong and knows that the most important thing is to protect your throat, and that words will come," she writes. "The main thing is to write good prose. It doesn't matter whether it fits in the traditions of Russian literature, whether it brings light to the soul or is in the service of darkness, whether it's moral or has no morals—it just has to be good and it has to be prose. Poetry—and good prose is always poetry—is what helps us transcend the prose of life."

The prose of the life from which she writes began very much like the life of her narrator: Polianskaya was born in the tiny town of Kasli near Cheliabinsk in Siberia, where her father, a former prisoner, was working for a top-secret military research outlet. "Of course, I don't remember that place," writes Polianskaya. "Memory does not retain imprisonment—but blood does, and this has determined the path of my words, and there is little I can do about that, even though I was among those who didn't learn anything new in April 1985," when much information about past political repressions was released.

Polianskaya's narrator is the daughter of a scientist who worked in one of the military-research outposts staffed with experts plucked out of Stalinist

73

concentration camps in the Siberian region of Kolyma, for the purpose of creating various weapons. It is no accident that the story is vague on the nature of the father's research; the only concrete detail in the story is the mention of Valentin Kurchatov, a physicist who played a central role in developing the Soviet Union's nuclear weapons. The narrator—who, like the author, does not have a conscious memory of living in the research town to which she returns—certainly knows little about the nature of her father's top-secret work. This knowledge, however, is lodged in her blood—poisoned, both literally and figuratively, by the work and the mysterious toxic accident that resulted from it.

Before attending the Literary Institute in Moscow, Polianskaya was educated as an actress in Rostov on the Don and worked as a company manager and a journalist. Her first work of fiction was published in 1983. She has published one book of short stories, Alleged Circumstances.

—M. G.

By the time the nurse from reception disappeared into the depths of the hallway carrying the hanger with my clothes, I had undergone a strange metamorphosis, of the sort that is possible only in dreams, where one reality easily flows into another with no gap in between them. For the first time in many years, I felt free and safe, quietly victorious over my life, which was left to wait for me out by the hospital entrance. And I followed another nurse without looking back, having finally handed over all of my duties and responsibilities, focusing on myself, my being, which was free as in infancy, knowing that no one could get to me here, that I was firmly protected by my illness, as though I had ended up on a mountain top that had been closed to all. It was long past time for me to come here, for out in the so-called free world I had accumulated more and more burdens that I could not push off, and Monday got stuck in Friday, October in September, nothing was ever completed, and my entire existence became inextricably entwined in deception of the sort that I could not be conscious of, the sort where, in order to survive, you pretend to be someone and then someone else and then someone else again, where you try to fit into the system of relationships that is crowding you, and you are consumed with the hopeless longing to take a dive or a turn or find a side street of life into which you can duck to wait out the stampede of marathon runners so that after they pass you can proceed in an entirely different direction, to an unknown destination, in complete solitude, in untouchable independence, sustained only by your personal time and your own fate, no longer within earshot of the stomping feet and the gleeful cries of victory and the grinding teeth of discord and hatred.

Indeed, what is there to do when lies are in the air and you don't know where society's lie ends and your own begins?—though yours is not a lie even, at least not a lie expressed directly through words: your words just work around the main idea, allowing it to exist, to penetrate easily the consciousness of the person you are talking to, even if this person is someone who merely happened to be there, for in any case you are painfully dependent on him, the one who just happened by. Only a child's every sensation is wet with sincerity, the dew of life. The longer you live, the deeper you are sucked into all the sly fabrications, the cunning game in which someone is always poised to take advantage of any misstep you might make. Only hysterics are sincerely sincere, but even they know whom they can and cannot take it out on, and I'm one they can take it out on because I make it easy on my enemy by putting my tail between my legs and running in search of my shell, which is barely slapped together and might just fall apart into a million grains of sand at the slightest gust of enmity. And now I have dived into my illness, which is every bit a shell: it will give me the opportunity to get stronger and gather my spiritual forces.

I am exhausted from being tired and afraid. On the one hand, I fear that I am about to be discovered, unmasked, exposed as always afraid that I'll step on somebody's foot or push somebody with my elbow. On the other hand, I am afraid that someone will push me or step on my foot and I'll take it all like I take things every moment of my existence, be it going to the shoemaker or simply talking with my flatmate. Yesterday, despite my best efforts, I bumped into her in the hallway. I'm sure she is stalking me. She has a nose for weakness, for someone she can show her muscles off to. I do everything to avoid seeing her, experiencing the requisite amount of timidity in mere anticipation, like Akaky Akakiyevich; I listen carefully for signs of her presence before diving into the hallway on my way to the kitchen or the bathroom; I make myself look busy or I moan, covering my mouth with my hand to indicate a toothache. But she has no compunction about ripping through the protective drape of my imaginary pain and sinking her claws into me like a tick, forcing me to stand in one place in anguish while she rolls her collection of complaints out before me. Unfortunately, she sees an empty place where my face should be and immediately starts filling it with her snake eggs so that, when I finally get away from her, I am left to do battle with all of the squashed emotions snaking through my heart. I heard the upbeat sound of the radio coming from her room. So having taken all the necessary precautions, I slipped out into the hallway—and again she appeared before me like a wicked witch in some stupid fairy tale. She appeared, her eyeglasses sparkling coldly, and bit into me with all she had. It turned out she had good reason for confiding, a tragedy even: her son is getting married.

"She is not one of us, if you know what I mean. She comes from poverty, squalor, a broken family, I don't even know where he found her. But he insists: 'I'm getting married.' What can I do? I've got to let the boy get married a little if he has the need. Can't argue with nature. You have to look for the good in everything: at least he is not going to be running around with whores, and this girl has her residence registration, so there won't be any unpleasant surprises in that department. So I'll spend a thousand on them—that'd still be better than having him going to prostitutes."

Her eyeglasses sparkled as she told me all this, submerging me deeper and deeper in my own trash bucket, which was pulling on my arm, and the only thing I could have done to rid myself of this sensation would have been to place the bucket over her head immediately. But I stood at attention, listening to the howling of the storm that was snowing me in, with sorrow in my soul and fear of the smooth, serious, flat face—until she released me with a majestic wave of her hand and I made a dash for my hole, the overflowing trash bucket still in my hand. And to think that I depend on this woman for nothing—her son doesn't "have a need" with me; she is not my boss or some other sort of authority figure—but the deep-rooted fear inside me asks no questions: it is like the color of my eyes—I can't just get rid of it.

As if by design, there was an empty bed by the window in the hospital room. I said hello to my roommates, placed my things in the night stand, and went up to the window and faced nature, which consisted of a pine forest in the distance, shaded by a thin coating of snow, and a set of dark tall fir trees.

There was a time when my parents lived in this town. Actually, there was no town then; there was a settlement where my father was brought on a sled, barely alive. A bit later he was allowed to send for my mother, whom he had not seen in almost seven years. I don't know what their life here was like. I only know that once my father was allowed to do what he loved, he came alive and buried himself in his work, shutting himself off from everything else—everything that made up his life when he was young. He spent many years working without a break, and when he came to—when he was granted a respite in the form of a serious illness—he saw that his wife had grown old and his children had grown up.

My sister ended up back in this town by accident, through a job assignment after graduation, and she is the one who had me admitted to this hospital, which is where she works.

Women like me—quiet women who had temporarily packed away their existence—were softly weaving a conversation behind me. When I turned around, there was a doctor standing by my bed, looking like a messenger from the snow. He asked me a few questions, which I answered with the joy of a person who is telling the truth for the first time in a long time.

"It hurts right here," he said affirmatively. "Don't worry, I've got you."

I wasn't worried; I was happy to be handing him a burden of which I had long since grown tired. From the moment I saw him, I knew that my doctor, Aleksey Alekseyevich, was a completely different kind of person than I. His eyes were calm and clear; his young face seemed friendly and disinterested at the same time: apparently, unlike me, he knew how to hold his distance. The hospital was the only place where he and I could coexist peacefully as equals, since we had an important common goal. Out in the free world, I would stay away from him out of my instinctive fear of self-confident friendly people.

"Well, so, we'll be operating on Monday," he said lightly, pulled my blanket up to my chin, and left.

"Oh, you'll be having an operation," one of the women said with respect, and I realized that I would really be able to capitalize on this upcoming procedure of mine. It would give me the right to stare out the window absently instead of taking part in conversation, or to read a book without being accused of being rude or proud.

So I cheerfully unpacked the treats my sister had packed for me; I would use them to pay for the happy chance at solitude. Sharing them says, I'm with you in spirit and all my pirogi, but please let my mind wander off in concentration and peace.

One woman was named Galia; the other was Maria. With a puzzled look on her face, Maria was holding the book I had lovingly chosen for myself. And I was already apologizing for this unfamiliar book, explaining its presence in my bag by saying I'd been extremely rushed when I was getting ready to come to the hospital, and I was already getting sad because even now I was not realizing my opportunity to do what I want and read what I want.

By the next day, we had learned a lot about one another and had become friends. Maria turned out to be happy and frivolous but with a dream in her heart, like the heroines of many of our movies, who are also divorced and also have casual contacts—until they stumble across a real person, who ultimately wastes no time showing up. Maria said that these endings were a big lie. Where she works, everyone is happy, everyone is kind, and everyone is single or has some odd marriage arrangement, and everyone is looking for happiness and getting nothing but a busy signal in response. Masha even gave us a demonstration: "Hello-o-o?" And the receiver answers, "Beep-beep-beep..."

Galia said that her life was like the movies. She had recently married a man with whom she had worked for many years. Petrovich—Galia's husband—had been married to a woman who also worked in the same collective and was disliked for being picky and zealous about the work. Nonetheless, when Petrovich divorced her and immediately married Galia, everyone suddenly took the side of his former wife, creating an atmosphere that was intolerable for Galia and Petrovich, so they both quit and found jobs in different places. Everything Galia said began with the celebratory words her mouth just couldn't get used to: "My husband Petrovich" or "Personally, my Petrovich," and the bulk of the information was contained in these very words and not in the statement that followed. Galia felt like a freshly minted duchess and couldn't get enough of her status as a married woman. The words "my husband" buzzed around the hospital room all day long. The words "my husband" pierced Masha's unmarried ears, and Masha, who could boast nothing more than "a certain person" who reliably visited her at the hospital, would make a polite face and wink at me. When Galia learned that I was married, too, she immediately switched her allegiance to me since I was someone she could talk to as an equal and discuss family problems. She looked for any reason to say the coveted words. If Serov was singing about the Madonna, it turned out that Petrovich the husband held the singer in high regard. If we had buckwheat for dinner, it turned out that Petrovich liked nothing better than kasha. If the window iced over, we had to breathe on it to make a peep-hole to observe Petrovich coming down the path. And Serov sang, and so did Alibek Dnishev and Sofia Rotaru,* and I wanted to take the buzzing radio box and yank out all its insides, take all these impossible songs that hurt my ears but to which my roommates listened faithfully, take them and wind them around some foul

---

*Pop-music stars.

broom like cobweb and shake them out the window. I wish someone would tell me where the inventors of these songs hide out, from whose reality they pluck all their quaint little peasant huts, all their old windmills, all their mellow chimes that even manage to get hold of the music, all their clean earthenware pots.

Feeling irritated and bitter, I wanted to say to my roommates, "Women, lies are in the air, in the music, in the clouds."

"I get in my car and go after you-u-u!" sings one no doubt innocent-looking charmer, and then another echoes him, "You are flying after me on your water skis!" and a third and fourth and fifth one all invite you to a carnival that no one's ever seen. Tell me, what does any of this have to do with you? What kind of madonnas are you? It's not any of our sorrowful silhouettes that they see through their windows, which are embroidered with majestic ice lilies. We slouch, we have our bags on wheels, which we puff and huff struggling to squeeze onto buses. It's not about us. Why are you letting them give you intravenous infusions from the airwaves, which swarm with germs, viruses, and deadly infections? They have erected impenetrable barricades between themselves and us, and these barricades are constructed of our very own bags, packages, bales. They don't write songs about your great joy at being able to snatch ten packages of Lotos laundry detergent when it's five per customer but you yell at the cashier in a feverishly pleading voice, singing a familiar song—I have a child who is standing right over there—and waving in the direction of a child who is indeed standing and is exhausted by the state you are in. They should write a song about the joy of having your teeth fixed after you kept putting it off until you had nothing left to chew with. A separate song about an overstuffed trolleybus, with a refrain that says, "If you are so smart, you should take a taxi-i-i." There are lots of topics like this to suggest to the smartypants who, in our day and age, write songs about bullfinches in the snow, chaffinches on the branch, and other magnificent images. Better to plug up your ears with wax than to hear the voices of these sirens. But no—the music has our hearing under arrest, and it bangs at our eardrums with all its shamelessness. And you, music—*et tu, Brute!*

In the mornings, the women prepared themselves for the doctor's rounds the way concubines prepare themselves for the master. They would prop their little mirrors up on their knees in bed and apply eye shadow to their tired eyelids and mascara to their lashes and remove their faithful hair curlers, which would spread out over the blankets like flocks of sheep. The radio would be chirping. One of them would stick her head out the window to see which room Aleksey Alekseyevich was in. Conversation would center on him, our Alioshenka: how attentive he is, how young but real, and he has a good wife, too, probably, because look at his nice starched shirts. It was the way maids talk about a beloved master: with pure loving care. He was the only man for us now: our Petroviches and "certain persons" were out there in the free world. Plus we knew that the feeling was mutual: Aleksey Alekseyevich was in love with his work, with our ailments—and by extension, with us. And he asked for nothing in return, not like on the outside. And his eyelashes were so long! Like a girl's! And his fingernails were clean! And his voice was firm but kind. Someone should make him some coffee for when he is on duty. Galia, tell Petrovich to bring a pirozhok for him. The man doesn't shut his eyes all night long. You know what? We should write to the radio station about him so they'll play that song, "People in White Coats." And to the paper, too. They say that they take this kind of thing—their rapport with patients—into consideration, so before you know it, they might add a fiver to Aliosha's salary. He stays at the hospital day and night, sparing no effort, feeling for us, such a sweetie.

I listened to their conversation, forcing a smile and thinking, Where can I disappear to, where can I find a place where I wouldn't have to be a part of anything, where I could let my face, my throat, and my soul rest? Is there a snowbank out there I can hide in?

As it turned out, what I was experiencing then, like all the feelings I seemed to be having during my first few days in the hospital, was nothing but a lie, an optical illusion in my inner eye that I mistook for some sort of discovery.

After replacing my city clothes with a robe, the hospital proposed to expose me further. For when patients are taken to their operations, they are naked, covered only with unfamiliar crackling sheets that go up to their chins. This was something I wasn't prepared for, and so on the day of the operation, my worldly disdain for the little things in life was replaced by unadulterated—I would even say innocent—fear.

With the arrival of fear, my book went into the night stand, where it fell apart into useless pages, dissolved into letters, and its words—those intelligent, perceptive words—could no longer support my confused consciousness. An icy drawing grew over the window, covering a landscape I no longer had any use for. Some people came in. These were the first people I could see clearly following my lengthy stay on a desert island. They were the last people; they would take me to the elevator and hand me over to sterile angels. The angels will carry me in the elevator up to the glass gates with the words "Clean Zone" and hand me over to god himself, and then I would taste an unconscionable, sterile dream from the mouth of a black rubber mask. I didn't want to know what would follow. I didn't want to look down at the place where my body would become even more exposed, where it would be opened up and uncorked. With my whole being I clung to these first and last people of mine, my roommates; I readily took part in the conversation, prompting Galia to say the words "my husband" again and again and pumping Masha for details about her "certain person." Then I thought of my old-woman flatmate; I thought of her with a pang of guilt, as though it were she and not I who would have to rise to the clean ozone zone tomorrow, and immediately I swore that when I returned from my unbelievable height, I would grant her the right to love her son the way she loved him, because in the final count what awaits us all is a zone even cleaner than the one where I was going the next day, and it will certainly cleanse us of all the delusions of our lives, will make us lower our loud, piercing voices, will shatter our vanity and our lies, and bring about an era of all-encompassing brotherly sincerity.

The doctors came on their rounds as always. A flock of white coats flew in, hovered over the neighboring beds, and touched down by me. Our Aleksey Alekseyevich stood out front, the leader of the flock, showing me off to the rest of them, but I was no longer looking at him; I was aiming my hope-filled stare at the friendly bearded face of the head of the ward, who was the one who would be operating on me. I was surreptitiously checking out his hands, which looked steady and were short-fingered and covered with short dark hairs. There wasn't a person in the world who was closer to me at that moment. He stepped forward, and I lifted myself on the pillows. He placed his kind hand on my shoulder.

"How are you feeling?"

"Good."

"Your sister said she was born here, in this area. I think your parents worked at the Center?"

"You could say that."

"Were they ever exposed to radiation?"

"My father was, in '51, I think. There was some sort of accident, and several people were exposed. They lifted them onto the roof right from the bin where everyone who worked in the mines threw their clothes, and then took them out by helicopter."

"Yes, I think I've heard of that incident. It's entirely possible that it explains your illness. So your sister was born before your father was in the accident?"

"Yes. My brother and I were less fortunate."

"I've heard about your brother. I'm sorry. Well, so are you prepared?" he asked lightly, smiling, as though he were referring to a short trip. At this point, a bravado reflex that was still in my blood from a former life responded to the familiar signal. "Always prepared," I said, raising my hand over my head.* "That's good," he said seriously, seeming not to notice my effort. The warmth emanating from his hand was so thorough and persuasive that I wanted to rub my cheek against it. For several hours in a row the next day he would belong wholly to me and I to him and then we would part forever, and this was truly remarkable. He took his steady hand off my shoulder, turned away, and immediately forgot about me. In the doorway, he and Aleksey Alekseyevich started talking about some Swedish medication, and the fact that he had already forgotten about me gave me added faith in his powers.

The women spoke to me in hushed voices that day.

"Aleksandr Ivanovich is a wonderful surgeon," said Galia. "My Petrovich has heard a lot of good things about him. He says he is the best one here. And he is a good person—spares no effort looking after his patients. I can't imagine why his wife left him."

"Think what you are saying," Masha reproached her, gesturing in my direction.

"So what? It didn't have any effect on him as a surgeon."

"But she doesn't need to know that." She nodded in my direction. "She should know only the good things."

"So I'm saying he's a great surgeon and his wife was an idiot. I'll point her out to you later," she promised me, and her certainty that there would be a later made me happy. "She is a nurse in gynecology. She is pretty. He isn't bad-looking either, can't say that was the problem, so I can't understand why she got it in her head to leave him. Yesterday Petrovich and I ended up riding the elevator with Aleksandr Ivanovich: he was going home, and I was seeing Petrovich off. The elevator stopped on the third floor, and she got on. Aleksandr

---

*A reference to the Young Pioneer's salute. When members of the Communist organization for ten-to-fourteen-year-olds are asked "Are you prepared to defend the cause of Communism?" they answer with the words "Always prepared," raising their hands over their heads to symbolize the supremacy of the collective over the individual.

Ivanovich straightened up and growled, 'Hello.' She said hello, too. And then they turned away from each other. We got to the bottom, and she shot out of the elevator and clicked down the corridor in her stilettos. Petrovich and I got off, too, but he was just standing there like he was stuck, watching her walk away. I felt sorry for him—"

My sister stopped by in the evening. "I looked at your test results, and everything is in order," she said.

"Obviously everything is in order. Otherwise they wouldn't be operating tomorrow. Listen, don't come in the morning, all right? I don't want you to."

"All right." She was looking at me pleadingly, and I couldn't wait for her to leave. I felt closer to Galia and Masha now than I did to my sister; there was nothing she could do to help me. Masha's "certain person" was already here, and so was Galia's Petrovich, and those two immediately made a nest in the corner of the bed and were talking softly about their home life. My sister finally left, and I took a sleeping pill and kept looking at Galia and Petrovich until I was in the very heart of their warm nest, where, without noticing it, I fell asleep.

A nurse woke me up in the morning. I opened my eyes, and she touched me on the shoulder again, sweeping away the snatches of sleep that were still hanging on to my eyelashes, and then I gave her a purposefully worried look. The nurse had an indifferently businesslike expression on her face that seemed to say that I had no reason to worry. But when she handed me the key to the bathroom, the gesture was confidential, as though she were a priest giving communion to a condemned prisoner. "No rush," she said. "You are second in line." I mulled over her words in the shower: if I was second, the surgeons must have had someone with a more serious problem to take care of first. Or it was the other way around, and they wanted to get warmed up before they got to me. When I returned to the room, the women were already up. The radio was considerably silent. My roommates met me with reassuring smiles, and I fashioned my cold lips into a smile in return. Aleksey Alekseyevich came and talked with Masha for a long time as he examined her tumor. I burrowed into the neatly trimmed back of his head with my eyes as I tried to guess what he would tell me. He paused by my bed and said, "We seem calm," and there was nothing I could do except confirm his observation. The same nurse came in again, gave me several injections and said, "Girls, do me a favor and take the food off the windowsills: the sanitary inspectors are coming around," and I started helping with the cleanup.

Half an hour went by. I lay there and snow kept falling outside the window, lowering me deeper and deeper, so that by the time the nurse wheeled in the stretcher, I had almost stopped being nervous and felt like I was making the transition from one snowbank to another. Now I was looking at the fluorescent bulb on the ceiling, feeling the sheet getting tucked in on all sides, feeling almost like a mime playing a king: I had nothing to do, but it was important that I be on stage. We left the room. Masha was standing by the elevator in the hallway talking on the phone. She rested the receiver on her shoulder and reached over to squeeze my shoulder lightly. And from this point on, everything was sterile.

At the elevator, two white angels handed my body over to two others in white. We went up to the eighth floor and came up to a glass door with a sign that said CLEAN ZONE. They changed the sheet, put foot warmers on me, and rolled me toward the operating room. The ceiling slid by like snow.

There was no one in the operating room. I rolled over onto the narrow operating table and started staring up at the circle with light bulbs until a large head appeared in front of it. It was the anesthesiologist. He said, "Hello," in a homey way. And I said, "Hello." He said something to the nurse softly, and the nurse addressed me: "Stretch out your arm." As she set up the IV and looked for the vein, the anesthesiologist and I chatted. "You look like the actress M." "Yes, so I've been told." "Really? And I was looking and thinking, Who is it that she looks like? Let's try on the mask now," he said, dipping my face in rubber. "Especially your eyebrows and your eyes—just like M's." *Fine*, I thought. *From this point on, I am not responsible for anything. This is peace.* And I turned my head away from him to enter the comfort of the operating table.

After it was all over and I was back in the room and awake from the anesthesia, I had my third metamorphosis in a few days: Now I needed no people—not the first people and not the last people, not my relatives—I needed no one at all. My soul was far away like the snow flying by the window; what was on the bed was an empty body, aware only of its own concerns, of the pain inside it—and there was no pain on the surface, because when the nurse made several injections into my arm, I didn't feel a thing. I lay swathed in a receding pain, a haze through which I heard my sister's voice asking if I wanted my lips moistened—but her voice met only a hollow echo in the hallways of my dream.

IRINA POLIANSKAYA

The radio was mumbling in the room: "…the development of chlorine-based manufacturing has led to an accumulation of polychlorinated compounds, which, even in tiny concentrations, act as immunosuppressants and in higher concentrations affect the central and peripheral nervous systems, the liver, the digestive tract and other organs…"

"Turn it off, for god's sake! I can't listen to this. I'd rather not know anything. Petrovich is right: he is always saying we're going to do ourselves in."

"At least they are talking about it on the radio. Last year there were those acid rains and we had to dig the potatoes all up to hell. They said it on the radio that we had to dig them up. The cabbage went to waste, too. May as well not plant anything. But we can't afford not to plant—the stuff at the markets is real expensive and has nitrates all over it."

"You can tell by the wasps: I always take the fruit that has wasps hovering over it, because they wouldn't hover over nitrates."

"Soon there won't be any wasps left either. There is salmonella in the chickens and the eggs, too. You've got to cook these chickens for an hour and a half and then get rid of the broth."

"After those acid rains, we suddenly got mushrooms this big growing by the steps. My Petrovich says we should dig them up, they're poisonous."

Poisonous. There was a mushroom that grew at the steps to our world, in the Land of the Rising Sun. My mother told me that after the news was announced people ran out into the streets for a celebration…Father, is this what you were working for when you stayed up nights, never saw the light of day, got no rest, let yourself go, and abandoned your family? Anesthesia covers my throat like a frost. What you did could only have been done under anesthesia, in a sad place where two-meter-tall attendants must have hit you on the head and forced you into a straitjacket.

"Look, I think she woke up. Are you awake? Are you?"

The next day Galia was released and replaced by an old woman named Maria Andreyevna. Masha sat down in the corner of my bed and said, "This is the last thing we need." Not seeing the understanding she was seeking in my face, she got up and started tidying the room for the doctors' rounds. This morning I felt closer to the old woman, so weak and helpless, than to Masha. Her addition clearly reinforced my right to stay in bed indefinitely, have the radio silenced and breakfast brought in. Aleksey Alekseyevich arrived, beautiful, calm and methodical, leaned over the old woman and submerged his hands in her wide, flattened-out belly. I could see his shoulder blades moving under his coat as though he were kneading dough, and I could make out the old woman's profile, her eyes directed at the ceiling in reverie. While the doctor was kneading her body, Maria Andreyevna never looked at him, as though the body weren't hers at all—and indeed, it almost didn't belong to her anymore. It was nothing to be ashamed of: it had given everything a body is supposed to give, and by this time the old woman could barely even feel the pain from her bedsores. All that was left of the body was the envelope, which Aleksey Alekseyevich was examining in conscientious detail.

The next day I sat up in bed, hanging my legs off and facing the old woman. I looked at her without interruption but could not catch her eyes, which wandered like a baby's. I was getting my sense of guilt back, and this meant that I was getting better. I could imagine how difficult it was for her relatives to talk to this old woman, because every word was a lie, even if they had unquenchable feelings of guilt in their souls. She was far from any earthly desires. Her illness had relieved her of having to care for her own body. Only in nature does a tree that has been struck by lightning exist on equal footing with new growth. Humans look at very old people with wonder and a condescending smile that says, "We'll never make it that far." Old people aside, generations just can't understand one another, because of their different life experiences. I remember I came running to a friend of my mother's with whom I had developed a fairly close relationship, to tell her of what then seemed like a tragedy of unprecedented proportions. Told what the problem was, she said with relief, "Thank god— I thought it was something serious." And I felt like a failed actress who had been booed off the stage, and for the first time in my life asked myself the question, Is my pain so bad? My mother's friend still remembered the language of childhood passions but she refused to use it just to please me, even though she suspected that at that moment she was losing me forever, for there is nothing worse than having doubt cast on the extent of your pain. Standing right up against my pain, I saw it as huge, boiling like a volcano, consuming my soul—but from the height of my mother's friend's life, the picture was different, and my tears looked light, like the bubbles in mineral water—the tears of seething, disorderly youth. The old woman named Maria Andreyevna was even higher, even farther—so far that she would never hear me scream.

Some relatives of hers came—with a lawyer. Two men planted

themselves firmly on either side of the bed; the woman lawyer, wearing a face that's seen it all, sat down and took some papers out of her purse and laid them out on the table; a third relative—a woman—perched at the old woman's feet and to alleviate her burning guilt started trimming the old woman's toenails. The men alternated between straightening the objects on the night stand and straightening up the old woman's pillows. They, too, still had lives to live, still had to drag the weight of their lives and their irrepressible lies uphill, to make the appropriate faces while playing a foul game—as the rules of the game demanded—and so they knit their brows and spread their feet, bent their heavy ox-like necks and dragged their chains and shackles on. The old woman strained and answered the lawyer's questions. The lawyer was forging ahead with her ball-point pen, addressing the old woman in a caring and loud voice and the relatives in a loud and official voice steeped in judgment.

A day later I was already walking around the room, and when I heard my sister's voice in the evening, I went out into the hallway. My sister, wearing her snow-white coat, was standing with Aleksandr Ivanovich, the surgeon; they were studying a Japanese phonoscope that my sister had somehow managed to buy. Aleksandr Ivanovich gestured in apparent surprise: "I see you are walking around already! Good." Seeing him now was what seeing an old lover must be like—it's all over between you, and you don't know how to act. Looking for something to say as I looked into his back receding into the hallway, I said, "What a good man, god bless him. Who knows why his wife left him." Frowning, my sister responded, "Do me a favor and stay out of hospital gossip." She added, more kindly, "I brought you some apple juice and persimmon: you should be eating and drinking more." I walked her to the elevator, and by the time I returned to the room, the radio was already boldly talking. Clearly demonstrates. Conclusively shows. Constantly building up. Reinforced by all available means.

Masha was spoon feeding Maria Andreyevna, who continued to look up at the ceiling in reverie but opened her mouth obediently like a child. Masha was saying, "And another one...there you go, good," and the radio was singing, "What are we to do with the apples in the snow?"

"To each his own," said Masha and winked at me, and I winked back.

We started working on the crossword puzzle—softly, trying not to disturb the old woman. Then suddenly, when we were stumped by a word, the old woman clearly pronounced, "Rutherford." Masha and I looked at each other, and the old woman repeated, impatiently: "Rutherford." To make sure, Masha read out loud again: "A British physicist, one of the creators of the study of radioactivity and atomic structure." She counted the letters and said, "That's right," and she and I looked at each other again, a bit confused, as though we had just been addressed by a Martian. Life never ceases to challenge my assumptions. Masha left for her treatment, and I tried to alleviate my guilt by making conversation with the old woman, who maintained a stubborn silence at first and then responded to my question—"You must be local, right?"—with the mumbled observation that all they ever fed you at this hospital was millet gruel.

There is a family that lives in our building: a woman, her daughter, and granddaughter. The mother used to be a university instructor; the daughter is an instructor now and bears most of the responsibility for their lives; the granddaughter—Tania, six years old—is not well, an idiot. The grandmother has lived her life already and in her soul has forgiven people for their idiocy and overconfidence. If you ask her a question, she will respond readily; if you get her talking, she will look at you questioningly and proceed to complain loudly about human idiocy—which she has already forgiven—the stupidity of people who think she needs sympathy, which, of course, is not heartfelt, because most people don't even have enough heart for their loved ones, and their sympathy, instead, comes from the impatience of their hearts. She waits out her conversation partner's turn patiently, patiently explains about Tania, who, incidentally—and this shows in the old woman's eyes—is no worse than your children, who'll grow up soon and become just like their idiot mothers, tactless and big-mouthed, while Tania is gentle and attentive—she is nature's answer to the kind of stupidity that is not obvious, not aware of itself. That's how the old woman discreetly brands us—and she has the right to, a right she gets from her pain, which is real and not made up. My mother does exactly the same thing when she is asked about my brother. The old woman tells everyone about the problems her daughter is having—she has some sort of female ailment—about how crowded it is in a one-room apartment, plus now Tania has picked up that dog she can't live without, but what are they supposed to do with a dog when they barely have enough to feed themselves? She talks about how it scares her that she might die, because there is no one to take care of Tania, since her daughter is always in and out of the hospital… And then, suddenly, the old woman clams up, turns her back to us and yells, "Tania, we are going home!" but Tania wants to keep playing with our children and she is laughing happily and shoving dirty snowballs in their faces as we look on with concern…And the old woman is right in her angry call—she is right because she can almost hear one of us whispering after her, "They've got no money—and look at them going and getting a dog." Sometimes Tania comes out on walks with her mother, but the mother doesn't buy our sympathy, because she knows exactly what it's worth. She tries to take Tania to places we don't go, but once we bumped into her on a narrow path and one of us, trying to demonstrate her loyalty to Tania, who happily ran toward our children, said, "Oh, look, Taniechka, what a nice doggie you have!" The mother shot her an enraged look. She was incapable of playing this game and feeding our sympathy. And she wasn't yet tired and resigned enough to forgive our awkward attempts. She didn't yet know all that Maria Andreyevna must have known to respond with a statement about millet gruel to my question "You must be local, right?" in spite of how difficult it was for her to return to the orbit of conventional human communication.

I turned to the window and said to myself again, Think, think, wake up, wake up—because you have just returned from the clean zone, where you barely existed, and not everyone has a chance to look at life from the outside like this, having *returned*. Could it be that everything would remain as it was? Could it be that life would continue the way sleep resumes after it is interrupted by the mumbling of a sleeping child—life as hibernation illuminated momentarily by the sound of the alarm clock? Would I continue to live with a soul filled with fear, as though danger were a wolf stalking me, its eyes staring me down like headlights at every turn? But what could be so dangerous when the equation with many variables has long since been solved, the solution is known, and the dream in brackets doesn't make one bit of difference? All this was easy to see from the vantage point of the clean zone, of course, but when you are in brackets living every detail, not noticing the punctuation marks—when you are living as though you were rushing to say a tongue twister before you choked on it—it feels different. Life was rushing by like a snowball rolling downhill, gaining weight as the snow outside the window kept falling and falling—and all this reminded me of something...The whole picture outside the window was somehow familiar, recognizable, not the way that any middle-Russian landscape is familiar, but differently—closer and more disturbing, like a dream I'd just had. My sister came by and I told her about this. I told her I had a sense that there was a tiny tower beyond the fir trees. My sister was strangely silent, and when I looked at her face I saw an expression of surprise that exceeded my expectations. I asked, "Why?" My sister inhaled quickly and said,

"No, you can't remember that. I don't even remember it, though I know that in the very spot where the hospital is now was the house in which we used to live. Beyond the fir trees was Kurchatov's house, which really does look like a tower; now there is some sort of cooperative in it. But you can't remember any of that, because you hadn't been born yet."

"Is there a river beyond the little house?" I guessed.

"A pond," my sister answered happily. "And a railroad beyond that."

"We never went that far—there was barbed wire."

Nature must have stored up a lot of frustration over the long cold autumn, which had rushed ahead of the calendar and undressed the trees before it was supposed to and dried the grass. Now the snow lasted and lasted, coating the horizon, obscuring the clouds over distant smokestacks. Only the forest still rippled vaguely, like the tiny photocopied text of a wonderful book I had just read, which told of this very town—and now its pages disappeared under forty-year-old snow. The snow covered the past of its heroes—they weren't made up; they had really lived—gently separating these people from their relatives and loved ones who still existed in their thoughts, taking over these people, leaving them only the strength to keep moving forward under the flow of orders and threats, plowing through the deep snow. The people fantasized about their own bodies, about the warmth remaining inside them, about stuffing their frozen hands inside their own bellies like muffs. They thought of how strange it was that life flickered inside their bodies, shivering in a transparent column, confined on every side like mercury inside a thermometer, and no matter what was done to it, it kept wavering among the seven marks of heat, but if it ever slid off this slope, it would immediately disappear under the snow of an endless winter. And when snow flew up off the ground, spring would roll in, and its emerald wave would roll over into summer, and then autumn would sweep away all the treasures collected with the sun's god-given help, and a new winter would bury them, but none of this taught us anything, even though this happened every year starting with the creation of the world. Snow was falling and saying to me with its whiteness, You must understand. Today the snowbank reached the windowsill of the physiology lab, where Masha and I went for ultraviolet treatments in the mornings. We sat there talking over the room divider. She said, "Where have all the street cleaners gone?" I said, "They must all be buried in the snow." She said, "What are they thinking in the Bureau of Life and Economy—how difficult can it be to make some paths?" I answered, "Must be the BLE is snowed in, too." "Used to be, people knew how to work," said Masha. "But now everyone's gotten lazy." Really—who could ever make paths as intricate as our thoughts, as our lives? We turned the hourglasses on the shelves by our heads at the same time—each turning her own—and another allotment of our time started falling, while outside the snow was already waist-high. Snowbanks would reach shoulder level in the sleepy and snowed-in wilderness of December. We turned the hourglasses over again—and now we were beneath the snow, along with the little glass jar full of dead time. Masha said, "Mine's cold already." Mine was getting cold, too.

"Nurse, you've forgotten about us! Take off the ultraviolet."

"I haven't forgotten. Wait a minute."

The sky was the same here as what had been hanging over Moscow for three months already. For three months the cloud cover over the capital had been making days and nights feel like dusty dusk. A dull, copper-colored reflection thrown by a funeral orchestra's brass stuck to the window glass, and neither sunlight nor starlight could break through it. A person stuck between the heavy brown sky and damp snow felt flattened and sleepy, and this might be why I kept feeling that one day got stuck in the last and felt suffocated in the stale air.

But now I was glad to look up at the calm gray sky, and I found it easier to be convalescing under it. It was good to look at the snow. I imagined how at four in the morning, my father, flashlight in his hand, was making a path on the way to his laboratory.

It will soon be a year that he has been waking up with the sensation of unbroken joy and physical health in his body. He leaves the house an hour early to give himself time to breathe the free frosty air; he often stops, turns off the flashlight, and dips his near-sighted stare into the dark sky with its smiling crescent moon, into the glowing snow which casts dark trees on either side of the path like shadows. He can see neither the soldiers in the observation towers nor the barbed wire separating people from people and trees from trees; he can hear neither the barking dogs nor the radio voice in the loudspeakers, because here in the colony he has finally found the freedom he has dreamed of for a decade, starting on the first day of the war and ending on his last day in Kolyma, when he and his colleague Moskalev, another inmate on the edge of starvation, were placed on a sled and taken to the station. Unlike Moskalev, he didn't need to send for his library from his sealed apartment in Moscow to feel free; it was enough for him to have this barely heated laboratory in a two-story barracks, to be given the opportunity to read scientific journals and to be allowed to resume his correspondence with a Norwegian scientist working on the same problem as he.

He opens the door to the laboratory, takes off his sheepskin jacket, and puts on a lab coat stained with chemicals. He can hear Tisyn, the genetics scientist, slowly climbing the stairs up to the barracks. Tisyn is toothless, with sunken-in cheeks, and the good food they get here has not improved his appearance. His wife still isn't here, though they say that Zaveniagin has combed all the camps; it's like Tisyna has vanished. More likely she's been snowed under in Kolyma or Vorkuta. People try gently to point Tisyn to look around among the outside employees, but my father, who is friendly with Tisyn, realizes that this man is a univalent element like Na or K. My father shines his flashlight at the clock: it's fifteen minutes to five; the lights will go on in half an hour. He has time to rest and think. Tisyn appears in the doorway, sweeping the snow off his felt boots as he walks in. A light shines on his face suddenly. Shielding his face with a mitten, Tisyn says, "Really, you are just like my investigator. Hello, Aleksandr Nikolayevich."

"Good morning, Anatoly Vikentyevich. I am sorry."

Tisyn sits down on a bench, puts his mittens together neatly like hands for prayer, and, with a familiar move, shoves them far inside his coat.

"You know, my investigator wasn't the nosy kind at all. He had a simple face—I would even say it predisposed one to trust him. A peasant's face. Sometimes as he leafed through my file, he would forget where he was and lick his finger before turning the page. But he had a famous last name: Bashmachkin. It struck me when he introduced himself: this was great Russian literature—which I had forgotten all about in those days—greeting me in my dismal underground. There is something about this that's more than a coincidence, I thought. During interrogations I would sit squinting at the light and let my lonely thoughts wander. Oh, Nikolai Vasilyevich Gogol, light of my life, I would think, if you could see your little person now, the one that our humanistic artists were crying over just half a century ago. Here he sits before me, basking in the light of his fame, directing the light from the desk lamp at my face—and he, like Akaky Akakiyevich of the same last name, feels no desire to wield satanic powers over the world—all he wants is a warm overcoat. So there he sits, conscientiously putting together the case against me so he'll get his overcoat, which will sooner or later be stolen from him by thieves in the night...It was as though time had been turned upside down like an hourglass, and our whole department had ended up on the bottom, with the head and the supervisors and the advisors landing behind bars while my Bashmachkin ended up at the top, exchanged his reddish uniform for a soldier's blouse and got to work as a writer. When he and I were saying good-bye to each other, he came right up to me and whispered, 'Don't worry, they didn't get your old lady.' I looked at his face with my inflamed eyes and I saw that my investigator was a redhead with blue eyes and a face covered with freckles. I trusted those freckles then, felt a weight off my shoulders—that they hadn't gotten my wife. Because someone like that, all freckled, wouldn't lie. It turned out he would—and did. This horse had already pulled on a jackal's coat—like an overcoat. Nikolai Vasilyevich hadn't dreamt of anything like that in his worst nightmares...What's that on your wall—a bulletin board?"

My father shines his flashlight at the poster on the wall.

"Three days ago we had a group of inspectors from Moscow here. I think they were sent here by mistake. They were less interested in the results of our work than in the bare walls—why don't we have any propaganda materials for all to see? So I have produced some propaganda for them."

"That's not what they meant. They thought the walls lacked for quotes from Josef and his brothers."

"The zoologists can hang up Josef and his brothers if they want. Here I am offering a simple and tasteful bar graph showing the relative resistance of atoms."

"How remarkable: the atoms are in the same situation as you and I—their resistance is behind bars."

"I have a more optimistic outlook on life: I think that what has happened to us will serve as a most powerful catalyst for human progress. And all the crap like your Bashmachkin will fall out as sediment. There you have a chemist's modest viewpoint."

"It would be interesting to find out the lord god's viewpoint, Aleksandr Nikolayevich."

"Most likely, it is impressionistic. He takes great risks with color. Currently he is attracted to shades of gray: he is trying to mix Leviticus with Bashmachkin."

"In that case the lord god is still priming the canvas, and the painting is yet to be done. Our children—I hear your spouse has received permission to give birth in Moscow? How very charitable of them."

"Leave it. They simply happened to have a need for you and me—that's the extent of their charity."

"Well, then, it was a pleasure talking with you. All the best, Aleksandr Nikolayevich."

"Be well, Anatoly Vikentyevich."

For another minute my father can hear footsteps overhead. Then they disappear: Tisyn has sat down in his chair and immersed himself in the study of his scary monsters—rabbits that have been subjected to radioactive exposure, mice and rats that have lost their fur and have bold spots on their sides but are incredibly tenacious, dogs and guinea pigs spreading out over the open-air cage like evil thoughts. My father doesn't know exactly what Tisyn is studying; it does not interest him—though, if he had the opportunity to look several decades ahead, he would become very interested in the subject, which will have a most direct relationship to him in the future. Meanwhile, though, Tisyn is sitting there on the second floor, tired and old like a parka, spinning the yarn of the future. My father shines the light at the clock again: the year is 1947, February 22, the time is 5:12 in the morning, and he does not yet know that in exactly twelve hours, his first daughter will come into the world. He loves this time, loves being lost in the snow, in his work. He is alone like Kay playing with the crystals in the Snow Queen's palace. He throws the sheepskin jacket over his shoulders, sits down in the rotating chair—a war trophy— and spends a few minutes warming his fingers over the spirit lamp. He sits slumped over the tiny fire, smiling the satisfied smile of a caveman who has made fire for the first time by rubbing two pieces of wood together. He is warming his large hands, which are no longer calloused, so that he can work to realize humanity's prophetic tales of rivers of fire and shores of mousse, lakes that go up in flames and cities that are flooded, and underground kingdoms. My father sits wrapped in the animal skin like a giant over a tiny fire that has already consumed so much and will consume more: the poor little house in the Penz governance in which he was born, the steep slopes by the Volga, where he spent his childhood and his youth, the pine trees standing on the shores like candles, the high waters in the rivers full of fish, the quaint little peasant huts, bullfinches in the snow, chaffinches on the branch, old windmills, mellow chimes, clean earthenware pots. He knows no doubts: his own scientific interests have happily coincided with the interests of the state—but the thing is that doubt lies at the basis of human nature, and nothing in nature disappears, nothing is lost without a trace: when my father reacted with his cruel time, doubt fell out in the sediment, which will yet be lodged in the bones of his children, in the hearts of his grandchildren.

IRINA POLIANSKAYA

He is sitting there peacefully, peacefully breathing onto his cold fingers, eagerly anticipating that any minute now the lights will go on and the laboratory will come alive, will fill up with people, and the breath of his labors will echo through all the world. When his hands are warm, he gets to work.

In half an hour, his footprints are covered with snow. In another half hour, a group of people, heads hung, walk through the snow in single file. People keep coming alone and in groups down the path they make—and then, again, the path is covered with snow. There is not a sound then, not a person—only silence, trees, snow, safety: the clean zone.

She Who Bears No Ill

Yelena Tarasova

If some critics are to be believed, this story is one of the most dangerous pieces of fiction ever written. "This kind of thing should not be printed," declares one (male) critic. "I agree," responds his more liberal-minded (male) colleague. "One can print anything, of course—but why?" Male critics are not the only ones who believe that "She Who Bears No Ill" should not be allowed to see light of day; indeed, in introducing the piece in the anthology of women's fiction that borrowed its name from the story, editor Larisa Vaneyeva acknowledged that "it was not without a struggle that we got this piece included." What makes the story—which Yelena Tarasova wrote before she was twenty-two—so frightening? Most who have written about the piece note that it is graphically disgusting—a shocking departure from the disembodied idealizations of socialist realism. But that's not all; the critic Pavel Basinsky claims that by portraying the soul as a mirror of the body, Tarasova has declared the soul dead. She has committed the sin of sacrilege not only against the heroic narrative of Soviet literature but the ideal of beauty in the Russian literary tradition itself.

In her autobiographical sketch, Tarasova writes, "I came into this world no earlier than September 1959 in the city of Rostov on the Don [in southeastern Russia]. When I was one year and two months old, I landed in the city of Makhackala [on the Caspian Sea], where I went on to fulfill the life program of a 'typical representative' under 'typical circumstances': I was an Oktiabrist and a Young Pioneer." Similarly, the narrator in this story originates in conspicuously normal surroundings. Tarasova gives every indication that the family is law-abiding and respectful of tradition and has been rewarded with typical upward mobility: for example, as we progress through the narrator's memories, the make of the family car steadily improves.

The narrator of "She Who Bears No Ill" is afflicted with a mysterious degenerative disease. The only affliction Tarasova herself admits to is an inferiority complex. Her autobiography continues: "I was not accepted into the Komsomol—they didn't consider me deserving—though I really wanted to be a member. Since then I have had an inferiority complex. I have no other interesting facts to convey about myself. Except, perhaps, that I did not take part in Alexander the Great's crusades; never crossed the Alps; had nothing to do with the signing of the Turkmenchai Treaty; and never skied to the North Pole—all of which I attest to, being of sound mind and body."

Not being of sound body—and viewing her still-sound mind as a burden—Tarasova's narrator is far less reticent regarding her origins, and she probes them to the discomfort of the readers and the critics. For a "typical representative," the search for origins is fraught with danger. In Soviet society the crime of "treason to the motherland" was punishable by death and family members were held responsible for one another's acts under this law, whether or not they were aware of them. In Soviet mythology, the motherland replaced god, and the family became a component part of the collective motherland. When Tarasova's narrator turns her back on her family to seek refuge in the insane asylum that she recognizes as her true motherland, she is committing something very much like sacrilege.

—M. G.

The gas was on. She threw a lit match into the oven. The flame caught noisily around the circle.

There. Nothing happened.

The bristle on her chin is slightly burned. The tips of her eyelashes are singed a bit. Even that wouldn't have happened if she hadn't crouched down—which was not at all necessary. It's not like she'd planned to poison herself with gas. So what was the point of doing that? That neighbor girl with her movie! She'd run in to tell all about it: "Oh, oh, oh!" It ended just like it was supposed to. Love, unrequited at first. Then he saves her and everything is great. An unsuccessful suicide is the moment of climax, melodrama's time-honored tool. Those who need that sort of thing sob quietly, swallowing their tears; those who don't, laugh for all to see. General delight follows. It turns out he loved her after all. All had been for naught, and everything is great.

But there are times when there is no other option.

But enough about that. She is baking a cake. That's all there is to it. What did the recipe say again?

…Three eggs mixed with a cup of sugar and a cup of flour, topped off. Add a cup of sour cream. A teaspoon of baking soda, neutralized by vinegar. Mix everything together and pour out into a buttered baking pan, it said something like that. Add the lemon syrup when the cake has browned—and back into the oven for another five minutes. It's fast, that's the thing. But you've got to have a taste for it: it's awfully sweet.

Getting up is hard: she's spent about fifteen minutes like this in front of a hot oven, spread out like a frog. She'd thought nothing of the sort. But she must never stop paying attention. Had she been lost in thought? She'd thought nothing of the sort. But now her legs are going to ache. She is heating up like the oven...Her eyes! She is losing her eyesight, she must remember that. The vessels in her face are going to burst again. Her nose and cheeks have long since become lined with red, and they get more so every year. She mustn't forget her age. Others at her age can still be considered young; for her it is practically old age. Were she sixty or so, she could almost be happy. But she is only thirty-three. The age of Jesus Christ.

So that's it! She wouldn't have even dared think it out loud. But it was bound to get her one way or another. The cyclical nature of "fateful" years. Where does it come from? It was one thing to believe in twenty-one, even to call it "Black Jack age." Back then she still had a chance. She could have stopped something, saved something, even if just her hair. And she did nothing. Then twenty-five. Then thirty. Little by little, she lost human features. Now it was too late; there were no chances left. But the hope thing has a way of happening over and over again. All the superstitions, the omens, the card readings, the palm readings, the fortune telling, the horoscopes start coming out. Next thing you know, she is going to go out to the market on junk day and go up to some smarmy little old man with a parrot on his shoulder and a hat full of rolled-up pieces of paper in his hand. The parrot will pull out a piece of paper that will turn out to contain a typed message with grammar mistakes. No, she won't do that—though that's all she has left. It's been a long time since her fortunes had anything to do with men—she only asked about change, about happiness of any sort, at least a little bit. And then another year would end and all its junk would be tossed in a trunk, and the last day would slam the lid down.

Here it is, the age of Jesus Christ. How trite—sickening, even. Now what? What sorts of memorable years lie ahead of her? Here: "In the middle of the journey of our life/I found myself astray in a dark wood..." That must have been thirty-five, the top of Dante's curve. That will be another year that will rip away at her soul with its failure to come true...According to Dante, she'll then have thirty-five years of torment still ahead of her. Fate may well turn out to be that mean—to keep her dying slowly for thirty-seven more years, keep her smoldering and smoking without going out.

What in the hell got into her—squatting in front of the stove? Now her legs...She is sitting on a stool, her heavy monstrous flesh hang-

　　　　　　　　　　　　　　　　YELENA TARASOVA

ing over the sides, and her legs hurt terribly. She hates it when they feel like cotton, but at least that's not painful. She's been rubbing and rubbing and rubbing them...Thousands of needles are piercing the soles of her feet, her calves and thighs. It takes a long time to rub down her thick purple thighs; to get at her calves she needs to bend over her belly, which makes her ears ring and glassy worm-like shapes in a pink fog appear before her eyes. The veins in her legs are pulling, hurting—and she still has half a day of walking ahead of her...Thirty-three years old! She must not forget that's old age.

...Hanging out all over...she asked her mother once what it could be compared to—hanging like what? "Like god's punishment" was her mother's nonsensical answer, which stuck in her mind and continues to come back in bad times. Her hideousness hangs like god's punishment over the home of her mother and father, brushes the edge of her sister's home, passes like a storm cloud over the friendships that have long since vanished into the distance. It hangs over everyone whose life is more or less closely connected with hers...And decay is the sort of thing that can attack what is healthy.

The decay in her soul is contagious.

She used to think that the soul is a reflection of the body and its shape, that it is equally palpable. When the body loses a finger, the soul loses one as well. But the body can use prostheses, while the soul remains toothless, legless, fingerless. The soul doesn't wear wigs; it is openly bald. Plastic surgery can correct a horrible nose, but the soul carries the scars from the operation. Everything that heals in the body continues to bleed and fester in the soul. That's what she thought when she was young, and if she were to remember everything now the way it happened, she would see her soul: a fat melancholy blob, always sighing heavily. Lids with shaggy lashes half cover its bulging eyes, which look like the eyes of a sad hippopotamus she once befriended at the Rostov zoo. She always found it standing, looking out with intelligent and very sad eyes from under blinking leathery lids; it steadfastly held up its huge heavy head. The other hippopotamus was meaner, bigger and darker. It rarely sighed and was always rubbing against the feeder, its sides covered with green excrement. She disliked it intensely for its carnivorous glare. Her grandmother was a janitor at the zoo then, but she died a very long time ago, and her husband, who watered flowers at the zoo, died, too. And what of her hippopotamus friend? It must have died, too. All this was more than twenty years ago. Is there another hippopotamus like that one out there somewhere?

Also, her soul is missing a finger on the right hand: it was slammed in the door of the family's old Zaporozhets. Her soul has a long bleeding scar on its neck, where the thyroid was removed. It's got bulging knots on its legs from varicose veins. Of its thirty-two teeth, only four remain, the rest having been claimed by decay. Its mouth is full of blackened shards. There is never a smile on the face of her soul or on her own face; it is a red, bumpy, distorted face covered with granulomas, inflammations, swollen lymph nodes…Decaying, distrustful, embittered, hopeless. Empty. It's all true: she and her soul are twins. She wears no prostheses or wigs, either. She bears the pain of her bad teeth, inflamed gums, and canker sores with a tormented steadfastness. She couldn't possibly go to a dentist's office, sit down in the chair, and open this kind of mouth. The dentist would throw up, and she would have to watch the look of distaste on his face as he poked around in the foul-smelling rotten remains of her mouth. She will not go. Or maybe she should? No. She couldn't: she'd change her mind at the door and leave. That's happened before.

Yes, the soul is a reflection of the body. Hers is hideous. It is huge, heavy, embittered, scowling like the bacilli being exterminated by cheerful antibiotic boys bearing a giant syringe in the color supplement to the magazine *Health*. Ten cheerful boys per syringe: the morbid fantasy of an artist whose last show took place too long ago.

But then what about the midget? He shows up next to her in the street every time she goes out. True, she is the only one who can see him. He is furious and agile, and he desperately flings mud at anyone who says something mean to her, and afterward, every time, he cries helpless, mean tears. In the end he always hurls mud at her. Then he leaves, smearing tears with his dirty hand…

Yes, the decay in her soul is contagious.

A baby oyster has attached itself to this hideous monolith—the neighbor girl. By some sort of accident she let the pip-squeak get beyond the threshold of her trashed room. But what if she infects her with her death? Will she be able to forgive herself? But no. Her brand of hideousness is acquired. It is not about being born a cripple but about slowly, deliberately molding yourself into a scary monster. It's about shaping the soul. It's about starting to decay. And the stupid little girl is trying to grab hold of anything of hers that's not attached: her habits, her words, her thoughts, her moods. She has no good habits, kind words, or peaceful thoughts to give. What a little idiot! Now she's decided she is not going to clean her room either. The mother is horrified and keeps screaming at her. But she shouldn't. If she hadn't started screaming, everything would have been back to normal by now. The girl would have gotten embarrassed about the mess when she brought friends home, and she would have cleaned up.

...No. This dirt is her possession, her ten-year habit. She has so little in life that she creates her own valuables, her treasures, no matter if they are laughable. She lets dust form a smoky layer over the shiny furniture finish; she lets moss collect in the corners. Her clothes and underclothes are strewn all around. Her shoes (when was the last time she wore real shoes?) sit on the table. The furniture is never moved because everything must remain in its place. Let her mother scream: she is willing to clean anywhere at all, to wash and scrub the pots in the kitchen, to shine the floor in the hallway, to wipe down the china again and again, as long as no one touches the dirt in her room, as long as no one enters this sanctuary of dirt so dear to her heart. But her mother screams words of hate, and her own allergic cough in the night is becoming unbearable, so now she has to clean once every three months. That shuts her mother up for a while.

But it's all right. It only takes three days for dust to start fogging up the furniture and the floor, for pieces of paper—ragged-edged scraps of her thoughts—to start flying off the cover of the secretaire once it's up again. This is how she reads books—writing down her thoughts in no particular order and with no direction: her doubts, her phraseological solutions if she doesn't like the author's, her own versions of epilogues and appendices if she feels something is missing. She doesn't write much: two or three words, two or three sentences, notes, words, exclamation points, and question marks in random order. In three or four months between cleanups, a great many of these scraps and snatches collect on the secretaire, on the chairs, and right on the floor. They mix with all sorts of trash: apple cores, orange peels, fruit pits, remnants of radishes. She never rereads these notes. Even if she tried, she wouldn't be able to: her handwriting is hurried and illegible; there are no dates, titles, or authors' names noted. Tiny wiggly letters jump all over the page: she knew she wouldn't be rereading this; it's just how she thinks. She crumples up the papers and stuffs yet another plastic bag full of trash, poems, thoughts, wiggles, and chewed-up cores and pulls the bag closed till the next cleanup. There are several of these bags, overstuffed to the point of bursting, behind the doors of the rolltop, and their number continues to grow. She likes hearing the rustle of the papers under her feet in the dark whenever she leaves her room in the middle of the night for any reason. She has no use for her parents' kind of entertainment:

backgammon, solitaire, Chinese checkers, television. She does not feel equal to the ways others enjoy life. She seeks her own sources of pleasure. Let them be what they are.

Meanwhile, the neighbors—the pip-squeak's parents—have stopped saying hello to her. She made every honest effort to scare away their daughter, to peel her away from herself: she drove her to tears, humiliated and insulted her, laughed at her. She even tormented her with her breath, trying to appear even more disgusting than she really is. The girl would get droopy-eyed and start bawling so hard that even she felt a pull at her jaw from the longing to cry together with the girl. The next day the girl would come again, her face preemptively pained, ready for new tears. God! Where did she get it? Where does a strong healthy snot-nosed girl get this desire, so much like her own, to have her nose rubbed in it? Where did she get this idea that joy equals suffering? This was about a year ago. Then, one night, as she was trying to lull an aching tooth that was keeping her awake, she thought that if she deprived herself of her one attachment, even if it was one-sided, then she would return to that place: *the* place. She needed someone to love her, to want to see her, to listen to her. Otherwise she wouldn't be able to hold on: she would hear *the call* too clearly if there was nothing to muffle it.

Meanwhile, back to this age "cycle": what does she have coming up? She can't think of anything. Maybe forty-five…How does it go? "They say that at the age of forty-five a dame is a berry again. Not a berry that's a bore but a good old Russian—" followed by a clear and unambiguous domestic Russian rhyme. And she? Will she still have hope at forty-five? Human beings are as given to hope as they are to making mistakes, but that is cold comfort. She knows nothing is going to change, but inside she keeps hoping, hoping for something. If hope were flesh, she would stomp it into the ground with cruel, brutally satisfying force. Then, whenever she saw someone else's happiness, her soul would no longer long for it, reach for it, hitting and scraping her heavy, pained body on the rough shoulder of the road. She always comes back to her own patch of dirt. She comes back bloodied and depressed, tied up in knots from her new pain…And she rubs her own nose in it. She forces herself to sit quietly, breathe the stale air, stare at her blue shins without ever raising her head, only sprinkling more and more dirt, trash, leaves, and dust onto her bald head, sprinkling and sprinkling…If she can stay like this, her unlikely reflection—the midget—will sit down across from her, hang his sinewy hands helplessly between his knees, no longer compelled

YELENA TARASOVA

to shake his hump. Cloudy tears will roll, will stream down his dusty face: there is nothing he can do. His eyes are pathetically sad. A child. His eyes are like a child's eyes.

Never. Never. She would be better off knowing and *never* again having hope for anything. A hunchback forever...No more fantasies! Her only dreams would be of chimeras, the instruments of her revenge—revenge on everyone, even those who have no fault...Beautiful, large green chimeras...But as for miracles, neither he nor she would hope for one. That would be better.

But she even envies him his hump. He probably hates her. She hates him, too. Why do monsters hate one another so? Theirs are similar fates, and it would seem that they should be together. Instead, they hate. They hate one another for the way they are treated: they are all pariahs...But doesn't hideousness have value of its own? Can't they even get anything for that? They need a place under the sun, after all. What a great consolation it would be to be one of a kind. In hospitals they compete for the grand prix in the following categories:

who is sicker? whose fits are scarier? whose labor is more painful? who gets more attention?

who? is closer to the edge?

Heart patients eat garlic, asthmatics secretly run out for cigarettes. Hell, what cigarettes? They'll run out into the snow barefoot just to have a higher temperature tomorrow! As for the pills, down the toilet they go.

At the other place, the value system was different. It was another hierarchy: the ones who were getting better, the ones who were almost well or entirely well were at the top. Every competitor's misfortune was placed on a scale opposite every other's. Mental handicap is not something you treasure; you try to push away from it by finding someone who is even uglier, even less fortunate. How mean the patients were about ridiculing those who were really insane. How they relished repeating words like *idiot*, *nut*, *insane*. (He who has lost his left eye mocks his neighbor for having lost his right one, doesn't he?) It seemed like there there these words even took on new meanings. That's probably what happened. Everything there was different. Still, this was strange, because they all had the same metal grate on the window separating them from freedom. In the spring, when the windows were opened, they would cling together to the warm metal stems covered with a skin of old, cracked paint, and together they would send out into the world a stream of obscenities, sweet from the taste of the free air. A busty attendant, whose instincts told her to make order in this place, would cruelly force them away from the grated spring, freedom, sun, and sky—all of them together. Then she would lock the window with the special handle-key that's used to lock all the doors and windows of that place.

How awful that place was! The very word "nuthouse" had an oppressive effect. Meanwhile, the place was perfectly normal. That is, it was completely normal. That is, it was too normal: solid walls, solid grates. Endless walls, locks, grates. They treated her will like a piece of aluminum wire, bendable in any direction. How she wanted to rebel! But she knew she couldn't, because they would bend her, trample her with their customary skill. She couldn't afford to give them such a trump card anyway. If you didn't want to seem sick, you had to obey everything: eat even when you couldn't look at food, never leave the room for patients under observation—not even to walk in the hallway, don't even think of it. Keep inhaling the foul odor of the sheets placed over the yellowish-pink rubber pads, the stinking bedding on which patients lay bound for days if they'd had the bad sense to "act up." As they lay there, they would be spoon-fed, and porridge, soup, and juice would be smeared from ear to ear all over the hate-filled faces tossing on the flat pillows. Don't tell your opinions to anyone; no one needs to hear them. Be quiet.

How she wanted to get up and give it to the aides who tormented the pathetic, transparent old woman Pirozhikha (everyone here lived under a pseudonym for local use exclusively, and names and last names did not exist). For no reason other than boredom and ox-eyed idleness, forcing her to have a fit. When the old woman started to spit and squeak something unintelligible in her thin, plaintive voice and with her weak hands toss back the junk that had been piled on her bed at the laughing, well-fed, the bitches would tie her to the bed with striped straps of cloth. Just because they were bored and hot. To everyone's delight, the old woman would keep chirping for a long time, lying uncomfortably on her back, her wet shirt riding up to her chin. No one even thought of covering her up. And if she, a new patient, had gotten it into her head to go up and strike them like she wanted to, they would have tied her down like the old woman Pirozhikha, on a stained rubber sheet. Then she, too, would have had to go on the sheet, also purely out of "boredom" and because they would not have untied her even if she had to go to the bathroom.

How the room stank of stale urine and dirt. The drafts would drag new waves of stench out of every corner. Her stained pillow stank. Her blanket was covered with yellow circles and ovals. The mattress was still damp from someone else. Oh, yes. It was that crying idiot over there, who'd been forcibly taken off the bed and made to lie on the floor.

The woman was still howling from the insult. (She herself had not ended up on the floor because she was from an intelligentsia family, from a warm and affluent home, so there was a chance that someone might get something for trying. It's true, someone did. Most of the other patients belonged nowhere and to no one. Except, maybe, on the men's ward, where someone's children found refuge from the draft thanks to the kindness of their loved ones and relatives.) There were four more people on the floor, their heads in the aisles, their feet under other people's beds. How they were stuffed in there! There were twenty-two beds, head to head, side to side, with three and four of them moved together.

God, why is she remembering all this? She should never cross the cutoff line of consciousness. She has a headache.

She has a headache. What was she doing sitting in front of the damned oven? What in the devil got into her? Now all night long she is going to feel dark blood pushing against her temples. She is home alone: her father is on a business trip and her mother has checked herself into a hospital to have a lipoma removed (it had become painful for her to sit down). What a gift it is to be alone in an empty, quiet apartment. She should just stay home all the time without sticking her nose out into the street. But no.

She has to finish the cake.

The syrup goes like this: grate a lemon, skin and all. Mix with a cup of sugar, place the sweet-and-sour liquid onto the hot dough, then put the cake back in to finish baking…She is nauseous.

Then she has to make the sauerkraut with sausages, iron a nightshirt, and drag all this to the clinic by visitors' hours. Plus she has to go to the other end of town to get the test answers for her nephew. The thing is, she doesn't remember a single function herself. Never mind the functions—she's forgotten the multiplication table. Now when she has to multiply, she adds like they did in school when they were first learning. The same thing happened with music: the only thing she still remembers is that the spiral of the treble clef starts on the second line. Now, when she needs help with the nephew's math, she asks the mother of her classmate. The classmate himself is someone she never wants to see again. But he knows exactly who is asking and keeps doing the tests for old times' sake.

At school and at the university, despite her laziness and failing grades, everyone expected her to have some sort of great future. Pity the person who is expected to have a great future! How happy she is that they no longer recognize her. They buy newspapers at her kiosk, take magazines, envelopes, things and change from her hands but don't recognize her. This makes her happy.

Expectations...Though no one was particularly surprised when she stopped coming to class following those grueling finals that dragged on endlessly because of her illness. But that's not when it began. It's just that her young skin held out for a long time, containing the decay that accumulated inside her with every passing year. People remember her beautiful face. No, she doesn't overestimate herself: she's not the only one who remembers it. It's true. But what a good thing that back then she already wasn't letting anyone take photos of her. How painful it would be to see the large, dark eyes that were once hers with her current bulging, always red bug eyes with their rough whites. Back then she had a wonderful—outstanding, really—mane of blue-black hair, a high, slightly concave forehead, a moderately sized nose, and a small mouth with slightly drooping corners—not because she was so serious all the time: it was just the way her mouth was. But by this time her figure already left a lot to be desired; it showed every sign of this syndrome with two names. (She has been told that it has a double name for the same reason as the Boil-Mariott Law does: two scientists in two different countries discovered it at the same time.) But she wasn't ugly, was she? There are people who are attracted to fat women—and fat women are always falling in love themselves, and they get married. But no one had any use for her. And back then she had no use for anyone either. People were happy to have her around, but no one sought a closer relationship or even a one-night stand. She didn't even have a regular girlfriend. She was alone. What's the problem? What *was* the problem?

There is one thing she knows about the present: she is alone because that's the way she wants it, because that's the way she's set things up. She wouldn't want it any other way. She treasures her aloneness, tends to it, cherishes it. But what about then? Why was she alone then?

Now she thinks she knows why, although she may have merely constructed a comfortable theory. As her illness destroyed her, starting with her hair and ending at her fingernails, a dull kind of hopelessness was eating away at her from the inside. It was a complete lack of spirit, a total internal nothingness that was almost palpable. Like the Bermuda Triangle, which eats ships and airplanes, it was a kind of emptiness, a black hole in which everything—any vibration, any sound—disappeared, everything died, in which light melted away. Nothing got a response. She merely pretended, played at being interested. She had no opinions or arguments. She could be foaming at the mouth trying to prove something one day, only to try to beat the exact opposite into someone's head the next. She could have been capable of betrayal, given the opportunity. But then given the opportunity, she could have done something supernoble, something sublime. So she avoided all opportunities to do anything lest she regret it or be ashamed of it later. There was a time when small children, puppies, and full-grown mutts had flocked to her, and she had loved them sincerely. Later, they met her indifference with hostility. Dogs would bare their teeth in soft but threatening growls. It began to irritate her when children cried. It was then that her first nephew was born. She hated his mouth, which was forever open. She thought that it was this particular purple boy with his big feet, big ears, and big mouth, that she couldn't stand. Then she realized that she just couldn't stand children, that they disgusted her the same way cats and other animals now did.

This emptiness must have closed in on her when she was studying in the physics and mathematics department at the university. Back then she didn't notice it at all; she had no clue about anything of the sort. She never pushed anyone away, but she didn't try to ingratiate herself either; she wasn't arrogant, but she didn't try to make friends. If someone had wanted to come in, she would have allowed it. But no one did. This was the way it was from day one: she preferred to sit alone at a desk, and in lecture halls she would sit by the window or the aisle in one of the emptier rows. She had her seat in every auditorium. For some reason, her right to these seats, which were among the most comfortable, was recognized by everyone from the start. There were times when it got crowded and people sat three or four to a desk, but no one even made a move toward the empty chair next to her: her bag was on it. It rarely occurred to instructors to ask someone to sit with her.

The department's population was split into the perennial elite ("high society"), the semi-high society ("spiritual plebeians"), the hangers-on (bloodsuckers), and the plebes. The lines were generally drawn by the "high society." She didn't belong anywhere. She didn't make it into any of these groupings. She was by herself. Members of the "high society" didn't consider her to be their equal and avoided her, though they were afraid to oppose her too obviously; the semi-highs didn't fear her one bit, but didn't get close to her either; the bloodsuckers openly feared and tried to please her, and the plebes hated her with a passion. This brought her real joy, real pleasure: she loved to bring the poverty of their minds out into the open and demonstrate the full extent of their stupidity to an audience, making them say all sorts of nonsense before they had a chance to even figure out what was going on. Unfortunately, there were quite a few plebes among the instructors—those who dragged in to put in the required hours, so unlike the few who brought true inspiration to their lectures. The punch-in/punch-out crowd feared her, so deft was she at making them slip up without even noticing. They got their revenge through failing her or giving her incompletes, but it was so easy to get revenge on her: she hardly ever studied, and when she wasn't prepared, she refused to answer questions, taking an honest fail over a pass she'd have to beg for. She liked things to be either black or white in her grades as in everything else: either excellent or fail. The instructors' petty revenge met with a formidable response: she made a laughing stock of them, though she wasn't one to say things behind their backs.

Her classmates liked repeating her words and witticisms, savoring the tricks she used to trip up the instructors imperceptibly but precisely. Nicknames she gave her enemies stuck firmly and followed them through the university from year to year.

She left school because it became so hard to study for an excellent from teachers whose self-esteem had especially suffered (*My tongue is my enemy*). She had to work like a dog, and the illness was already beginning to affect her: she had headaches and dizzy spells. Formulas leave no room for expansive speeches; they demand learning by rote. Meanwhile, she tired quickly and was always sleepy whether she had had four hours of sleep or twelve. Sleep brought no relief; it didn't even alleviate her physical exhaustion. After every exam, she spent two weeks bedridden, unable to lift her leaden head off the pillow. She got three extensions on her last set of finals. In the end her steel-trap memory, which had amazed even her, began to fail drastically. She couldn't even remember the information on a page she had just turned. Just six months earlier, on a bet, she had recited the entire contents of a page of unfamiliar text, including the punctuation, after three readings. Now it seemed like that must have been someone else. She ended the finals in the hospital. She was horrified, depressed. From her parents her ineptness in getting a higher education earned her nicknames like *plebeian* and worse. The best of familial intentions dictated that they hold back none of their disappointment, as though an idiot who is told he is an idiot often enough will get smarter. All this weighed on her poor head, which was losing the last of its thinned hair while her memory lost the names and faces of her classmates. She cried a lot and made painful attempts to gather her thoughts, reconstruct, remember, or find something. She was afraid she would lose what was left of her memory and ability to think. She didn't notify the administration, so no one at the university knew she was in the hospital. She tried to keep her parents' visits to a minimum, too. Cruelly, painfully, she deprived herself of the sympathy and understanding of eyes and words that were warm but so hurtful...*Rub your nose in it...There! Again...And again!* Then her source of comfort appeared as a big, fat, and wonderful surprise—a diabetic Jew. He was old and sickly, a tireless joke teller who savored witticisms, word play, and refined vulgarities disguised as elegant ambiguities. He had curly hair and a plum-like nose and a really genuine accent and really genuine jokes populated with Moishes, Khaims, and Saras. Every day he would tell her new ones on any topic, with never a repetition. He never sympathized with her; he just listened attentively to all her achy complaints and her despair and then told a joke that would make her burst out laughing at the time of his telling it and then every time she happened to remember it, which was always at the most inappropriate moments. She laughed during the doctors' rounds, during examinations, when she was getting a shot. The doctors were simply amazed, and she was happy that sleep had gotten easier and even enjoyable. She ate in the cafeteria with the heavy old man named Nison; they strolled the hospital hallways together, shuffling their slippered feet. In good-natured moments when he was about to tell a joke, he would pinch her fat sides. They would spend hours talking about everything: diets, science, taboos, customs, bazaars, literature, religion. Without even noticing it, she adopted all his gestures and speech patterns, the singsong intonations of Jewish speech, and even his sense of irony. She started pinching the old man's sides. Most amazing, she remembered everything he told her, absolutely everything. One day when her relatives came to see her, wearing the dim expressions of hospital visitors, she said that they were free to plug up their ears if they were easily embarrassed, to close their eyes if those started coming out of their sockets, to leave, finally, if they were ashamed for her, but she was going to tell jokes anyway because she was ill and had the right to do as she wished. They listened to the first two jokes with sourly sweet smiles on their faces. After the third one, they forgot about propriety and laughed. She told jokes for about an hour, not forgetting a single one. The five of them walked up and down the same path in the park about twenty times, crying from laughter and scaring birds.

It's been over ten years since that time, but even now, on first meeting, she is often told that she sounds Jewish. She doesn't mind, though she does nothing to cultivate the accent.

She didn't go back to the university. She didn't get a job. She breathed the air. She enjoyed herself. She met people and more people and more people: anyone, through anyone. She had fun.

Oh, look at this! She totally forgot: she should have saturated the cake about ten minutes ago. Where is the potholder? Oh, where in the world is it already? The hell with it, it will still be edible. She baked it for an extra ten minutes because of—but then her mood…Now is the time to remember that today is her birthday: those very thirty-three years. Not that she forgot—though she did want to. Others forgot; they almost always forget—even her mother forgets the day she gave birth to her. About two months after her birthday, she remembers and feels guilty and then goes a week without screaming, and there is peace and quiet in the house. Herself, she never reminds anyone about this day. No, she doesn't, uh-uh. Who needs it? Really, how could anyone look at her and think of birthdays? A birthday is something light, happy, joyful, and one look at her is enough to wipe a smile off anyone's face. So this is how she is celebrating her birthday. She is even baking a cake, though it is not for her. But what's the point of lying to herself? The reason she was sitting in front of the oven is that she is thirty-three today and no one remembers it, and she wishes she could forget about it, too. That's the reason she crossed the line, too: started thinking about things she'd forbidden herself to remember, things she must not remember: the building with the burning windows. But now that she's gotten started, she can let herself remember that the kind old Jew died. He went into an insulin coma; there was nothing they could do for him. What a good birthday party, what beautiful guests: useless, bad memories. That's all right, tonight she'll get to the business of imagining chimeras, and she'll try to come up with something outstanding.

How careless! It must be her good mood or something. She's really burned her hand with the frying pan. She should rub egg white on the burn, but there isn't a single egg in the apartment. Shit! She should at least stick it under cold water. It's always like this! She is apparently programmed for misfortune: she is even unlucky in small ways. Now

YELENA TARASOVA

she's burned her hand—and the thing is, all her cuts, all her injuries turn into wounds that don't heal for months—what are they called, tropic or something? Now she has to protect the injured hand, which will just lead to another odd habit. She has plenty of those already. She has a special walk that spares her achy legs and a bite that protects her inflamed gums, and lots and lots of other habits. Indeed, she must make a very interesting spectacle when she is marching down the street. She wears soft slippers or semi-athletic shoes that are loosely laced and a dress that's shiny on the stomach and at the hips. Step-step, step-step. She walks, rocking from one foot onto the other, holding her hands away from her body, turned out and away. Jealously, she watches for looks that turn to her shapeless, heaving body. Greedily, she stares into the eyes that pause on her thin wrists and shins, on her shiny, sweaty forehead. Sometimes she can feel with her back that a mother-and-daughter pair or a couple of older people that have just passed her as though she were nothing special, without even a glance in her direction, have stopped and turned to follow her with their eyes, whispering something curious and sympathetic. With a sudden jelly-like heave, she turns to face them and tries to catch the meaning of their grimaces, capture the looks that are now running away, hiding behind a newly indifferent back, escaping on convulsively hurried feet. These are people who are tactful in their own interpretation of this word. They are the ones she dislikes the most. It's hard to take a straight-on stare, but it is worse when she knows that these "tactful" people, once they've glided behind her back, will start staring at her in as "well-mannered" a way as one stares through a grate in a zoo at a sleeping hippopotamus spread out in its own green excrement. And they justify their own animal curiosity to themselves by shaking their reasonable heads like Chinese dolls and clucking sympathetically, salivating condolences: "Poor, poor woman! What a shame, what a shame!" Then even those who didn't notice her at first, those who accidentally failed to register the heaving hideousness of her body, stop as though before a live post with a sign saying SPECTACLE! The stares directed at her back make her skin shrink, become too small. She has come to understand the straight backs and independent stares of actors from the lilliputian theater, to realize why they never walk alone. She has always tried not to look at them, and when she saw one, she would immediately turn away. Looking at cripples was taboo. Let there be just one less stare that they—the ones without legs or arms, the blind ones, the ones disfigured by birthmarks—have to deal with.

It's as though she had known that she would be stared at the same way.

Sometimes they will intentionally catch her eye, carefully survey her blotchy skin and her shaved chin and triumphantly throw some hurtful and very loud words at her: "What a cow!" is the least painful of the things she has had to hear. Then they laugh at their own joke, laugh cheerfully and loudly, whether they are one, two, three, or even more. Sometimes they push her, apparently intuiting that she is not very stable on her achy legs and knowing how amusing she will look doing a heavy dance with her arms spread out in an attempt to keep her balance. Sometimes it seems like she has worked out a firm resistance to the insults, the hurtful comments, and bazaar screams, so that nothing can break through her fat concentration, the massive fog in which she drags herself around the streets, noticing nothing and no one except the eyes at her back...Sometimes...Sometimes her soul howls and cries. And the pathetic angry midget crouching beside her starts jumping up and down, jerking his hump.

The mirror...If there is a strong gust of wind, flocks of birds will fly out from the forested black crevices beneath her eyebrows...A menacing thousand-year idol. A stone creation...Scary...She should never look at herself.

Until recently she held to a base, instinctive sense that naked flesh was taboo. From the time she reached the age at which children realize they have a sex, no one ever saw her undressed, not even her sister or her mother. The public baths to which she and her sister were taken when they were children were a nightmare. She remembers some kind of fumes and stone benches, the hollow din of metal basins, breasts, hips, loose hair, shiny faces, pink backs, and buttocks disappearing into the fog, voices, laughter, the sound of water. Where did she get this idea that flesh was taboo?

Now she thinks that it marked the beginning of her escape—her escape from nature, from flesh. She tried to separate herself, fence herself and those around her off from the laws of the body, build a tall barrier to divide once and for all the spiritual—the things that made people human—from their material, animalistic beginnings. Maybe this is where she got her dislike, her distaste for infants: they were too sharp a reminder of the ways and means through which we come into the world, and, like little animals—cats, dogs, monkeys—they sucked nipples. The ways and means were something she found out about at an unusually late age, and she immediately tried to put the

YELENA TARASOVA

information out of her mind. The knowledge broke her tender, anxious connection to her parents, for she could never forgive them or herself that she tumbled out into the world—into the hands of a midwife—covered in blood and water. But it was about twenty-five years ago that she found the words to describe what disturbed her connection to the world. She read somewhere: "It is somehow inhuman that a human being, a creature possessed of imagination, fantasy, technology, and so many nuances and shades of feeling, is born and gives birth in such a primitive way...like a horse, a dog, a cat, a pig..." And she tried to free herself of the sin of being an animal, to escape this frightening essence, the mystery of birth.

It was then that she made friends with various cripples, monsters, and just really ugly people—the ones she felt would be deprived of this animal joy, the conception and birth of children. She started hating her body. She cut into her fingers with a dull knife, she put lit matches out on her palm, she poked at her veins with dull, rusty pins, and once she branded her hand with a knife blade that she had heated till it was red. Her hands were covered with scratches, pricks, and boils. The bluish-white scars are still visible. Her relationship with her parents, which had never been easy, congealed into hatred. She did only what she was forbidden to do: she didn't go to school and she dropped out of music school as well, even though she had only a year to go. She sought out beatings. No one in her family had ever given much thought to whether children should be beaten: they beat them and that was that. Now her father and mother would drive themselves to rage in an attempt to beat tears out of her. At times one of them had to drag the other away from her. She stood the beatings with a cruel sense of satisfaction: it was her *parents* beating her, the ones who conceived her, gave birth to her, and betrayed her—by giving birth. They had taught her children's songs about a tree that was born in the forest and encouraged her to identify with the baby Thumbelina born of a flower, and with the little tin soldier. They fed her fairy tales in which everything was so light, clean, and clear...

Following the beatings, she would lock herself in her room, where she ripped away at the blanket with her teeth, tending to her pain in a way they could not hear. Then she would spend several nights mending the blanket—until the next beating...And she continued to be friends with those with whom she was forbidden to spend time, continued stubbornly to wear rags, and in school, following long and insistent hours of forced cramming, she continued to announce simply "Unprepared" in every single one of her classes. And again she would go home to beatings that lasted until she was black and blue and bloody, until a neighbor happened by to rescue her. Even her sister, who had grown accustomed to protecting her own hide at the expense of hers (she would tattle to their mother, blaming her for infractions either of them was guilty of, knowing that the first waves of anger would come out in the first blows and she would get away with a lazy kick, neither painful nor frightening)—even her sister started sticking up for her. But she would have none of her attempts at helping, because she knew that her sister was already going on dates and she had even seen her kissing. How could she accept help from her? No. She was better off alone. In her better moments, her mother would utter endearments and try to kiss her daughter's angry eyes but was met with such cruel resistance, such harsh words, that it was almost enough to provoke another beating. Sometimes it did, and again she had scrapes, bruises, and aching cheekbones. It was in these moments that she felt like she had escaped—or nearly escaped—her essence, escaped those who gave birth to her, escaped the blood of her birth.

Now she hated books, which had been her great joy and pleasure. They had betrayed her. She made pronouncements that would have made the Grand Inquisitor proud: "All books must be burned, destroyed." Yes, they had lied to her. She never read them anymore. She moped around the apartment with nothing to do: she had given up music, she didn't do her homework, and she didn't read. More and more often she would wander into the kitchen and probe the insides of the refrigerator, dipping into pots with a ladle, a spoon, or simply her hands, ransack the cupboards in search of sweets. Half an hour later she would return to the kitchen and start all over again. To make matters worse, food always seemed especially tasty and sweet after a beating, so, crying, she would chase her hurt and sadness with food, dripping tears on every tidbit she placed in her mouth. She would sit in the kitchen and eat and eat and eat, occasionally getting water from the tap to wet her numb lips and smarting scraped cheekbones. She ate lunch, breakfast, and supper alone so that no one would see how much she ate. Sitting at a table littered with dirty dishes, trash, and the remains of others people's meals, she would shovel huge pieces of food into her mouth and swallow almost without chewing, for fear that someone would come in and catch her. She consumed her endless ration in this filth, and so for a long time she considered the process of eating to be something unclean, untidy, shameful, something that needed to be kept out of sight and not

YELENA TARASOVA

dragged out for everyone to see during family dinners, holiday cele-
brations, and banquets. She didn't want to know that people can eat
beautifully, and so she noticed only the ugly: people grabbing food
with their hands out of a common plate, people smacking their lips as
they chewed, people noisily swallowing their tea, people licking their
fingers and burping.

Soon she gained so much weight that neighborhood kids started
taunting her with the nickname Bomber. But she couldn't stop, so she
kept eating. She was horribly ashamed of her body. And when she
made the transition from being a fat little girl to being a fat young
woman, she became doubly ashamed. Going outside was torture. If it
had not been absolutely necessary to leave the house on occasion, she
would have stayed in, guarding her four walls. She kept thinking that
this was temporary, that it would pass by itself, disappear somehow,
and then she would be able to go to the sandy beach as she had
before. She would once again be able to drop her dress on the sand
and go out into the sea without having to meet ridiculing stares, see
laughing faces, hear the cautionary statement that is considered the
height of witticism across the world and across all age groups: "Don't
go in or the sea will overflow."

She loved the sea. She liked the sensation of weightlessness, of
being light; she liked the smell of iodine, salt and seaweed. But now
she had only the night sea—a black sea with a long stripe of moonlight. Infrequently, her father would give in to her insistent, pestering
requests and start up the old Zaporozhets to drive to the beach on a
hot August night. They would fall asleep there on benches, on fold-
away cots, or in the car until the sound of the morning surf woke them
up. Under the rays of the morning sun, the awareness of her hideousness would return. She would sit in a sweaty heap under the scorch-
ing-hot blue car roof, angrily and enviously watching the others swim
in the transparent morning water.

This was when the first signs of her illness started to show. There
were only a few then, and they were minor: red welts of scar tissue
appeared on her body; her skin became sensitive and oily; a dense
fuzz started growing on her chin.

Yes. Then she was ashamed of her body. Now, on the other hand—
now she relishes exploring her hideousness. How did this happen? As
she lay in the observation room of that place with grates on the windows, pretending that she was able to fall asleep, that she wasn't
scared, it occurred to her that there was no one in this place who was
nude or naked in the usual sense. True, there were totally naked

women walking the hallways here, some of them freely and some shrinking in shame. Fresh nightshirts were given out only once a day—during the doctors' rounds—and she was always seeing naked body parts that are usually covered. But in this place no one paid any attention to this sort of thing, as though this was the way it should be. Maybe it is. Everything is bared in that place, everything is naked flesh; whatever you do, whatever you wear, all gestures and all movements are reduced to naked flesh. You can run around on all fours if you want, and no one will think it unnatural. In this place she reexamined many of her values, reevaluated many of her concepts, thought a lot. It was better not to use your scared-to-death brains in this place. It was best to try to go with the flow: to eat and drink, to go on walks when you were taken out with your shift under the watchful eyes of three or four sturdy aides, to take part in dances improvised to a rhythm beaten out with palms, to join everyone in laughing at Pirozhikha, the transparent weak old woman, to help catch red-haired Anfisa in the hallway and bind this strong, resistant idiot—happy with her lot—to the bed. You might want to join everyone in stealing fruit sent from home to the weakest and most helpless of them, who offered no resistance. You might also earn an extra walk by helping the dumb, bored aides in the cruel games they played with the patients. God, the things they did to them! And all these things, including groveling, were encouraged as manifestations of good sense, indicating that her mental health was returning.

For god's sake! Who was she to complain to? The doctors, during their morning rounds? No, someone else would have to do that, someone healthy, and not in this hospital, not in this one. The patients in this one were capable only of answering questions with dumb and disjointed statements and jumping away and trying to stuff themselves under their beds to hide from scary medications and painful injections. At two o'clock in the afternoon, the doctors would leave, having earned their daily pay, and a new seventeen-hour-long prison nightmare would begin. In a fit of rage *they* could kill, could bite off a hated attendant's ear—and the incident would live on in hospital lore for many years—but they never harbored, never repressed anger. All their anger showed on their faces, sounded in their voices. But they harbored nothing...THEY BORE NO ILL.

She lived in a constant state of animal horror, afraid of everything. She feared the woman who had come to her on the first night, sneaking by the sleeping patients to kneel by her bed: "You are a goddess. I know that you are a goddess. You have come to save me. They want

YELENA TARASOVA

to poison me here. They've been preparing my poison. But you will save me, I know. I will always be beside you now. Don't cry, please. Don't cry. Don't try to talk me out of it, I know that you are a goddess anyway! Will you save me, will you let me stay beside you, will you let me?" She left as quietly as she had come, and a minute later she returned with her bedding and made her lair right under her bed. They kicked her out, but she kept coming back. The next day, after lunch, she came bearing her uneaten meal with a drumstick she'd somehow managed to get…But she rejected this willing slave because she feared those quiet, pleading eyes like she feared everything else.

This was also when she first saw Kandalarova. The sight didn't just frighten her; it astounded her. Kandalarova's huge body, the color of fumed oak, towered on the hospital bed like a series of improbable spheres, looking like a chaotic pile of some half-empty bags and certainly not like a human body. When this enormity stood up on its elephantine legs, its head would soar up to the ceiling, looking down with enraged red wild eyes. The biggest robe on the ward was barely enough to cover the powerful torso; the legs, which were not covered, looked like crooked, knotty tree trunks. They didn't really, but there was nothing else to compare them to. Her tree-bark-covered heels scraped the linoleum when she moved around the hallways, because there were no slippers her size either; her unforgettable "panties" hung out from under the short robe and down to her knees. But there was a sort of harmony in her whole being, a harmony of horror, of hideousness.

About three months after she was released, she ran into Kandalarova in the street. Kandalarova was wearing an overcoat and a pair of inconceivable boots—but at least they fit. But she looked very mediocre: the horror had disappeared, and so had the harmony. What had changed? She got to thinking then. It must have been their *motherland*—whose name, like god's name, is not to be said aloud—that undressed all its children, bared the horrors, and gave them singularity. She came home after that encounter, which left her with a strange sensation, like with a nut…A nut: a second ago you could hear the kernel inside. You bite in with a cracking sound, and your teeth find nothing. Bitter black dust gets on your tongue, hangs for a minute over the empty inside of the nut, suspended in the air…

When she came home that day, her parents weren't there. She undressed, lit a candle, turned out the lights, and stepped up to the mirror.

This was the first time, the first time she heard from her flesh, which she had tried to run away from, to escape for all these years.

This was when she heard *the call* in her blood...

It all must have happened because she feared her future. She could see it, and she feared it. It took a battle to get her released from that place; it took pressure from above, where her worn-out, lobbied-out parents had come via some intricate passageways: that place is exceedingly easy to get into and exceedingly difficult to get out of. When she was being evaluated for release, she named the reason. It was false, of course: she said that the man whom she loved had married, taking away her last chance at marriage. That was it: the failure to satisfy the ordinary female needs—to be married, have children, keep house. All in all, through all the torture of cross-examinations and second opinions, she never had to say one word that was true. But these people's ideas of mental health turned out to be just too strange. On the other hand, perhaps their ideas were just right, maybe too right: if they could see that a person was capable of lying to save herself, then she was well, completely well. But what if she had told them that she felt nothing at all—no joy, no pain, no love, no anger? That inside of her she had zero, a deaf vacuum, a black hole that sucked everything in and gave nothing back, not love and not hate? That she filled her days with imaginary feelings: anger, irritation, arousal, pleasure? That she had to tell herself, Here I should feel this, and now this...She jangled the composite parts of her feelings like triangular plastic parts of a child's puzzle in her hands. This is how you make a wolf, and this is how you make a giraffe and a house. Now you can take it all apart, break it up and put the parts back in the box. These were all her feelings, all the emotions that she constructed in the course of a day and tried to believe in. At night she shoveled them into a box like a pile of useless junk. She was twenty-seven then, is that right? She had loved no one. Ever. She wanted to but couldn't. Another handicap. She would even have settled for unrequited love, as long as she felt something. She'd been exhausted by that big round zero, which changed shapes like an amoeba and could deceive anyone, but not her. She had nothing left besides the body, with its aches, its fears, its lameness, and its illnesses. Also, she had her fear of the future. One evening then, she came to a calm, clear, cold decision: she didn't want a future; she wanted to slash her veins. She had to do it that very day because later she might not be able to bring herself to do it: she could see the encroaching wretchedness and knew that in the future it would rule, wield absolute power over her. Having made this decision, she used her building blocks to construct the desire to realize it while she still could.

YELENA TARASOVA

She swallowed a bottle and a half of her pills, chasing them with water. She opened a new pack of imported razor blades. She walked around, waiting for the pills to take effect. She felt a prickling and pinching sensation in the soles of her feet and in her hands, she felt dizzy...It was even pleasant in a way. The layered air distorted the outlines of objects; she felt heat, then pain in her stomach. Slowly, savoring the moment, she rolled up her sleeve and took aim—it was still scary. All right, it would be easier with her eyes closed...How odd: she felt nothing. Her hand was lying on her knees, the blood streaming down onto her robe, crawling down her shin, starting to drip onto the rug now—she should roll up the rug. There was less prickling in her hand, and her head became clearer. For some reason she got a cramp in her arm up to the shoulder, and she was having convulsions, but the long bloody strip didn't hurt at all. The blood was this really red color red. It was congealing on the rug, and she was thinking she should roll up the rug...Jelly...God, she felt nauseous. She lay down on the couch, barely able to hold back the nausea at her throat. What was that? The doorbell? She would never open the door. Let them ring. They'll get tired of it and leave...She heard the jingling of keys; now someone was in the apartment. Why, oh why was she so unlucky—now they were going to come in and see everything. God willing, it was too late.

It was her father then, coming back for some documents: he'd forgotten his driver's license in his other jacket. He came into the room. Right away her insides were wrenched out of her. A hot, bitter white liquid was coming out of every opening, including her nostrils, pouring into the disgusting, already darkened bloody jelly on the rug.

She never lost consciousness. She remembers the pain in her stomach, the neighbors who materialized out of nowhere, her mother, an ambulance. Everything seemed to appear at once. She sat on the couch, ready to go. She had rolled up the rug herself. She put on a new robe. They wanted to carry her down on a stretcher, but she declined. Overcoming weakness, suppressing the shudders going through her body, she walked downstairs.

They pumped her stomach. They hooked up an IV and gave her glucose. The hospital was calm and quiet. Her parents came in. She fought back her delusions—she kept hurriedly unbuttoning a shiny black satin vest at her chest to prevent something terrible from happening—and said that she would never forgive them for having interfered, that they would never forgive themselves. They would be sorry for what they had done. Because she would never be able to do it now.

Never. She had no will power. And this had been her only chance to escape her frightening future. She kept clenching her teeth tighter and tighter, starting to grind them...She couldn't speak anymore. She was fighting the black vest, which kept being buttoned up...

Now there is nothing she can do except groan in front of the oven and dream. She is not dying, but she is living her death...She is baking a cake. That's all.

Speaking of which, she should have left by now, but the damned sweet dough isn't done yet. How she wishes she didn't have to go out into the street. What could be worse than having to walk again under the stares fixed at her back, plodding through the anticipation of insults. She is going to have to take six buses today. She has never been able to drag her heavy body onto a full bus on the first attempt. Once she does get on, other passengers shove her, nudge her with their elbows, push her up against handrails and the backs of seats. God forbid she should happen to step on somebody's foot: "People like you shouldn't use public transportation. You might maim someone." When someone steps on her foot, that's her fault, too, and she doesn't even have the right of response with the stock bus brush-off: "If you don't like it, take a taxi." All she can do is look at the culprits sternly while her midget shivers, hanging back and crumpling his cap in his hands, his head lowered. She wants to take his nose in her fingers and squeeze it hard to make him cry, to get revenge for the dirt he has thrown in her face. But she understands him perfectly; she knows that he is desperate because he is helpless to help either her or himself. She forgives him.

Every time she goes out, she feels doomed, at the mercy of the mob. But what if her stomach were flat and smooth and she could cover it with her own two hands—could become this cruel, heartless, and rude? If her nape weren't this fat? If she still had thick jet-black hair, if the whites of her eyes were still bluish and smooth, if her fingers were not bent by arthritis—would she be this mean ? The young beautiful girls with long legs and shiny eyes are always the most cruel. They laugh louder, more exuberantly than anyone else, happy to show their beautiful healthy teeth and their pink gums, to turn their faces, covered with a silvery pink down, toward her. Because their hair has not lost its shine to seborrhea, because it shivers and plays in the sunlight, they can laugh at the bald top of her head with its scaly skin. They nail her to the cross of her hideousness with their mercilessly clear eyes. They are the worst.

Funny, she used to think that she would never be able to harm

YELENA TARASOVA

others in petty ways. Now she gets great pleasure out of cheating her customers out of kopecks when they pay for magazines, pens, or envelopes. She stares them down from the depths of her kiosk, eating away at their smooth skin with her eyes; she huffs and puffs, intentionally fussing and letting her lips loose to show off the rot in her mouth; she tries to breathe in their faces—those beautiful happy scumbags, who are guilty of nothing. If someone rushes her with the change, she intentionally loses count so she has to count the change three times over. She readily gets into fights and starts yelling, spraying her spit. And if someone leaves her a tip, she throws the change out at them, aiming for the back. There, this is her great future. Why did they stop her then?

Scum, scum. Beautiful scum! God forbid any one of you...She shares their world only because she doesn't have the strength to get out. She escapes only in her dreams. After every new insult she escapes quietly and without a trace, so that her corpse—something even more hideous than she—will never float up or get dug up anywhere, bloated and puffy. If someone were to die every time she imagined this, their city would turn into a city of corpses. She imagines escaping quietly, inconspicuously. She lives her death the way others live their hopes, their troubles, their relationships to reality: their vanity, their income, their clothes, their worries, their vices, their love, their fame, their studies. She lives her death—a quiet, inaudible, imperceptible death. Her long-held grudge against the world demands neither hifalutin funeral speeches nor tears nor pangs of conscience for those who have hurt her; she needs no recognition of her rare qualities, no sympathy, no understanding. She just needs death. She searches her memory for a friend in some far-away town whom she could trust with a pack of letters written two years ahead so he could throw one in a mailbox from time to time, sending bitter words of hatred to her hometown to leave no doubt that as long as she was full of hatred and anger she was alive.

She works her imagination until it is exhausted. Her fantasies do not just come into her head; she summons them like spirits. She has her regular death delusions: deserted beaches, pits full of quicklime, aerial ropeways, abandoned mine shafts, precipices. In addition, she has the most beautiful visions percolating, boiling over in her head as in an alchemist's laboratory. She imagines them taking shape from purple smoke streams: palaces and cathedrals, medieval castles and gothic chapels. The main thing is not to populate her dreams with people: she doesn't want to see the happiness of others. And she cannot let herself see herself in them, or the intricate constructions will collapse into heaps of dust and dirt. That's how it has to be: not a soul. Empty except for her incorporeal spirit wandering amid the splendor...Empty palaces and castles. Armchairs, couches, and chairs with no one sitting in them. Deserted park alleys. Deer, birds, butterflies. Beautiful. Nothing ever happens. Why should it? She constructs her own louvres, hermitages, peterhoffs from her own blueprints. She chooses curves in the rivers' paths, valleys and hills in which to make parks. She was once awed by the parks in Pavlovsk, and she tries to recreate their spirit: brooding trees, thoughtful groves, philosophically resigned meadows. On the inside she has to think through every detail, she cannot leave either the high-ceilinged halls or the modest dressing rooms or the libraries until she has found a color solution, ripped down the wall hangings three times, ripped up the upholstery, reshuffled the most minute details of the cloth patterns, changed the wood carvings a hundred times, rehung the wallpaper and relaid the parquet floors. Details, details, details...Every nail, every piece of wood...Outside her lowered eyelids is her dirty room: more and more scraps of paper fly off the rolltop, covering the floor; gray dust covers her scattered clothes, the moss-grown floor, the bottles of medicine, the books, which are with her again now that she allows much of what was once taboo.

And the neighbor girl is the only one who remembers her birthday. She is going to come tonight, bearing touching and laughable birthday wishes. Still, what's she supposed to do with her? What's she supposed to do? Because today she is thirty-three, that evangelical age when one has to make decisions. She must not infect her with her death. She must not. Let her live a real life, with sad sorrows and happy joys. Yes. Today she is going to kick her out rudely. Rudely. The hell with her. As for herself—what can she do? She'll return to the place where she is meant to be. She'll return to the Call...once she is rid of this attachment.

It was a year ago, on the day before her operation, that she realized that she would return. They were supposed to take out her thyroid and had already been preparing her for it for a week. She was preparing too, in her own way: getting herself together.

On a hot August night, when a scorching darkness lay heavily on her chest, she remembered that place. It had been a hot night then, too. A thunderstorm was starting. Rolls of thunder provoked confusion and fear in the brightly lit rooms. Suddenly, a small epileptic woman started convulsing in the tight confines of her ropes. This was not a

YELENA TARASOVA

seizure. Her fragile naked spread-out body was bending, trying to free itself. She started howling. She howled louder and louder. Then she started growling. The she howled again, long and slow, like a dog. The three-story building, flooded with bright electrical light, was awake. A few minutes later they could hear a response from downstairs: a bass howl from the men's ward. Anguish crept from floor to floor.

Suddenly, a heavy pale woman started shaking in excitement. She was one of the four who slept on the floor. She squatted and abruptly flung open her robe, exposing full white breasts with bluish veins, and started hurriedly feeling for something on her smooth skin. Then she found it and squashed it between her nails. Then she quickly moved her hands over her body and through her hair, throwing imaginary insects on the floor and squashing them. She could see horror in her face.

Kandalarova started heaving on her bed, with its mattress net hanging down almost to the floor. Her lips whispered something disjointed. Her giant hand flew from one shoulder to the other, from her forehead to her navel. Kandalarova was crossing herself, crossing, crossing herself endlessly...How she feared her then.

She recalled the horror of that night as she lay on the surgery ward the day before her operation. She could not lie there any longer. She got up noiselessly, went out of the room, went down the stairs to the first floor. How was she to get out? One of the planks across the entrance had been lifted up: would she fit? She got through, scraping her belly and losing several buttons off her robe. It was difficult to get her bearings on hospital property at night. There was an electrical glow in the distance—was that what she was looking for? There would be a thunderstorm tonight, too, like there was that night. She heard the roar of thunder. That's why it had been so humid! Tomorrow they were going to operate on her, and she had to go there...She plodded without knowing the way, unable to see anything in the dark, stumbling over tree roots. She saw a dark bulky object, the outline of a crane over her: this was where they were putting up the new surgery building. She would have to go around it. Suddenly a strong gust of wind blew brick dust into her face...Lightning. Thunder. The storm.

By the time she got there, she was soaked. Her large slippers were sticking to the wet ground. There it was, that place!

It was huge, engulfed in the blinding flames of electrical light, which forced its way out every crack, a mysterious ship setting off into the night...A thunderstorm. The trunks of old trees were creaking. A slow, anguished howl was coming through the windows, as it had that night.

A thunderstorm. The branches of large trees were swaying. Her nameless *motherland* was calling for her in wild, dark voices...Come back, come back, it's all a lie. Come back quick. Get on all fours and start howling...Bite the ground until it hurts, until it bleeds...It's all a lie—all the hopes, all the dreams. Everything that's whole and everything that's broken is a lie. The truth is here. This is it. Get on all fours and into the bushes. Run!

The CALL sounded in her blood. Everything is a lie. Her dress is a lie, so off with it! Running on all fours, naked, dragging her fat belly on the ground, scraping roots of trees, jiggling her thighs, letting her jowls and lips hang...

Come to your senses and leave, before it's too late. Before it's too late. In another minute, you'll start howling. Turn your back, even if it creaks, even if it makes a grinding sound. Turn around! In another minute, it will be too late.

Everything was over, over, and again she was plodding through the mud, dragging both her feet. The rain poured down on her, and she licked raindrops off her cracked lips. Now she knew that she was destined to return. She would return when her blood spoke, responding to the unintelligible call of its *motherland*, whose name, like god's name, is not to be said aloud.

Yes, now she has reached the age of the human god. But he was slender and healthy when he was crucified at thirty-three. In all the depictions of him, his face may not be beautiful, but he is wiry and slender in a youthful way, and his whole body—still warm—says he wants to live, he wants to live!

It's not even that she doesn't want to live; she can't live. And she can't seem to die. She'd settle for being crucified instead of him, the human god. But no one would worship this kind of deity: gods cannot be disgusting...Hers would be a red-purple, bloated carcass hanging off the cross...It seems people only trust things that are beautiful and healthy.

She trusts nothing. When even Kandalarova kept crossing and crossing her huge belly on that night of horrors.

If she could believe, maybe it would be easier for her now. All she has left is dirt growing in her room and populating her imagination with ghosts: her heavy soul, the hunchback midget, Lazarus, Christ and Pontius Pilate, and the reflection of her own body in the mirror—Lady Ragnell turned into a disgusting monster by fairy Morganna; palaces, castles, parks. And if she follows the CALL, they might all come alive, turn to flesh.

Perhaps hope will turn to flesh as well.

And then she could stomp on it with her feet...

This should be it. She can take out the cake now, and then she'll get dressed. Her mother is at the hospital, waiting for her, waiting to see her own hideous monster. How they all love one another when one of them is ill! When she herself is in the hospital, her father, who used to beat her unconscious, doesn't know what to do with himself; his heart starts acting up. He cries tears of joy when she is released and their current Volga (which has replaced the old Zaporozhets), sparkling clean, takes her home.

Back home, the vicious circle closes again.

Back are the half-forgotten words of hatred, the faces blue from screaming. One day she feels a chip off a tooth on her tongue, and she walks around depressed and certain that she can salvage nothing anymore. She cannot get plastic dentures, which would bruise her bare gums, for her soul. Lady Ragnell cannot be brought out from under the spell: she did not meet her Sir Gawain in time. She will remain a slobbery monster with red, inflamed eyes. Nothing could be made better now, not even if a noble knight were to appear and want to kiss the monster's flat lips. There will be no magic: her soul has begun to resemble an empty skin and has lost faith in deliverance. Everything will be as it was.

Everything will stay in its place.

Again, she will throw her best defense in her parents' faces: "I was offering you a different option. You didn't want it. You took me to the hospital. So you saved me! I told you you'd be sorry. Now bear it! Or else kill me: it's up to you." She will walk from room to room in a fury, driving her parents to a frenzy, to rage. She will grow incensed herself. She will respond with rudeness and filth to anyone who speaks to her. A string will tighten inside her, set to break during the approaching fight. She will scream and scream. And she will feel sorry, endlessly sorry for her parents.

...What's better: a vicious circle or a prison nightmare?

Or, maybe, there is another way? Maybe she could at least try one. Like this, at least: "How they all love one another when one of them is ill! When she is in the hospital, her father doesn't know what to do with himself; his heart starts acting up. He cries tears of joy when she is released, and their new Volga takes everyone home. No one is more dear to her than these people: her aging mother, her ailing father, and she, their biggest pain of all..."

The oven belches acrid smoke. It smells of burned dough and sugar.

The cake is completely burned.

Another way. There is no other way anymore. Everything will stay in its place.

She won't go anywhere today. She burned the cake. The burn on her hand has turned into a huge blister. She has spent the whole day in the dark room without turning on the light.

And she didn't come today. The neighbor girl didn't come.

No one came.

And she burned the cake.

Now what? What's next in the cycle? Thirty-five, the top of Dante's curve. Then what?

A fat hideous woman will howl on a crazy thunderstorm night. Her huge bulging eyes will reflect laughing smiles, bared pink gums. And this woman will be I.

I am shewhobearsnoill.

Speak, Maria!

Tatiana Nabatnikova

Everyone in Russia knows what a collective farmer and a laborer look like: they are several stories tall and made of steel, and they are forging ahead, muscular arms linked in a show of strength and solidarity. And everyone in Russia knows what a collective farmer or a laborer sounds like: like any formulaic Soviet story, produced by an educated city-dweller who wrote in the name of the heroic working class. Tatiana Nabatnikova, a native of the Altai region of Siberia, was taught at Moscow's Literary Institute to pro-duce those sorts of stories; they were what brought authors honors, awards, and membership in the Writers Union.

Nabatnikova's project is a different sort of narrative, one where the writer represents herself not as the medium but as a catalyst: she merely says, "Speak, Maria!" What emerges is not a steely vision of strength but a story of powerlessness, of strength lost—never learned in childhood, smashed by an abusive husband, sucked into the "Earth's weak spot," or, perhaps, sapped by "humanities types" like the writer to whom this mono-logue is apparently addressed.

Before becoming a writer, Nabatnikova graduated from the Novosibirsk Electrotechnical Institute. Her fiction was first published in 1980. She has published three books of short stories: Short Stories, A Home Education *and* Each and Every Hunter. *She lives in Cheliabinsk, a city in Siberia.*
—M. G.

Sometimes I lie awake, alone.

He-e-e-e-ey! is a silent sound. It soars, grows, multiplies under the dome of night. It rolls and thins out. It melts. It is my vain, unquench-able call.

I have a memory from my youth. We disappeared from the gradua-tion ball. He rolled out his motorcycle, and I climbed into the side car in my white dress. We rode for a long time to put a sure distance between us and the village, the people, the lights, all sound. Neither of us said a word once we left the celebration to vanish into the night. Language was turned off; it had no application here.

We rode and I shivered, sensing that I lacked the requisite courage.

Then we stopped. It became quiet.

All the silence, as much as there is of it, gathered here. We sat unable to move a finger, pressed down by the silence, lowered along with the ray of our headlight to the bottom of the cosmos. Only the space claimed by the light—a tiny piece carved out of the huge darkness—was ours. We folded into ourselves like snails and hid, holding our eyes in the safety of the light, afraid to turn them outward into the darkness.

I knew I would have to be the one to break the silence. I would have to get up out of the side car, step out into the night, into the steppes. He had no right, he didn't dare prompt me. I had to do it of my own free will.

I stalled, scared.

He didn't turn off the headlight, and I knew why: to keep a separation between light and dark. He was letting me hide in the darkness. The darkness would help, but everything else was up to me—that was the just and honest way to do it.

But I didn't have it in me. I grew into the side car; he remained in the seat; we were each alone. We would have had to get up to be together. There comes a point when love demands a scary, sacred sacrifice. Remember the Nogei bird carrying Ivan across the precipice in the fairy tale, turning its head from time to time to get its sustenance: a piece of meat, a drink of water? Then the meat in Ivan's bucket is exhausted, but the Nogei bird turns its head, opening its hungry, thirsty beak insistently: Take your knife out, Ivan, and cut a piece from your body—or you won't make it across the precipice.

Doesn't leave much room for *pleasure*.

I sat there, small and contemptible, holding on to the side car for dear life.

He understood. He sighed and turned the ignition key. We returned into the world, the undemanding world of the comfortingly familiar: the noise of the motor, the wind, the lights in people's houses.

The next day we left for different places. We never saw each other again.

I looked for him later, wrote letters someplace, but there was no trace of him. By the time I had the money and freedom to go in search of him, so many years had passed, transforming my face, that I no longer dared appear before my beloved: it would insult his memory of me. Also, he probably had a family, a happy family (nothing but happiness could possibly have been awaiting the family of my beloved).

Happiness was something I didn't know how to do.

TATIANA NABATNIKOVA

One person in a couple has to know the recipe. Then the other one can learn. Neither my husband nor I knew the recipe.

We have this Uncle Kolia Butko who has worked out a theory of gravity (the existing one wasn't good enough). According to his, bodies don't attract but push one another away because each one emanates a force, crowding the other bodies. The other ones, then, resist. The Earth has its own resistance to the pressure of the sun and the stars, which creates optimal conditions for us human beings between these two battling forces. Though this isn't true everywhere. The Earth has a weak spot in the Bermuda Triangle, in his opinion, and that creates a kind of trap door there. In the Apennines, on the other hand, there are some heavy-ore deposits that have a great deal of resistance and simply force things up out of that place. And the weight of objects on the earth's surface should change with the time of day: during the day, when the sun's pressure is stronger, things weigh more. ("Uncle Kolia, have you checked this thing out?" "Nah, haven't gotten around to it yet.")

The thing I find most appealing about Uncle Kolia Butko's theory is the idea that bodies take into consideration each other's forces and use something akin to diplomacy to find mutually tolerable positions, setting what Uncle Kolia calls "the square of distance" between them. It is this "square of distance" that I hold dear. It applies to people's relationships, too. The optimal square of distance is a point of balance of different forces, where they do each other the least harm. I didn't set it with my god-given husband. But now he is dead.

Uncle Kolia explains the chaos of Brownian motion by the fact that such a large number of particles can't find a "square" that would be tolerable to all. So they are forever pushing one another around.

That's what I see when I look at people: Brownian motion.

Uncle Kolia's theory has many other benefits: he can use it to explain high and low tide or substantiate the existence of Mercury's ring, and he is willing to throw in a perpetual motion machine for good measure—a wheel that uses its own weight to keep rolling. True, his prototype can only go downhill, but he says this is just a flaw in the handmade model, and he hasn't been able to get factory equipment for his wheel because he's been slighted by everyone he has written to.

Uncle Kolia keeps hoping that physicists will be brought to the collective farm for the harvest so that he can corner them and make them explain how it is they figure seasons work—because if in the summer the Earth gets closer to the sun, then summer should start all around the globe at the same time, when in reality it comes in turns, first in the southern hemisphere, then in the northern. Can the slant of the Earth's axis really account for the differentiation in the orbital distance between the Earth and the sun? But Uncle Kolia keeps being tormented by all these different questions and we keep not getting any physicists for the harvest because they keep sending humanities types like you. Of course he could go see some physicists himself, but Uncle Kolia just doesn't have the time. I didn't even go to search for my beloved, which was the question of my whole life—surely he can live with some questions in his mind.

If I'd gone, if I'd scraped up the determination to drop everything and go on a wild goose chase, I would have become stronger precisely by the measure of this act (and any subsequent act, if any followed), the way muscles get stronger from exercise.

Or I could begin even earlier: if I had gotten out of the side car...

No, even earlier, some time in my childhood when I stood still instead of yelling "Hooray!" and running and taking something by storm and overcoming obstacles...

Maybe all our troubles start in childhood. Take my late husband, for example. Look, he was born—a boy, a joy—they named him Roman and expected only the best for him. But that's not the way it happened. His father was arrested, as a lot of people were then. His mother, left without her "square," tried to keep her equilibrium for a while, and then lost it. She started getting sucked into the weak spot in the Earth's resistance. No, not in the way you are primed to understand it. Good things happen to people in many different ways, and so do bad things. Her life became dependent on her breakdowns the way electrical power lines are dependent on their posts. A sort of reverse gravity. Her breakdowns sustained her spiritually, and she preferred them to all other kinds of sustenance, the way an Eskimo prefers slightly rancid meat. Little Roman was her most available victim, and she haunted him like a predator: one misstep of his—and she got her breakdown. She would raise her voice to the highest level, right up to the ceiling where it no longer fit (and flattened out into nothing), and curse him this way and that, all on one note, grateful to be liberated, freed from some intolerable internal pressure. Then she would enter another boring stretch of electrical power lines, an expanse of sagging cables, a vegetative state that lasted until her next opportunity to express herself.

Little Roman knew already that this was "bad." He was three, and he looked at his mother, paralyzed, and the key to all his future life

TATIANA NABATNIKOVA

was growing firmly into his spine: the knowledge that "bad" was ALLOWED. Moreover, that overcoming the prohibition of "bad" can bring unbelievable joy, which cannot be had any other way. It's like nuclear energy: you've got an ordinary substance, not fuel—but there is an awful force concealed in its atoms, and if it's let out then no kind of oil or TNT can even compete with it. It was like that with my mother-in-law, may she rest in peace. She had no talents, no skills, no special brain power—no spark and no fire. But she extracted the forbidden force of the conquered "bad" from the gray dust that made up her self, and out of it grew the disgraceful mushroom cloud under which my husband grew up. My late husband. After that he wasn't happy with anything his whole life. He couldn't be satisfied. And I didn't know how to save him. Falling was the only thing that tasted sweet to him. But in order to fall, you need to start up high. He never had any height to begin with. All he could do was spread himself out over a flat place. So I sent my daughter to my mother's to grow up. By the end he was half insane, and I was afraid of him. He needed to kill me. There was nothing else that could have given him the energy that sustained his spirit. Because I didn't toss him petty fights like you'd toss logs into an oven. He was freezing. He got the psychic chills, see? I would wake up in the middle of the night and see him lying awake on his bed, his chin resting on his hand, looking at me so heavy, sullen, like stone. His other hand would be hanging down to the floor. It was this monolithic stare that woke me up.

But he didn't have the strength to kill me. All he could do was dream. He liked telling me about all sorts of crimes that supposedly happened somewhere in our area. Then it would turn out that he'd made up half of them himself and exaggerated the other half. He lived these FANTASIES. Vodka didn't do anything for him anymore. He would drink and drink without finding the edge he could come up against and hold on to. He was in free fall, and there wasn't a single thing for him to grab on to. I watched all this with horror, though the horror was dulled from our whole life without a "square of distance." I'd been sick myself for a long time. There was no way I could not have been: I saw the psychiatrist say on TV that the necessary conditions for health are a job that you like, good friends, and a happy family life. I wanted him to die myself; I'd wanted it for many years. I wanted him to be killed. I'm scaring you, aren't I? I lived my fantasies, too. I think I fantasized about this for such a long time and so hard that my thoughts finally congealed into a dense lump, so dense that it materialized. That's how you make butter, you know: you keep churning and churning, and then finally it hardens. My thoughts congealed into a dense lump and passed from the world of ideas into the material world. On the thirtieth day of a drinking binge, he hanged himself. I woke up and saw him hanging. Right there.

I'll skip the details. You have no use for them.

But I won't lie to you: after some time, when the dust settled, I became happy. I breathed easier.

And stupid me, I didn't try to hide it. I told lots of people everywhere: I feel so good! (If I could remember now everyone I told and take my careless cries of joy back from them!) I didn't know then how dangerous this was.

He started coming to me in my dreams. I would see him standing in a crowd, pretending that he couldn't see me but really thinking up something to do to me. And if I turned away, he would attack. I would be shaking and I'd wake up so I could hide from him in THIS world. I would walk around in a disgusted sort of fear for days on end and say bad things about him to anyone and everyone I happened to talk to.

Which is something our ancestors commanded us not to do. No! But we've ignored so many commandments with no harm to ourselves—how was I supposed to know that this one was so strong?

You smile…I understand…We're all educated, but we've all got some part of this education we forget. Because life is stronger anyway. Obviously, it's silly to believe in dreams. Uncle Kolia Butko laughed, too. I see, I see: his self-rolling wheel and squares of distance aren't funny, because they are from the material phenomena department, but as for dreams, those are just ignorant superstitions.

But there is another person who came to me in my dreams: the beloved of my youth, from all that time ago. My love for him, it had its head cut off so suddenly—it's like if you cut off a rooster's head, the bird will still run around for a bit and then fall down on the ground, headless, and keep fluttering for a long time.

Sometimes I would dream that I'd stayed in the office after a collective farm meeting, and it was night, and I was wandering down an empty corridor. I looked into some room and saw—stupefying joy!—he was waiting for me, my beloved. But then people showed up, and they had my damned late husband with them, and I was embarrassed to tell them to go away because I recognized my spousal duty. And people kept talking, and my beloved awaited my decision, and the less it looked like we would be together, the paler he got, the more apathetic, like he was withering, disappearing, until—look!—the room was empty. And this is one thing I can't forgive my damned enemy for.

TATIANA NABATNIKOVA

Or I'd dream that I was on my way into town, and the bus was full of people from our village, and suddenly I saw that there was a tent on the bank of the collective farm pond, and he, my beloved, was standing by the tent. He was looking at me from afar, and it was clear that he was here because of me. But I was embarrassed to tell the bus driver to stop, so I betrayed him again, and again his image paled, faded, and disappeared. And I stayed on the bus but I sensed there was a deadly danger behind my back. I turned around and—oh, my god!—my damned husband was sitting right behind me, staring at me with his mean eyes, and close by was his mother with the same sort of mean face on. I was trapped. I wanted to jump up and run down the aisle, but there were people all around and I felt self-conscious. So I sat there, keeping up appearances, anticipating the knife in my back.

And again I would tell one and all: Thank god he is dead, the bastard, he just about stabbed me in my sleep last night.

And then I realized that because of the things I said he would come back even meaner and more dangerous in my next dream.

Which is exactly what happened.

And so our mutual hatred kept growing. Yes, I mean MUTUAL: it's like his dreary spirit was hanging around here and knew about all my hatred and was getting its revenge (I don't know if he can—if we are not only what you can touch, if we are some kind of intricate nerve that's invisibly grown into another world and is sucking juice out of it like a tree sucks out of the ground with its roots, like an umbilical cord that someone can step on and break in the other dimension somewhere...).

There is this superstition that if you are being haunted by a dead man, you should go to church and give money to poor people. But I couldn't let myself follow some superstition; I was embarrassed the same way I was embarrassed and scared to get out of the motorcycle side car, the same way I was embarrassed to stop the bus and run to my beloved in plain view of everybody, the same way I was embarrassed and unprepared to leave my hated husband and go someplace else. I spent my whole life in captivity of one sort or another. I wasn't the master of my fate; rather, my fate pushed me aside so I wouldn't be underfoot. Doesn't it sound like I spent my whole life following a set of superstitions we call "propriety"? Everyone chooses his own superstitions to follow. And I couldn't find any excuse for going into town to give out money in front of the church. I would rather have let myself die than break the habits of my consciousness.

And I was dying, because I was weak, unable to act. My beloved was right not to have come looking for me. I am nothing, and he realized it all the way back then, in the steppes.

I was dying, yes. I had marked two years of living without my oppressor. I should have been happy, but every day my body was getting heavier and heavier, and I was more and more tired at night. I could barely remember what youth had felt like—when you walk without feeling your feet, a little like running and a little like flying. Where did that kind of lightness come from? Your soul was ahead of you, and you were following it. Your soul was in a hurry.

But I got so much heavier, though I hadn't gained any weight. Nothing excited my spirit anymore; the only things moving inside me were percolating concerns about food, repairs, income—and even if I never ran and just walked, I would get so tired of dragging myself around that by the end of the day I could barely move my feet. I would fall down at night and go to sleep. But I never felt rested. If I could have, I would have slept and slept during the day, too.

And so it went. I had a stomach ulcer. I had an operation. I had varicose veins. I had one breakdown after another. It happens like that, you know: you've got a mechanism that's been working fine, and then one thing breaks and you fix it, but in the process you invariably move something or disturb something in another place, and it just keeps going.

I couldn't run anymore, and I didn't want to either.

Then you know what I figured out? It was his evil spirit over me. He was the one stepping on my umbilical cord, on my intricate root in the sky. So I stopped getting my sustenance, the stuff that kept me alive.

Spiteful bastard couldn't be satisfied with the fact that I couldn't be with my beloved.

I admit, of course, that I'm weak myself. I said that already. There are people who seem to have such thick umbilical cords to the sources of their strength that no one can stop the flow. They could live in the desert and still have full lives. As for me, I have tightening of the arteries of the spirit—that's my ailment. Go ahead and ask me why I lived with him, with my foe, ask me what held me there. It was our notorious lazy *maybe:* "Maybe it will be better tomorrow—and come to think of it, Friday wasn't half bad."

I was afraid of change. So I didn't go anywhere. Plus, I don't like your town, I hope you don't mind my saying. Which brings me back to Uncle Kolia's immortal "square of distance." Like the Earth—the way it has its atmospheric coating—every person carries with him his own force, which shouldn't be crowded: it needs space like we have in the village—you walk around and your "square of distance" makes itself comfortable. In the city you can't take this "square" into consideration because there is no room for it. If you are walking down the street, it's crowded; if you squeeze onto a tram, your poor "square" will get dented and damaged—which is how people get heart attacks. When I'm in the city, I think I can almost hear those squashed "squares" squeaking.

Here it's quiet.

So I lived with my foe.

If you want to know something interesting—Uncle Kolia Butko doesn't get sick. He has this furious spirit boiling inside him—the theory stuff—and he gives it all his attention, forgetting about himself. Try asking him, "Uncle Kolia, how's your health?" and he gets insulted. "Sickness is dumb," he answers. And you know something—his step is light.

One day I happened to look at a childhood picture of myself. I saw eyes dense as oil spilling out over the edge. And now what have I got? Eyes get shallower with time, like rivers. That's my own brand of ecology.

So. This is what happened to me then. I was on a bus, and it was dark, so you couldn't really tell people's ages too well. If you could see their eyes shining—ghosting—it was enough. It was a bus traveling at night in a strange place, between cities. A young man got on and sat down next to me. He had no luggage, just his working papers, which he took out once he sat down, read the notation about having voluntarily resigned, stuck them back in his pocket, and looked around with the victorious expression of a person who has acted with determination. And I saw that he was going to run out of room on his working papers very quickly, so much potential determination was in that face. Then the bus started moving, and I discovered that my seat didn't recline. He suggested we trade seats, but I wouldn't accept his offer. Then he generously got up and went somewhere into the back of the bus, leaving me his seat to use for free, without having to be in his debt. That was the kind of sensitive person he was. When the bus stopped, he went out to smoke a cigarette, and when he got back on, he gave me a serious, caring look that stayed in my heart. And again the bus rode for a long time through the night, passing the lights of lonely snowed-over villages at long intervals. The motor droned on monotonously, and all the passengers slept—except for two guys sitting behind me, who'd just been released from prison and couldn't get enough of talking softly—about freedom, about transport, about canned fish in tomato paste, which they called "red fish," about timber cutting and the temper of their equipment. Near as I could gather, one of them fixed a tractor that had been written off, but then the tractor died anyway. He spoke with pain of how much he had loved this tractor, because he couldn't stop being human just because he was behind bars, so he had to have something to love. I was half-asleep. Then I saw my young man walk through the darkened bus up to the driver, blocking my view of the road; the driver slowed down, turned on a dim inside light, stopped, and let the young man out forever into the dark winter desert by a turnoff with a sign pointing toward an invisible village. Passing by my window, the young man raised his head and sent the long ray of his farewell stare straight at me, putting quite a bit of his heart into it. The bus started moving again, the light went out, everyone kept sleeping in the dark, but I was really agitated. You see, this look of his—he took it out of himself and sent it off into the silent darkness, with no hope of a response. You understand? It's like using all the energy from a power plant to create a radio signal and then sending it off into the cold cosmos without out a response. It was free, you see. Yes, maybe he felt sad for my youth—gone, lost to him. Maybe he was using me to send love to this inaccessible youth of mine like food to the hungry, this generous man. He shared pure warmth with me. It was like before there were matches—the way people saved the flame and passed it from one person to another. And it gave me something I hadn't had: warmth, excitement. I got my spirit back.

I understood then how people live their love.

And you know what happened then? I suddenly realized that my late husband had left me alone—and I had forgotten and forgiven for all the grief he had caused me.

Was one look from a young stranger enough to chase away the man who was haunting me? Is that what happened?

Then my ailments disappeared. I mean, I thought of them one day, and it was like they'd never even been here. You don't have to believe me if you don't want to. I am alive; the world is full of anxiety; and I hear an eternal wind inside of me, you understand? And my step is light.

And that young stranger doesn't even know what he did for me.

But now I know what to do. Some nights, when I lie awake, I gather all my love into one bunch, I gather up all its unused force, and I send this ray toward the point at which my memory is aimed: to the beloved of my youth.

TATIANA NABATNIKOVA

He-e-e-e-ey!

This is not a call anymore; it is the opposite of a call.

And somewhere, I don't know where—doesn't even matter—he will wake up in the morning, full of joy and strength.

III. Experiments

Mashka and Asiunia

NATALIA SHULGA

By the time I was given Natalia Shulga's phone number, my search for les-
bian-themed short fiction had yielded nothing but surprised (and invari-
ably curious) stares from literary friends and one tortured coming-out
opus. I was told that Shulga (whose name I had never heard) had a man-
uscript on the topic, and that her writing was "interesting." The number I
was given for Shulga was wrong, but after a couple of hang-ups and much
pleading on my part, I made staticky contact with the writer and explained
that I was looking for "lesbian fiction" ("lezbiyskaya proza") and her work
had been recommended by a mutual editor friend. When Shulga arrived at
my apartment a few hours later, bearing the manuscript, she confessed that
she'd heard me say "Belgian fiction" ("belgiyskaya proza")—a measure
not only of the poor quality of Moscow phone lines but of how unprepared
the Russian ear is to hear the word lesbian. *Standing in the doorway, she*
explained that once she had hung up and conveyed the content of our con-
versation to her husband, he figured out that I must have meant lesbian
and not Belgian. A young man then appeared in the door frame, and
Shulga introduced her husband. I was unprepared for that.

In spite of the unquestionable gains made by the Russian gay and les-
bian community in the last few years, the concept of lesbian continues to be
entirely alien to mainstream literary discourse. In the total absence of vis-
ible lesbians in literature—either as writers or as subjects—it is remark-
able that in 1992 the twenty-two-year-old Shulga presented this story as
her thesis project at the Literary Institute (where some readers compared it
to "The Song of Bilitis"—probably the only piece of lesbian literature
familiar to them—while others seemed to miss the lesbian content alto-
gether). It is not at all surprising, though, that the piece has never been
published in Russia and that both the writer and the narrator are noncom-
mittal about the basis in fact of this story composed of fragmented memo-
ries that just might be dreams. Writes Shulga: "This piece was conceived
as a film script a long time ago—about six years ago, when I was still
planning to become a scriptwriter. I never wrote the script, but the idea
wouldn't leave me alone; I began to feel that it was frightfully important
for me to write this story. The hero of this story has a prototype, but not in
the sense that I am just Mashka and she is just Asiunia. She recently read

the piece, by the way, and saw nothing of the kind in it. Which means that the story is not a document but the product of an inflamed imagination— though there was such a town and, most important, such a 'game of cats.' Cats are my favorite animals. I have an Egyptian named Asya."

I last saw Shulga when she and her husband, Denis Klimanov—a writer and Literary Institute classmate—reviewed this translation in the summer of 1993. Shulga was visibly pregnant. The couple announced cheerfully that a child was due in the fall and that they now had their own apartment, which they shared with Asya the Egyptian and Asya the prototype, who had moved in after getting kicked out of her parents' house in the small town where she lived. I took the news as a fitting, if by no means definitive, epilogue to this "product of an inflamed imagination."   *—M. G.*

I

"Let's play cats," she suggests when we aren't even going to play anymore, and I am thinking of going home altogether. But if she wants to play, all right, I'll stay, except that I've never heard of this game—is this when you play with a lot of cats or something? No, Mashka responds, two is enough. Hurry up and say yes, because I can't get home late!—Is that because of me? What does your family have against me, anyway?—I'll tell you later, or else we won't have time to play cats, because you don't even know how yet.

Asiunia

I was sick of living at home—no, I wasn't hurt or misunderstood. Until I was five, I never noticed other people's homes at all, and then I looked and thought, What if I went and lived some place else? Maybe it would be a hundred times more interesting?

Then I walked down the street looking for a place to stay, but it was hard to choose because other people's homes were all so new, so strange, and I wanted to go into all of them. So I walked and peeked into windows and cracks in fences like an ill-behaved child. That would make it easier to choose.

Mashka

Finally, I decided: I had to write something brilliant. I was eleven years old when I thought about it and decided, "It's time." Before that, Asiunia had come by.

"Mash," she said, looking to the side, as though she had done something dishonest, and everything inside me died from her voice. "Mash," said Asiunia, rocking from foot to foot in the doorway as though she were in my house for the first time. "I read your notebook yesterday. You left it on the bench. It was an accident. There was something about music in there."

"Oh, for god's sake, who cares..." I swallowed, and then I was too scared to say anything else.

"You are brilliant," Asiunia said, resigned. "But that's all right," she said apologetically. "You aren't mad that I read it? Except I couldn't figure out who the sharps and the flats were. If they are cats and dogs, then why don't they have normal names?"

"They are musical keys—they are all like that."

Asiunia was agonizing, getting ready to confess to something else secret and bad.

"I felt really bad for the gray sharp," she said. "Why did you make it so he died? You've got talent, but you're writing stupid things."

She said this very seriously, like she wasn't talking to me at all, like she wasn't ten years old and I eleven.

The next day, I thought, I should write something for real. Not because of Asiunia—I don't know why. I didn't believe her about the brilliant part.

Mashka, fifteen years old:
"They asked this one guy, 'You want a cherry-colored cat?' This was in the States, I think. He said, 'Of course, I want it.' And he paid money. Then time went by, and they gave him a cat—a regular one, not cherry-colored at all, but black. And they said—"

She turns toward me, and at the same time she is pulling down on a huge crooked apple tree branch. The branch is making a suspicious cracking sound, and the apples are raining down onto the ground.

"You listening?" she squints. "A black one. And they said, Didn't you know that cherries are black around here? And he—"

At this point everything collapses into a heap of leaves, apples, and Asiunia.

"Where are you?" I'm scared. "Are you alive?"

She is sitting on the ground, alive and well, and she is cursing, too! Really, she is the only one who ever had that kind of luck.

Asiunia, six years old:
There were all sorts of holes in the fences, big ones and little ones— look all you want. I saw other people's yards, dog houses, sometimes

little withered flowers close to the ground. None of this could make me pause for long—it had been around all my life, it was all familiar. I don't remember how many holes I'd counted when my journey ended. Instead of another dog house, I saw somebody's surprised-looking eye, which was examining me very, very closely.

"Why are you peeking?"

"Why are you?" came the response from the other side.

Mashka, fifteen years old:

Asiunia, unfettered, removes a dried leaf from her hair.

I turn away and walk through the weeds toward the fence; she runs after me. "You make up God knows what!" Asiunia screams, shaking me. "I just knew that you were saying to yourself, 'That is going to be the first line!' "

"Well, I think it makes an excellent beginning."

"About the tomcat? Well, good luck to you!"

The apples flop into the bucket, bouncing off its walls. She has her back to me, and she is reaching for the top branch. "Asiunia," I warn her.

Without turning around, she mutters under her breath: "I, for example, have an idea, but you don't write about this sort of thing... There was an artist, he wasn't from a rich family, this was in the eighteenth century..."

"In what century?"

"In the eighteenth."

"Why?"

"What difference does it make? For God's sake, don't write about it if you don't want to. I'm not going to tell you."

"Asia, please— I'm a tactless idiot. I won't do it again."

"Oh, never mind! You have no use for it anyway."

"But what if?"

"It will never get published," Asiunia sighs knowingly.

"I don't care."

"Do, too, care. Because what would be the point then—to do something for me, like a favor?"

We walk along the fence. Asiunia has calmed down now, and I can hear her munching on an apple behind me. "You are a khemul, that's what you are," she says. "You have only a little time left to hang out here, and you aren't doing anything—"

"And what's a khemul?"

"It's you! You only have a little bit left, better hurry to get finished."

"I haven't even started yet. What are you, serious? Who needs this?"

NATALIA SHULGA

That's when I get an apple core thrown at my back. I can understand her, but this is too much. Even Asiunia herself is embarrassed.

"So what's wrong?" I ask.

"Sometimes I really want to hit you," Asiunia informs me and runs ahead.

Asiunia:

This is the first summer we are together. Just like I have wanted for a long time—with no outsiders. Her family will be here in August, which is when the business with the house will get decided; my relatives will hardly be around, thank God. My mother has beat it—I mean, she is alive and well, and it's not like I don't know where she is—she's with her people. She is lying low; I haven't heard any rumors about any of her conquests. Am I supposed to be suffering? Mashka thinks I am, because normal families don't act like this. Some don't, but we do: grandma has abandoned us until fall, there is no way she'll show before then; that leaves my sister Marinka, who is busy setting up her life and can't run away like everyone else. My irresponsible relatives are just what we need, dearest Mashka—what a joy.

Then it was only two or three days till her arrival—I didn't know for sure how long but I could feel it because I couldn't do anything right and I had time to think as I tried to fix things: Mashka wouldn't approve, she would want to see me suffering over my mother and not noticing Mashka's own arrival, but that wouldn't be fair. I wouldn't be able to pretend, and why should I? My mother left the same way before, a year ago—though that time she warned us in a letter she left on the table—and then she sent a birthday present, and my brother never even knew, because while he was at summer camp, my mother had enough time to go and come back.

It was the usual: summer, and I was lying around on the couch, not feeling like going anywhere. Maybe Mashka will come by to get me, I was thinking—but with a strain somehow, more out of habit. On days like this, they didn't let her out of the house; they said, "Mashka is resting," because she might have problems with her heart if she ran around outside in the heat for a long time. (The problem was not Mashka but her relatives; they were all heart patients and otherwise respectable people who believed that children under twelve should "rest" during the day.) They never opened the shutters on hot days, so it was like it was always night in the house, where there was a table, a mirror, and a German painting of girls in a meadow, which you couldn't see in the dark.

"Come in," an invisible Mashka says to me. "The aunts won't be here now. It's a good thing you came to see me."

When it's dark their house is different—it gets bigger and, most important, as if we were there at night. Though the shutters have long, narrow cracks which are all lit up brightly, and some of them make thin lines of light on the floor. When we weren't playing cats, what were we playing? We hid in the dark rooms, of which there were suddenly more and which you could only tell apart by their smell: the little room behind the stove smelled a lot like medicine—I think, because there was a medicine cabinet in it. I finally found Mashka, and she said she wasn't going to run around playing hide and seek anymore, that she bumped into something and hit her elbow on the edge. "Where? Show me," I went up to Mashka where she was sitting on the floor by the cardboard and the boxes. I couldn't really see her, and because of that I felt especially bad for her somehow. "Where, here? I know what that's like—awful, like getting electrocuted." Mashka didn't say anything. "Are you mad or something?"

"Go away."

I wasn't surprised and didn't go anywhere, and we sat in the dark and little by little we started talking again, and I even started laughing at Mashka and mumbling all sorts of silly rhymes like, "The doggie has a pain and the kitty has a pain but Masha's getting married and she only has to gain." Mashka said she is never getting married, that's one thing that sure isn't going to happen—God, that made me happy! That means she is going to come here every summer for her whole life, she is not going to get away from me! She said, What am I, crazy, that's not the reason she's not going to get married. She just isn't into it, thinks the whole thing is disgusting. If she feels like it, she is going to get children from an orphanage or some place. We were going to make some other sort of deal, too, but we didn't have the time because I had to leave before her relatives got home.

What's going on in my home right now reminds me of the story "My Heart Is in the Mountains," which our English teacher once translated for us for no particular reason on the last day of classes before vacation. It's also got a child who drives the adults crazy and they fight with each other, and there is nothing in the house to eat. Our mother is coming home today, and Andriukha is bugging me and Marinka in turn, whining without a break, and finally declares that he is hungry; in addition, the fan is broken and it is hot, and Marinka is studying for her exams and saying she can't remember anything at all

NATALIA SHULGA

and why don't I stop hanging out on the couch and at least go do something. I get up.

"I'm hungry," Andriukha is whining. "I'm going to up and fall over—then you'll see."

"What are you just standing there for, Asiunia?" Marinka picks up in the same vein. "I can't take it anymore. Give the child something to eat."

"Not as though we had jam enough to spread on his back," I say, kind of like in that story—though not really, of course.

Everyone is silent.

"Marina," my brother starts in again. "What a bitch. I'm hungry."

"Damn!" My sister throws down her notebook. "Give him something already—we must have something—He keeps whining and whining. Why does it always have to be me? There is some fish there somewhere."

"It's raw," I say, slamming the refrigerator door for emphasis.

Marinka gets set to yell at me but changes her mind and adds lazily, "So helpless. It always has to be me. Aska, you are big and healthy like a horse—"

"I want something to eat but not fish."

"Then what do you want already?" Marinka screams finally.

Then I notice something out the window: Mashka is coming.

I scream that's it, I'm out of here, gone. Meanwhile somebody is already pulling on the gate and shaking it. I run out onto the porch.

"Let's go. I've got money," Mashka says with no introduction.

She's got on some sort of strange dress: it's not ironed properly, somehow too long and too adult. I check it out and say where did you find it, is it some sort of inheritance or something…Can you wait for me?—All right.

A couple of minutes later I come out, and she is already gone.

"What if they hadn't let me go—would you have left?"

She is all cool and collected, walking just ahead of me, dragging her skirt on the ground, and says, Of course. Then I ask, Where are we going?

"I told you already: I've got money."

"But looking like that—"

"That's right, we're going into town."

The conversation continues in the same nonsensical vein. Plus, this dress—you can see all there is of Mashka through the sleeve, all she has to do is raise her arm; I bet she knows it, too, but if I said anything now, she would just leave, and then what would I do?

Then I say, Fine, but first we have to go to the post office to pick up a package from my mother. I look to see if she is buying it, and it looks like she is...

"Why, did it come? Maybe we'll stop by there later?"

"Oh, no."

There, she is doing like I said, I knew it! There is nothing she can say: it's a package from my mother. Mashka drags her feet, doesn't say anything the whole way, but that's fine, because just a couple of days ago she kept demanding to know why my mother was gone and if she ever wrote. Now, when we get to the post office, I'll make something up. We still have to get to the top of the hill, turn the corner, and walk to the end of the street—we've still got time.

Soon I notice that Mashka isn't just quiet; she is demonstratively quiet. She is checking out other people's houses and yards, like she's got nothing better to do. I think, If she didn't want to go with me, she could have just said so—there is nothing here to look at, everything is familiar as can be: some windows higher, some windows lower, my favorite house is on the other side of the street—the wooden one with a balcony, the only two-story one. There was one time Mashka said, I wonder when it's going to fall down on top of us, meaning the balcony. It really is pretty old. I've never seen anyone standing on it.

She says to me, I think somebody saw your mother in town at the bus stop or maybe by the bakery. I don't want to talk about this, who cares where they saw her? I'd rather talk about where she got the dress; it's crap, of course, a piece of junk, but I like it, except it's too bad Mashka looks like she is going to a funeral, after all it's not like I asked... Suddenly, it becomes unclear where we are going at all.

"Probably home already," Mashka ventures.

"You know, I think my mother is here, so I don't want to go home right now. It would be better to go hang out someplace."

Mashka agrees, and we go in no particular direction, which turns out to be to the construction site nearby, climb up on top of a pile of sand, and discuss how you can't build a nine-story tower right here, on the edge of a ravine, because before you know it, it will go and collapse. Suddenly, Mashka says, "Remember you said they wanted to build a building that had apartments that were two and three stories each and had stairways—maybe that's what they're building?"

"We can check," I say. "Let's go."

Then they finished this ten-story tower so fast and got people living in it so fast and gave it a name—Akhmystovski—so fast that we didn't know what hit us before we were on a bus in the heat and we didn't know the stop or the address.

NATALIA SHULGA

She rushed by me with a wave of her hand—at once "Come on!" and "The hell with everything!" and I ran and caught up with her.

For a while we ran together silently; she didn't look in my direction. Finally, I asked, Where are you dragging me? Instead of answering, Mashka tripped, scraped her knee real good, and started howling in pain. "Must be God's punishment." Mashka raised her head, surprised: Did I really ask you to come? odd..."Very odd!" I squatted down next to her, waiting for an explanation.

"You see," Mashka shrugged slightly. "To be honest, I didn't have to ask you to come. Forgive me?"

Then, probably to quiet her conscience, she added: All right, let's go together. On an overstuffed bus, hanging off the step, I kept up my thorough and vengeful questioning: Where?...That's no reason...I wonder when you had the time?...We got tossed out at the last stop, and Mashka ran across the construction site, toward the five-story "Akhmystovski" buildings, dropping answers as she ran: Yes, he plays...Must be a wedding or an anniversary of some sort, how am I supposed to know.

We ran up the stairs, out of breath. Voices broke through unintelligibly from upstairs, reflecting off the walls, like in a well.

"They could at least put in an elevator." She slowed down.

"Don't hurry," I prompted, dragging behind her. "It's not like it's your wedding, is it? You'll get there."

She grabbed on to the heating pipe and stepped aside.

"Shall we take a breather?" I yelled.

Mashka was hanging over the windowsill and looking down.

And then there was the sound of a funeral dirge!

I took three steps in one and looked out the window to see a crowd in front of the building, the coffin cover propped on two stools and a hapless orchestra, which had started in ahead of time.

One of the musicians, with a drumstick in his hand, was standing a few steps away on the road. I saw Mashka flying down the path, and I was only afraid of one thing happening—that Mashka would jump and cling to this guy's neck to the sounds of the funeral dirge.

A day later I opened the gate and saw her on all fours, crawling around a huge funeral drum, which was on its back, and next to it were an awl, needles, and some rolls of thread, and the drum itself had a very noticeable hole in it, with ragged edges. "And what kind of shop have you set up here?" I said. Mashka didn't turn toward my voice. "Hey, you drumming expert you, where were you after the funeral, when I didn't know how to get back! What about the guitar—did he play his guitar for you? I can't believe it, he never goes out with anybody without his guitar. But he is the creative type, you should keep that in mind. Not only is he a restaurant musician—"

"What are you going on about," Mashka said without any inflection.

"By the way, despite his advanced age of thirty-five—"

Mashka turned toward me. She looked exhausted. "What do you think," she said, "we can do about this hole? I have to take it back in half an hour."

I was stubbornly silent.

"Well, we are seeing each other," Mashka added reluctantly, "at the construction site."

"I knew that; that's where everyone goes."

Mashka looked at me pleadingly.

"All right, I'll do it," I couldn't help myself. It's not like she'd gotten me to feel sympathetic...I kicked the drum with my foot. "It's heavy. How did he break it—with his head or something?"

"Asiunia," Mashka said, with feeling. "He didn't break it with his head. He broke it doing honest work at a funeral. Please do it in half an hour."

I dragged the drum toward the gate.

Then I dragged it through my whole garden, trying not to drop it onto any of the vegetable patches. When I got to the fence, I dropped it into the poison ivy.

For some reason, Mashka's date didn't go off as planned that day, and I got away with it.

Mashka:
This happened so long ago that Asiunia doesn't even remember whose parents we were allowed to go to the river with, and one of our mothers was standing on the shore—if it was mine, then I don't have to describe her, but if it was Asiunia's, then she was tall, awkward, like Asiunia is going to be really soon now, and then I'll never be able to get used to her: "You are really looking like a woman now or something," and Asiunia smiles guiltily, like she is trying to say, Well, it's not my fault that I grew * * * But for now, she hasn't grown all that much, she is not all that different from me, to look at us, we look like sisters, our coloring being almost exactly the same.

Asiunia:
"To be honest, I wouldn't especially want to have you as a relative—

imagine having to be in the same house morning to night: you'd go crazy and take off."

"Enough already. I'm going to get a sunburn sitting here with you," Mashka gets up from the blanket, and next to her is my mother's completely motionless back, which is no different from the rest of them—and as I survey them, Mashka goes down right to the water and starts strolling along it sort of reluctantly and demonstratively. That's what she is like now—last year she was horribly shy. "Cats can do anything, that's what's so great about them." The only thing is, there is no way to get them in the water—and that's just like you: just look at how you test the water off the shore with your paw, such a collected and careful Mashka, almost a stranger. Me, I learned to swim a long time ago, but you just won't, no matter what.

Jellicle cats are white and black,
Jellicle cats are of moderate size;
Jellicles jump like a jumping-jack,
Jellicle cats have moonlit eyes.

Mashka paddles up to me somehow, grabs on to my arm, then my shoulder as hard as she can… "That's right, hold on to me!" Everything is getting wobbly in front of my eyes, it is hard to swim with her after all, I should turn while we are still hanging on. "You know, we're almost there already, get off and swim yourself!" Instead of doing that, Mashka sort of jumps and hangs herself around my neck, and I immediately go down, under water, and Mashka scrambles up me, she scratches me trying to hang on, and I can't even yell at her.

Mashka:
Asiunia's mother shakes out the blanket and quickly gathers up all our junk, swearing under her breath: now they want to drown each other here, what will they think of next.

I start thinking this is fun. Family like this is hard to find: everyone is staring at us, and she couldn't care less. She didn't even yell at Asiunia, who is sitting there breathing on her arm, the poor thing. "Well, shall we go?" Asiunia sighs deeply, grabs on to me but for some reason she's not getting up, she can't manage. "We're leaving," I say. "If you want to stay, that's fine, there are five thugs checking you out already. Well?"

Asiunia:
It's not me, it's you they are checking out: you walk by them, and it's

more like they don't find you attractive. And I just keep sitting there, I don't even feel like getting dressed, and I can't get warm, and the wind—my legs are covered with goosebumps—and I fold into myself, into my knees, I shrink. I wish they wouldn't call me at all. I'm going to try not to move and sit here for a long, long time, and when it gets toward evening, I'll try to drown without Mashka's help, and then she'll be surprised.

Why don't I make it so that I am invisible and right under your nose—the main thing is for you to bump into me in the morning and scream in shock. And then I would jump up and start comforting you: Mashka, you idiot, that's just what you are.

Mashka is really crying now, lowering herself onto a wet wooden bench. Where are we? In her bathing hut, where it's always dark, wet and great except that the shower leaks a little bit. "Stop it or I'll stick you under the water!"

"I," Mashka quiets down right away. "I was going to wash anyway, you know. Go check if there is water in the tank." And she is looking at me as though she were ashamed or she were getting ready for some sort of trick. For some reason I don't want to leave. "Fine, we'll just check from here." We barely manage to turn the faucet up by the ceiling, and ice-cold water soaks us—Mashka, who is naked, and me, with my clothes on; now is probably the only time and place when I could hug Mashka and hold her against me, but Mashka spoils everything because she starts asking, How did you manage that? I thought we were really going to drown this time.

This is the right place to tell about her house. It worries me when it appears: it's at the end of some street—Mashka's street—and then there is something like a puddle that never dries and a garden.

It's no fun living in a corner house: all sorts of characters are always hanging around it, walking by the windows, climbing into the garden to get some cherries. No one thinks to think that it's your garden and not just a couple of trees on the corner. Two of the walls of the house—white and peeling, with the windows close to the ground—are not protected in any way, which is also bad, because you can see everything. They've added something on the side—a greenhouse or a terrace, you can't tell what: something with glass and dust but always guarded by a dog on a short chain. "There is something valuable in there," Mashka assured me, and once, after she went there—if she wasn't lying—she immediately informed me that there were caged canaries and three scary big-nosed birds called the oak-beeks living there, and on the mud floor there is a packing box that's got either lizards or snakes. The menagerie was property of Mashka's adoptive grandfather, who occupied the other addition and was always fighting with everybody; their yard must have re-divided into "ours" and "not ours" about ten times, and Mashka almost never went to the "other" addition.

It turns out there isn't much to love about this house, except maybe its family history, which doesn't go as far back as I would want it to in the case of Mashka's house, but no one ever asks me what I want for Mashka.

Since it was built by her great-great-grandfather's family at the turn of the century, the house has been divided and subdivided in every direction. It had something like fifteen rooms and half-rooms, and it usually had three or four families in it, not counting tenants and visitors. When Mashka was there, it was clearly designated who occupied which part of the house; Mashka didn't have anything to do with this, the designation was simply necessary because no one wanted to have anything to do with anyone anymore and didn't con-sider one another family anymore, and really, what kind of family is it: the brother of the second wife's sister—and what am I, his grand-daughter? They kept trying to divide up the yard and build two new porches to give everyone his own entrance to his own half—his third, that is. Then they boarded up the middle part, demolishing the "cen-tral" porch because one of the families moved without selling their part. This left Mashka's aunts on the left and the birdhouse proprietor on the right, and the two sides fought from time to time. I didn't notice when it changed suddenly; one time when she came Mashka said that the "other" addition now had strangers living in it, and now there was no way to find out about the canaries—maybe they are still living there and reproducing, I can imagine this very well, except they must be crowded in the greenhouse.

Maybe there was never any reason for Mashka's family to be fight-ing with the owner of the addition—but it was customary to say that he tortured his birds and was tremendously miserly: "Verochka had to study music, and he wouldn't lend us his piano temporarily." (Verochka was Mashka's mother, and the piano was German, black, with Mozart on the lid, brought from Germany like all the furniture in the "other" addition and some of the furniture in this one. Many years later, it was discovered in the boarded-up part of the house; it wasn't working—the keys collapsed heavily under your fingertips, making no sound whatsoever. "He was always saying, 'I won't give it to you, we are going to use it ourselves, my wife and I are going to play.' So who played?—the mice, and they ate all the padding.")

"There is a piano in the other addition, it's black and it's got Mozart on it, it doesn't work but sometimes you hear two or three random notes because a mouse runs over the mallets in the dark—and it probably gets scared." You can feel whatever way you want about this house: you can love it or not, but it seems it's better to stay away from it—by going away for the whole year, the way Mashka does, or going away forever, like her parents, or even trying to sell it, which her family has been trying to do all the time recently. I can imagine what kinds of problems they will have: it will be even worse than when the other addition was sold. They are saying that ever since the "strangers" moved in, they've been fixing things: the floors started to fall in right away in the half that was sold, and it started smelling like the cellar—in other words, everything was falling apart before their very eyes. Before they can sell the rest of the house, they need money to fix it up, but where are they going to get the money without selling the house? It's a vicious circle. In the end, they will just board it up and leave it alone, and every so often a mouse will run over the mallets, a canary will fly out (in the light, it will be white instead of yellow because it will have gradually lost its coloring in the dark)—all this will really happen, Mashka, if we don't do something right now, if we don't, first of all, make a deal that you will stay with me.

My sister comes home from work and declares, We need to talk.

"Asiunia, where have you been, I was calling you. You are practically grown already, and look at how you are spending your time, always playing some kind of strange games with this Mashka of yours. You do everything like your friend, who, by the way, wants nothing to do with you." She follows this with numerous examples of Mashka's betrayals and dirty tricks—all of which are, alas, true, all having taken place—and then Marina goes on: "You shouldn't trust girlfriends at all. At your age what a girl wants for another girl—well, she doesn't wish her ill, exactly, but she doesn't want good things for her. If you ever even get a boyfriend, your Mashka will up and steal him from you, you'll see."

"What boyfriend?" I say. "Why are you meddling, anyway?"

"I'm meddling because I have a right. Mashka makes up all sorts of garbage for you, I've seen that notebook of hers—"

"What notebook?"

NATALIA SHULGA

"About the cats!"

There was such a notebook. I never thought that Marinka would stumble upon it. It had pictures of all the cats that were mentioned in our game—to make it easier to find them if they ran away—and there was an honest price written underneath each one: the white cat was the most expensive (it had a line of zeroes stretching across the whole drawing), and that was, as was also noted there, just the price per half hour. It wasn't because the white one was a beautiful and rare cat. It was because the white kitty kept having kittens but she didn't really know how to do it and twice she almost died, and we didn't want to lose her because of somebody's whim. The white kitty lived at the end of the street, and we saw her often, which is how we got her. Mashka always played her.

"But this is almost lethal for you," all her friends and doctors would sigh. "Not to mention that all the kittens had to be drowned."

But Mashka the white kitty just rolled her eyes tragically, all the while showing off her leg in the most lascivious manner.

"Local residents start complaining in the spring," I would continue, trying to talk sense into her. "The floating kittens get stuck at the turn, and people have to push them forward with sticks. Someone could file suit against you, you know."

"It's all the damned tomcats," Mashka would quickly say then. "They won't leave you alone, and they don't want to pay either."

"Tomcats these days, girlfriend," one kitty complains to another. "They won't leave you alone, and they don't want to pay either. They took me for a ride yesterday, they took me for a ride again today. I'll go again tomorrow."

"If she so much as tries anything like that," says Marinka, "when her parents get here, I'll tell them you play whorehouse."

"Yes, but only one for cats," I could have said, but I didn't want to get into it with her.

I'm having strange dreams. I am coming home when I see a crowd all standing in line like to the Mausoleum, saying, Your sister is going to leave us forever, and we are all here to say good-bye to her. I say, Well, let me through, I'm family, too, after all. All right, you may go up to the window and talk, but don't take long, because everyone is waiting. And I hear Marinka's actual voice, but she is going on about god knows what—that she wants to leave us, like our mother, and go live with some other family. And I can do that, too, but not now, because some time has to pass. And then Marinka tells me different things to do—

look after my brother and my father, and if Mashka agrees to marry me, make sure she doesn't have too many children, because that's dangerous, and besides what are we going to do with all those kids?

She is calling for me from the other room: Come, I brought them all here. She is stretched out on the floor, and the whole litter is running around her.

"Aren't you cold lying around here?"

Mashka catches one of the kittens and places it on her belly.

"Watch him walk on me! This is another cat game. You know, it feels great when they walk on you. The little ones are better—they are more careful, and the big ones can scratch. Just imagine how he touches you, all light, pushes down with his paws, and falls over. Try it when you are alone sometime. You'll like it. Where are you going, stop!" She catches one of them by pushing him to the floor with her foot.

"Why did you get all these stupid kittens? They aren't going to let you take any of them with you."

"By the time anyone gets here," Mashka says, "they are all going to grow up. And I don't have any use for them when they are big!"

Five minutes ago we almost had a fight when Mashka was trying to teach me the rules of *that* game. She kept breaking them herself: when she was a tomcat, she would order me around brazenly, but when she was a kitty, she would play me for a fool. As soon as I would get into it even a little bit and forget about the game, Mashka would make up some other scummy rule, or say, Let's finish playing tomorrow.

II

The problem is that I have lost the ability to recreate what happened exactly, but at the same time I have only myself to rely on. I can't imagine going up to Mashka now and asking. I could do it, I should, even, for who can answer if not she—but you know what would happen? She would definitely say, No way, not even in my wildest dreams. And she would say that her first—she wouldn't even talk about me and her, instead she would just talk nonsense, made-up things about her adventures that very summer—and they would be lies and yet not. Go figure now.

If she had her father's last name, she would be Maria Feldman. That's what she says. This isn't the father who dragged her family to

Leningrad but the other one, the real one, whom I've never seen. Mashka announced, He was beautiful, so I am going to get prettier still, periodically. She was standing in front of a mirror that opened up like shingles into two panels, and the left one reflected an empty vial and a thermometer made to look like a Kremlin tower while the right one reflected the inimitable thirteen-year-old Mashka. I couldn't tell much about her "breed" (her word), but her coloring was dark, her eyes seemed dark, too...She was standing there in just her skirt, turning this way and that. "But they can see you through the window!" Mashka backed up to the middle of the room, ran her hands over her ribs—she hardly had anything there—and then said, "Well? It's already hanging a bit there. I'm really changing, aren't I?" and something else, too. I couldn't say anything to her. I want to see her again in the left half of our mirror—now. I wonder, incidentally, what ever happened to the "Kremlin tower"—I don't remember anyone breaking it or throwing it out—why would anyone throw out a thermometer? For some time now, objects that once or twice managed to be reflected in the mirror together with her have been disappearing mysteriously: someone is taking them away, methodically but not all at once. What for? She *might still come* for the May Day holidays—

—which are the words with which the day began, opening on every side and multiplying, and that day could be called,

The Day of the Railroad Angel,

meaning a time when all the conventional indicators—such as letters and phone calls—say that there is no way she could be coming, but I begin waiting for her fiercely, as though remembering and trying to make up for all I have missed during the year—From the top of the hill, I can see a stained-gray strip of trees (it could be green, red, blue—what difference would it make?); toward evening, unbelievable numbers of thugs start gathering down on the street, and I am afraid to let them see me, so I make a huge circle on the way home, stretching this day impossibly, when I should really be doing the opposite—trying to live it out as quickly as I can, because it is really involving and exhausting me.

THE DAY OF THE RAILROAD ANGEL can be heard beyond the house: a chorus of out-of-control station gossips are discussing the possible consequences of the collapse of the bridge over the river—it's so old, how could it not collapse when trains start rushing like crazy on it back and forth at random without any schedule. I fear that that's exactly what will happen. "But how will we get to the other side then—I mean, that's the only way to get to the spit when you still haven't learned to swim."

"I haven't, but you are afraid of the bridge—that a train will come without you noticing and you won't have time to jump away toward the edge."

"Oh, just hold on and stop talking, no one is going to go hitting like some thug in your mother's imagination—"

"Your tenant is the thug—remember that—you better just say what will hit me—a stick or a rail."

—No one is coming, but what if she does come but after the bridge has already collapsed, when I am sick I can feel how fragile everything is, and the bridge can definitely be finished off just like that, all you have to do is touch it exactly in the middle, and they go sending the fattest train down this bridge, and it may as well fall into the river, because it's going to Pionerovka anyway, and that's a camp where I was in August, and it would be better if there weren't any trains going there—

—Mashka came by foot twice in the morning that time and sat in my lap—

"We didn't get hit by anything?"

"I don't think so. But you know, they just keep coming, so let's hurry."

And as I make my way home, railroad angels negotiate unintelligibly over my head, and what if no one comes tomorrow?

The thing with the funeral drummer didn't end just like that. Five days later she came and announced that she was "going to go again" to the Akhmystovski buildings, because they've got to be "celebrating nine days"[*] (that's what she said: celebrating), but she was shy and I had to go with her.

"But it's somebody else's wake," is what I think I said, dumbfounded. "What do you need there?"

She needed "any trace at all"—I mean, the expressions she used really got me!—of the funeral musician, as though the guests at the wake would have to know something about these traces...God, Mashka!

"Who are you going to ask? This is stupid."

We'll see, they might just mention it themselves...

---

[*] In Russian Orthodox tradition, nine days and forty days since a death are commemorated as milestones in the soul's departure from the body and the world.

NATALIA SHULGA

A wake with a funeral orchestra! I was thinking, Is this character that she needs so much the center of the universe or something? She'd imagined a wake with a funeral orchestra, and now she was eager to see whether it would come true or not.

But the main thing—and the worst thing—is that starting at this very place I can't say exactly what happened. Sometimes I could swear that I walked with her across the empty lot toward the Akhmystovski buildings, and right then and there, right in the yard, I saw clouds of dust and an orchestra in the dust, and a really fun wake (there was even a flag hanging at the entrance—or maybe they forgot to take it down after the holiday)—I want to remember and Mashka won't do it, I'm warning you, she won't, and I'm not good for much.

Some people might find it strange that there are just the two of us— me and Mashka—and everyone else just keeps coming in and out of the house (the garden, the town, the building where they are having the wake—for the life of me, I can't remember who the wake was for, if we were there just the two of us). Unfortunately, I do know: there were probably lots of people there, and they probably kept talking to us, not letting us have either a real conversation or the thing that I don't even know what to call or what to make up to call it if I can't call it by name—but then again, what can you expect of people who were invited here? If you get right down to it, we were the ones who hadn't been invited, Mashka, it's just that ten days or so later you came and told me.

Last year I didn't know how to greet her. I sent the stupidest telegram imaginable: I'll meet you at the railroad station—and then went and overslept. Mashka ran over here herself, knocking on the window at six in the morning, waking everyone in the house; I ran outside in my nightgown, too sleepy to remember what it was that Mashka was "guilty" of, and then I did remember, but not right away, and not easily. Mashka was the same and different; she shied away from me. I rushed to "forgive" with all I had. Mashka acted dignified (the idea even occurred to me that maybe she'd been testing me or something— with her letters). She told me about how she went to that character's house, where he kept up with his tricks and demands ("So I got undressed so I wouldn't look like an idiot"), and Mashka didn't pause here for a second and kept telling the story, as though it weren't me she was talking to, snickering that "they didn't do anything special to me" and wouldn't give me a chance to find out properly, and I thought,

The hell with it, that just means that it wasn't that bad! and she sensed it: What difference does it make to you what exactly? It was nothing special, really. And it didn't take that much for me, really. You know, I'm very gifted!

"Tell me everything—now—or else—"

There kept being things that were forbidden: no drinking from the water pump ("There were these people who kept drinking and then were sick forever with dysentery"), no going beyond the green house. We did anyway, because there was a carousel beyond the green house—a wooden circle, sloppily nailed together on a pole: you grabbed on to it, hit the ground with your foot and went around in a circle. She was a showoff on this "carousel": she would get going and lie down on the circle and scream, The sky is turning, or would reach over to grab a blade of grass on the fly, and one time she cut her finger pretty bad, but she didn't let on. I couldn't look at the sky or cut my finger on the fly—I felt queasy as it was: what if it's too much and the thing breaks off the pole and flies off—where are we going to end up? When her parents came, the "carousel" would get canceled. They wouldn't let Mashka go out, and she'd be so upset she wouldn't even want to see me. She managed to escape—with a little help from me— by undoing the latch—"Just for a little while, in case they notice I'm missing!" First thing she wanted to catch a tomcat. She got him up in a tree and was waiting there, having forgotten all about me. Then she figured it out: "He can't get down!" and ordered me to drag over a long board, which the two of us held at an angle, and the cat went to climb up higher but then suddenly grabbed on and slid down and that was the end of him; she and I were left alone and immediately disappeared for three hours, and they were looking for her all up and down the street.

Starting at a certain point, a neighbor girl about a year older would make periodic appearances. She had all the luck: she lived across from Mashka's house, and all she had to do was cross the street... I could see it clear as day: she was going to seduce Mashka for herself! Plus the neighbor had a tomcat—that very one—and he let her put him in a box and play cat house. One time when I couldn't take it any more, I sneaked into the neighbor's yard and broke their cat house all to hell. No one saw me, and I wasn't scared of getting caught. I felt like throwing something at the tomcat, but I didn't have the guts. I remember all this: the heat, the narrow yard, the box in pieces, the tomcat stretched out in the sun—but why and how Mashka came back, I don't remember. It was soon. Maybe she and the neighbor girl couldn't agree on something about the tomcat and Mashka decided to trade him in for me. But the neighbor girl didn't go away just like that; she changed—grew older and more clever and shrewd; she needed Mashka, and we had an underground war that lasted several more years. The girl would tell Mashka things, and Mashka would hurry up and tell me. She—the neighbor girl—was the one who "opened her eyes," of course. She also told her, in strictest confidence, that apparently Mashka's stepfather left here because of my mother, and that's how he ended up in St. Pete. "It's not like she was chasing him or anything," I said to Mashka. "If he hadn't wanted to, he wouldn't have left."

Also, when she was about ten, Mashka told me about the "madman" she met in the elevator who stopped the elevator between floors and wouldn't let Mashka out for a whole hour. When Mashka finally came home, her parents started screaming, Where were you when we just sent you out for bread? Mashka answered honestly: In the elevator, where there was this madman, and he said, Touch me with your hand, but Mashka wouldn't, she wasn't about to take that gross thing in her hands. Then the parents said the "madman" was a criminal who would go to jail. Mashka didn't believe them: how was he going to go to jail, it's not like you can just go out in the street and catch him. "But did you remember what he looked like?" From here, I think, Mashka lied: she said her parents wrote a letter to the police so they would catch the madman.

So while she was confessing—by the time she confessed—I remembered this story. Mashka would never in her life have even talked to him, never mind the things she'd just been telling me about. This is stupid—here is Mashka, and she is the same, nothing has happened to her, she doesn't seem any different, "and what's so bad about what they did," and in the end she started screaming at me: Go ahead and check! Go as far as you want, if you have to.

I got scared and didn't say anything. She had to leave that time—almost right away—a couple of days later, to go see her other relatives, and I'm ashamed to say that I could hardly wait, but as soon as she left, I started writing her letters, each better than the last, here's just an example: * * *

"Mashka," I am at the post office, sending a telegram with all the money I've got. "I want to remind you about how we went to the Akhmystovski buildings the third time. You got a postcard in the mail that looked like this: on one side it had two stamps and that's it, and on the other an invitation to the commemoration of a stranger's forty days, which come after the nine days. I didn't have to go, but I went to keep you company, and a good thing I did. We went up to the sixth floor, as usual, and rang the doorbell, and someone screamed that it's not locked, come in, who is it, and so on. That was one big apartment. See, I told you, Mashka, that we've got these two or three special buildings that have apartments that are three stories each and have two baths on every floor? yeah, Asiunia, but what a crappy layout— look where the bathtub is—right in the hall!

"'That's just because we haven't put it in right yet,' the hosts explain. 'We wanted to put it in, but then we had the nine days, the forty days. Come on in.'

"'Would you tell me please,' Mashka leans forward.

"'Mashka, you have two holes in back,' I say softly.

"'Hush,' she says. 'Tell me, where may I see the orchestra that was at your funeral recently?'

"The hosts get insulted, as well they should, and go on up to the third floor, throwing 'Oh, you' over their shoulders.

"You and I look for a spot in this sad celebration, but there are people everywhere, setting up tables and putting flowers in water, and I say, 'But are they going to feed us, Mashka?'

"The hostess comes back and says, 'No, that orchestra of yours is gone, the funeral guys just left. What are we supposed to do with you? You are too young to drink.'

"Mashka says, 'Give us a separate room so no one goes in, at least not without knocking.'

"I'm surprised but the hostess isn't, and she takes us up to the second floor and up higher, to the fourth floor, and up higher, and invites us to climb up to the attic. 'No,' Mashka says, 'this won't do at all, we have very special business.' And the hostess leaves.

"'What are you up to now, Mashka, where are we?' 'This is where we are going to have our wedding,' she answers, but quiet, so the hostess doesn't hear us, because she'll get insulted: 'I promised you we'd have a wedding if we didn't find the musician, so here.'

"What's that on the window, I say, to stay completely calm. Is it a box or something, where, right there, on the window. It's kind of dark here, turn on the light. It's a box of paints, a set of them. Better you should paint me for this, because what if the musician shows up and I'm not made up.

"Good, because I like to make others up, and I'm good at it. Close your eye, what color do you want? Whatever.

"It was a real wedding. I painted all over Mashka with a brush, but then she suddenly opened the door and went God knows where. I'm going to look for the musicians. Don't you want to get dressed? Then they won't see the painted parts, so what's the point. Quiet, Mashka, there are guests and corpses there, are you afraid of corpses? Yes, come with me, I'm afraid of all of them. You and I went looking for the hosts and the guests. But everyone was asleep all in a row, it's a good thing they opened the doors for us ahead of time.

"When we left, it was still early."

I get a handful of change back—enough to buy her something, too.

Mashka:

My house is nothing at all like the way Asiunia sees it. The main thing is, you can't live in it no matter how hard you try. I don't see how anyone could buy it, because you can see this quality right off. In addition it's hard to sleep because of all the noise and the banging from the station, and you can only really sleep when there is a break between trains, which can be three hours sometimes and sometimes a little longer.

Speaking of tenants: Her mother was a tenant, which everyone knows but it's kept a secret, and the apartment she rented was across the fence from Asiunia's house (so meeting people through the fence must run in the family). Asiunia's father looked like a non-Russian, and non-Russians often addressed him in their languages; but Asiunia doesn't look like him.

Asiunia's birth was preceded by an incident with a neighbor named Roza, who lived across the way. She was sixty or seventy years old, and she fell in love with Asiunia's father. Truth be told, she was just crazy, off her rocker, and it didn't make any difference to her what kind of bizarre things she was doing. After Asiunia's parents got married, Roza would stick pins in their porch every day in order to get Asiunia's father. Asiunia's grandmother would take the pins out and put them in a box. Finally, they caught Roza on the porch, and people could hear them screaming all up and down the street, with Roza screaming, Give him to me, you this way and that, why aren't you letting me through to him? The grandmother says, Look for yourself, Roza, what kind of match are you, plus he's got a wife. Roza got up from the porch, went out the gate, and started singing her song again: You are my sunshine, apple of my eye, **Anna** (Asiunia's grandmother) is mean and won't let me through to you when I bought her onions, paid thirty kopecks, bought her garlic, and you are the apple of my eye, you are priceless. Too bad no one really remembered the words, so it's passed on in an altered version. People asked what's with the thirty kopecks, but no one could remember, and maybe Roza really did lend it. There were no more pins after this, and it is also remarkable that Asiunia's mother didn't figure in this incident in any way because she was in her last month of pregnancy and wasn't going out.

Asiunia insists that there was never any Roza incident but that a day or two before she was born there was a corpse that was floating down the creek and got stuck under the bridge by Asiunia's house. Someone went out and saw it and pushed it through. They say it was wrapped in something and came with twenty kopecks. This story used to really scare me. I was scared because they pushed it through instead of pulling it out and burying it for real. Plus you have to not be scared to take a stick and reach for and touch it and push. The bottom is dirty there, covered with slime, and there is a shiny coin on the bottom—it fell out of it. *Dowry*.

"Do you have a dowry?" my Asiunia asked after I said yes.

"Yes," I said. "A whole addition full. Furniture and dresses. They are too big for me, but you know I look good in things that are too big."

"But of course," my Asiunia said, touching me.

Asiunia:

I think I came to see you in St. Pete? If I've never been there, then why do I remember the big round square in front of the station and walking around it a couple of times and being hot in the sun and having no place to change, and not knowing how to find you in the city?

There was a conversation, but it would be better if it had never happened: "We are free to choose." Choose whom? I could choose you a couple of more times, but don't test me anymore, I beg you, I have no way to protect myself from you, and I doubt you want to hear this; stop, then, get a hold of yourself.

"All right, imagine that I even do find some sort of dowry, that there are the means, that it can be kept secret from the family—"

(Here I tense because I know what's coming—and sure enough!)

"For example, I find somebody just for show, so it's like everybody else. But really—"

Fine, but we'd still need our own house. The best option would be to buy the addition—no, your whole house, so that the one addition would be yours, the other mine, and the middle would belong to whomever you find for show and your children and all the other perfectly normal stuff; part of the middle—the part that hasn't been lived in—you will rent out, and the one for show will be kind of like a tenant, too, and if you want, we'll evict him somehow in the future. Somewhere, I don't yet know where, there will be a long dark hallway leading to my half of the house, which will always be open, so that you could come anytime and even by accident happen into my half when you were planning to go run errands—I'd like that even more. Of course, either way you wouldn't be able to get around the tenants' half, but that's all right, I consent, you can write it down that way. This is what the house will look like if you look from above:

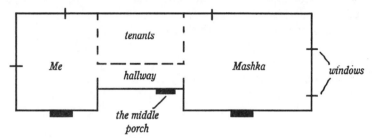

Though no amount of rent money will make this possible.

It is customary, at least among decent people, to despise tenants.

Marinka was standing with her back to me and moving a plate around in muddy water, which had been poured into another plate especially for this purpose.

"He was here yesterday already and brought money for three months."

"That creep?" I screamed. "Is that the best we can find?"

The plate plopped down into the water.

"Asiunia, be quiet! Maybe you are going to start paying rent now? Or looking for tenants yourself? He is a creep, she says. What do you want from him—to be godfather to your children?"

"I'm not having any children!"

"That's for sure—who'd want you, always jumping all over everybody!"

I turned off the television and it got suddenly quiet, as if I had turned off Marinka at the same time.

I opened a wardrobe drawer and, digging through a box of Mashka's letters, stumbled upon a picture from a hundred years ago. Mashka is eleven years old, hideous, like a little rat. The likeness is amplified by a broken tooth (she just *had* to smile—there is a person with no hang-ups!) and the uneven trim of her bangs. Looking at her in this picture always makes me feel better: who else really needs her—who except for me?!

We would go wash together, too. There were lots of people, the place would be full of steam, I would feel sick. I would lean against a wall somewhere, suffocating, falling, and see Mashka, her head thrown back in the shower, bangs stuck to her head and pouring down with the little streams of water. And again I would compare her to our peers and repeat to myself that yes, she is impossibly hideous, flat, awkward, with ribs that stick out—and I want her to stay like that, if not forever then for a long time, because I sense that as long as she is like this, everything will be the same.

Asiunia, fourteen years old:
The street light is so dim I can hardly see their faces.

I take giant strides toward the log, slouching—but I don't care!

"Ooh! Look at who is here!" They sing from the log and move over to make a place.

"Let's go, they are looking for you," I nod in Mashka's direction.

They sing some Gypsy song as we leave. Something about asking someone to dance and someone demurring.

"I think I got it," Mashka stops. "No one is looking for me, right? Who could be looking for me?"

"No one," I smile shamelessly.

Mashka smiles a little, too, as in, All right, then, I'm going?

I let that go by.

"So, exploring the local population, are we? What are your impressions?"

"Quit it! They are regular people."

"Your—international efforts," I say, stuttering, "will be appreciated by future generations."

She raises her eyebrows quickly: this was unexpected.

"Go home," I say softly. "You'll write something. You said you'd write something about the cats!"

She shrugs and turns back toward the log.

I don't like rereading letter number two, "Dear Asiunia." The one I wrote—and didn't send—is better:

"Masha, I've lost my mind. I can't sleep. I want you now, here, with me. What you wrote about your business with *** makes absolutely no difference. For me, you are forever. The only thing is, I can't understand why you just have to seek out and get into all kinds of crap, it's like you look for it and won't rest until you find it, and then you come crying to me. Remember how I wanted to come but you..." From here I'd better explain in my own words because otherwise it wouldn't make sense. Usually it was hard for her to get away even if she was with her class or someone's parents—but this time she suddenly managed to get out and not just anywhere but to Moscow for school vacation. Right away, right in the street, having fallen behind her classmates, she met some "actor" who had two months to go till the army; she followed him to his "theater" and, according to her, spent the whole evening sewing some curtain. The actor then followed her to St. Pete and tried to seduce her like he was supposed to—this, Mashka spent a long time describing, her voice shaking because what if somebody finds out? So nothing really happened! I dunno. What if you start avoiding me or else what if you are scared of me? *I couldn't take it, you know, there is a reason I keep coming here!* and I had to stroke her hair and cry along with her and say that she is still, to me—but this was something you didn't want to hear, Mashka, you let me know I was going too far.

"Do you remember, at least," I say now, when I have the nerve because you are not really here, "how you came running that time at six in the morning and what you said and what you did?"

"No," Mashka says to me. "On that exact day I had my last music exam, so I couldn't have come. I was living in Leningrad—in a suburb, actually, a half hour by train. And I wasn't the age I would have had to be for this to have happened. You forget that we aren't the same age: you were born in seventy-this while I was born in seventy-that, so I was this old already and planning to quit music school.

"I told you already, I wrote that I won't be doing the music thing anymore. I did it for five years, now it's time to quit, no one asked me if I wanted to study. At this point you would remind me, of course, about how they would come to *** every summer to get me and how we would go into the woods for the whole day and how you could always get permission to go with them. That doesn't mean anything, I mean, it doesn't mean that they always understood me. At this point I guess I can write about what happened with the letters: they accidentally got some, the very ones, and then my family decided that *everything just stayed like that between us*—like in the letters. And then you say they are sensitive and kind. Like hell!

—Your Mashka."

Mashka, *** years old:
I started taking the train to Z.V.'s house. She lived in an old building with high ceilings: you always had this urge to divide the room height-wise and make an attic. She was unhappy that I played with no count. Once I came pretty late and fantasized about being kept here overnight, even though I knew it was stupid because there was no room and plus they would worry about me at home—even before that, I dreamt that I did spend the night there after all and that I slept in the grand piano with the cover open, on the strings (they didn't have any other place—they had two instruments in a small room). I didn't like playing with count or without, but I liked going there to that building, passing some semi-basement windows every time, where the third one down had a display of things made out of tree roots: snakes and dragons, and you are always walking fast and can't tell what's what, and Z.V. is always mad that you are not on time, and if you then play without count again... And when you are walking home, the only things in the window where the snakes were are glasses of salt—in the third one down and in the fourth, too...

Asiunia:
Just between us, Mashka was a genius, at least for a while. She was just full of serial stories that she was planning to make into a movie or a play or something. Speaking of which, that crappy game could have made a novel, too: the main character would still be the white kitty; for a long time, Mashka would hang an old fox collar off her skirt so that at least the lead would have a real tail, and others would get a hold of it, but very rarely, while the tomcats were tailless and pushy, only thinking about wanting a kitty, and once they jumped on a kitty none of them would even think about caring about her future at least a little bit. I was sure that if it was just once with just one tomcat, there would likely not be any consequences, but there were five tomcats in the game, and at least three of them were in love with the white kitty.

I remember the first time the white kitty showed up. For the first six days, she came to sit for a portrait, which would be copied over into the notebook. I was afraid that one of our artists would try to seduce her for free, so I took it on myself, and I drew as best I knew how, but the portrait wasn't working out—it was distorted, and I managed to exhaust her pretty well, keeping her from morning till night for six days. It's a good thing that it used to be her job—modeling—so she didn't rush me and kept saying that for some reason

NATALIA SHULGA

everyone always takes a long time to draw her and it never comes out looking like her; then I got the idea of making her out of clay, which took another week—soon I abandoned everything and thought only of her; she kept coming patiently, and asking, But when am I going to get a job? You promised! and then I became one of the tomcats and decided to test her in prose or maybe in verse because I couldn't give her a job without testing her first! But my verse wasn't descriptive; more like, Why must you fly around like snow, clawing at my heart, oh, I wish as a kitten I had been drowned. The white kitty just laughed at me. Say the beginning was, "Do you not love me, oh you snow-white cat." She would immediately change "snow-white" to "mangy" and would make fun of me: "If you do, then tell me won't you, Why did you not put out? Why must you fly around like snow..." Go and try to draw her under these circumstances! She really looked like a street cat, and I didn't want to see her like that, and I knew she was doing it on purpose, and all this hurt, especially because I never did manage to describe her—not in verse, not in a drawing; and the white kitty kept saying, You really should hire me! I would be terribly profitable for you. I know all there is to know about all the tomcats in the neighborhood, I can do anything—except swim, of course—I have a wealth of personal experience, including living with a therapsid once even.

"You really are a liar, Masha," I interrupted. "That's some sort of nonsense."

"Why? A regular therapsid, a perfectly normal animal, of the Therapsida order. I was the apple of his eye! I lived in his house."

"So how was it?" I asked, not knowing what else to say.

"Boring," the white kitty wrinkled her forehead. "He would go whole days without saying a word. Then at night he would sit down to stare at the fire."

"In the wood stove," I added a detail. "Did he propose to you?"

"God forbid! He didn't want to insult me. He was old and ugly. I can't describe it," Mashka repeated. "He kept saying, Soon we'll be extinct. He got his wish finally: I buried him on Thursday, put him in the ground myself—you know where? In our garden, if you go past the bathhouse—right there, where the phlox are—but you better not go or you'll get scared." Then we went there right away, and I put my arms around her there so she wouldn't be scared either, told her that I love her forever, that she is *** I knew what she wanted to hear, so I wanted her to swear right there, right on the grave, because there were some things I wanted to hear her say, too.

The white kitty jumped out of my lap, no, slipped out of my arms, I'm sorry, she said, I have to tell you something. Exactly one day before the funeral I went to hire a funeral orchestra. It was missing a percussionist and a German grand piano, and I said that there could not be a grand piano, but they proved it to me one-two-three that they couldn't make nice sad music for the therapsid without a grand piano, and if she wants to, the lady of the house can play herself—they've heard her play. She refused to play, of course—not with four years of music school and a three* in her specialty! The situation with the percussionist was worse—they couldn't do it without him at all; then someone just happened to whisper a hint—that there is one who is not exactly a funeral musician and sometimes just for the love of it he plays restaurants, which is where she could find him now; she didn't believe them but went looking anyway. "And then I fell in love with him." She could have lied, could have said that nothing happened—but she even hinted that the drummer's instrument was really poor and cracked during the funeral; plus, the musician seems to have dumped her, go find him now. But the main thing is, the therapsid left her an inheritance which she gets only if she goes and gets a job with us at the cats' house, which is what she is doing now as we speak!

You couldn't tell yet what was going to be where; there were some roughly marked-off little cages of the future—some were empty, others piled with junk. Mashka ran ahead, peeking into door openings. Farther down, the rooms didn't have floors for some reason—only deep pits full of water with pipes rising out of them. "This doesn't really look like your famous building. Hey, where are you?"

"...can't tell yet," Mashka called back. Her voice seemed to be coming from above. It appeared she had climbed up onto the second floor and was running around there all happy about some round hole in the roof.

"I don't like it here!" I said.

"Hey, no, it's all right!" That's how it always is—she likes all sorts of dumps full of empty bottles and other junk. Where does she get this? She comes from a perfectly tidy family. Whenever Mashka's mother would come from St. Pete, she would start cleaning like crazy first off—shaking out all the rugs and inevitably washing the tenants' half, which had clearly not been washed by the recently departed ten-

---

* The equivalent of a "C" on a five-point grading scale.

NATALIA SHULGA

ants and had something awful going on in it. Mashka would show up on one porch and then the other, looking devastated and carrying a wet rag or a dirty broom; there could be no talk even of running away with me until late at night because Masha would clean for an incredibly long time because she couldn't stand to do it. I would see her to her door and she would walk away down the wet hallway, drawing a slow line behind her with a disintegrating rag: "You keep sweeping and spreading dirt all around here—what's the point?" I resolved that when we lived together she could sweep whenever she felt like it and it wouldn't make any difference to me (incidentally, we also adapted all sorts of trees—of those we could climb—for our home, and there was never any need to clean up there). But in general, Mashka is hard to please: she likes that unfinished building, for example, or just the opposite—some totally uninhabitable ruin. She found one like that pretty far away, by the bridge, almost outside of town; it was an old boaters' house, which had burned down but not completely—even had a roof, apparently. Mashka drew it in my notebook and suggested we go see it. So we wouldn't get lost, we walked right on the rails, which were covered with black oily slime; closer to the bridge there was a freight station, and the pot-bellied tank cars looked like they might take off from there any minute—we would have to dive under them and jump out the other side bent over, so as not to hit the cable; the rails were definitely oiled, and Mashka was walking on the rail ahead of me and I was watching so she wouldn't step on the points. Beyond the station, a bit to the side, we'd see a concrete fence with buzzing electrical towers behind it, where there are cherry trees that we often pick cherries from, and then Mashka always warned that we could get electrocuted. Then we'd have to walk on the rails again, and it's not far to the bridge—and then she said, her voice lowered in glee, that I was about to see her favorite places. The road ran along an embankment, and we saw, in turn: a spoon that someone had placed on the rail to be flattened out; a roll of cloth so torn up there was nothing to pick up; then a dog cut in half—but a very long time ago, and this was the front half, almost a skeleton, with pieces of grayish-yellow fur hanging off in places. "Poor doggie," Mashka let out. "Isn't it great here? Have you ever seen a cat skeleton? It's the worst! You better not look at one, it's got this scowling kind of face—" Mashka half-closed her eyes. We passed the dog, stepped over a fresh tar puddle; now there were short dusty shrubs on either side of the railroad, and beyond them there was the river, and which side is your house on—this one? I don't really recall, said Mashka, it was on this side one time and on the other side the other time. She was pulling my leg! There was no house on any side! She was testing me as usual.

"If you are testing what I am willing to do for you—" I started speaking, more or less firmly, into her back; Mashka paused, rubbed one foot against the other, spreading tar all over it, and kept going—

Mashka:
We go out through a door that isn't there onto a floor that consists of maybe two bricks that haven't fallen through yet, and from there it's a narrative in pictures—do you mind if I sketch it all right here? or I would forget that also: you can see through two stories that the room upstairs used to have yellow flowered wallpaper and the other has photographs on the wall, which didn't even get ripped down, and really it's odd that the building collapsed on the inside while from the outside it's perfectly normal—there's the room with wallpaper, a stairway next to it but no landing, but there are banisters bent in the air, too bad the remains of someone's kitchen don't fit in that corner: a gas stove… all right, that's another drawing, while here we will have: junk on the remains of the stairway, you dictate and I'll draw. So, what do we have—*Milk, Pegasus cigs, Eggplant Caviar,* a mailer, what was once condensed milk, *Losk shoe polish*—some of these things I don't know how to draw, so I'll write on the drawing—now the far corner with the remains of the kitchen: here I am drawing the corner of the building, which still has a bit of the floor on this level and that level, here a gas stove has attached itself like there's nothing wrong, and it's got a frying pan on it; on the floor below, it's just like this—a wardrobe with a mirrored door, and over our heads, in the corner, there is a blue stripe, it's somebody's sled hung up in between the windows—that's odd, it must have been a communal apartment, in which case this was the hallway. Underneath there are windows like we've got on the terrace (with only half the glass, if that much), and where we are standing used to be the door to the apartment, except without the walls and ceilings you can't tell what's what and the whole building seems like a three-story room, and, by the way, there may be no door here but there is still a chain lock, so maybe there's valuables in there for the taking?

Asiunia:
Maybe there's valuables for the taking? I could understand if you had the wrong house. It had been represented to you as a boaters' house—which is perfectly plausible: there was a boat by the bridge

and we saw it—when we were younger, we used to run away and come here to "ride" the boat out to the end of the chain—the sound of water and steel, the boat jerking as though it were alive, just don't fall into the water, because there is no one to rescue you; when a train is going over the bridge, everything around shudders and the boat shakes, and the water splashes over the edge, and in another two or three trains, everything will turn upside down, and the sun is going crazy in the water, and Mashka is hanging over the edge, dreaming at the very end—and there was a boater, too, that's for sure, because once he showed up suddenly, as though he had come from the water, and started screaming, What the hell is going on here, get out of the boat this minute!—and we ran to where he couldn't see us and watched him fumble with the locks in a proprietary sort of way, taking off the chain—and then he finally took off in one of the wooden ones, but, thank God, not in "ours." How sad that his house burned down! But still, this isn't his house. You've got to agree, Mashka. It's possible, certainly, that he was rich and just concealed it from everybody— I mean, he lived alone in a luxurious wooden communal house, where he lived in some of the rooms and used others for fixing up his boats, or maybe even building them himself—or maybe he just outlived all the other tenants, because himself he had no age and he had been taking people to the other side since before there was a bridge—what a scary idea, you never could have made it here to see me back then. On the other hand, if the bridge went and disappeared some wonderful summer, then you would never leave and together we would live through the long and painful period of the apples growing ripe—we always picked them for her "for the road" and dried them and made preserves for the winter, the roof would be covered with them, but by fall rotting apples still covered half the garden—a red polka-dotted rug under the anise tree, yellow and green under the "crossbreed." Toward evening the multicolored shadows from the poles are boundlessly long; during the day they are covered with gray dragonflies that take off with a crackling sound. It is almost that time when she leaves—I don't understand why Mashka has to go someplace every year. Mashka "is a student, she goes to school," but is there ever a real, honest-to-goodness reason for her to leave? Why go to school God knows where, why such a long distance? It was never clear where she disappeared to, by the way. If it had suddenly come to light that it was not Leningrad, I wouldn't have been surprised. There was never any sign that she came *from* somewhere; she talked little about "her" city—or suburb, wherever it was she lived—in other words,

Masha would just take off and disappear shamelessly for a long time, and it was like she wasn't anywhere. She could have been doing it on purpose to spite me, in order to "test" me again or to "make it clear"— The white kitty sneaked a picture of the therapsid into her room. It was not discovered right away, although she never tried to hide it—to the contrary, she hung it in the most obvious place, on a totally bare wall right over the couch. The picture itself was in a thick gilded frame with doohickies, with the therapsid's tail curled and his face sad and even somewhat mysterious, despite his being, you know, a beast. The white kitty would say, This is the work of a well-known master! She knew that personal belongings were not allowed—and especially a therapsid! The tomcats will take one look and flee, is how I put it. I was wrong: the picture came in handy for her. She never parted with it—if she was going to someone's house, she would take it with her and hang it up over the bed ahead of time. It was the picture that gave the white kitty's visits their charm; it served to begin the acquaintance: goodness, who could that be—a relative of yours?—which is when she would extract the therapsid's "family album," from her inheritance. I saw it only once: one of the pages had a picture from a textbook on it: a very sad therapsid is coming out of the water at sunset, there are fish splashing, butterflies flying all around it—the therapsid's neck is all covered with butterflies, and he has tears in his eyes, and there is a caption: He is all alone in the world, all his brothers and sisters are extinct—and I think it was this caption that got the tomcats—or maybe it just appealed to them that the therapsid hung over the couch like a stone visitor while they were alive and visiting the white kitty. She was allowed to keep the picture. "Don't you dare come alive," I warned the therapsid. I didn't know whom to fear, what would be worse: ten tomcats or one live therapsid; incidentally, I had a dream about him, and it was most peculiar: I dreamt that I was sitting in Mashka's garden and he ran out as a lizard, all nimble and everything, and green, and jumped onto my belly and started digging a hole for himself really fast. "What do you think you are doing?" I screamed at him, and he paused and answered from inside me: the white kitty and I need a home.

In reality, even though he was dead there were traces of him everywhere: something would start looking like him—the bridge, a cloud, or an abandoned building—and I think Mashka noticed about the bridge, too, because she was always scared to stand on the rails and look along the railroad *as though through the therapsid's skeleton*—then the train would appear suddenly on the other side, and the only way

NATALIA SHULGA

to survive is to get down and lie on the rails, touching your face to the dog, the spoon, the cloth, and becoming one with them so the train won't notice you.

"A burned-down building is like a therapsid: you can't live in it." Mashka is tired and doesn't want to talk to me anymore. From the side, the bridge looks just like his back, with his head hidden on shore. There is a soft, steady buzz coming from the ground, going through me and ending in the sky, reaching beyond the bridge in an expansive white line. I bragged to Mashka that I knew when it crossed the sound barrier: I could feel it. "Oh, it's when it's like a shot!" It's not like a shot, you just have to close your eyes and imagine it going through you, everything filling with the soft scary buzz, then the thick wide line cutting through you at an angle, and then there is the fast *thoroughness* of all the trains passing after she leaves, the forgotten rails drowning in tar and growing over with grass at an unbelievable speed, and grayish-yellow-colored dogs coming out onto the railroad, lying down on the rails themselves, and I am pulled to go with them, but I don't have the nerve. (We were walking down one of those rails and moved the points for the hell of it, then looked and saw it was a dead end! Mashka: Too bad!)

Unbeknownst to us, the white kitty got hold of the notebook, which ceased to be a document: it started filling with trendy pictures, sketches of local life—the white kitty turned out to have a talent, say maybe it was she who painted her therapsid but didn't say so out of modesty. Now anyone could make it into the notebook along with the kitties—mostly it was the visiting tomcats: the white kitty just couldn't contain herself, she had to draw everyone to have something to remember them by—and to remember "our" house she drew a portrait of a green-eyed receptionist sitting by the phone. Some pictures were touchingly tacky—for example, a tomcat and a kitty sitting on the floor, he holding a red goblet in his paws (when have we ever had red goblets?), she detached, looking off to the side, as though she had nothing to do with any of this. All the cats were big-eyed and dressed in human clothes or totally naked with fluffy tails. *Touching your face to the dog, the spoon, the cloth, and becoming one with them, along for the ride, so you will never die and the train won't notice you.*

You never know how it started: we were supposed to be together the whole summer—and now where is it? Nothing is going right. Mashka doesn't come out for days at a time. She took her own letters from me for some reason, and now sits there going through them, and when I come over, she is always grouchy, complaining about her own handwriting.

"So drop them!"

"No, why don't you read them to me instead?" she offers out of the blue—no, why don't I leave instead. (I look over my shoulder at the three-paneled mirror, where the Kremlin tower is registering the appropriate amount of heat, and there is Mashka's hair pin and scissors. "My hair's really grown out. Mash, let's do something about me." Where did I ever get the idea that she could cut in a straight line?)

"I brought you something," and I take out a wrinkled blue rag. Mashka goes to try it on reluctantly; it's the dress the white kitty always wore in the game (what the hell is she rereading this for: my dear, my beloved, I have never, no one else—so, you are going to camp? shame on you, you should be drowned, and for how long? oh, that's not very long!)—and then Masha comes out, all wrinkled blue silk ripped—and this kind of fabric used to be fashionable, silk dresses were considered the best for going out, that's what you wore to birthday parties. I inherited the dress from my sister—and then the cats got it. It wrinkles and clings to your legs.

By the way, the cat book contains a warning: "There is a tree on the therapsid's grave planted in his memory. It is called a melba tree. The apples are very tasty, but the therapsid will stalk you from his hiding place in the tree roots."

It's odd, but I never got the opportunity to spend the night at her house, when that's the only thing I ever wanted—or for her to be allowed to sleep over at my house, which was also forbidden: "My parents say it's not appropriate when everyone has their own house." Over the course of these days, I never asked her once, and Mashka didn't let on either, why, I have no idea; it's getting darker little by little, we move from one room to another, meanwhile Mashka announces, You can't sleep here—there is nothing to sleep on, here "the wall has eyes" (a scary story about a dead relative), here Mashka herself used to get scared when she was little because they would hang slaughtered rabbits up from the doorjamb—they'd be all skinned except for their little paws left on like gloves; sometimes they gave Mashka the cut-off paws to play with when they dried out, and she made all kinds of pillows out of them for her dolls, but I don't remember Mashka playing with anything like that, she always liked everything to be live, I'm a cat, you're a cat, the most honest kind of game! There are several other games like everyone else plays, and we played them, too: The Bird in a Tree, where you have to touch wood and then

NATALIA SHULGA

you're safe where the cat won't get you; but if every bird is in a tree then the cat can eat any one he wants. You shouldn't touch the melba tree, though—Mashka informed me separately later that it is "off limits." * * * Meanwhile she's led me through all the rooms, there aren't any left, and all I have left to do is turn to leave like I can take a hint; no one is going to be extending any invitations to me tonight, and I say the first thing that comes into my head: I could give a damn that there is no place to lie down and about the skinned rabbits, who knows when we are ever going to have a scary house of our own again.

"Oh, but why?" Mashka responds. "I believe you wanted to divide it but first buy it. To buy it we need money, and to get money we need a tenant, or whatever it was you said. And as it happens, somebody came by earlier today—"

(And here I am overcome by this odd kind of joy like everything just worked itself out, thank God, and nothing bad is going to happen anymore; everything is clear without saying anything, and everything is as it ever was: the best kind of dress is silk, the best kind of tree is a palm tree in a metal bucket, from Germany or someplace like that, which used to be in a vat that had the number 226 on it and was painted with oil paint, it was from the other addition, too. "This is imported," as Mashka puts it; once upon a time it looked good on top of the piano, but now it has withered, and the dried little stump is still sitting in the corner of the large room—and when Mashka starts moving it out into the middle of the room, and when it finally goes over and she runs to get the broom, I ask her what all the commotion is about. Mashka answers, without batting an eye, I've decided to "let in some tenants," just for three days, no big deal, they are just passing through, in three days exactly they will no longer be here—and then something fairly believable about the lack of vacancies at the hotel, about some kind of horrible complications, and all this is further confirmed by the fact that she wastes no time dragging in a bucket of water and starting to scrub the floor.

"You are not getting away with it," I say without much confidence. "Because you aren't the owner."

"So what?" says Mashka. "They don't care about that."

They don't care about a lot of things, but you can't do this, they must have been joking...

"Look it," says Mashka. "Either you stop getting in my way and leave, or start helping. They are supposed to come right about now."

"They?! Are there a lot of them?"

"I'm going to let them have the other addition. There won't be a lot of them, so they'll fit, though I only have the keys to the inside door—but that's all right, they'll just have to use our porch."

"Do what you want. But I'll stay, all right?" Mashka seems to be agreeing to everything quietly; she gives me something to do right away, then right away calls me over: Why am I not doing anything? We won't manage in time! Then she takes the key and takes me to unlock "that" addition—we open it and come right up against a plywood wall; beyond it there is some sort of wardrobe right up against the door, and Mashka is afraid that we won't be able to push it out of the way—and as soon as we are able to budge it, she squeezes through the hole and says to me from the other side, It's got a clock on it! and glass shelves—the clock was built right into the wardrobe, but Mashka embellished a little about the shelves, there were just shards of them left, but there was a low round table in the corner and unbelievable dirt and dust all over the place.

"Do they really have to be right here—"

"No, and where do you want to put them?" Mashka asks indignantly. "They asked for a separate room themselves! What, do you think this is not good enough?"

There is no arguing with her on this point, plus everything up to this point has been going like we wanted, except too fast and weird.

"Maybe no one is going to come?"

"Maybe they won't," Mashka answers calmly. "But that's unlikely. You go lie down for now."

"But where?"

"In the little room, there is a fold-away there." That means behind the stove, where it smells like medicine; *they* might come very late but they'll definitely have to walk past me, and I'll hear them, tell their footsteps from Mashka's feline jogs from room to room—to straighten out the tablecloth and dust the windowsill—and back; except it really is impossible to sleep at her house, and I call her to come and talk to me, but she has no time, no time, and I fall in, and sometime in the middle of the night I suddenly realize that I've long since slept through it, *everyone is here*, there is a night light on in the large room, and they've dragged the wardrobe in there and the sole round table from that addition, and there is a statue on it—Dresden china all threaded through with cracks; a boy with a frightening stationary stare is threatening the dog. Mashka rushes in, tries to please everybody, pours tea into little teacups—the guests can't get enough of her, keep asking: what a good girl, how old are you? no, don't answer that, play something for us instead on the piano with the black Mozart, but you have to wear your best dress.

"The keys don't work," Mashka demurs. "And where are you headed, and what do you do?"

"We are headed for entry examinations in the down-and-fur trade school that is located in your wonderful town; in the future we'll be selling furs. That will be me, and my comrade—the one slouching over there—he is kind of like a music student but he doesn't want to play anything, he just keeps checking everything out."

"Oh, you must be joking!" says Mashka. "He is probably the best musician in the world! I beg you, tell me, what does he play?" They tell her softly. Mashka shrieks and faints, I think, though I can't see because they are in the way, but a second later she is laughing already, pouring tea, saying, Would you like to hear a story about the three tomcats?—Yes!—Well, listen then. Three tomcats are sitting around when they hear, Meow! Oh, the eldest one says, my kitty is here, I think I'll go give it to her. He leaves, then comes back; the others ask, Is everything all right? Fine. So they are sitting there... They are sitting there, and the night light is getting dim now, because she didn't have anything, so they brought this with them. Mashka keeps trying, now bringing her drawings out to show them, now coming out in a different dress suddenly—now running to me, sobbing, My god, he is not feeling well, do you have anything for a headache?

"Me? This is your house!"—Mashka drops something, then digs through rustling medicines; I jump up: Listen, quit running back and forth! Or else introduce me to them already. Fine, Mashka says to me, get dressed and let's go, and leads me I don't know where in the dark, because there is no electricity in that half. "Allow me to introduce myself, I..."

"It's too late for introductions," I am told. "We'll have time for that tomorrow." And Mashka says: Did your light go out? I'll bring you a candle! I can find anything in the dark, I've been living here—but she can't find anything and she asks, Where is your comrade, the one that was sitting looking away, the one who is a musician or something?— He's coming, he'll be back, just wait a bit. Sit down here, if you want, I can't fall asleep anyway, keep seeing God knows what. Mashka: You shouldn't be afraid, there is nothing here—but in the garden there is a forbidden tree called the melba tree, which has very tasty apples, but there is a danger so it's better not to touch.

I told you then: we'll have a wedding, and we did, and I wouldn't dream of refuting that; you are silly—everything will be like we agreed: this house and the additions, but you are not going to want me without a dowry, are you? I am supposed to inherit the "other" addition and everything in it, you said yourself those dresses look good on me! How long can we go on sketching tomcats, you agreed to have tenants, I wasn't just handed my inheritance with no strings attached, this is no joke, but it's not bad at all, I'm gifted, you know that!—Do you want me to do everything for you? and I get scared that she will say yes! but of course she doesn't and instead turns off all the lights in the little room and lies down on the edge of the bed and says sleepily, Wake me up in two hours. I can hear falling apples hitting the roof, rolling down, and getting stuck in the gutter.

I should just go now and tell them everything myself, and the hell with the damned addition! No, I'm scared, because they are really having fun, they've laid furs out on the floor and are waiting for the hostess, because she did promise, and they have the piano playing and the canaries have woken up in the greenhouse and are singing, and candles are lit—or would it be better in the dark, when you don't know how many of them there are, and what to tell whom when all they want is some kitties and they want no explanations—as though we didn't know before that letting someone spend one night wouldn't pay for the addition, but this way, sure: a line of zeroes across the whole page, nothing bad is going to happen to you, nothing worse than a live therapsid in the garden behind the bucket (he is eating currants right off the bushes, he only likes red currant, won't even look at the black ones), and now it's even worse: the ground is covered with apples, and even those are all small, all anise apples dented every which way, all covered with worm holes, and half rolled off into the poison ivy. I don't really think Mashka would get upset; in the dark we look alike—almost like sisters—all I have to do is climb over her and walk down the hall: it's me, meow—me, Mashka, the white kitty, come out if you are not asleep.

(The hallway is rocking for some reason, and it's got big flashes and metal planks—maybe they are banisters and I need to step carefully, because one misstep and I'm in the water, or the train will sneak up on me without lights and strike quietly, and you're history—who is going to pick you up here?—you'll lie around here until morning.)
    "Who is it?"
    "It's me, the white kitty, meow,"
    "It's you making all that noise, not letting people sleep?"
    "I fell down."

"Come here." There are so many of them, they won't let me explain anything, they are checking—Where does it hurt, here?—That's all right, I can take it, tomorrow Mashka will wake up and stroke all my festering wounds and when I'm getting married I'll have no pain.

I wake up alone, dressed, lying on top of the blanket; Mashka is not here. She is not anywhere in the house. "That" addition is not locked, and there is no one there. I find her at the station, I manage to spot her in line to the ticket window, and I push through and drag her out by the hand, What are you doing, I scream, did you buy a ticket already?—Yeah, I did, she answers in a tired voice. I just want to kill her, but she can barely stand up: Let's go sit down, she says.

I fell asleep right away and I dreamt of Mashka.

She came and asked me as though nothing had happened, "Asiunia, can you let me stay in your apartment?"

"What?" I say, without even getting up from the couch. "What do you need an apartment for?"

"I want to stay here and not anyplace else," she pauses and adds plaintively, for some reason, "I mean, you do take tenants."

So I don't have to answer right away, I ask, "Don't you like it in your town?"

"I'm tired of it."

"You just get things into your head, and the same thing will happen here."

She looks at me like she is begging me, like that time. * * * "You really love our town that much?" I ask. It sounds dumb.

"No," Mashka admits truthfully. "It's pretty boring, and the streets are kind of dusty..." ("And there is no one but you," I fantasize.) But Mashka doesn't say anything else and falls through into the darkness somewhere, and in her place appears my four-year-old brother Andriukha, and he screams, It's snowing! And I woke up at two in the morning. There was a branch with large apples on it outside the window.

Well, what is it with you; I don't even know what to call you! She is sitting with her eyes closed. She says that I'm the one who's cracked: she bought the ticket in advance, a few days ahead of time, and that's the way everyone always does it. There is a molded plaster ornament above us on the ceiling, and there are angels flying around the ceiling, flapping their wings. I'm staying, she says, and we're going to go home now.

Asiunia, eleven years old:
The middle part of the house is always boarded up. When we played in the front yard right under those windows, Mashka would stand on her toes and peek into the cracks in the shingles. "I can't see anything!" And she would make plans to climb into the little room—at night, through the window. She called the room "Where someone died," and I would get scared.

When they opened up the middle part, they didn't find anything special: dust, trash, no furniture even.

In the Here and There

VALERIYA NARBIKOVA

If it is fiction, then what kind is it? This is the sort of catechism question that could serve as a starting point for a story by Valeriya Narbikova, whose work has frustrated scholars' attempts to place her in the context of contemporary Russian writing. Narbikova's first publication, the novella "The Equilibrium of the Light of Daytime and Nighttime Stars," which appeared in the journal Youth *in 1989, came recommended by Andrei Bitov, one of the country's most respected writers and critics and a mentor of Narbikova's at the Literary Institute. Bitov's introduction was uncharacteristically inarticulate. The venerable author admitted that it had taken him several years to get a taste for Narbikova's writing—and now that he had he was convinced it was worth a read. He urged readers not to reject it merely because it was "different fiction"—a catch-all term that has come to describe the work of a dozen diverse writers—but to read it if for no other reason than that it was the voice of the "mute generation."*

The novella was an instant success, winning the journal's Publication of the Year award. Subsequent novellas—all of which are similar in length and style and share an absence of traditional narrative—have puzzled and alternately charmed and infuriated critics and readers. Still, while Narbikova's writing, with its unrelenting word play and defiantly eclectic literary and historical allusions (mixed with pure arbitrary fantasy, such as the andy-baby in this story), is firmly embedded in the language and culture of Moscow intelligentsia of the "Stagnation Period," her voice is no more typical of her generation than it is of any other. Her detached virtuosity leaves some readers angry and others awed. "If there is anything I understand in the labyrinths of Valerlya Narbikova's writing," writes Pavel Basinsky, "it's that the outrageously dry and unerotic quality of her writing (the apparent plentitude of erotic scenes notwithstanding) takes its root in the absence of the male in our lives—or, perhaps, in his facelessness."

On the other hand, Yelena Gessen saw Narbikova as the clear leader of the erotic movement in Russian women's fiction, arguing even that "Narbikova's fiction achieves an almost Socratic coming together of Eros and Logos."

Larisa Vaneyeva, the editor of She Who Bears No Ill, *one of the first anthologies to include Narbikova's work, wrote an introduction full of*

undisguised awe: "Her apartment looks like a gallery: Valeriya is a tal-
ented visual artist. One can only wonder, comparing her painting style with
her prose style. She never touches a brush to canvas. How she writes her
unusual, virtuoso texts is another mystery. All we know is she uses a soft-
lead pencil and writes so illegibly that she has to retype her stories right
away."

The author herself seems entirely unwilling to shed light on her creative
process. "There are writers who like to read what they've written, and there
are those who simply hate to do that," writes Narbikova, who lives in
Moscow. "When I read what I've written, I think, How did I manage to
write that? Now I would never write that. Good thing I already wrote it, so
I don't have to write it now. Meaning that when I start to think about
what's missing in some one of my pieces, I think about it not from my own
point of view but from the point of view of my favorite living and even dead
writers, because there are more favorite writers among the dead than
among the living, which is a sad point concerning the dead and the living.
And I start to think that, say, Nabokov may not like this, though he might
like some one thing—he might, or at least I would like it if he did. But
Pushkin wouldn't like it for sure. Because he is simple and clear. And why
would he, so simple and clear, like something so complicated and unclear?
And how could this be transported through time to be appreciated? That's
what contemporaries are for. And it is thanks to my contemporaries that I
start to understand what it is I have written anyway. What is it, anyway?"

If it is fiction, then what kind is it? —M. G.

Something always precedes that which follows. Here are three
examples from an entirely different novel, with the first example illustrating the relativity of place, the second illustrating the permanence
of time, and the third illustrating (see below).

Example one:

One day V.N. and I.K. arrive in Sympheropol by plane late at night
(at 2300) but need to proceed to an entirely different place, 80 km
from Sympheropol. The only means of transportation to this place is a
taxi at a cost of 80 r., but, as this amount exceeds the cost of two plane
tickets from Moscow to Sympheropol, they, having solved the simple
arithmetic problem in which the question is Which is more expensive—by air or by land?—turn down the taxi driver's offer not because
of the staggering cost but because they stagger at the realization of
the accessibility of travel by plane and the inaccessibility of travel by
automobile. They board a trolley and, for the cost of 80 kop., proceed

to Alushta so as to make a circle and reach the desired destination by sea. In Alushta, having been assured that no means of transportation operates at such a late hour, they decide to spend the night somewhere on the beach. But the beach, which is divided into segments, is locked, and they depart for the woods that cover the mountain, with the intention of lying down somewhere in the bushes. The mountain is in the very center of town; rather, the town is situated on the mountain. Having put some distance between themselves and the center of town, they discover a very dark and discreet place on the warm soil, covered with warm pine needles and soft cypress branches. They sit down and when their eyes get a little bit used to the darkness, they are able to see that there is a road a bit below them, about 50 meters away, and a bit above them, there is some sort of structure (a building?). To be precise, a building and yet not. In the darkness it appears to be of three stories or possibly four but at the same time unfinished and seemingly uninhabited, not fenced but somehow official in appearance, possibly a tailor shop or a post office, though nothing indicates that either is the case. It is definitely not a hotel or a movie theater but a building of unknown purpose. But because it is still dark, V.N and I.K. decide that when it gets light they will determine with certainty what kind of building they are spending the night by. They drink two bottles of Gyrdzhaani[*], which they have brought with them from Moscow, and fall asleep beautifully right on the ground. When they wake up at six o'clock in the morning, they see this "building" in the soft gray light of a southern morning, but they are still unable to determine what kind of building it is. As they pack their bags and collect pieces of paper and empty bottles (their trash), they exchange ideas about this building but find none of these ideas satisfactory.

"It's not a post office."

"Nah."

"It's not finished."

"Why not? It's got glass, and that over there looks like a curtain."

"It looks somehow unfinished."

"A creepy kind of place, what did you do with my bag?"

"I slept on it, it's kind of scary."

"You lost money out of your pants pockets, a weird kind of place."

"Let's get out of here fast."

Wrapping up quickly, they practically roll off the mountain, beating

---

* Georgian wine made in the area where the two are traveling.

it from the inexplicable place with the inexplicable building. In the end it cannot be explained what kind of place this was, unrecognizable not only in the dark but in the light as well.

Example two:

As they await the arrival of their friends bearing beer, V.N. and I.K. look longingly upon a pointy cape that cuts into the sea somewhat more abruptly than the rest of the shapes, which are elliptically semi-circular. From their location at one point, they are looking at another point located at a distance of 5 km from them; they are looking from Novy Svet to Sudak, and at this point, being absolutely real in Novy Svet, they can distinguish absolutely no people in Sudak, and have only their knowledge that the concave shore and the pointy cape over there constitute Sudak. Having lost all hope that their friends will ever return with the beer and having held a lengthy discussion on the topic that it would be faster to go themselves, they find themselves, albeit not too soon, in Sudak on the very point they observed as but a point from Novy Svet. But now Novy Svet, the place where they were not too long ago, appears to them as a point. It is difficult to say in which point they are really real, since only about six hours passes between Novy Svet and Sudak. But if we ignore that time, which is merely a grain in the sand of time, merely a drop in the ocean—the ocean of time—then it turns out they are really real in two points at the same time.

Example three:

A person (a relative?) attempts to write the life story of an author on the basis of a novel that has accidentally made its way into his possession. Details that appear to him to be entirely autobiographical horrify him, and he imagines the rest of the author's life by filling in details from the book. When the author learns of this, he is horrified by the way in which people in general (relatives?) read books. The author becomes very agitated and refuses to acknowledge that the details were entirely autobiographical, but this begs the question of why the author found it necessary to camouflage everything so carefully in his novel if those details were not autobiographical...

1

...if it's a thought, then what kind is it? They had covered kilometers by walking from one room to the other.

"You just don't give a damn about anything," the older sister said to the younger.

"About what?"

"About anything."

With every word they moved farther apart.

"What did I ever do to you?" said the younger sister and sat down.

"You didn't do anything to me," answered Yezdandukta.

"Then tell me, what did I do?"

"I'll tell you. You—you, Petia—are intolerable, and I only tolerate you because you are my sister."

"I know, it's not like you'd marry me," said Petrarka. "But we are related."

Yezdandukta didn't answer this. She stuffed herself into a sweater, pulled on a pair of shoes, and when she was already standing in the doorway she said, "So this is how you treat relatives?"

"Tell me, What did I do that was so bad?" said Petia.

And as the door was shut on this question, the question was left stuck in the door.

It's a city fall like...if it's fall, then what kind is it? The *beautiful* sun, moving across a *luxuriously blue* sky, shone its rays straight down onto dirt that had been turned up: potholes, boards, pieces of paper swollen from rain. And the wind, going over the garbage dumpsters in a *slight* gust, showered the pavement with watermelon rinds, fruit pits, and apple cores—the *generous* gifts of fall. It is not like winter, when garbage, frozen into the ground and covered with a *thin layer of snow*, weakly sprouts *early* growth, but precisely fall, which is so *plentiful*. And the day is pumped full of sounds, each of which is a *triumph* of conscious *human* activity: the sounds of trolleys and trams, which *celebrate* the *power* of *humankind*, that of which *humans* are capable on this *morning* that is both *beautiful* and *sunny* at the end of the twentieth century.

Petia fell in love with Boris. She knew that she loved him and only him, that she knew that she loved him and only that.

Boris was late. They were supposed to meet at the front of the platform at the first car of a train, and the train was already at the platform, but it had arrived in the opposite direction, and the first car was at the rear of the platform, and now Petia didn't know why Boris wasn't there and where he was and whether she should remain at the front of the platform or go to the first car at the other end of the platform. All this was so terrible that Anna Karenina should immediately have jumped in front of the train which she was riding to see Vronsky when she was late to see him—and not only should she have jumped, but she should have jumped together with Vronsky's mother, who was riding with her, so she would not be tormented by her throughout the length of the novel and so Vronsky would be left without Anna from the very beginning and could grieve for her through the whole novel and not just in the last chapter. Boris found Petia in the middle of the platform, where she stood the way she stood: like a shadow. And as soon as he saw her, he heard: "Don't go!"

"I'll come back soon," he said. "In three days."

and a minute later she said, "Don't go!" And he said:

"I'll come right back."

and right away she said, "Don't go!"

And while she was trying to talk him out of leaving, the train left and Boris stayed. The train left without Boris, it left absolutely empty, and jumping in front of it would have been useless, since it could not have killed anyone because it was light as a feather. But Boris was left with a heavy heart after the train left so lightly and so quickly.

Petia had already loved Boris an eternity, which had rushed by in the month they had known each other. She needed to see him every day several times a day. Her eyes were empty from happiness, and there was not a thought in her head except for the thought about Boris.

What impressed her about Boris was what had not impressed her at all at first. At first she had not been impressed at all by his appearance, but later any man who resembled Boris the least bit became worthy of her attention, especially since Boris's appearance was fairly typical among men: he had straight hair, a straight nose, light eyes, and light hair. If he was forty, he looked younger than his years, but if he was thirty, he looked older than his years. In general, his appearance was such that any man's appearance could have been reduced to Boris's appearance. At first she had not been impressed at all by his work. If Boris's appearance was typical, then his work was absolutely atypical: he didn't go to work. What he had the opportunity to make at home he wouldn't have had the opportunity to make at work; at home he made sculptures that rang, shone, walked, sat, and one of which carried a name: *The Eyes Are the Mirror of the Soul,* featuring a perfectly ordinary pair of doll's eyes set in a perfectly ordinary mirror, and this was precisely the work that impressed her in a way in which it had not impressed her at first. Even her first night with Boris, which ended in the morning, seemed entirely unimpressive to Petia during the day, and in the evening she didn't call Boris. But when her head filled with the ways in which she had not been impressed with Boris, she fell in love with him head over heels.

As for the sculptures that Boris made, they would have sold out all over the world as well as at the store Art World, but Boris never traveled anywhere, unlike Gogol, who traveled, as did Turgenev and Dostoyevsky; like Pushkin, he didn't travel; he traveled to the country, of course, and to the Caucasus, but never beyond Mikhaylovskoye or Bakhchysaray. Right away Petia fell in love with this one temple, the model of which Boris didn't show her right away but only after he fell in love with her himself. From the outside this temple looked like a regular nine-story tower, a white concrete-block matchbox, not a bit different from all the other nine-story towers in Moscow; but inside it embodied the outside of the Kolomensky Temple: in other words, when a person ended up inside this concrete-block matchbox, what appeared before his eyes was a concave Kolomensky Temple: every protrusion of the Kolomensky Temple became a concavity of the Boris Temple, and under the roof of the nine-story tower was a concave dome, which was blue with gold stars.

After Boris didn't leave by train, he left almost immediately by foot; he and Petia parted at the railroad station to meet again tomorrow at Petia's house, after her sister left.

Yezdandukta could not forgive Petia for the Korean airliner incident, as though it had been Petia who shot it down. It so happened that a month before Petia met Boris, the Korean airliner was shot down, and Petia and her friends pretended to be the airliner, which wore dark "spy" glasses on its nose. But then the "airliner" demonstratively removed the spy glasses and shyly donned a pair of regular children's prescription glasses, whereupon everyone started crying out of sadness for these glasses, and the glasses broke, so the "airliner" couldn't see anything and started tripping over various objects—shelves, chairs, tables—and then with some difficulty made its way to the bathroom, and as soon as the door closed behind it, it noisily fell into the toilet, and then everything became quiet and everyone could hear the peaceful murmur of water in the toilet.

"Idiots," said Yezdandukta. "This will get you nowhere fast."

"Where?" asked Petia.

"Why are you asking me a question I already answered for you?" And after a brief silence, she answered again: "Nowhere."

There was nothing repellent about Yezdandukta's face; it was even attractive. It attracted so it could repel. It attracted the way the face of a little animal that's been artificially bred by human beings attracts through its anomaly: a small nose becomes smaller and smaller in the process of breeding until it disappears entirely, and eyes become bigger and bigger and the ears thinner and the neck thicker. Plus,

Yezdandukta applied her makeup in an unfortunate manner that made everything that was already small seem even smaller and everything that was already large seem even larger.

...if it's words, then what kind of words? The kind that would reach Yezdandukta before Boris called, the kind that would get her so she would leave right away, without saying one rude thing to Petia.

As though to be spiteful, Yezdandukta was getting ready as if she were going to a ball: first she put on one skirt and one blouse, then she put on a different skirt and a different blouse to go with it. She drank tea and then went back to finish it. Along with her unfinished tea she finished her uneaten sandwich. When Petia jumped to the phone when Yezdandukta had already picked up the receiver, when Petia said, "It's for me," when Yezdandukta had already hung up saying, "They hung up," Petia sat down by the phone in total despair the reason for which was Yezdandukta. As the reason, she was walking back and forth for no reason and caused Petia pain with this unreasonable walking. Having lost hope that she would ever depart, Petia thought only of the hope that she would depart. The reason for Petia's pain was Yezdandukta, who couldn't depart, and the consequence of Petia's pain was Boris, who couldn't arrive. In the end the cause and the effect got so confused that Boris, who couldn't arrive, became the cause of her pain, and Yezdandukta, who couldn't depart, became the effect of this pain, and the fact that Raskolnikov killed the old lady was the cause, and the fact that he was condemned to hard labor was the effect, and the killing was the crime and the hard labor was punishment, but it would be better if he had labored first and then killed the old lady, and would be better if the Decembrists* had been exiled first and then had come out onto Senate Square, and the scariest thing was when the effect traded places with the cause, and more than anything else Petia was afraid that first Boris wouldn't arrive and then Yezdandukta would depart, that first Napoleon would be sent to St. Helen and then he would conquer the world.

"Nowhere," said Petia when Yezdandukta asked her where she was going today.

"Just like this," she answered when Yezdandukta said, "Are you going to walk around all day looking like that?"

And after Yezdandukta said nothing else and Petia said nothing

---

*A group of Russian officers who led a military uprising against the Czar in St. Petersburg's Senate Square in 1825. Five of them were executed and 121 others exiled to Siberia.

VALERIYA NARBIKOVA

else back, Yezdandukta left almost immediately, and almost immediately there was a call from Boris.

"Well?"

"Where are you?"

"Is your house across from the post office?"

"Are you by the post office?"

Petia named the floor and the apartment number. And as soon as she opened the door for him and as soon as she had had time enough to close the door and as soon as they hugged, they didn't stop hugging, all they did was hug something awful and kiss right there by the door next to the coat rack: "Take your coat off already." "Take yours off." Boris kept his coat on while Petia was wearing a nightgown in which she was as hot as though she had been wearing a coat, and in the rear of the "coat" she had a giant hole, and when she stuck her face in a coat that was hanging on the rack, Boris unbuttoned his coat while Petia kept wearing her holey "coat," and then he used the hole in her gown, this absolutely obvious hole in the plane, to reach space, he used a vacuum to reach a depth. "Tell you later," he said when she asked, "What are you doing?" because he had sighed in such a way that it sounded to her like he couldn't breathe. "Tell me now." "Later." And later, when they were drinking wine and Boris was looking around her room, which he was wild about right away, with its poems pinned to the wallpaper after they were just written and were still drying and with its cast-metal butterfly that looked real from afar because it even had metal antennae, Petia asked:

"What did you want to tell me when you said you'd tell me later?"

"I'll tell you later."

"When?"

and when they left the building together to avoid being caught by the sister, Boris saw a hole in the fence that led to the opening of a concrete pipe, and when Petia and Boris climbed through the hole in the fence they ended up inside the pipe, when they traversed the hole in the plane, they ended up in the deep darkness of space, they reached a depth through a vacuum, together they ended up inside Petia in the hallway by the coat rack, and now they were together and kissing inside Petia, bending their necks to fit in the pipe.

"Got it," said she.

"Cool," said he.

And they did it again: they climbed through the hole in the fence into the pipe.

"You think the laborers know about this?" asked Petia.

"About your holey gown?"

"Now it seems to me like everyone knows about it, like you f— me publicly through the hole in the fence."

If it's the height of happiness, then what's higher? the shortest route to happiness begins with happiness itself. It's not the kind of long route they took in the last century, when they began with a light gust of wind and ended with a storm; this begins with a storm and ends with a storm. If Petia's love had begun in the nineteenth century, then it would just be reaching its climax at the end of the twentieth century, because in the last century Boris would just have had time to notice, first, how *silky* Petia's eyelashes are and how *radiant* her skin is, and Boris would be moving toward his happiness without rushing, in total harmony with nature, and some moonlit night or during a thunderstorm or at noon, he and Petia wouldn't let their happiness get away and their happiness wouldn't let them get away. Boris was hugging his girl who was no longer a maiden and the fact that he wasn't her first and the fact that she wasn't his first—and what came first was that, second, she was his first love and that, first, he was her first love, and the fact that during her first year of college she had her first man, who was a second-year student for whom she was his first—that was secondary.

Petia fell asleep thinking of Boris, and when she woke up because she was thinking of Boris, she couldn't fall asleep for thinking of Boris. The earliest thought, which was about Boris, got her out of bed, and she didn't even think of thinking other thoughts. She valued her thought about Boris so much that the only thing more valuable was Boris's thought about Petia. If sex as a physical characteristic in the nineteenth century became sex as a concept in the twentieth century, then Boris as a person in the last century became in the present century, in the transition from past to present, the concept of love, because before Boris Petia had no concept of love. Petia thought Boris, and for her he became not merely a proper name—Boris—he became the proper name for her love and her own proper name, and not one language—not even the "great and mighty" Russian—had a name for it, only the dead Latin language, which no one spoke, could unite Petia and Boris into one whole and name this whole properly: *borisus*.

...if it's a life, then what's it like? it could be lived in such a way that wasn't the way of—like it's long but not in such a way as to always be ahead of you.

Boris's home was his castle, and in his castle Boris was at home. It had a piece of metal garden fence, the Kolomensky Temple in a box, a tree stump—all this luxury. And the model of "the temple from inside" was as tall as a person, and when Petia and Boris entered the inside of the temple, their heads ended up right in the dome, and the dome was close enough to kiss and all the stars were close enough to kiss, and Petia kissed one of the stars. There is no feeling that cannot be expressed through words, but there are no words that can express the feeling and the kiss that has left its imprint on the lips and on the plaster when the plaster carries the imprint of lips the way the sky carries the imprint of a pink cloud washed out by the wind the way plaster carries the imprint of pink lipstick washed out by the rain. Petia showed Boris how red her throat was; it was painful for her to swallow after the kiss. Even feelings as hot as theirs were powerless here, where only warm beer could make the throat better, warm beer being more powerful than the hottest of feelings. Petia lay down, and Boris went to warm up the beer. She drank a glass and then another glass, and the third glass affected her in such a way that when Boris touched his lips, ice-cold from ice-cold beer, to her lips, warm from warm beer, because of the colossal difference in temperature Petia and Boris tried another remedy, namely that she took a mouthful of water, except this was not water, and when he said "Spit it out if you can't swallow," she couldn't answer right away because she had her mouth full and only after she swallowed did she answer, "I can."

As they tended to themselves at this rate, time didn't stand still either, and the speed of this treatment speeded up time to such a degree that when they looked out onto the street they saw that where it had been light it had become dark while under the street lights it had become, conversely, light.

"What are you going to tell your sister?" asked Boris.

"I was at a birthday party," Petia replied to Yezdandukta when she showed up at home in the morning.

Between Boris's question and Petia's answer stretched a night so happy and truthful that Petia couldn't be truthful with Yezdandukta because this truth would not have brought happiness.

"I couldn't," Petia replied to Yezdandukta's reproachful "Couldn't you have called?"

"I did," said Petia when Yezdandukta said, "Did you even think of me?"

Petia did think that she would never tell her sister the truth about Boris because Yezdandukta would think it wasn't true and it was better to have Yezdandukta thinking that what isn't true isn't true than to have her thinking that what is true isn't true, which would truly be worse.

And when it was morning, it was like a morning that can only be on a day like this one was, when everything is like it is when everything else seems to be so unlike anything that it can change nothing.

When Petia didn't come home at night for the second time, Yezdandukta told her for the first time, "This is the last time." Petia left the house and was free to head in any direction. She headed not in the direction of the store, where her sister had asked her to go, but in the opposite direction. And when she was crossing the street, a trolley came to a stop so abruptly that it seemed to be acting like a private car. Petia boarded the trolley, which had been hired by Kostroma and Dyl.

"We could have gotten a private car for three rubles," said Dyl.

"I like getting a trolley for three rubles," said Kostroma.

Kostroma handed three rubles to the boy driver, and the trolley headed for the grove, which was not a glassy grove or a wooden grove but the Silver Grove, possibly named so because of the pine trees, which could get to looking pretty silver in the winter or because of the silver creek or possibly because of the thirty silver points and the wooden house that had been given to Kostroma's grandfather by his place of service for his faithful service. He did as he was told. And what he was told, he did. He looked to the future so intently that his eyes had gotten glassy in the way the grove wasn't.

"Is your grandfather home?" asked Petia.

"He's on assignment," answered Kostroma.

"Dyl," said Petia, "I don't really feel like going with you. I was on my way to the store."

"What do you need at the store?" said Kostroma. "We've got everything at the place."

"You got bread?"

They were walking to Kostroma's grandfather's house—Kostroma's "grandhouse"—and talking about love.

"Kostroma, do you love your grandfather?" asked Dyl.

"What about you, Dyl—do you love your grandfather?"

"My grandfather was killed because of your grandfather."

"So was my grandmother," said Petia.

"Your grandmother would be old enough to be his grandfather's mother."

"That means it was like killing his mother—the worst sin of all."

"She wouldn't be old enough to be his mother, she'd be more like his sister."

"So it was like killing his sister."

"Even if it was like killing his daughter, that wouldn't change any-

VALERIYA NARBIKOVA

thing," said Kostroma. "I won't let you kill my grandfather."

"Who said anything about killing your grandfather?" said Dyl.

"Petia, do you have any plans to kill his grandfather?"

"Then why are we going there?" asked Petia.

"Did you think we were going there to kill his grandfather?" said Dyl. "We are going there to drink coffee."

"I won't let anyone kill my grandfather. He's like a baby now, just born into this world, still washed in his mother's blood."

"We're sick of you with your grandfather," said Dyl.

"Then leave me alone."

"Why are we going there?" asked Petia when they were already in front of the "grandhouse."

"To get the suitcase," said Kostroma.

Climbing up to the second floor, which Kostroma was temporarily inhabiting, was like literally getting into the grandfather's head. "Show us the suitcase."

The decor of the room was quite extraordinary for an ordinary person. What was extraordinary was that perfectly ordinary chairs, couches, and wardrobes were tagged like migratory birds, presumably to prevent the furniture from flying away. Petia sat down in a chair, which was tagged and numbered, and while Kostroma was crawling underneath the (tagged and numbered) couch, Petia looked out the (tagged and numbered) window, where she saw trees, which were tagged and numbered, and she saw fallen leaves that belonged to the trees that belonged to the house that belonged to Kostroma's grandfather, who did not own any of these belongings. The grandfather is going to live here until he dies, and when he dies another grandfather, exactly the same and a little different, is going to live here. And in this space, which was permanent—with permanent furniture, walls, and stories—the only thing that was temporary was the person, namely Kostroma's grandfather. This permanent decor, created once and for all, would allow only the kind of grandfather that was created in its own image. This was not a place where a person chose his decor but a place where the decor chose its person. And all those people the decor chose were mortal, while the decor was immortal. Even if this decor were buried, the numbered tags would remain and descendants could use them to recreate the chairs, wardrobes, etc.

Dyl just couldn't believe his eyes when Kostroma opened the suitcase. Kostroma opened it and then right away—*bang!*—closed it. And Dyl imagined that he'd imagined it. Petia didn't see that Kostroma opened the suitcase because she was looking out the window, and when she turned back toward the suitcase, it was already closed. It was an old-fashioned little suitcase with metal corners.

"Give me three rubles for the trolley," Petia said to Kostroma. "And I'll go." Kostroma stuck his hand in his pocket uncertainly, certain that he didn't have a three-ruble bill, and pulled out his handkerchief and his money along with it. And when he gave Petia the three-ruble bill, and she turned to—he opened the suitcase and when Petia looked, she saw that which she had only heard about before.

"Petrarka," said Kostroma. He said it loud and formal, but suddenly something happened to his voice and he said "Petrarka" again, but this time much softer. Kostroma picked up the suitcase like a jewelry box and presented it to Petia, who smiled because it was stuffed with treasures, which appeal to all kinds of women—czarinas, whores, and maidens—but at the same time the contents of the suitcase could not be called treasures. That is, there was gold there and there were diamonds, but these were not decorations—that is, since they were in a jewelry box of sorts they were decorations of sorts, but they were not the normal sort of decorations—rings, bracelets, and pins—these were decorations of precisely the abnormal sort: medals.

"Who does all this belong to?" said Petia, and her question was barely audible, but Kostroma heard her and gave a barely audible answer: "You," but Petia did not hear him and said, more softly still, "Who?" but Kostroma did not hear her and said nothing else and it became so quiet that nothing was audible; that is, what became audible was that nothing could be heard. But when the metal jingled when Kostroma put down the jewelry box, absolutely everyone heard it. And Dyl asked Kostroma, absolutely calmly, "Where'd you get it?" Kostroma looked at him calmly and said, "Have you heard the joke about 'Where'd you get it, where'd you get it?' " Kostroma told the joke: a person is running down the street with an ax in his hand, and another person is running after him, screaming, "Where'd you get it?" The one with the ax stops, bops him on the head with the ax, and keeps walking like nothing happened, walking and muttering, "Where'd I get it, where'd I get it? I bought it, duh."

"So that's what you are going to be muttering when they bop you," said Dyl.

"Why would they bop *me*?"

"What'd you think—that they give out medals for this sort of thing?"

"Maybe they give out medals posthumously."

"Maybe they aren't real," asked Petia.

VALERIYA NARBIKOVA

"What do you mean, not real?" Kostroma answered indignantly. "You think I would give forgeries to a beautiful girl?"

"Who's the beautiful girl?" Petia asked him.

"You, you are the beautiful girl."

And Dyl and Kostroma looked at Petia, whose face looked like a very feminine boy's face.

"You mean I'm not a beautiful girl?" asked Dyl.

And Petia and Kostroma looked at Dyl, whose face was so feminine that to look at his face, he looked more like a girl than like a boy, but for some reason, Petia's boyish face was attractive while Dyl's girlish face was repellent. The fact that Dyl was of the male sex and had many of the features of the opposite sex did not become him, while the fact that Petia was of the female sex and had features of the opposite sex became her so much that Kostroma became transfixed on her face, and her face became flushed. Kostroma himself blushed frequently and this was especially striking because by nature he was white: he had white skin, white hair, white eyelashes, and white eyebrows. And if he had been a girl and could apply makeup to his eyebrows and eyelashes, then they would have been noticeable, but since he was not a girl and could not apply makeup, what was noticeable was that they were barely noticeable.

"Are you trying to say that the entire suitcase belongs to Petrarka?" said Dyl.

"I said that already."

"Are you in love or something?"

"Is love a crime or something?"

"Wait," Petia stopped them. "I'm already in love."

Kostroma and Dyl looked at her as though she were guilty of a terrible crime.

"I'm in love. Is that a crime?"

"What do you mean, you are in love," said Kostroma. "With whom?"

Petia said nothing and stepped away from the suitcase.

"When did you fall in love? When they shot down the airliner, you weren't in love."

"Not yet."

"But that wasn't that long ago that it was shot down. When did you have time to fall in love?"

"Recently, almost right after it was shot down."

"It hasn't even been a month since it was shot down."

"No, it's been two months already," said Petia.

"Has it really been two months already?" said Kostroma.

"Two months exactly," said Petia.

"So you fell in love right away after the plane thing?"

"No, not right away. A month later."

"Who is he?" asked Kostroma.

"Who?" Petia was confused.

"Who?" Kostroma said again.

she said Boris—she said that it was he—that he and she—that without him she—and that when he is not, she—and that it can only be he—that she would have never—but he—and then he too—and she...

"Yeah, that's it," said Kostroma.

"What's 'it'?" asked Petia.

"The real thing," said Kostroma.

"The real thing deserves a Gold Star,"* said Dyl.

"The Admiral Ushakov Medal!"

"The Georgian Cross!"†

"They are all yours," said Kostroma and laid the medals at Petia's feet.

"Bring it out," he said to Dyl.

"Where is it?" asked Dyl.

"Under the couch, on the right."

Dyl reached under the couch, got out a bottle of cognac. "You've got glasses here, too."

"Get out the glasses. Get out whatever is under there. There's some sausage."

"Why don't you lock the stuff up under the couch?"

"What am I supposed to do—lock up a hole?"

"A hole is exactly what you are supposed to lock up."

They cut a few pieces, they filled the glasses, and they drank a shot each.

"To 'it,' " said Kostroma. " 'It' is such a rarity these days. 'It' is a great service to our people."

Five medals appeared on Petia's chest at once.

"But really, love is such hard labor, such hard labor," said Dyl, "that you deserve the Labor Veteran medal. And you can be awarded the Gold Star," Dyl got talkative, addressing Kostroma. "Because you are in love."

"No, if only one person is in love, it doesn't count," said Kostroma.

---

*The Gold Star, or the title of Hero of the Soviet Union or Hero of Socialist Labor, is the highest military or civilian honor.

† A prerevolutionary honor.

VALERIYA NARBIKOVA

"Anybody can fall in love with somebody. Medals should only be awarded for the kind of feeling that affects two people," reasoned Kostroma. "Really, medals should be awarded not to people but to the feeling, and people should only serve as representatives of the feeling, the same way that medals are awarded for deeds and people serve as representatives of these deeds: if a particular speed is achieved, the Labor Veteran medal is awarded; if a certain time is achieved, the medal goes to the time."

"If they are for the feeling," said Petia, "then half the medals belong to Boris."

"Half belong to him," concurred Kostroma.

Nothing was left out—everything, including the unfinished bottle and the sausage, went in the suitcase.

"You going to invite us to your wedding?" asked Dyl.

The taxi driver got them from the grove to the boulevard in a few minutes, and they gave him a few rubles when he stopped by the university where Petia and Kostroma were studying and Dyl used to study but dropped out but he could reenter while Petia and Kostroma could, conversely, drop out, and they crossed the boulevard toward the New Art Theater but the "old" one was worth two new ones put together, and Kostroma recited a verse:

A leg in the distance is the same leg,

And eyes in the distance are the same eyes,

And a star in distance is still a star,

But love in the distance is also love.

Dyl looked at Kostroma, who had no love either in the present or in the distance, and who would do well to give up writing poetry.

"Recite something else," said Dyl.

Kostroma recited something else.

"Now sing something," said Petia.

So, with song and poetry, they arrived in front of Boris's building and looked at his apartment, which was on the first floor, even a bit below the sidewalk, but not in the basement. Petia looked down into his window, but he wasn't there.

"Should we wait?" asked Kostroma.

They hung out in the cold and Kostroma started reciting another poem, but Petia gave him the kind of look that made him stop and say that he hadn't finished it yet.

"If we had private property in this country," said Dyl, "we could go into a private café and warm up."

"You can't go into a state one?"

"No. It stinks in the state ones."

"What stinks?"

"The stuff people eat, that's what stinks."

"So it's the food that stinks."

"I like it when food smells instead of stinking."

"I wouldn't oppose everything becoming private property," said Petia.

"Who would?" said Dyl. "Everything should be private property except for borders, which should belong to the state."

Petia thought a bit and said, "We can go to my house," because she thought that her sister wasn't home. Having spent what they had to spend, they rode the Metro to Petia's house. And when Petia started to open the door, it was opened from the other side by Yezdandukta, and that wasn't bad, because she opened it and went back inside, but then from the other side came Boris. At the sight of Boris, Petia should have fainted, and the fact that she didn't faint and that she kept standing and that she even took a step forward; she should have become speechless at the sight of Boris, and that she said, and that she answered, and that she later asked—apparently, from the minute she saw Boris, she did not stop talking and only she thought that she was still and silent, because in reality she was walking and talking, and she thought that everyone was walking and talking, when in reality everyone was still and silent. Yezdandukta started asking, and Petia started explaining, but Yezdandukta couldn't understand anything and asked only for an explanation of where the medals came from, but Petia couldn't understand where Boris had come from, and when Yezdandukta had her question met with Petia's answer—"From outer space"—she met Petia's question with Petia's answer: "From outer space." And Boris didn't understand that the medals were for love and kept slipping away from Dyl and Kostroma like a fish—one minute they had him and the next minute he was gone—but when he understood that they were for love, the medals began shining on his chest like fish scales. Petia never stopped laughing, because her love was endless and this was the end of love. Yezdandukta, who was absolutely white, said, "Go away," which absolutely everyone heard. And Petia asked, "Who?" And she answered, "Everybody." And Petia and Boris, their medals jingling, headed for the door. Dyl and Kostroma headed for the door. And when everybody was going down the stairs together, Yezdandukta stuck her head out the door and said, "Boris, may I see you for a minute?" And Boris turned around and headed back for the door, and when the door shut after Boris, Petia wanted to go right back and open the door with her key, then she wanted to ring the doorbell, then to kick the door in with her foot, but when Kostroma said, "Come on, we'll wait downstairs," Petia followed Kostroma, and once downstairs, they started waiting. The first minute was like any other minute, but when five more minutes had passed and Petia started counting the minutes—"how long has it been?"—"Ten minutes"—and five more minutes had passed, Petia felt that it had already been an hour and she said she wasn't going to wait one more minute, and in exactly one minute they left, and in exactly one minute Boris came out. He stood in front of the door for a few minutes, then walked a full circle in a minute, then, after thinking a minute, he decided to go back in for a minute.

2

...whereas those who cannot have children can have an andy-baby, which is a small metal figurine that speaks—or a different sort of andy-baby can be bred in an egg by taking the egg of a black chicken, replacing the egg white with sperm, plugging the egg with damp wax paper, and placing it under a pile of manure on the first day of a March moon; following a gestation period of thirty days a monster resembling a small person will appear; it will need to be fed earth worms and bird feed...and as long as it is alive, you will be happy.

"Do you know at least where we are?"

"Na-ah."

"This is a stadium."

"There is a big field, but there are no bleachers."

"Maybe there are bleachers on the other side and we are on the opposite side."

"Bleachers should be all around the perimeter of the field."

"And we are outside the perimeter of the bleachers."

"There's fog there."

"What kind of fog?"

"Nighttime fog, and the bleachers are in the fog."

"Then why are there stars?"

"The stars are in the sky; the fog is on the ground."

"Then what's in the sky?"

"Stars."

"And on the ground?"

"Bleachers."

"Is there a sip left in there?"

"Are you kidding?"

"Last night I had a dream about a woman who was really beautiful with brown eyes and a red dress, and she said, 'When you are unhappy or when you are happy, think of me, and I'll come to you. She had an eye in her forehead in addition to two eyes in the usual places, and the eye in her forehead kept falling in toward the back of her head, then floating up like a bob, as though in some sort of little pipe that led to the back of the head, and then it would float up to the surface of the forehead," Petrarka was relating with feeling.

"Do you love him?" asked Kostroma.

"Boris is my love," replied Petia.

And Kostroma, anticipating that Petrarka was going to say something else about Boris, said something else: "See that, toward the sky? That's the barn where they keep the inventory."

And insensitive Dyl said, "Anyone can tell that Petrarka is in love."

From where they were sitting, not only could they not see a barn, they couldn't even see bleachers, and they could only see the stadium in their imagination.

And Petia became so emotional because of the things that were visible and invisible that she was lifted up almost half a meter off the ground, and when she landed—no, when she was still between the ground and the sky—during the moment of landing—no, when she had already stood up, she said, when she had sat down, "I love Boris."

she talked and she could barely talk because she was overwhelmed by love, and she said nothing except that she loved Boris, and her speech was less like a speech than like a melody—tah-tah-tah-tah— some melody known to some bird, and the idea contained in this melody was so simple that one wanted to fall in love with some bird in the Caucasus that loved some branch in Esher and chirped, from the moment she greeted the sun with joy in the morning and until night: "I-love-bo-ris." And if the bird's song were a ship signal or a trolley jingle or the sound of a car braking in the sky, this could have struck a listener, but in the fact that a bird sings or a girl loves, in the very melody as idea or idea as melody, there was nothing striking. So she loves. So she sings.

"I'll never love anyone else. Never," said Petia. This new song was even more touching, and when she said, again, "Never," it started snowing, and closer to the sky, it was more like snow, and closer to the ground, it was more like rain, and it became very apparent that there are several levels between the ground and the sky. This was apparent from the point of view of a person, but it would have been good if it had been apparent from some other point of view as well.

Petia came home not too late, but later than the time at which Boris

    VALERIYA NARBIKOVA

left and earlier than the time at which Yezdandukta went to sleep.

Yezdandukta was glowing like never before; that is, Petia had never before seen Yezdandukta glow like that. She was washing the dishes and flying around the apartment, and as she flew she glowed, and as she washed she said that she and Boris had discussed a variety of topics including the topic of her dissertation and that the topic had changed after her first advisor died, and now the topic of her dissertation was "The Topic of Nature in the Philosophical Love Verse of the First Half of the Nineteenth Century," and that by the second half of the day, when Petia and her friends came home, they had not had time to finish discussing this topic, and Yezdandukta asked Boris to stay a minute but they began discussing an entirely different topic, and Yezdandukta had told him that she was very happy that her sister had a regular friend because her other friends were entirely irregular, "and you are gone with them all night long," she said to Petia, and Boris had said, "You have a very talented sister."

"When was I ever gone all night long?" asked Petia.

"You were gone two nights in a row," said Yezdandukta.

And then Petia didn't say that during those two nights she was gone to Boris's and that she had lied until now, that she lied before and now she was not lying, that she loved Boris and he loved her and that they had loved each other two nights in a row and that she had lied about the birthday party; and instead of the things she didn't say, she said:

"Did you feed him soup?"

"I hope you are not in love," said Yezdandukta.

"With whom?" asked Petia.

"Say, with Boris."

Petia asked, "Which Boris?" simply because she couldn't talk to Yezdandukta about her Boris but could easily have talked to her about Boris Godunov or about Boris and Gleb* or about a generic Boris. But Yezdandukta didn't want to talk about a generic Boris and started again talking about Petia's Boris, and Petia accidentally let herself say, "You are probably in love with him yourself."

And suddenly Yezdandukta answered her all serious and quiet, "If he loved me as a person just a little bit, I would be willing to love him forever."

Petia had not anticipated this.

"What do you mean, as a person?" she asked a question.

---

* Russian Orthodox saints.

"Just what I said," said Yezdandukta.

A huge moon was shining in the window, we know what kind of bird this moon is, we know nothing, Petia went to her room, jingling the medals, and a diamond sparkled in the moonlight like in the sunlight, and love was like friendship, sister like brother, mother like father, a fool like a fool, and before going to sleep, Petia thought that when she dreamed of Boris not as a person but as an object or an animal, such as a can or a turtle, she knew for certain in her sleep that this can or this turtle was Boris, and she related to them not as she would to a can or a turtle but as she would to a person—"Is that what Yezdandukta was talking about?" thought Petia. But that's not what Yezdandukta had been talking about.

And then she started missing Boris so much that she got depressed, and not just about Boris but about one's place of residence, the country, where nothing could be changed because if everything started being changed radically, if everything became private property except for borders, which belong to the state, then this couldn't be done peacefully and everyone would fight and kill one another, and why couldn't the borders be opened so that she and Boris could go to, say, Japan (say it to whom?) with a show of his sculptures and then come back in a year and paint a painting or maybe start painting it in Japan and at least finish it in Moscow, and why does just going to Japan have to take half your life, because first you have to finish and then you have to get hired-admitted-recommended-whatnotted; and as for Japan, where the culture developed something awesome over the three hundred years that the borders were closed—well, Japan is small, it's an island and a disciple of China, whereas we are part of the continent, part of Asia and Europe, and our culture isn't sleeping either—it's just that life is dying out. We live as enemies and all that's left to do is fool around. It's a rare country where no one lives because everyone's struggling, a country of experiments—but life is not an experiment; life is the only life for life. All around there are Little Oktiabrists in place of children, Young Communists in place of youth, members in place of people. Petia thought that Boris put the Kolomensky Temple in a box on purpose, so that it couldn't be seen from the outside and could only be seen from the inside. And while Petia was lying in bed unable to sleep because she was exhausted from all these thoughts, Boris, who was exhausted at the airport, fell asleep, because he kept being unable to fly out with his temple in a box, and not even to Japan but to an Asia that was merely Central.

It would be wrong to say that Boris flew out of Moscow early in the

VALERIYA NARBIKOVA

morning; he simply flew away from a dead city, as if he were its soul. He had purposefully not told Petia that he had to leave because he really wanted to leave by plane and he remembered how he hadn't left by train when he told her that he had to leave. But he'd left her the key to his apartment, and Yezdandukta had said that she would give it to her that night along with his regards, but whereas she gave her his regards, she decided to wait until morning to give her the key. And while Petia slept the morning away, Yezdandukta didn't waste a minute. She arrived at Boris's with the intention of instituting her version of beautification: to arrange the chairs beautifully and fold the linen; she went so far in her cleaning that after she washed the floors and the dishes she started on the windows. She got them to such a transparent state that the street started looking especially disgusting through the transparently clean quasi-basement windows. She moved the sculptures aside, and everything that had been moving around and jingling was now standing still and silent. When Yezdandukta returned home in the evening, she started telling Petia about her day methodically, but Petia was rushing her with her questions because Petia was impatient to find out where Boris was, but Yezdandukta had no patience for being interrupted by Petia when she spoke, and because Yezdandukta wanted to tell everything in order and Petia's disorderly questions interrupted her, Yezdandukta lost her train of thought at the most interesting point in the story, where she was talking about the airplane, because when Petia interrupted her with the question "How could he fly out?" and Yezdandukta answered "The usual way—on an airplane" and Petia started asking questions— "When did he fly out? On what airplane?"—and finally Petia said "There is no way he could have flown out on an airplane," Yezdandukta was at a loss for words at first but then answered calmly, "He flew out yesterday, and he landed today." "But why did he go by airplane?" said Petia. This made Yezdandukta laugh. "How else was he supposed to get to Central Asia—by train?"

"Why Central Asia?" asked Petia. "He should have taken the train to Riga."

"That's correct. The train goes to Riga, and the airplane goes to Tashkent." Petia immediately started hating the airplane that goes to Tashkent and had already landed—not because it was stuffed to the gills, and not because it had dirty seat covers which don't get aired out or disinfected, not even because there are cockroaches running around and flies flying around in the airplane—flies in the air while the airplane is in the air—but she began hating it as a means of transportation that takes off and lands, quickly and conveniently—"Use the services of Aeroflot; it is always at your service"—she hated it for these services, and even though there is service on the train, too, there is more humanity in a train, and if you ask, like a human being, "don't go," it won't go while the plane will go like an ass, and there is even more humanity in automobiles because if you ask a taxi, "Don't go," it definitely won't go, but the most inhumane means of transportation is your very own pair of feet, which can carry you away like wings.

After the airplane, Yezdandukta didn't even remember about the keys, and Petia didn't ask, and Yezdandukta didn't say, and Petia never knew. She remembered about the keys after Petia had already left, and she decided that she'd tell Petia when she came home, especially since she'd told Petia before she left, "Don't be late coming home." At school Petia went to a seminar devoted to the work of a male writer who was Kostroma's classmate and a female poet who was Petia's classmate, and the seminar was led by a young male critic, an upperclassman who said right away that when the heroine of a story is referred to by her last name and the hero by his first name, that's bad, and it's better when the heroine is referred to by her first name and the hero by his last name, and it's better still when the heroine is referred to not by her full name but by her nickname, like Tania instead of Tatiana. This proved to be the most germane topic because no one said anything on any other topic. And only at the very end did someone say that the young poet's work had a manly strength to it, and then in parting someone called her an accomplished poet. Following this depressing experience, Petia and Kostroma walked out into the yard, where the one who was awakened by the Decembrists and then awakened someone himself was standing.*

"Shouldn't have gone waking one another up," said Kostroma, pointing at the statue, which was all small and ugly with three tulips growing out of its muddy shoes and a hose stuck between its legs.

Then they discussed the topics of who awakened whom and who slept more and who slept less, and "Napoleon slept very little—only three hours a day—but walked around a lot, always out in the battlefield," and "There was someone else who would only sleep during the day and then keep everyone else awake at night," and "Nowadays people like to sleep a lot, and if they didn't have to go to work, no one

---

* Aleksandr Gerzen, a 19th century Russian writer held in high esteem by Lenin, who once said that Gerzen was "awakened" by the Decembrists.

VALERIYA NARBIKOVA

would ever stir," and "Why would they stir—there's no point—you may as well sleep."

Dyl came up. "What are you sitting here for?" he said. "Let's go." And they went. How clean was the air, how good it smelled.

"What's this smell?"

"Thyme."

"Like you've smelled thyme?"

"Like you bet."

"Like where?"

"Like at the drugstore," and there was such longing for everything to be precisely clean and good and not precise, like at the drugstore. Petia soon got rid of Dyl and Kostroma so that she could go look in Boris's windows, which were transparent like glass and dirty like the air. Boris had flown away, and everything was meaningless, and there was no place to go, and Petia went home.

It was already late at night when Yezdandukta said, "I completely forgot—Boris left you his keys."

"When?" asked Petia.

"There you go again," said Yezdandukta, "asking pointless questions."

"What questions?" said Petia because she was very nervous.

"Stupid ones," answered Yezdandukta and went to bed.

Petia didn't go to bed for a long time and spent a long time sitting in the kitchen and wanting to ask her sister about the details, but Yezdandukta stayed away. But as soon as she came out of her room, Petia asked her, "When did he leave the keys for me?"

"Yesterday," said Yezdandukta. "Oh, and I didn't tell you—" and then she said something so frightening that Petia shivered: "I went to his house today and cleaned up a little—but that probably doesn't make any difference to you."

"That's different," said Petia. "So how was it?"

"Fine," said Yezdandukta and went back into her room.

"Everything will be all right," thought Petia as she was falling asleep. "Everything will be wonderful." And the wonder took her away all right, to a wonderful place far, far away, not so far from home, into the area of sleep, which area could expect precipitation and light frosts in some spots, and all handicapped spots were occupied, and where there was spot color, in the most interesting spot in the dream, where Boris usually appeared, he had not yet appeared in the dream, and for the first time in their relationship, he was to appear not at the point where space intersected with time, not at the point where two o'clock in the afternoon intersected with Gogol Boulevard, not at the point where the clock said five-oh-five near the zoo, but he was to appear at the time of the rain—on time—and he could have been on the street, out at sea, or in a café, anywhere she would have found him at the time of her dream, say, at three o'clock. But he was nowhere in the dream, not at four o'clock, not at five, and only when it was nine o'clock instead of seven, and the door was closing behind Yezdandukta, all this early-morning activity, which was crowding into Petia's head along with the sunlight and the alarm, caused Boris to appear.

At first Petia didn't believe that it was indeed he; he could have been in the air or in Central Asia, but his standing in the doorway seemed so improbable that it seemed more probable that this was a dream in which she dreamt that she woke up—and the fact that the furnishings in this dream were the same as in waking life meant nothing. And only when Boris started talking to her sister and Petia sat up in bed did it become clear that this was indeed Boris talking and Petia was indeed sitting up in bed. This was no dream. She threw on a robe and went out into the kitchen. She wanted to kiss Boris, but not in front of her sister. The three of them had coffee together, but they didn't have a real conversation on any issue because Petia and Boris had their own issues, and Yezdandukta and Boris had theirs, and Petia and Yezdandukta had theirs, which was that they didn't discuss any issue because they didn't discuss the issue of relatives, of which they had none, and they didn't discuss the issue of love, of which they had none, they almost never discussed any literary issues, and various issues of homemaking were unpleasant issues, although sometimes they had discussions like: "Did you buy it?"—"I didn't buy it."—"Why not?"—"They didn't have any."

Yezdandukta left for work, but Petia was so afraid that she might come back at any moment that she said to Boris, "Maybe we should go to your house?"

"Were you there while I was gone?"

"Didn't get around to it."

But Petia said that her sister had gotten around to it and had even gotten around to cleaning up a little. Boris wasn't happy to hear this and was even less happy to hear that Yezdandukta had heard nothing about Petia's love.

"Why are you hiding me?" asked Boris.

"She wouldn't believe me anyway."

For a minute Boris forgot about his worries because Petia started

VALERIYA NARBIKOVA

kissing him, and then he forgot everything because Petia remembered to tell him her dream.

"Imagine," she said. "We didn't have to set a place, we didn't have to agree exactly about whether we were meeting on the boulevard or at the Metro station; we only had to set a time, say, for example, 'Let's meet at three,' and wherever you are at three, that's where I'd be. Imagine if that were true."

He said, "Great," because it was great that they connected, and the point of their connection wasn't a boulevard or a movie theater but the most tender point, which was so inflamed that there could be no comparison at this point, and from Boris's point of view, all of Petia was in this point, which became the point of departure for the rest of her body, which extended in all directions from this point, as though pushed by a centrifugal force, and from Petia's point of view, her whole body was directed toward that point, as though pushed by another, centripetal, force, and when she no longer had the strength to contain this force, she said "That's it," because she had come to this point and he had led her to this point. Time rolled over and out, and he said, "I'm going to go," when Petia asked, "Where are you going? And what about me?"

"You sleep some more."

And indeed he left, and indeed she fell asleep, and in her sleep she heard a ring, which in reality was a telephone ring, and it was her sister ringing.

"Did Boris leave?" asked Yezdandukta.

"A long time ago," answered Petia.

"I made soup, and I'll take it to him."

Petia didn't try to determine where exactly Yezdandukta had made the soup—on the Metro or at work—but she marveled at the thought of homemakers who make soup right at the station.

"Don't worry about it," said Petia. "I made some soup myself. I'll just let it cool a little and take it to him."

"You made soup?" Yezdandukta's voice expressed genuine surprise.

And in order not to make her sister angry, Petia said amicably, "So you just keep working and don't worry—I'll take it to him myself."

"I'll be home soon," said Yezdandukta and hung up.

And Petia started cooking soup at an amazing rate. And cabbage and carrots started cooking at this rate along with potatoes, which were cooking at the same rate with which Petia was circling the pot, poking carrots with a knife—Is it cooked or isn't it?—and she still had the onions, which had to be sautéed separately, together with the tomatoes, of which she didn't have any. Finally, the carrots became tender and the onions golden, and it all became soup, which didn't have time to cool before Yezdandukta, who was going to "be home soon," came home. So Petia placed the little pot into a bigger pot into a cold tub, but all this was cooling so slowly that she took the small narrow pot and placed it into a wider pot and placed the shower head on the bottom of the wide pot and turned on the cold water, and when the soup had cooled off in the shower and a carrot started spinning in a liter glass jar, it looked like an aquarium with exotic fish that had to be fed, and Petia sprinkled some parsley on top, and when she was already on her way out the door, she bumped into her sister on her way in the door, and said, "There's soup in the pot I made."

And Boris wasn't at all surprised to get Petia's soup, and maybe he wasn't happy either. But they were both happy when they, having found themselves at the end of the line to get into the Yakor restaurant, were told that they would be served but to warn people not to get in line behind them. An hour later they were allowed to come in and warned that there wouldn't be time to serve them before the clean-up hour but that during the clean-up hour they would be given appetizers and wine and that after the clean-up hour they would be given the hot dish. And there was something else to be happy about: Those who'd had time to eat before the clean-up hour all left, the restaurant emptied out and began to resemble a deserted beach as well as the pages of French writers—Maupassant, Proust—as well as Russian writers—Bunin and everyone else. And this was something to be happy about until a woman with a broom and a dustpan showed up and started sweeping under the tables, and Petia said to Boris, "What do you want to bet that she'll say 'Pick up your feet'?"

But she didn't. Bent at the waist, she moved through the room without a sound. She was the wife of an alcoholic, mother of two, grandmother of three, aunt of one, and the bearer of an old noble name, which was a coincidence. And the fact that there wasn't even a hint of fish in this restaurant, and the fact that there wasn't even a hint of winter outside, and the fact that the cleaning woman was worn and dirty and the waitress girl was all skinny and weakly and was poking the champagne bottle open so awkwardly, and the fact that there were sturgeon bones hidden under the slice of sturgeon for an unknown reason—the reasons for all of this were unknown to anyone except the sovietikuses, who knew the reasons for this whole setup. The wine was called European, and it was a cheap, faceless wine, which may as well have been called Asian, African, American—

"When did they discover Australia?"—"In the 19th cent."—or 19th Cent. Australian wine: this wine was wine as a concept, just wine, not wine as a generalization that encompasses a variety of wines, the same way that cognac was a concept, just cognac, and there was only one vodka. And not just in the restaurant—right next door, in life, what was fruit? it was apples on the store shelves. The stores, unlike flora and fauna, were completely devoid of distinctions of kind, order, or breed, and there was only one sausage, which had no variations, kinds, orders, or breeds. But there were so many names of dishes on the menu! And if one imagined that each dish had a taste and a substance, then the appetizers were tasty and the dinner was substantial. Petia poked at the caviar and licked it off the egg without really tasting its substance. On the menu of Soviet life, as on this menu, names served as substitutes for substance; for example, a sweet name like Sturgeon Baked in a Pot was, in substance, pieces of some tasteless mystery fish that resembled sturgeon only in someone's very active imagination. But wine and champagne can inflame the imagination to such a degree that everything seems very tasty, and even sober cold stew seems drunk and aromatic. It's not like they'd come here to eat, after all! then why? just to hang out. They could have eaten at home—half a liter of soup each. But they hung out until people started coming; after the clean-up hour, there were as many people there as if they'd been showing a Western.

Petia and Boris left the restaurant to the sounds of an orchestra playing something that may well have been the anthem of the Soviet Union. The backdrop against which they were human beings was a street, and it was inconsequential that it was Gorky Street, because what was Gorky today had been Tverskaya yesterday and would be Lah-lah tomorrow, and everything would end and everything would change, and the only thing that would remain would be beauty (the landmark examples of art and architecture)—no, only love would remain, as the poet said when he was speaking the truth, and since the time when he said this—a hundred years later—love has remained while revolution has come and gone, leaving behind flags, prisons, and monuments, and the cult came and went, leaving behind monuments that were like prisons (and not at all like landmark examples of art and architecture), and what will be left tomorrow? flags?

3

On the last night before the New Year, having begged a book off of Kostroma for only one night, Petia had conscientiously digested it by morning, and only in the morning did it become clear to her that at the very beginning of the book Martyn received an anglophile upbringing so that in the end he would become a hero by moving to Russia despite the fact that the memories of it he had brought with him were automobile, tennis, soccer, rubber balls, and baths, which he liked, and were not the Pushkin nanny with her knitting and Russian folk wisdom, sayings, and riddles, which he didn't like. The book was a faint Xerox that had fallen victim to a binding job that hid parts of words, forcing the reader to guess that *-ch* was *which* and *-nt* was *runt*, if only because *cunt* would be as far away from the writer's mind as he was from Russia. But the book's appearance—the absence of margins, the ratty binding, the faint print—were so appropriate to its content, its pitifulness amplifying the nostalgia for Russia that, maybe, the publisher could have made some money by releasing some bad copies. And in the morning, when Petia's eyes began closing of their own accord, she thought that it wouldn't be so easy to make books badly at Ardis*, where they were used to making books well, but this "bad" book was so "alive" that Petia thought with tenderness of all that was bad but "alive": the ceiling, which was overly "alive" with its cracks and water stains, the wallpaper, the plumbing, and all sorts of little things, and she was already falling asleep when the telephone cut in with a ring that was so alive that it could have meant only two things: that her sister wasn't home, since she wasn't picking up, and that it was her sister calling, since she knew that Petia would pick up, which Petia did.

"Did you finish it?"

"Oh, it's you," said Petia.

"Let's say one o'clock at the school," said Kostroma.

Petia tried to postpone the meeting until five, but because this was not an ordinary day but New Year's eve, Kostroma said, "No, five would be too late. The book's not mine."

"All right, then three," said Petia.

So they settled on three. But before three Petia didn't fall asleep because the thought of having to be there at three wouldn't let her sleep, and she called Kostroma a couple of times to reschedule for one, but Kostroma wasn't there and she got angry at the complete futility of such a meeting on such an important day. In addition to this meeting, she had two important things to do: pick up the holiday food

---

* A U.S. publisher of Russian-language books.

VALERIYA NARBIKOVA

bonus at Yezdandukta's office, sew metal decorations on her dress, and meet Boris, with whom she had planned to bring in the New Year with Yezdandukta.

At three o'clock the meeting occurred: Petia handed over the book, Kostroma put it in his bag, and this would have been the end of it if Kostroma hadn't asked, "Where are you headed now?"

"I have to pick up the bonus at my sister's."

"And then what?"

"Finish the dress." And Petia told him about the dress: that it was made of pieces of fur and silk and was supposed to have these metal decorations that she hadn't had time to sew on. "What about you?" she asked.

"I'm going to Dyl's. We could go together."

"Where is he?"

"In the center of town."

Petia called from a pay phone and everything fell into place: Yezdandukta had already gotten the bonus, and Boris would come at eleven.

"Let's go," she said, because there was still time.

But it turned out that Dyl resided not in the center of town but in the center of the outskirts, because after they went there they kept going and going until they got to a huge Stalin-era building that was the only such building in the area. There was a park across from it, and there was a monument in the park. They entered the building, but not from the side of the entrances but from the side where there was a stairway built on the side, and at first they had to go up this stairway to a door, which Kostroma opened to a stairway that went sharply down into total darkness, where there was a door. Kostroma knocked and Dyl opened the door. This could hardly have been described as a room. But there were curtains and there were beds, of which there were, for some reason, four, and in the middle there was a painted old-fashioned school desk, and on the walls over the beds there were those things that they put flags into, and when Kostroma came in, he said, "Why did you stick sticks in the flaginas?" because there were fir-tree branches sticking out of the holes.

"Because," answered Dyl.

"You gonna sleep on needles?"

"I'll sleep on another one."

Petia walked around and looked around and this was not a room but something gross, and she just asked Dyl, "Why are there so many beds?"

"Four people can live here," Dyl explained.

"Who do you live with?" asked Petia, who had never before been interested in Dyl's life.

"By myself," answered Dyl. "But I pay for four."

"So you pay four times as much?"

"No, twice as much."

"Why?" Petia was surprised. "If it's five rubles for one, then it should be twenty for four."

"I pay thirty."

"So you pay more than four times as much?"

"No. Exactly twice as much, because it's fifteen each."

"I wonder who rents this out."

Kostroma got some fabulous bottle out of his bag, and at this point Petia may have lost interest because she didn't repeat the question and Dyl didn't repeat the answer.

Kostroma started opening the beautiful vessel while Petia opened the curtains to discover that there were no windows and the curtains hung on the bare walls.

"There are no windows," said Dyl.

"That's scary," said Petia.

"I was scared, too. That's why I hung the curtains."

Dyl, who was so pretty, living in such an unpretty place was not a pretty picture.

"Where did you live before?"

"On the shore," joked Dyl, but, jokes aside, he could have lived on the shore before.

It was hard to be joyous in such a joyless place, and Kostroma, who may have been trying to get Petia to enjoy herself, said that he and Dyl had decided to make an andy-baby. She started asking about the andy-baby, and Kostroma started explaining that he and Dyl wanted a baby but they weren't homos, and Dyl wasn't a woman, and Kostroma wasn't a girl, and by March they would track down a black chicken and steal its egg, and whoever got to it first would fertilize this egg or maybe they'd both shoot into it, and then they'd look after this egg and then they'd have a monster of their own, and then they'd be happy whereas now they were unhappy without an andy-baby. And when Kostroma wrote *android* in Greek, Petia realized that she was getting limp from the port and then she managed to think *borisus* in Latin, whereupon she fell asleep...As it happened, there were one too many beds and in his sleep Dyl thought that he saw Kostroma sleeping on two beds at the same time in two bodies, but of the three of them Kostroma was the only one who didn't sleep at all that night, on any bed and in any

VALERIYA NARBIKOVA

body. At first he thought that he should wake up Petia and take her home and then he thought that it would be better not to think about it.

Anything can be the case except what cannot be the case. At midnight the clock's hands kept going but Petrarka didn't come. So Boris and Yezdandukta filled their glasses. And had a drink. And wished each other—what? A Happy New Year, that's what. That's the kind of holiday it is—people drink, wish each other a Happy New Year, and go home. Which they didn't. Supper followed. The two of them ate everything and went to bed with full stomachs. He screwed Petrarka's sister, and there can be no memory of this. Boris remembered this around six in the morning, in a three-ruble private car, around eight. He and Yezdandukta had woken up in the same bed and he hadn't even known what to say to her, the same way that he hadn't known what to say to her before he did it, and he did it because he didn't know what else to say, but after he did it, he didn't know what else to do and what to say, so he fell asleep and by the time he woke up there was nothing left to do and nothing left to say. And when the car stopped at a light and he looked up at the red light, he remembered it all in this light: that Yezdandukta had been a virgin. He even remembered her admission that he was her first. She dropped it so matter-of-factly that it sounded like people get new hymens every year and at that moment it sounded to him like he was her first in the new year, which was understandable, especially since the clock hand had only gone halfway around. But now he suddenly realized that this admission was not made in the new year, that it was made in general. There had been every sign that he was her first. The only sign that hadn't been there was he. He had clearly been absent from this incident and from what she said and he said and she asked and he said and, having said it, fell asleep. A virgin at thirty-five in the new year at forty in eighty-five, and in the mouth, too.

Still, it's odd that everything can be going one way, going along and then stopping and then something else entirely starts going. Petia opened her eyes, but it was so dark and there was no sign of light that she shut her eyes. Then she opened them again, and again it was dark. In this darkness, where she couldn't even see anything, she understood where she was. And stirred. Then a light went on, but it was small. And the people were small and their shadows were big. And the shadows were smoking. These enlarged shadows exhaled and the smoke was a shadow of itself.

"We slept through the New Year," said Kostroma.

"What time is it?" asked Petia.

"Seven of one."

"One what?"

"One eighty five."

"Idiot," said Petia.

She said it and started crying. She cried so hard that it was hard for Kostroma even and hard even for Dyl. She cried at the desk, smearing her makeup all over her face, she slumped over the desk with her face in her sleeve and shoved Kostroma with her elbow when he tried to sit down next to her, and then, having cried her eyes out, she slammed the desk top.

"Is there water here?" she asked Dyl.

"Over there," he said.

And she went over there. Over there was a toilet and a shower—all stuffed into one closet, all trashed and fucked up but she didn't give a fuck.

"Take me home," Petia asked Kostroma.

"You just fell asleep," said Kostroma. "What's so terrible about that? You'll tell him, and he'll understand."

She said, "Idiot," again and he quit trying to comfort her. But he took her home, where Yezdandukta opened the door and Kostroma left. Yezdandukta had no intention of concealing anything. She told everything right away, but everything seemed so unbelievable that Petia didn't believe her. Yezdandukta said that she'd never done anything with anyone and that Boris was her first and that they did it that night for the first time. Petia was shocked that Yezdandukta and Boris did it, but the very assertion that her sister was a virgin was shocking. This was more an aspersion than an assertion. And Petia sat down in the kitchen and stayed sitting. And then later she was in her room and stayed lying. And she tried to think but she couldn't think of anything. She thought that she wouldn't have killed her even if Yezdandukta weren't her sister, because Yezdandukta was an idea and how could you kill an idea? And another idea: He didn't want to but she wanted to, and it all just happened, she didn't want to and he wanted to, and it happened, they both didn't want to, and it happened. She tortured herself like that.

Having spent half the day in bed like this, having cried her eyes out, washed up, and started crying again by evening, Petia was saying to herself, "But I love him, I love him terribly, and he loves me, and we love each other, so why is everything so awful?" She went to Boris's, and it's not even clear how she got there: when she left the house, she didn't know yet that she was going to Boris's, and when she answered her sister's question by saying, "For a walk," she had no idea that she

VALERIYA NARBIKOVA

was going to his house. It took her a rather long time of using different means of transportation, which didn't even represent the fastest way of getting there, and at first she was not even going to his house but in his general direction. And once she found herself in his general vicinity, she then somehow found herself at his house, and when she saw that his light was on, she got so happy that when she showed up on his doorstep she was boundlessly happy. Boris was surprised at all this happiness, which he didn't understand. There is only one way to say "I love you" but there are many different ways to say "I'm angry," because there aren't many reasons to say "I love you"—in fact, there is only one reason, which is love—whereas there are many reasons to say "I'm angry"—too many to say them all at once. Boris at once said he wanted the reason Petia didn't come on New Year's, and Petia immediately said the reason was that she "just fell asleep." This reason didn't sound like the main reason to him and it sounded to him like the main reason was behind this reason, and the main reason was that she was "really sleepy." None of this was any reason not to come to New Year's, but there was no other reason. But when Petia told Boris that she knew everything because her sister had told her everything and begged Boris to give her just one reason this happened, Boris said, "I don't even know—no reason."

That this was followed by "love" was bad—that is, during "love" it was "good," but it didn't get better following love. And even after Petia swore to Boris that she loved him and only him and would never love another, this promise didn't make Boris feel better, because it would have been better without this promise because he had felt better before, when she didn't say this and things were good. And when she asked, "Is this good for you?" and he said, "It's good," this wasn't the best answer, and when after this she said, "But do you feel better now?" and he said, "Maybe better," she thought that really he felt worse because she herself felt worse, and she decided to go home, because she thought that would be better.

And when she was going home alone because she'd said there was no need to take her home and no need to catch a cab, and when she got off the Metro, she was horrified by the thought of how horribly she wanted to stop loving him. She knew that she loved him and only him and would never love another. That's exactly why she wanted to stop loving him—so that she would never love anyone. She knew for a fact that she would never love another, and so she wanted to stop loving him forever. She decided that she would try her hardest to stop loving him so that she would never love anyone. And this powerful thought sapped all her energy, and she fell asleep because she didn't have the energy to read more than a few pages by a powerful writer from a powerless country.

4

What began as a joke for Dyl and Kostroma soon became no laughing matter, namely the matter of acquiring an andy-baby. It's a fact that the first day of a March moon occurs in March. There has never been a March that didn't have a March moon. And there has never been a moon that didn't exist in March. Kostroma bought the chicken ahead of time at a bird market, albeit a black one, since the chicken also had to be black. He took it to his grandfather's country house and kept it in his room. But she wasn't laying anything. At least she hadn't laid any yet. Kostroma reported this to Dyl, who became concerned: "Think it's dyed?"

"Why would it be dyed?"

"Think it's old?"

"What difference would it make whether it's young or old? I was thinking, maybe it's a hermaphrodite?"

"I doubt it," said Dyl. "Let's wait a bit more—maybe it will lay one. If not, we'll sell it and get another one."

So they waited. Nothing. The next Sunday Dyl went to the market, but even the black market didn't have any black chickens. They decided not to sell the chicken and wait for the first day of the March moon. As the calendar would have it, this day coincided with the grandfather's birthday. Kostroma was surprised at the coincidence. But Dyl said that this was no coincidence because if they'd decided to make the andy-baby the previous year then the days wouldn't have coincided, because the first day of the March moon moves around while grandfather's birthday stays in place, and the following year they wouldn't coincide either.

"But we decided to make the andy-baby this year," said Kostroma. "So it's a coincidence."

It started snowing. They were standing in the garden in front of the country house, looking up at the sky in which they couldn't see the moon, which was hanging around somewhere behind the clouds.

"There isn't any coincidence because nothing's going to happen," said Dyl. "Have we got an egg?"

"It will get laid—today."

"What's the occasion for that—your grandfather's birthday? I'd cancel birthdays for grandfathers like that altogether."

"And what would the occasion for that be?"

"The occasion of his putting my grandmother and grandfather you know where."

"As a member of the party, he was carrying out the orders of the party."

"I'd cancel birthdays for parties like that too."

Suddenly there was a flicker of the moon in the sky under the snow—that is, it looked like it was snowing right on the moon. And then they heard so much clucking that Dyl and Kostroma ran from the garden and into the house. And sure enough—it'd laid an egg. It was full like the moon and it even had some smoky clouds that looked like moon mountains that you can look at from Earth.

It turned out that it's easy to start loving and not at all easy to stop loving because Petia fell in love with Boris for no reason and she had to stop loving him for a reason and this wasn't so easy. When Petia loved Boris, she didn't realize how many things she loved about him; she didn't love his appearance and his actions and his talent separately because she loved him wholly, as in *borisus*. But when she decided she should stop loving him, she had to stop loving everything separately—his face separately from his art separately from everything else. When she told herself that she didn't love his face and didn't love kissing his face, she started loving his art even more and was ready to start kissing the Kolomensky Temple in a box. But when she told herself that she no longer loved his art, that it had all been done before in art, that she loved the art of the canon, then she wanted more than anything else to love him separately from his art and against all canons. Basically, Petia didn't know how to stop loving Boris. Sometimes it seemed to her that this was simply impossible, and then she started hating him because she loved him so much. Love had been but one feeling, but trying to stop loving him turned into an endless pit of feelings. Basically, trying to stop loving felt the worst, worse than any feeling, except maybe the feeling of having no feelings.

She got worse. The first time she got worse was when she found herself at Dyl's for the second time. His hole hadn't changed a bit except what was now sticking out of the flaginas looked less like branches and more like sticks, and the desk had been shoved over to the side, but the curtains were the same, and everything else was the same and in the same place. On their way there, Dyl had told Petia that soon he and Kostroma would have their own andy-baby— "Remember, Kostroma told you at New Year's?" Reminding Petia about New Year's was a crime on Dyl's part, but for her part, Petia shouldn't have been on her way all the way out to Dyl's place, because Dyl's place was the scene of the crime, because it had been a crime on her part not to come home at New Year's.

"Tell me about it," asked Petia.

And Dyl happily started telling her that andy-baby was growing and would soon be hatched, and then they'd be happy.

The egg was sitting in a pile of manure, and they'd eaten the chicken. "Did you kill it?"

"It happened all wrong," said Dyl. "Kostroma and I had planned to kill her the right way, like you're supposed to."

"Which is how?"

"Which is how it says in the book, the manual for slaughtering domestic animals, but his grandfather got ahead of us. It tells you everything: The right way to kill a cow, a chicken, a pig, so it's not painful for them and it's not painful for people to watch."

"So his grandfather killed it?"

"Seems like he killed her in such a brutal manner that she swallowed her tongue. I think he tortured her to get her to tell him everything."

"What?" said Petia.

"Everything she knew. You know what her skin looked like when his grandfather finished plucking her? Kostroma said it was like a mulatto's, and grandfather said he was going to make soup."

"Did you eat it?"

"I ate a little."

"Did it taste good?"

"Nah."

By the end of the story it was already the beginning of April, during which Petia and Boris never saw each other—that is, there was never a time in April when they ever saw each other—and so April came and went, and then came May, and as soon as Petia came to Boris's, right away she noticed a new work of art, but she didn't ask about it right away because right away she asked, "Do you love me?"

"I love you," he said.

"I love you forever," said Petia. "I love you more than you love me."

"I thought you didn't love me anymore."

"I love you more than anyone else in the whole world."

"You are lying to me."

"If I stop loving you, I'll never love another."

And Boris said, "You will."

And she said, "I won't."

And he said, "Yes."

And she said, "No."

And he said, "What are we arguing about?"

"I was unfaithful to you," said Petia.

"Why?"

"I did it on purpose."

"Why?"

"So I'd be worse."

Petia said that when everyone around her got worse she had to get worse, too, and if everything got better all by itself then she'd get better, too.

"It will never get better all by itself," said Boris.

"But you were unfaithful to me, too," said Petia.

"But I didn't do it on purpose," said Boris.

And during the act, she demanded to know whether he'd enjoyed himself during the act with Yezdandukta—"Did you do the same thing with her as with me?"—and to shut her up, to make it so she wouldn't say another word, he put it in her mouth, and with her mouth full, she said, "I love you."

This was the last thing he heard, because when he saw that she was no longer in the room, he heard the door shut.

The fact that Boris was Petia's love and the fact that Petia was his love were inarguable. She loved him, yes. He loved her, yes. But love didn't love Petia and Boris—historically, love had not loved them. *Historically* not in the sense of stories—romantic, sentimental, or realistic ones—but historically in the sense of the history to which they bore witness, and as witnesses they could testify that this historical moment was not too auspicious for their love. Of course, theoretically, it's possible to love during practically any historical period, which is what they did—they loved—but love didn't love them, being historically in opposition to them, because on New Year's Eve Petia had been reading a book that could have been a household book, meaning that it would be in every household, in which case there would be no need to digest it in one night, but this book wasn't in every household or in every other household but in the other man's household, even though the writer, whom Petia loved, loved his country, which was far away from him, and the country loved its writer, who was far away from it because both the country and the writer were Russian, but the writer distanced himself from the country, the Russian way, and the country distanced itself from the writer the English way. And the fact that love, historically, did not love Petia and Boris, was bad; it was also bad that love loved them pornographically—meaning what?—meaning generic characters in a generic setting in the act of lovemaking.

Suddenly, at dusk, an internal force caused the egg to explode with andy-baby's appearance the shell turned to dust in a single moment. There was the force, there was the shell, the shell splattered—and *bang!*—Kostroma had never seen anything like this, and Dyl never saw anything like it, and when Kostroma started telling about it, Dyl started asking questions.

"Like dust," said Kostroma.

"You said before, like a fountain."

"It splattered like a fountain, but what was in the air was glass dust, and when the dust settled—"

"Too bad I wasn't there."

"You know car windows shatter at high speed?"

"The speed of light?"

"Not necessarily the speed of light—the speed of 80 km an hour."

"Oh, yeah! Incredible speed," laughed Dyl.

"Don't you laugh. For our cars it is incredible, and on impact glass shatters and turns to dust."

"Regular glass?"

"No, not regular glass. I forget what it's called."

"But the shell wasn't glass. Glass is chemical, and the shell was organic."

"How do you know what the shell was made of?"

"I know."

"So what's it made of?"

"Egg shell."

"That's the thing. Seems that andy-baby was writhing around inside the egg at an incredible speed."

"You know what it's like?" asked Dyl. "Think about it." And after thinking about it, he said, "It's unlike anything."

"Looks like it," concurred Kostroma.

"It's not even possible to imagine," said Dyl.

"Imagine: the shell turns to dust, and andy-baby is standing there."

"And then what?"

"You won't let me finish," said Kostroma. "Then he disappeared somewhere. He just hatched and disappeared, and I didn't even get a good look at him."

"Well, is he vertical? Like a person?"

"So what if he's vertical? A chicken is vertical too, standing on two feet—but it's not a person."

"But what's he look like at least?"

"I'm telling you, I didn't get a good look," said Kostroma. "I didn't have time, plus it was dusk, and what can you see in the dusk?"

What happens in the dusk is testimony to the fact that nature has no color, only the concept of sunlight, the physical mystery of the eye, the shifting of the spectrum in fog when yellow looks reddish and green looks yellowish, and what of the traffic sign that warns of a road narrowing—does it denote the narrowing of the road in perspective rather than the physical narrowing of the road? And an object at dusk is undefined in that it lacks clear definition—that is, its outline pulsates and the object breathes *optically* at dusk, and it is this *optical breathing*, rather than color or shape, that indicates the presence of the object and the near-absence of distinction between an inanimate object and an animate object, or the absence of—having lost its color, the chair loses its weight and its legs become thinner and the table's corners soften. And Kostroma stared at the ceiling at dusk, which arrived an hour later this time, because this time was in May and the last time was in April. He heard a radio somewhere far away, but he couldn't tell not only where it was but what it was saying. And he stretched toward the sound, and the sound turned out to be nearby even though it sounded like the radio was far away somewhere. The sound was right next to the couch, but Kostroma was looking for the sound on the ceiling when in fact it was on the floor, and when Kostroma shifted his eyes from the ceiling to the floor, he saw andy-baby, who was making the very sounds that sounded like the radio. The resemblance was striking: it sounded like a far-away station that's being jammed, and it was impossible to tell what language it was in, but it was clearly human speech, or at least speech resembling human speech. Kostroma listened to andy-baby talking and looked at him. He was hard enough to hear and even harder to see, but Kostroma was able to see that he seemed to be folded in half along the nose line: in profile the little monster looked enough like a person, but when he looked him straight in the face, he appeared as a fuzzy line, and the very concept of looking "straight in the face" became a bit fuzzy; this line had no eyes, mouth, ears, or anything. So just as Kostroma was silent before andy-baby appeared in the room, he didn't say a word to him, and the next day he didn't even breathe a word to Dyl, because he wanted Dyl to see and hear everything for himself, so he said, "Let's go to my place."

"Can't hear you," said Dyl.

And Kostroma didn't say anything to that.

5

The summer was short like a winter day, like a flash in the pan, fly-by-night, by all accounts it was soon nothing but a memory of summer, a summer that came and went, that ended as soon as it began, like a summer shower, which was soon replaced by the autumn shower, which starts during the day and lasts long enough to cover the autumn evening, which is long enough that the rain is frozen by morning and stays in the air like snow—no, not like snow: it really is snow rather than a likeness of snow, because it is now really winter, not to be likened to anything but last winter, which was not as cold, white, clean, and good as this winter, which is, on the contrary, definitely worse than the last.

Petia still loved Boris but hadn't seen him since the last time he had seen her. She didn't see Boris, but she heard a lot about him from Yezdandukta, and Boris was hearing a lot about Petia from Yezdandukta, but it's better to see once than to hear a hundred times, so in late winter, when Petia heard about him from her sister again in early spring, she went to see him that very day.

If consciousness is superficial, then what's it like? smoking is bad for you but dying is good, good to pump the last drops of energy out of the earth, good to split the atom, good to go faster and faster, farther and farther, to build the kind of plaster nightmares that the future of humankind, which will be approaching extinction, will have as a monument for the rest of its time, a monument to power, as in nuclear power, a monument built by whom?—well, whom?—by us. What do we need water for? To drink it. No, for the monument to drink it, and we can drink what's left over, except that nothing's left over—not for us, not for the fishes, not for the flowers—but look at him, the man of the future: naked, wearing headphones, holding a bomb because he has armed himself in order to disarm his opponent—but who is his opponent? he himself, disarming himself—and where is he going? he is going back from the future into the present, and soon we are going to meet. Hello!

"Hello," said Petia to Boris.

She had accomplished a lot in a year of trying to kill her love; what was left was passion. She had pumped out the love and pumped up the passion, like in the country where we live, which is divided into sixteen colonies, which are definitely colonies, because only colonies can be pumped mercilessly like this, like from the Baikal and Siberia, from the Baltics and Ukraine—we pump everything we've annexed. And we are getting pumped like one giant colony, which consists of

VALERIYA NARBIKOVA

sixteen colonies, including oil, animals, water, hell—everything!—"I can't live like this! Now what?"

"What did you say?"

"What?"

Is it nature that's sick all over? No, it's man that's sick all over himself, all over his heart—but who's healthy? life is evaluated when it is over. We are disintegrating! Not only do we not love—we don't listen, we don't look, we don't want to see,—"I can't live like this!"

"Did you say something?"

"What?"

Boris had done a new painting and hung it up; it was simple like any masterpiece, but it wasn't a masterpiece just because it was simple. It was painted on a magnetic piece of metal. On a light blue background that was almost white, there was a path that wound as though in the air, and in its most invulnerable spot, almost at the horizon line, Boris had attached a little island made out of thumbtacks, which flashed fiercely in the rays of the setting sun, and there were little human footprints on this path, but there was no human in the painting, as though he had just walked on the path and left fresh footprints, and it was as though he had walked on the thumbtacks as well and there were footprints on the horizon line in the corner of the painting, where the thumbtacks ended, and these footprints were all sticky, wet, and bloody, and some of the thumbtacks, where he had stepped, were bloody too. Petia didn't tell Boris anything about her love, because her love had been like a flash in the pan, fly-by-night, by all accounts it was now nothing but a memory of love, a love that came and went, that ended as soon as it began, and in this memory they were both cleaner and better.

Petia walked around and looked around and said, "You've done a lot of work and gotten a lot done."

"Yeah, I've done a little work," said Boris.

"Is it true that you want to marry Yezdandukta?" asked Petia.

"Did she tell you that?" asked Boris.

"I want you to tell me."

"She is a good person," said Boris.

"Do you love her?"

"I love her as a person."

"Remember I told you that I'll never love anyone again?" said Petia. And Boris answered, "You will anyway."

"No," said Petia. "Never. Because I don't want to."

"Someday you'll want to anyway."

"We're going to die anyway," said Petia.

"Someday we'll die."

In the light of a sunset that was real and not painted, they were both alive and not painted, and the love that had historically not loved them was real and not pretend, and Petia and Boris hugged in a way that was simple and not complicated. They simply hugged to say good-bye, which followed hello, which had come and gone, which ended as soon as it began, and after Petia left and took a few steps on the boulevard, she returned with such passion and she and Boris started kissing until it got dark and then until it got light. And at dawn, when she was barely alive from love, Petia said to Boris, who was nearly dead, "Why am I thinking about war—why? Do you think there's going to be a war?"

"No. I try not to think."

The street sweeper started shoveling snow over their heads as though they were underground, which in fact they were, as though he were burying them, and Petia never said to Boris "I love you" even once all night, and he didn't say "And I you."

Are we not dead because we are still alive, or are we still alive because we are not yet dead?

There were many familiar faces but it was hard to tell who was who—like in a dream. And the temple, where Kostroma was standing and where people were crowding, was flooded with this cool light, and some of the grates had ice on them, and it was sad, and there were many fresh flowers, like at a funeral, and when they carried in the stretcher and were carrying it over people's heads, everyone saw a person sitting on it, and the person's face was distorted by makeup—that is, part of his face was covered by a mask that had been put together sloppily of pieces of cardboard, cotton, and thumbtacks, and his skin was covered with chalk. His head was out of proportion to his body, as though his body belonged to a different head or the head to a different body. And when they carried this in on the stretcher, there was a whisper—"Linen, Linen"—but the head looked nothing like the Linen on the coins or on the medals or on the posters—or the Linen on the medals looked nothing like this Linen. And then they turned off the light, and when they then directed a stream of light so that the head cast a gigantic shadow on the wall, and the shadow was the exact Linen profile, everyone recognized Linen. And they carried the stretcher around the room along the walls, and people started throwing flowers up in the air, showering Linen's shadow with the shadows of flowers. A funeral dirge sounded, and it had a vulgar twist. This

226   VALERIYA NARBIKOVA

twist—this vulgar effect—was created by the shattering of symbols—that is, when the cymbals came in over the tooting of the horn, the cymbals shattered into a hundred pieces. The sound of symbols shattering during a funeral dirge woke Kostroma up, and when someone pinched him hard on the thigh because he was wearing his underwear to a funeral, he woke from the pinch, and he was indeed wearing underwear.

It was snowing outside the window, and it was morning while just a minute earlier in the dream it had been night. Kostroma thought about Petia and about the fact that she had many men and that different people had told him that they had seen her in different cities with different men at the same time. And Kostroma thought about how different Petia was, and then he thought that she was always the same and only the men were different and then that the men were the same and she was different. Then he thought that the cities were different and then that the cities were the same, and then he thought the same thing that he'd thought in the first place except all at once—at the same time. And he was so thirsty and so loath to get up that he took a deep breath of air, which was fresh and cold like water, and he thought that when we don't have enough water, we need it like air, and when we don't have enough air, we need it like water, and when we don't have enough bread, we need it like water and air, and we can do without everything else, but he couldn't do without water, and he went to take a drink, and then he kept going and going and going, and then spring came and the snow began to melt and the sun began to shine and the birds began to fly and the wind began to blow and the girls began to— and Yezdandukta told Petia that she was marrying Boris in the summer.

6

Summer was at the height of summertime. No one had gone anywhere this summer: not to the seashore or anywhere. People were walking around in the rain, carrying umbrellas to protect themselves from the rain and not from the sun, and when it started clearing, every object took on sharp definition in the sunlight, and when Yezdandukta showed up in the doorway in the morning and said, "Today," Petia know that meant that today there had been a transfer of power. And even though Boris still had power over Petia, there had been a transfer of state power with one power structure departing and another arriving—and what was one to expect? after all, any new power structure is an unrealized old one. And the old power structure was the dark side of love that had accomplished nothing. Let there be new life! let it be better, cleaner, and richer! let it be! long live the king after the king is dead! what does that mean? that means that Yezdandukta went from sister to wife, and Boris went from lover to husband, and Petia went from lover to sister—what a change! and there was an acceleration of blood flow, and blood was rushing and flapping like a bird, and could it be that soon we would all fly? it would be better if we all took a flying leap instead of taking flight.

"Today?" Petia asked Yezdandukta. "Yesterday you told me that it would be tomorrow, and now it's today already."

This was the beginning of the end already!

Petia didn't have to spend much time looking for Kostroma and Dyl; they were in place, and Petia, having informed them that it was "today," undertook a taxi offensive. The world can be conquered, but only in a taxi—not in an airplane or a tank, which are the wrong means of transportation for conquering the world.

"Drivers of Taxi Park Five, do you recognize me?" "Yes, yes, yes!" The world can be conquered only by the meter—a kopeck for a kopeck, a ruble for a ruble, an eye for an eye, a tooth for a tooth!

They flew in the taxi and conquered Europe, Italy, and the America that's beyond the horizon in the newspaper, the newspaper being precisely the horizon that shields everything that's beyond the horizon.

Be happy, ye conquered nations whose lives will be paid for by the meter, be healthy!

"Don't drive yourself crazy," said Kostroma to Petia. "What do you need him for—Boris!"

"I need him because, and he me, and the two of us, and if only we—"

"Don't cry," said Kostroma.

"How can it be," said Petia, "that even the smallest mistake is the end and even the smallest infidelity is the end?"

"You'll marry someone else," said Kostroma.

"Never," said Petia. "I'll never love again."

"You will," said Kostroma.

And the taxi was flying like a bird, like a plane, where are you taking me? do tell!

And when they ran out of fuel and when the driver said how much, none of the conquered people could see any of their conquerors, who'd made a ring around Moscow on the Ring Road; the people were carrying heavy bags to the store and full bags from the store; their arms felt like they were about to break; they walked in the rays of the setting sun, and there were red rays on their faces along with yellow and pink rays and the entire spectrum of rays to which their skin was receptive, and they walked the way that was almost the same way they had walked yesterday, thinking not about the transfer of power but about the beginning—the beginning of next week—because power had been transferred in a peaceful manner, by the meter, paid for by the passenger. Long live peace!

And the new life got under way in the way of long-forgotten old life—like the time when Petia stayed at Boris's house for the first time and there was a whole world of stars outside the window, she now stayed at his house not like that time, because this time was after her sister's wedding, and the stars shone like that time, but this time Petia lay under the blanket like the sister of her married sister and Boris lay with Yezdandukta like the husband of Petia's sister. But all the sisters and brothers up in the sky, pagan ancestors' brides and grooms, were all in their own constellations, living lives that didn't change. The meaning of this is that the stars above stay the same when the people underneath change. And so they lived—Petia at Boris's instead of Boris, and Boris at Yezdandukta's instead of Petia. "What if Yezdandukta loves him like she loves me?" thought Petia, "and Boris loves her like I love her, and Boris loves me like he loves me, and I love him like I love him?" Less than a month later, Petia found out what Boris's love for her was like. When Petia saw Boris in the doorway when she was getting ready for sleep already, he said he had come to get the colored chalks and started going through the drawers and couldn't find the box. And Petia put on a sweater and started looking for the chalks, too. They never found anything. There weren't any chalks. Petia sat down on the bed and started drinking milk out of the carton.

"Want some wine?" asked Boris.

He opened a bottle, and she drank some from the bottle.

"Should I bring a glass?" asked Boris.

"Bring one for yourself."

So Petia drank out of the bottle and Boris drank out of a glass. She had no doubt that love would follow the wine. They still loved each other despite the fact that love didn't love them—that is, they loved each other physically, not platonically—never like Plato, never like a man loves a man, never like Socrates loved Socrates—and when they had physically tired of love, Boris left and returned not less than a month later, when, physically, fall had already passed and winter had ended when nothing could change physically in their love any longer, when at dawn one day Petia suddenly woke to the monotonous sound of a radio that was on somewhere outside the window. And she opened her eyes and saw andy-baby—whom she only knew existed because

Kostroma had told her—standing in front of her. He stood there, and she could hear that he was talking but couldn't tell what he was saying. Suddenly, he said in perfect Russian, "Hand over the medals."

"What?" said Petia.

And he repeated harshly, "Hand over the medals."

"What medals?" asked Petia, even though she got it right away: the ones that flashed in the moonlight that time, the ones she had half of and Boris had half.

"Medals?" said Petia.

Andy-baby shot the word *medals* into her ear, possibly shattering her eardrum, because there was definitely an explosion in her ear. And Petia brought out a sweater that was all covered with medals, and andy-baby shook the sweater, and the medals flashed and fell to the floor with the first rays of the sun that flashed on the medals. Andy-baby got the rest of the medals without even bothering to wake up Boris; he just showed up by his bed in Petia's room, where Boris slept, and, after toying with Boris for a bit with some easy-listening music, he branded Boris's memory with seven exact-time beeps, which made Boris shiver in his sleep, but it was as if andy-baby had never been there.

Having come upon a sleeping Kostroma, andy-baby came up close and got talkative.

"Go knock off your grandfather."

"No," said Kostroma.

"He is a bastard," said andy-baby.

"I'm no bastard—to knock off a bastard."

"He knocked people off," said andy-baby. "Go knock him off."

"Then it will never end: we started knocking people off and we can stop, because it's time to knock off knocking people off."

"Then I'll knock you off."

"Knock it off."

And andy-baby pierced Kostroma's body with the pins from the medals. He used the medals to pin his insides to his skin. And he used the diamond pin to pierce his heart. And he dragged him down to the river and let him go with the current. And Kostroma started floating. He floated in gasoline circles, of which there were plenty in the water. And when Kostroma's funeral was over, when his body had floated off and the cries of the people seeing his body off had almost faded, because it was already late winter, his body, floating into the distance, was covered with junk—with Little Oktiabrist star pins and Young Communist pins and factory pins all over, all over other unprecious metals, all over at the end of March.

VALERIYA NARBIKOVA

Touched: Little Stories

NINA SADUR

Nina Sadur is best known as a playwright, a leader in post-perestroika Russian theater. But her now best-known play, Chudnaya Baba *(which has been staged in the United States under the title* Wonderbroad*) was banned for years for what the censor termed "mysticism." The "little stories" that follow, combining the most socialist-realistic of details and language with an ever-present mystical "it," can be read as an ironic answer to the censor. In the introduction to these stories in the anthology* She Who Bears No Ill, *Sadur writes:*

"Why wasn't my fiction published?

"Because it couldn't be. It's harmful.

"I know the term to break through. The term social layer. The term socialist realism."

She has refused to "do" socialist realism in order to break through to the social layer of comfortable, approved writers. Now, she writes, "It has become fashionable to resurrect the landmarks of our culture from the ashes, to use old blueprints to build demolished cathedrals where nothing is left. Does that mean we are going to live surrounded by replicas? Gradually, the copies will grow over with time and we will forget that there was ever an original. It's better than an empty space. Every people has to have a culture. And we will."

By taking up the topic of the unknowable "it"—which was an integral part of the Russian literary tradition before socialist realism was decreed the only acceptable way to write—and by taking it up in the style most familiar to Soviet readers, by placing it in the most mundane of the details of their lives, Sadur is committing herself to building this new culture, to filling the empty spaces within it.

Nina Sadur was born in Novosibirsk in 1950 to a poet and a teacher and graduated from the Literary Institute in 1983. She lives in Moscow with her mother and her daughter, who is also a writer. In her one-paragraph autobiographical statement on the back cover of her collection of plays, Chudnaya Baba *(Moscow, 1991), Sadur wrote, "I have basically never been published." Her fiction has since appeared in many journals and a few anthologies. She was nominated for the 1993 Booker Prize for her novel* South. *Her plays are now being staged throughout Russia and the former*

Soviet Union. In the face of her newfound recognition, she writes, "Unfortunately, I can forget nothing. I remember everything." —*M. G.*

There is something to all this, of course. You can't tell what right away, can't even say what exactly is strange, different from ordinary life, unlike anything that we do in life—and if you bury yourself in real life, then you don't even have to notice that *it* is always with us, watching our every move. It is like summer air: at first it looks normal, clear—but then suddenly everything tenses and shudders as though you were looking not at reality but at a picture of reality, but really it is just hot air swaying, weaving, and streaming.

But humans need to run away from it, and our age, the most truthful and humane of ages in its relationship to the human being, has closed its eyes to it, to protect the human being from phenomena that are hard to understand and have no application in life.

Those who insist on trying to touch *it* are lost souls. They will either go insane or die or drink themselves into oblivion.

It Glistened

Here is what happened to this girl I knew at the trade school. She had a guy, Alik Gorokhov. To look at him, he was pretty plain. At the summerhouse, where they met, she didn't even notice him. Plus, he was there with his girl. They sat there making shish kebab. Truth be told, my Olga is a determined kind of girl, and she doesn't waste any time. So she sat there relaxing and checking out the young men who'd gathered for the shish kebab. Suddenly, she felt this stare. She looked over and saw Alik looking at her. Well, my Olga just snorted—he was all skinny, all kind of gray, with just his nose red from the cold. She had a little to drink and then went out the gate to walk by the lake. She heard someone about to catch up with her—and somehow she knew right away that it was Alik, chasing after her.

"What do you want?" said Olga.

"Nothing," answered Alik.

So they walked down to the lake. Olga hates being pursued by young men she didn't pick herself. Olga's a looker, she dresses well (her mother works in a department store), and the way she is, she doesn't hurt for male attention.

"What do you do?" Olga asked him.

He answered that he'd tried to get into aviation school but didn't get enough points on the exams and now he'd get swept up by the military.

By the time they got to the lake, it was late and pretty cold. They wandered around the beach. There were no people around—just dogs running around checking them out.

And by the time they got back, everyone had gotten drunk and Alik's girl was sitting motionless by the fire. She wasn't bad-looking either. She'd been sitting by the fire when those two were strolling about the lake, and when the gate shut she didn't even turn her head. As for Alik, he walked through the gate and stopped short as soon as he remembered about his lady.

"I have to see her home," he said to Olga. "But I'll call you tomorrow."

"That's the last thing I need," said my Olga.

"Give me your number," said Alik, and Olga gave it to him just to get rid of him.

He got his lady and they left.

Then he started calling Olga, and when she didn't have anyone, she'd agree to see him. They would go out, see a movie, sometimes drink a bit, and Olga was bored to death. Meanwhile, he kept trying to talk her into marrying him.

Then one time they went to somebody's house, and Olga saw this cool guy and started hanging all over him and then got drunk and kicked Alik out. When she woke up the next morning, she remembered the whole thing and decided to call him just in case, being that he was a person after all.

She called and he said that everything was fine, everything was good, and everything was cool. Another month went by. Olga and the guy, naturally, split up, and she was waiting for Alik to call because she didn't like being alone. She'd been bored with him, sure, but she was used to him anyway, and so she was waiting.

But he wasn't calling. Olga got all mad, waited a bit more, and then called him herself. They got together and went out as usual. He walked her home. Everything was cool. Then she went and called him again. They went out again. Same thing again. Then she called again. And he goes, "I have a new girl. I'm going to marry her." Olga went and searched out his crowd just to check out this girl: she was as hideous as they come. And that's when he got his draft notice. The ugly duckling saw him off, and Olga went up to him on the platform and said right out, "She's not going to wait around for you to come back, but I am." He didn't say anything. And that's exactly what happened: the girl went and got married, and he came back to nothing. Olga started calling him again, they'd see each other again, go out.

And he always agreed to see her but never called her himself and always went out with her reluctantly. Olga would cry and rage until finally she managed to stop calling him. And then it started: she started being able to sense him.

Say we are walking somewhere. Olga's talking as usual. The she gets all quiet and says, "Girls, we're about to run into Alik." We say, "Come on, get him out of your head." Then *bang*—Gorokhov himself is walking toward us. We'd get so scared we'd be shaking. They'd stand there and stare at each other like two rams. We'd pull them apart somehow, then yell at Olga. Time passes, and she senses him again, and we run into him again, some place he never even used to go.

She dropped her studies; we had to give her our notes. She sent all her guys away. We told her that was the wrong thing to do. "Find yourself someone already," we said. "It's painful to even look at you anymore." She said, "That's what I think too, but I can't. They've all stopped paying attention to me." This was true: after a certain point, guys started running away from Olga. They might have it in them to go out with her once, but when it came to going steady—no, thanks.

Meanwhile, her thing with Alik was getting to be like a horror movie. She didn't just sense him anymore; she could see him now. "Today," she'd say, "someone close to him has died. But he doesn't know yet. But he is going to slip and twist his ankle, and then they'll tell him at the hospital." Naturally, that's exactly what would happen.

One day I came to see her when her mother wasn't home. Olga was sitting there by herself. I said, "Either you've really turned into an idiot or you're going to call him again and start over." And Olga said, "I don't want to. I'm not attracted to him."

Then I didn't know what to think.

"Then why the hell are you sensing him all the time?"

She just shrugged and didn't say anything.

Then one time we were going to the post office, and by this time I was scared to walk anywhere with her anymore in case she saw Alik again—and sure enough, Olga started shaking, grabbed on to me, and said, "Around the corner." I looked, and he was standing there, all hangdog like some old geezer—and I mean he was a young guy, our age. And I got the idea that he was forcing himself to wait for somebody he didn't want to see.

Then Olga caught up with me but I didn't let her get any farther. I said, "There isn't anyone there. Let's go back." She believed me and we went in the opposite direction. But I was all shaken up somehow, so I put her on a tram and went home.

Six months later, Olga got married after all.

At the wedding she took me aside and said, "I got sick of all that shit and decided to forget about it." I said to her, "Thank god!" And she said, "Alik's going to be a cripple soon anyway." That's exactly what happened. He was run over by a car and got first-degree disability. Meanwhile, Olga had a girl, named her Marina, and got divorced, but she is fine because her mother helps her out a lot and Olga's reregistered at the trade school. And that's how it all ended.

The Cute Little Redhead

We had this other girl, Natashka Soloviova. She wasn't a Muscovite herself, so she rented a room from this old woman. Actually, it was more of a corner than a room. The old woman had a one-room apartment. She let Natashka live there for fifteen rubles. In theory it was fine: close to the Metro, and the old woman fed Natashka pretty often. But the woman herself was weird. Natashka said there were times when the woman refused to take her money no matter what. She'd give her the money for the month, say, the fifteen rubles, and the woman would start screaming and throwing the money all around like an idiot.

Natashka would say, "What's the matter, Granny? Did you forget? I haven't paid you for November yet."

Or the woman would spill some flour, like by accident, and then scream that Natashka pushed her and now she had to sweep out the flour. And if you've ever had to try to sweep up flour, you know it's worse than death. But Natashka would start sweeping: what else could she do?

Other months, the woman would take the money and count it a hundred times and keep mumbling that it wasn't enough.

This woman had a cat, of course. No, he wasn't black—just a regular gray cat called Murzik. He'd go off for weeks at a time and come back through the window. His face would be all ripped up, he'd be dirty all over—a scary sight. Basically, a regular street cat.

Then my Natashka noticed that when the cat wasn't around, the woman would take money for the apartment. And when the cat was home, she wouldn't. Also, she noticed that with the cat around the woman was different. With the cat around she was more together somehow, meaner, and she worked more. The woman was a fast one—a reseller—and she was active. She'd be making noise in the kitchen, fighting with somebody. Also Natashka noticed how the woman would say, "Good sign or bad?" She'd say this about all sorts of things that only she noticed. Something she'd put on a shelf would lean to the side, and she'd go up to the thing and ask it, "Good sign or bad?" Once a basin fell over in the bathroom. Natashka jumped right up at the sound. The woman ran into the bathroom, saw the basin on the floor. She looked at it and asked it, "Good sign or bad?" Natashka came, too, and thought the whole thing was too funny. I mean, the basin can't talk! It was lying there on the tile all quiet, with the woman standing over it demanding an answer. Natashka gave such a guffaw! The woman jumped right up, turned to her, and just stared. Then Natashka got all scared.

This woman wouldn't let Natashka have us over. But one time I needed to get history notes from her right away, so I came over. But I just couldn't stand being there! I just couldn't! Natashka even said, "Why are you so jumpy? The old woman's fine with you, I'm surprised even."

True, the woman didn't say anything besides "Hello, girl," and went right into the kitchen and didn't even stick her face out like old women always do, sticking their noses in other people's business. But I just couldn't! I said, Give me my notebook and I'll go. I took the notebook, went outside—and right away, right there on the porch, it let go. Like I hadn't even felt anything: no fear or anxiety or horror. It got easier to breathe. I laughed even. What a trip!

I said to her, "How can you live with her?"

Natashka looked away and said, "It's fine."

And I said, "What about at night?"

And she said, "I got some tranquilizers. I take three pills and I'm dead to the world."

"Oh," I said. "I see. But still?"

And Natashka looked away quietly, like someone wasn't letting her talk.

But then we found out about everything. Natashka got married to Serezha Koloskov suddenly and moved in with him and then told us everything.

This old woman had cordoned off half the room with a curtain to give Natashka her separate corner. And every night someone would be squeaking in the woman's part of the room, and the woman would either fight or consult with these squeaky voices.

Natashka would be dying of fear every night, and in the morning the woman checked her out, like did Natashka hear anything or not? Of course the woman knew perfectly well that Natashka could hear everything, but she needed Natashka not to let on, and Natashka understood that.

But then there was one night in October. It was raining heavily, the wind was blowing, there was thunder coming from somewhere. Natashka lay down to go to sleep. She hadn't gotten her pills yet, so she had to go to sleep on her own.

Then she heard someone moving around: it was starting. She heard one voice start squeaking, asking something, from the sounds of it. The woman started tossing and turning, mumbling something sleepy. The little voice left her alone. And the rain was getting heavier and heavier, hitting against the window ledge like crazy, like in some sort of hell.

Natashka pulled the blanket over her head and lay there. Suddenly the voice started squeaking again—and the thing was, you couldn't tell what it was squeaking about, but you could tell it was words, you just couldn't tell which ones. And she really wanted to know what kind of words these squeaks were. The voice was like from a cartoon except scarier because it was clearly live. And she really wanted to be able to tell what it was squeaking about. It's like this kind of voice shouldn't know any words, but it's saying something, and that's funny and scary at the same time.

Natashka pulled her blanket down a bit, raised her head off the pillow, and listened. By this time, they'd really gotten going! The woman was thundering in a low voice, and the little voice was reprimanding her like our trade-school principal. The woman was turning about on the springs, muttering, whining, but the little voice wouldn't let up, kept hammering away at her.

And Natashka—maybe because she'd gotten used to it, or maybe because she'd gotten into the whole thing herself after all—sat up on the bed, shaking, her teeth chattering, feeling that her own eyes were burning now, and she couldn't do anything about it—she was feeling pulled toward the curtain so hard she felt like her insides were getting yanked and she just couldn't hold back.

The voices had gotten real rowdy now, and the rain was forcing against the window, and everything was cracking and moaning. Natashka was sitting there and suddenly she saw the curtain flutter like there was a breeze in the room. Which was impossible because the woman was afraid of drafts and all the windows were closed. Natashka wanted to lie back down quick but suddenly she couldn't and just kept on sitting there like she was under a spell. And the curtain kept fluttering until—leap!—Murzik came out from behind it on his soft paws. He saw Natashka and stopped, looking at her with his big eyes, her looking back at him. Murzik stood there awhile, glanced back at the curtain, then squinted, yawned, came up to Natashka, jumped up on the bed, sniffed Natashka, and started singing. Natashka petted him and he was rubbing up to her, pushing his head against her hand. Meanwhile, behind the curtain, the voices were squealing. Natashka held him against her and shook. And Murzik was looking over at the curtain, moving his ears and hitting the blanket with his tail. And Natashka was holding him tighter against her even though he had fleas and was dirty and hung around garbage dumps. She didn't care. She had tears running down her face, which Murzik thought was funny, and he kept sniffing her cheeks. Then he got bored and wiggled out of her arms and left—jumped down onto the floor, stretched, and went back toward the curtain, and Natashka literally collapsed onto the bed, all wet, and she was out.

Then the woman looked at her special somehow, like she was asking something with her eyes. And Natashka sensed that today she could say, "I heard, I saw." Like the old woman was letting her. But Natashka didn't want to say anything, and that was that. Every time she remembered how she sat there crying, she just couldn't talk! The woman danced around her all morning long until Natashka left for school—all in vain. Then Natashka got herself those sleeping pills and started taking them, and everything seemed to get better.

At our trade school, we have this one class where we make all sorts of models, little things and parts of things. I was making a stairway for a building, for example, but then got crazy busy and ended up getting a three.* The point was to use matches, cardboard, and wire to make a tiny stairway like in a real building except for people the size of infusorians, approximately. Anyway, I got a three. Natasha, on the other hand, was supposed to make little itsy-bitsy suits for those little infusoricks that were going to be climbing my stairway. So Natashka did even worse, getting a two because a shirt sewn from a handkerchief disappeared without a trace, and the little suit didn't count without the shirt. She got so mad looking everywhere for this little shirt and the thing is, she felt bad about the handkerchief because she wasted it and got an incomplete anyway. But then she made a new shirt and they passed her. But she was almost kept back a year.

So a month passed peacefully. The woman didn't look at her at all, and Natashka just kept swallowing her sleeping pills and walking

---

* The equivalent of a "C" on a five-point grading scale, where 5 is an "A" and 1 and 2 are failing grades.

NINA SADUR

around like a freak because the pills were always working and she couldn't think straight, slept on her feet, and was always looking off into the distance. Natashka used to put those pills on the chair by her bed. One day she saw the old woman standing there turning the pills around in her hands, sniffing them, holding them up to the light, trying to taste them even.

"What are you doing, Granny?" Natashka asked her in a sleepy voice. She always had a sleepy voice now, and at the school they'd started calling her Sleepy.

"What are you looking at?" said Sleepy.

"Your medication," said the woman.

"It's medication," said Natashka.

"What for?" asked the woman.

"For a cold," lied Natashka.

The look the woman gave her! Then she made a grimace and growled, "The dream of the soul! Demonic scum!" and threw the pills down real hard and then spilled flour again and made Sleepy sweep it up. Of course, it took Natashka half the day to sweep it up because she had no energy, she was so sleepy.

That night Natashka lay down to go to sleep but couldn't find her pills. And she got so scared! She realized that the old woman had stolen them. And then it started: the voices squeaking, the old woman fighting with them, the curtain dancing. Natashka was shaking under her blanket. She pulled it over her head and stopped breathing. And then she heard—*tip tip tip*—somebody run up to her and stop. She could sense him there but she couldn't even cry from fear. She bit her fingers and lay there, staring into the darkness under the blanket. Meanwhile, he was standing at her feet. It got quiet in the old woman's part of the room; Natashka could even hear her breathing in her sleep. But he just stood there. Natashka started pulling her feet up away from him little by little; she wanted to curl up, and then he went and pulled on the blanket. He pulled lightly, but Natashka grabbed onto the blanket, too. He yanked, but she didn't let go, and she realized that she was stronger and got less scared and even started getting mad that he was playing pranks down there. But then she felt that her hand was going numb and she had no more energy and her whole body was prickly and she lost feeling in her fingers. That's when he yanked, and the blanket slid off her face. So she decided to peek at her feet—to see who was yanking. She rose a bit and saw an itsy-bitsy can't say what: he had a little face, and he was kind of red, filthy, wrapped up in some rag.

She thought the rag looked familiar, so she looked closer and saw that it was her little shirt, the one she'd almost gotten kicked out of the trade school over. The shirt was too big for him; he barely stuck out of it, and the opening had already ripped down to the chest (she hadn't hemmed it), and there was red fur sticking out through the opening, like on a man, and the shirt itself didn't look like anything anymore, except like he'd been rolling around drunk in it in the gutter. He was standing there pulling her by the blanket, scowling, sticking out his lips, not even noticing that she'd been looking at him for a long time now. Natashka opened her mouth but couldn't sigh. She saw that he looked like her a little bit, and she felt a little tenderness, and at the same time she felt scared something awful. She wanted to catch her breath, so she gave a quiet little sigh, and he shuddered because he saw her. He lowered his arms and stuck his little eyes out at her. And he wouldn't leave. He stood there, then started scowling, glowering at her, and Natashka could see that his face was like hers—his little nose, his eyebrows like her own! His shirt was sliding off his shoulder, and he kept pulling it on, embarrassed and nervous, scratching himself, hemming and hawing, while Natashka was lying there with her mouth open and her eyes bulging out. This went on for a few minutes until Natashka heard a whisper right in her ear: "Ask or else!" Then hoarsely from fear, she growled into this face, which was real despite being tiny and dirty: "Good sign or bad?"

And then without hesitation, like a trained pet or a Young Pioneer, he answered her in his little voice, "A little bit good."

Then someone hit her over the head real hard and she fell down, squeezed her eyes shut, and when she opened them, there was no one there except for Murzik sleeping by her side.

When she got up in the morning, the old woman was walking around mean as a toad. This happened to be rent day. Natashka gave her the money. The old woman took it, counted it, and said, "Not enough."

"There's fifteen there," Natashka said.

"What am I supposed to live on?" the woman screamed.

"What have you been living on?" Natashka screamed. "I always give you fifteen and I'll keep on giving you fifteen!"

The woman got all mad, banged a frying pan, spilled some flour, and started mumbling. Natashka took the broom, and the woman grabbed the broom away from her and threw it out the window, like she'd really gone off the deep end. So they stepped on the flour all day long, got their footprints all over the apartment, got flour on all the rugs. Natashka didn't know what to think.

And then literally two days later Serezha Koloskov proposed to her, and she moved in with him.

That's it.

Rings

There is something to rings, of course. Same as with dreams. If dreams reflect one side of our lives, then rings reflect the other.

Dreams give us pictures, and we begin to understand issues that life only hinted at or events that didn't happen like they should have in life. Rings, on the other hand, are silent and encircle all of life without singling out specific events. Rings manifest only during life's principal moments. I could give a lot of examples regarding dreams and rings, but I'd get confused. So I'll just stick to my own love and my own friendship.

My most favorite friend Liubka Vakheta, she is three years younger than me—she's seventeen. We live in the same building, and she introduced herself to me in the elevator. I was in the eighth grade then, and she in the sixth. She caught up with me in the entryway and said, "Excuse me, are you going to come out and play today?" I was surprised because she was just some snot-nosed sixth-grader. But then I got used to it, and now our own mothers mistake us for each other because we've gotten to look alike. My Liubka is a bad influence; I skip classes at the trade school because of her. But then I look at my classmates and see how they all do what they are supposed to, while I have a holiday every day thanks to Liubka. She doesn't know anything. She doesn't know what year the war was. She says, "Twenty million..." I say, "That's right—were killed." She says, "Then who is president in America? Kennedy or somebody?" I say, "Hello! Reagan!" And she says, "Then why was I thinking Kennedy?" She is real beautiful, Liubka, she's got sharp little teeth and really blue eyes, and she dreams of drugs, and she is always shaking with feeling, and she doesn't want to lose weight. She eats so much that I've never seen anybody eat so much. Her clothes don't fit her anymore, and she comes over and asks for candy and then eats everything, but it's better that way, because I do want to lose weight. Liubka got into trouble in Cherniye Zemli. She is always getting into trouble. But in Cherniye Zemli she got into real trouble for life. She and I fell in love then: I with Levan and she with Sasha. But I'm more worried about Liubka, because she is crazy. This Sasha, he was all right basically, he didn't do anything mean, he was polite and proper. But he talks to Liubka like she is a prostitute. When what she is, is innocent. And that's low. In Cherniye Zemli, things were going all right between them at first. He was really into Liubka, but when he found out she was a virgin he lost interest, and that's when she lost it. The boys from their group lived in Camp Two, and at night Liubka would ask one of our boys to go with her, across the whole field to Camp Two. She'd pick someone who was drunk, and they'd drag themselves that whole way over the ruts in pitch darkness. She'd get to the platform on the other side and she'd get rid of the drunkard, and Sasha would say to her, "All right. I've got thirty minutes for you." And then afterward she'd walk back. But that was nothing. We were helping with the watermelon harvest there, and Liubka found a ring, a little black one, kind of crumpled with a watery dirty little stone. She and I had a little laugh about it, and she stuck it in her coat pocket and forgot about it. How can you find a ring in the middle of watermelons? Only Liubka can do something like that.

Then we came back to Moscow, and Liubka started getting ready to give herself to Sasha since she didn't have any other choice because he wouldn't be just friends with her. Her mother took up smoking, her father started taking heart medication, and her grandmother lost the use of her legs. Liubka can't keep a secret. She'd go up to her mother and say, "Mama, buy me a pair of white panties." Her mother would burst into tears: "You think I don't know what you need white panties for? You stupid cow! Get yourself another guy if it's going to be like this. This one's scum!" And Liubka would call him, and they'd have a conversation like this:

"Hello, Sasha."

"What do you want?"

"Why don't you ever call me?"

"Don't have the time."

"But everything was fine between us in Cherniye Zemli."

"You said you'd do it and you haven't."

"But you know that I'm still a virgin, and you won't have any fun with me because I don't know how to do anything yet."

"We should try it first and then talk."

"But you'll dump me right away. I can't take it."

"Then stop calling."

That's how he talked to her. So I called Sasha and said, "First, please don't tell Liubka that I called, and second, I want to let you know that corrupting minors is against the law. Just so you know."

And the next time Liubka called him, he said, "Don't call me anymore. I'm not attracted to you."

Meanwhile, the ring was sitting in a pocket of a forgotten coat.

Now, about Levan. The reason he's got a name like that is that he was born in Georgia, where they all have names like that. But he is Russian—baptized, even. He is married. I fell in love with him by accident. It was after Liubka got wild. She would go to Camp Two, and I'd be left alone, and Levan would be sitting by the fire, and he wasn't like other boys. Plus, he is married, and he's got a wedding band on his finger, a silver one that's like two snakes with a slit between them. There is the slit in the middle and two identical snakes on either side. At first I thought it was two rings, like a set, but it was one band with a deep slit. Liubka said to me, "It's all right that you make out. But no petting!" She said that to me! Really! The thing is, you can't argue with her because she starts shaking and calling you names. She is like that. If she sees a street peddler selling something, she'll buy it for sure no matter what, even if you beg her not to on your knees. And then she'll say, "You were right. He ripped us off." But arguing with her is useless because she starts shaking and yelling, and it's better to just let her do her thing. So she'd be shaking and screaming that don't I dare go petting with Levan, and I'd calm her down a little, and then we'd go to the club. The collective farm had a club. It was always dimly lit. We'd be sitting on a bench, all our girls would be in front except for Liubka and me in the back of the room— I mean, the club. Then Liubka would say, "Listen, Lariska, why do you and I have to suffer this kind of pain? Look: we're the best-looking, the tallest, the best-looking and the best-dressed!" And then she'd throw herself at me and start kissing. Plus, she would kiss me in a totally obscene way, the idiot. Everyone would be looking at us, and Liubka would just be clutching on to me for dear life like she was drunk. Liubka is beautiful, but our boys act kind of weird around her. They started getting weird around me, too, but I didn't care for some reason. I kind of lost interest in them because of Liubka.

Levan, meanwhile, would keep telling me about his daughter. He has a little daughter and he loves only her. He'd say to me, "When you and I get married, I'll make three hundred rubles a month and I'll teach my daughter foreign languages. And you'll probably laugh at me." I couldn't imagine that kind of life very well. What's that supposed to be: me, Levan, and his daughter with foreign languages? What about my daughters? But I didn't push the subject for the time being because I was preoccupied with Liubka with her treks in the night fields. The thing was, she'd lose our drunk boys in the fields and come back crazy herself. Plus there were the locals from the collective farm. Plus wolves. And they all found out about our Liubka. And were closing in. But we left for Moscow in time.

Then in Moscow I had a dream. I walk into a room and I know it: I've been here. The room is real crowded. There are a lot of overweight aging women. I sit down on a chair, and I know that I have a joy. And that all these women have gathered because of my joy. Then Levan comes in. He comes in from behind and I can't see him, but he's come in because everyone has gotten quiet. And my joy, I got it from him. I turn toward him and see, suddenly, how he is standing there—actually, he is sitting too—and I get up and walk toward him and say, "See, Levan, everything turned out like I wanted." But he doesn't say anything to me and leans back like he's been killed and throws his head back, and his lips open up in pain, but he can't say anything and he closes his eyes. I start screaming and bothering him—to get him mad at least—but he gives to the touch, and only his face has turned into a grimace because he is about to start crying. This was my first dream about Levan.

The next day he came to see me, and we had a nice time fantasizing about our life together, and we made out and Levan said that he loved me. And at night Liubka showed up, and we went to the bar but didn't stay long and went back to my place to talk about our lovers. That night I had another dream. There are a lot of people again, everyone is screaming, I'm trying to get away from them, I'm arguing with them, and Levan is sitting on some bench again, half-dead. I push my way through to him, but along the way some woman wounds my leg at the hip and there is blood. And I scream to Levan, "Why are you sitting there, Levan? I'm bleeding! Bleeding!" And he is silent again, and again some force is leading him, and again he gives to the touch and only grimaces like he's going to cry. Finally, I get right up to him and show him how my leg is bleeding, and when I say, "Look here," he looks. But if I didn't say it, he'd just keep sitting there rocking and throwing his head back and grimacing. He looks at my leg but doesn't do anything. Then I take his hand myself and put it against the wound and say, "Stop the bleeding." And his hand just lies there against the wound where I put it. But something black begins to trickle out through his motionless fingers and flow down his forearm to his elbow now, and that is really scary.

That night I said to Liubka, "I think you and I are going to die."

Liubka got all happy and jumped all over me: "Oh, how great!

Larisa, my darling, let me kiss you. I love you so much no one else loves you like this. You are so beautiful. And Levan is an idiot! A married one! Yuck! He is ugly! A man. And you and I will be so beautiful in the same coffin, like twins." I said, "What about your Sasha?" And Liubka said, "I'll call him tomorrow. I can wait. And then you and I will die." And then I dreamt of Levan again. Again there are all these furious people saying, "How can he do that?" about him. And I squeeze through the crowd and see Levan is standing in some doorway or something, turned sideways, sort of toward us but more toward the room that he is coming out of. And where he is coming from it's really dark, and someone is holding on to him and only showing him to us a little bit, and his legs are weak, and he is rocking and smiling, willy-nilly, from all our light and noise. I know that I need to call out to him and then whoever is in the dark room will tell him to answer softly, meekly, raise his face and whisper something. And I really, really love him, I love him so much I don't know how to love somebody this much in life, I love him with the kind of love that I won't ever be able to understand in life, and that becomes the only thing I can think about—how I can remember this love so I can do something. And I start thinking about that really hard, and I take my eyes off Levan, who is rocking in the doorway, all meek and like he didn't come out of the darkness of his own free will, and I think, "What do I need that for? I could live this feeling! I could find a good guy, have children. And what do I need this for?!" And then I look up and see that the doorway is empty and the door is half-closed, and Levan is gone, and there is a trickle of smoke coming out from under the door.

Then I woke up and went to school and couldn't look at Levan. By this time, he and I weren't seeing each other anymore either. He'd started avoiding me and spending all his time with his wife. He was afraid of me. Then Liubka and I went for a walk. It was real warm, so she put on the coat she'd worn to Cherniye Zemli. We were walking down the street and all the men were looking at us, and Liubka was getting drunk off their looks and was walking this real show-off walk with her hands in her pockets. And suddenly she pulled out the ring. Then we remembered Cherniye Zemli. Liubka started shaking and said, "Oh, Lariska, Cherniye Zemli. I'm going to die of love." Then we looked, and there was a thrift shop in front of us. Liubka was getting all worked up, so she said, "Hey, let's go in. Maybe they'll give three rubles for it. That'll pay for coffee."

Now, I knew there was no point in arguing. We went in. Liubka handed the little ring over to the man in the window and he started looking it over. He kept turning it and looking at it, and I was getting real mad and saying instead of wasting our time here we should have gone to a bar, and then the man stuck his head out and said to Liubka, "Young lady, would you come over here?" Liubka went over, he said something to her; she shrugged, and we went on our way. He'd told her to come back tomorrow. But she couldn't come back tomorrow because they came for her instead. They came in a car with guards and took her to the thrift shop. And kept her there a long time, till she really lost it. She got all messed up in her lies because she'd decided to lie about the ring just in case. In the end they took the ring from her, and instead of giving her money—well, this is where it gets like science fiction or something—they put Liubka and her whole family on the government's payroll and said that Liubka's children and grandchildren were all going to live off that ring still. Now we have whatever we want. And Liubka is getting fat because she eats so much. I've never seen anyone eat so much. Put something in front of her, and she'll eat it. And we don't know how we are supposed to live now. Because Liubka doesn't wish to go to "just some trade school," as she puts it, anymore, which means she is spending all her time on this Sasha character now. And Sasha's behavior has been odd. When he found out about the ring and the government payroll, he said, "Make sure I don't ever see you again, you whore." And then—and then—then Levan comes over. I wasn't expecting him. I didn't know he was going to come. He comes over and takes off his coat and comes into the room, and I'm feeling real weird that he came over. He comes into the room and goes up to the table and sees a book and reaches over for it, and suddenly something on his finger just sparkles something fierce! Really bright, really crude! I pulled back even. I thought, "He can't be wearing a ring, and certainly not a signet ring like that! He may have a weird name like Levan, but he's got taste." What was it? It was just a moment, I don't know myself what kind, but something crude and powerful shined right into my eyes. But I looked closer and saw that it was just his silver wedding band. It just sparkled like that for a minute. And now it looked different to me, like the silver had just told me something and was now cooling and getting duller right there on his finger. Two snakes—Levan and his unloved wife with a slit between them—and me, unloved by anybody. And I got it. I got everything. If the band is like that and Levan wears it, then nothing's going to happen. Nothing. I don't know how to explain it, but nothing is going to happen. Ever.

Two Fiancées

This one guy surprised us all. And the thing is, he was perfectly normal, psychologically speaking. Anyone will tell you that. But what he did remains unexplained and inexplicable. Before he went into the military, he had a girl. He wrote to her practically every day, but then she got married anyway. And wrote him about it. Then he went and hanged himself.

If he'd hanged himself in some bathroom somewhere, they would have taken him down and resuscitated him. But his unit was in the forest, in some wooded locale or something, and so he sneaked past the guards one night, went into the forest, and hanged himself. First they had a search on for him as a deserter, but then two days later they found him suffocated. We all went to the funeral, including that Natasha of his, who was indifferent, except sad just like another human being. She said, "Yes, it's too bad, but I have everything: I have a husband and I'm going to have a child. I feel bad for Kolia, but I am not to blame." And as it turned out, she really wasn't to blame. Because it turned out that Kolia had another fiancée just like her, that he made an agreement about getting married with just like with her, and that he wrote frequent love letters to just like to her. She, by the way, came to the funeral, too, and her grief was significantly greater than Natasha's.

It was resolved to compare these letters and his relationships with both of them, and it turned out, again, that he acted exactly the same with both of them, loved both of them the same, and wanted to marry both of them.

What was strange is that he hanged himself when he still had one fiancée left, Galia. Because there was no evidence that he loved Natasha more. But he hanged himself because of Natasha, who soon forgot all about him, and it ended up that he only punished his mother, who grieves for him as her only son whom she has lost forever. I mean, he only had one mother and two fiancées, so it would have made more sense if he'd hanged himself over his mother, but not one person in the world will ever do that even though everybody loves their mother more than a hundred fiancées put together. We started thinking maybe he went nuts because of his difficult life in the service or something. Maybe they are beaten and tortured there. But that's not it, either, because they don't even go nuts in Afghanistan; our guys only go nuts in Germany. This one friend of mine had a brother who came back from Germany and, just like all the other guys I've seen who come back from Germany, he came back nutty. And they can't even tell you how they got that way.

Before the military, this guy was normal, but when he came back, he had the mental capacity of a fourteen-year-old. One day he had a fight with his sister, so he put on this fancy brown raincoat of his and his hat, took a cane, and got ready to leave. I looked at him and couldn't believe my eyes: he was just like Shtirlits, the secret agent from the movie. I said, "Gena, where you going?" And he said, "I'll go get some air; my wounds are bothering me." I said, "Gena, what wounds? And what do you need a cane for?" And he said, "I have a field wound in my leg. I have to walk with a cane." I shrugged my shoulders, and when he left, I said to my friend, "What's with him?" And she said, "He went nuts in the service. He became different. He hasn't got any wounds. But he likes to walk around alone with his cane all night long, sometimes till morning. He doesn't have anybody—no girl-friends." I said, "All right, what does he like to talk about, discuss, what's he interested in?" And she said, "Nothing." I said, "Well, the cane, it's totally the limit, of course. I mean, it would be different if he'd been in Afghanistan. I've seen guys who came back from Afghanistan, and they're just like regular guys except more tense, but that's understandable. And this one here—he served in Germany in peace time and went nuts. And he isn't the first either. Germany's the only place they come back from like this. What do they do to them there?" Another time I came over and Gena was sitting there quietly, not reading, not talking, just sitting and that's that. I went to walk by, and he looked up, and I jumped: his eyes were white! Just totally white eyes, like he was wall-eyed. I said, "Gena, what happened?" And he's looking at me like he can't understand anything. I say, "Earth to Gena!" So he caught his breath, looked at me with his eyes regular, and said, "Screw off. I've got a bullet in my gut." I said, "Take your cane and go for a walk." And he said, "Don't you know I'm not supposed to move, bitch? The bullet will go through my gut, reach the heart, and I'll be *kaput*." Then I was real surprised, because before he used to be polite and now he was insulting me.

But then it turned out that he didn't have any bullets anywhere in him but walked around with a cane because he had fungus on his feet and the fungus on his left foot got so bad it got in the way of walking. That's why he used a cane. They all get fungus in the service because it's filthy, and then they go nuts over it.

But Kolia with his two brides is still a puzzle. Most guys try to get themselves a girl before they go into the service. It's like a rule. They need to have a girl waiting for them, because they don't know what's going to happen to them. So Kolia got himself not one but two girls, like getting overinsured. He's the one who got all the insurance, and he's the one who hanged himself. That's just too weird.

Silky Hair

There was a woman who had a son whom she loved very much but who was always getting sick. The doctors told her that if it kept going like that, the boy would be developmentally challenged because his body would get tired and worn down fighting disease all the time. She tried everything, but the doctors couldn't help her, and then someone told her to go to a fortune teller.

The fortune teller told her, "Someone is drinking his young juices." She lit a candle, took the woman's hands in hers, and looked her in the eyes. The woman was real scared, but she was willing to go through anything for her little baby. Then the fortune teller closed her eyes and looked like she went to sleep. The woman sat there listening to the candle crackling, got tired, and started pulling her hands back little by little, but the fortune teller gave a sob, knit her eyebrows, and wouldn't let go. So the woman got quiet until the fortune teller opened her eyes and let her go.

"You got in my way there," said the fortune teller. "But basically, see for yourself. Here's what I found out for you. There is a dahlia with a stem reaching down into the garden. There is a button lying at its root. That's a curse. But you can take the curse off if you get the button and throw it as far as you can with all your might."

"Oh, come on!" the poor woman exclaimed. "How am I supposed to find this garden without an address or anything?"

"Didn't go outside the line," said the fortune teller. "So it's somewhere on the outskirts of Moscow. And the other thing I can tell you is that the curse was put on by a woman kind of like you, around your age."

"What does she look like at least?" asked the poor thing.

"That's where you got in the way," said the fortune teller. "With the jerking. You are defending her yourself somehow—since you didn't want me to see her face. I can only tell you that she's got long silky hair."

And the woman said "Oh!" because she knew who it was.

She said, "Thank you, Granny, here is the money, thank you for everything."

The fortune teller said to her, "You've got to go at night, dig up the button and throw it as far as you can with all your might."

The woman said, "Fine."

The fortune teller said to her, "But then if they take the button away from you, that will mean not just the death of you but your child, too, and all your grandchildren to come."

The woman said, "I understand. Good-bye."

Since she lived alone without a husband, she took her child to some friends' house for the night, telling them some lie in explanation so they would agree to take the boy. And then she went to the place. She had figured it out by the hair, who it was. It was Yelena, the best and closest friend of her youth whom she hadn't seen in ten years. She had never thought that Yelena could do something like this, and if the fortune teller hadn't told her about the hair, then her boy would have just gone on getting sick till he withered.

When she got to the place, it was still pretty early, so she started wandering the streets, and as she was wandering, she was overwhelmed with memories of her youth, and she got bitter. "My little boy is all I have," she thought. "And why is it that the people you love the most are always trying to take your last thing away from you? What did my baby boy ever do to her?" The thing is, she had really loved the man that she got the baby from, but the man, of course, went back to his wife as soon as her stomach began to grow. He said to her, "It's not mine, and anyway, it's six of one, a half dozen of the other, so why should I trade? It's the same thing here as there." And now it turned out that her best and closest friend nurtured a hidden hatred for her, too. Then night came, and the woman went up to the gate. She saw there was a light on in Yelena's house, and the light from the terrace windows fell on the garden. "Of course, Zhuchka is long since dead and the new dog is going to bite me," she figured, but she stepped bravely forward into the yard, and the yard greeted her with silence. Yelena didn't have a new dog. The woman tip-toed into the garden and started looking around for tall plants because even though there was some light, it was dark down on the ground anyway. She saw there were some flowers swaying on their tall stems in the middle patch. She started moving toward them, but then she heard the shed door squeak, and she crouched down in fear.

She sneaked right up to the porch where she figured she'd wait a little longer, until they turned off the light in the house. She crouched behind the porch, waiting. Meanwhile, there wasn't anybody in the shed except for a baby pig, which had made the squeaking noise. And then Yelena herself came out onto the porch, and in the yellow light from the terrace, the woman could see that her friend lived well and had blossomed in carefree bliss. The woman was half dead with fear

NINA SADUR

crouching behind the porch. And on the porch, Yelena started brushing her silky hair. She was brushing it out, and a light breeze blew a strand past the woman's nose, and she sneezed from the surprise of it. Yelena froze with the comb in her hand, and the woman stood up, and they saw each other and they both said, "Oh!" Yelena dropped the comb, and they both ran into the garden. The woman fell down, Yelena tripped over her, and they were both straining toward the dahlia, struggling, rolling around in the patches, all the while unable to say a single word. But because my woman was desperate, she had enough strength to wiggle out from under Yelena and stick her nails into the warm loose soil. So she was digging with one hand and using her other hand to fend off Yelena, pulling her hair, shaking her as she wiggled, also reaching for the dahlia.

But the woman had already dug down to a big flat button which she could now feel with her fingers. She squeezed it in her hand and jumped up. And Yelena, stretched out on the ground, was looking up at her and breathing quietly. "Give it to me," she said.

"Why did you do it?" the woman said.

Yelena got up, brushed herself off, and didn't say anything. Then the woman stretched out her arm to throw the button with all her might, and Yelena said, "If you do it, then my son will get sick and he'll be very, very sick."

"Why did you do it?" the woman asked her again.

Yelena looked down but didn't say anything. And the woman stretched out her arm again, and Yelena started moaning and covered her face with her hands. Then the woman started crying and said, "I'm gonna throw it anyway."

And Yelena said, "No, put it back. Or my son will get sick."

And the woman said, "I should take a look at your son."

And Yelena said, "Don't go in there."

But the woman ran toward the house, ran in, and the first thing she saw was her own photograph standing on the bureau with a needle stuck in her heart. And Yelena was saying nothing again, just looking down with hair falling over her pink face.

The woman yanked the needle out of the picture and said, "Aren't you ashamed?"

And Yelena said, "Give it to me."

But the woman went to leave the house so she could throw the button. Yelena got in her way, and there was a commotion, and Yelena's little son woke up in the other room and started calling, "Mama! Mama!"

"Quiet," said Yelena. "You'll wake up my son. See, I told you."

And the woman said, "My god, what's all this about? Lenka! Lenka!" But Yelena was just avoiding her with this smile on her face and muttering the same thing over and over again, "Give it to me." And the baby was crying and calling his mama. And the woman said, "Where's what's left of your conscience?" And Yelena said, "Mean is god, mean is the spirit, be it on earth, or in heaven be it." Then the woman was engulfed by fear and started shaking, and her grip started loosening and letting go of the button, and Yelena was encouraging her: "Give it to me. Give it to me." But then some kind of force threw my woman out of the house so that she hit the doorjamb and scraped her shoulder, but still she got out onto the street and threw the button as far as she could with all her might.

The Bad Seed

The man is strong. He is beautiful, tall, and mighty. He has dark eyes and a hot mouth. When you see the man, you freeze and forget who you are. But the man can't make you happy. That's the way he is. I thought about this for a long time until I figured out why that's the way it is. The man arrives like a hero and covers up all the ugliness of the world. When he comes, lights go out and everything withers so the only thing left is the ruddy heat of passion. But he can't make you happy. He just can't. That's the way he is. He is not at all what he seems. He is ugly, short, and petty. He comes and gobbles up everything. I work and work and deny myself everything, and then he comes and gobbles it all up. Or he doesn't come at all, in which case there is no reason to live and no reason to keep washing the foyer because there is no one to gobble up your salary. Which is tiny anyway—seventy rubles plus another twenty from the Yermolov Theater. And no days off, though this has a profit side, too, because children drop lots of coins during the matinee—it comes to half a ruble a month. Plus there is candy, apples, pins, cookies sometimes. And handkerchiefs, too, embroidered with names: "Liuba Vakheta" or "Mitia Mishutin." But you can't tempt a man with a handkerchief. Because he is a tempter himself. That's the way he is. He was bitten by the demon of treachery, and ever since, he's had to put on masks. He is sincere in those masks, thinking that they are his face. But they are his masks that he puts on for us. The eyes are his, and everything else is a mask. That's why you can't have anything work out with a man. That's the way he is, I figured out: he wears masks. He hides his eyes. When in reality he is an ass, a bastard, a rogue, and a mercenary. And a drunkard, too. And the only way to be with him is to kick him in the head to make him know his place. Otherwise, he'll come and gobble up and drink everything. He is like a fiery pit, swallowing everything—pieces of food, wine, silver—and filling up with dark juices. He is trouble. He can be touching at first. He'll breathe right in your soul. He'll say something and look right in. He'll touch it. And he's got depth! And he's got all kinds of mysteries, the ass, all tragic, calling you to go to his death with him. But he'll kick off on a featherbed by his wife's side. She'll give him a mustard compress as a farewell gift. And he won't even call before dying, the old bastard.

There are no old men, only old people. Men are all treacherous, willful, tall, and wearing masks, going around gobbling up everything. They gobble us up with all our innocence, our future, and our bones. They infect us with death and depravity. They drink us up and crumple us up like empty milk cartons. They are not shamed by us because we aren't anyone to them. They are shamed by god. They say, "I have fallen in love with this woman. Let it work out." It won't work out. It won't. They know this, but they start in anyway. And they don't fear god. And god knows that the man has been bitten by the demon of treachery, of lust and flight and willfulness and freedom and treachery. How could the demon even stand to bite into such slime? It would have been better if he'd bitten the woman so she'd corrupt the man and take away his innocence and his future and drink him all up and then leave him to grow old alone. So that men would become women and women would become men.

Men sometimes have moles. But these are masks, too. You can't trust them. The man is good for your health. But he is dangerous. He is a beast. He swallowed a scorpion. He stings. He stomps on the woman and torments her and teaches her everything and then despises her for learning all his vile games so well. Men have desires for our daughters who are still not grown. They are monsters. They should be beheaded—right away. But even they can elicit pity, because any mask has to be attached with a string—and it always is.

From all the man's dangerous living he gets worms in his brain. And they eat away at his brain in all its nooks and crannies and suck the gray matter, and the man becomes even more of a beast. And when he is lying down asleep, the worms peek out his ears: a worm in the left one and a worm in the right one.

Conceit and cruelty. But the rogue man sleeps without his mask, and his face is hideous, and the sucking worms are peeking out and squeaking about how tasty he is.

Mean Girls

As salt burns in a fire,
So you will burn for me.
—a spell

His jacket was rustling from the wind and the rain when he burst in. His sunken cheeks were a bit flushed from the cold. He was a beast. He had the face of a beast. The reason was, he was German, born to a German woman in a prisoner camp in 1947, which made him fourteen years older than us. He wasn't attractive the way he was, with his German hair and the eyes of a beast, wiry, forward, and hoarse.

We were drinking, and he kept looking up at me with his pale eyes. I would lower my eyes and press my knees together. And then Emka says to me, "He is mine." Fine. But he is fourteen years older than us. First of all, there is something of a fascist in him—probably because he was born in a camp. He is a baby who grew behind barbed wire and turned into a beast.

We were drinking vodka and he was looking with his transparent eyes, and I could see glimpses of madness in them, and that gave me the chills. But Emka started showing off—she let her hair out and was smiling and joking and then they went out on the balcony. And when they came back, he gave me a mocking look and his pale lips were twisted in disdain. He put his hand on Emka's shoulder and sleepily patted Emka's blouse with his pale bony hand. I saw the faint freckles on that hand, and I couldn't drink anymore. Emka was rubbing up against him. I was pressing my knees together. Outside, a winter storm was whistling. That's how they looked when they came back from the balcony—flushed and frozen, and microscopic prickly little snowflakes were sparkling in his white hair like grains of salt.

Then we found out that he was going to be at Gena Galkin's. Emka said let's go to Gena's, and I said no. But we went anyway. Emka is wild. Everything happened exactly like before, including the storm, and something sparkled in his hair again, refusing to melt. He was the only person in the world who could hold on to snow. And then suddenly they split off like a couple and started walking around just the two of them, separate from us, in the wet winter dusk. But Emka is a wild girl, and even though she says she won't cheat, that's only good for two years or so. He had three children and made a hundred forty a month, and still Emka got rid of her guy because of him. In the end, he said, "I am leaving everything for you: my children, my apartment, my lifestyle. I have nothing to lose. If you leave me, I'll kill you." And

NINA SADUR

he was right. Plus, he beat her. Emka, she can really get going, so this one time she got drunk and started screaming. He said, "Be quiet. The neighbors will hear you." But she just kept screaming and stomping her feet. He said again, "Be quiet. The neighbors can hear you." She kept screaming. Then he started in beating her. Emka fell down, got quiet, covered her head, and just lay there while he kicked her, barking in German, till she was bleeding. He just about killed her, the beast. They'd only been going out six months and he'd already beaten her three times. Emka said, "His blood is pale like water. He cut himself when he was shaving, I saw." She thought they were going to have a life. She said, "He's not going to beat me anymore. We're going to have a life." And I said, "But I know you!" And Emka said, "You are wrong. He's got something that other men don't have. It always holds me back." And I said, "Well, well."

So then they rented an apartment. They made all the arrangements, burned all the bridges officially, got through it all and rented an apartment: empty, except for a couch and a table.

And then look—there was a candy box on the table. And it had two chocolates in it. I wanted to take one, but Emka ran up to me and wouldn't let me. I was surprised, and I looked, and saw she'd gotten all pale. I said, "What's the matter?" And Emka said, "Don't eat it." And why was this? I like chocolates. And these were good chocolates, expensive ones. And Emka said, "Don't eat it. There's something wrong with them."

Turns out this is what happened: when she and Harry rented this apartment, the box was already on the table. And all the men got sick off the chocolates—but this we didn't find out until later. There were exactly two chocolates in the box. Harry took one and ate it, but Emka didn't because she's got an allergy to sweets. Then they started cleaning up, arranging their things, and two hours later Harry got a bad headache. They went to bed, and Harry tossed all night and was delusional. In the morning, there were two chocolates in the box again. They each thought the other one had done it. They fought and then figured out that neither of them had put in an extra chocolate. They decided that the owners of the apartment must have a key and this must be their idea of a joke. They changed the lock. Then Harry ate a chocolate and got a headache and tossed and cried all night, and the next morning there were exactly two chocolates in the box. Then every day got to be like that. Harry would say, "I may have to spend my life doing it, but I'll get those chocolates." They checked the bottom of the box and studied the box in every other way but didn't figure anything out. Naturally, they couldn't have any kind of life anymore. Harry went mad. All his energy went into the chocolates. He dropped everything. He was suffering. He became all transparent, like a blue flame. He couldn't do anything. He was in agony. He knew what was right for him and he wanted to prove it, but he became like the fire over an alcohol stove, and everything inside him went out.

I went up to the box, opened it, and was hit in the nostrils by a stuffy chocolate smell. It was an ancient smell, from far away. The two dark chocolates lay next to each other. It was like it hit me. I got it all. I didn't tell Emka anything and quietly closed the box.

I looked at Emka in a completely new light. She was already pregnant. She was standing by the table in her housecoat, and the buttons on it were already straining. She wasn't made up, and she looked at me all simple forever. I saw that she was no longer a friend to me. I tried not to step away from the table. We were chatting like always, but she suddenly said, "Why are you looking at me like that?" After that I lowered my eyes, but Emka was saying very little and kept pausing for a long time, but I wouldn't leave. I tried not to step away from the table, and Emka sensed something and started breathing fast and playing with the buttons on her housecoat and looking around the empty room scared.

Then we heard the door shut and Harry's fast footsteps. He was literally running. Emka didn't know what to do or what to be afraid of, and her eyes bugged out and there were tears in them already. But till the last moment I made no move, so I wouldn't give myself away. But when he was already at the door, I ran up to the table, opened the box, grabbed the chocolates, and swallowed them one after the other. My throat hurt from the big chocolates, and I remembered that pain. A faint taste of chocolate slipped through my throat, but I remember that it hurt, and I'll remember that. I even got tears in my eyes.

He ran into the room mean and wiry in his rustling jacket, all white and transparent like an alcohol fire. And he saw two women in tears. He stopped dead in his tracks. He looked with his pale eyes like a madman, and we looked at him through tears. He looked and looked, and then he began to see it. A thin kind of blush started showing on his sunken cheeks, and his thin lips opened up: "Oh, so that's what you are," and he whistled.

And then, softly, softly like a little white rat, I breathed on him: "Harry-eee..."

The Blue Hand

Marya Ivanovna hated her new flatmate, Valia. Valia was weak and thin and liked to drink wine and had men friends. Marya Ivanovna had done time in prison for theft and hated anyone who hadn't done time. She was scared and crippled forever by prison. She liked stealing, but she thought all other vices were bad. She hated Valia all the more for being young and weak. Marya Ivanovna had a husband, Ivan Petrovich, whom she made piss on the floor in the bathroom when it was Valia's turn to wash the floors. Ivan Petrovich pissed like he was told, but he had a good heart. He had six fingers. His right thumb split into two useless little fingers in the upper phalanx. They had a daughter. The daughter had a husband. And they had a daughter, Marya Ivanovna's granddaughter. There were a lot of them and only one Valia, a thin, scared, young girl who drank.

This is how the torment went. Marya Ivanovna promised she would clear out space for a coat hanger but didn't and put another wardrobe there instead because Valia was such a drunkard. She filled the utility closet with some kind of stuff to make sure that Valia's potatoes would die from all the chemicals. Then she got into shifting her weight, sniffling and moaning, crouching down and stomping her feet, exclaiming, "Gaaahd!" She said that she was entrusted with millions and ask anybody in half of Moscow and they will tell you that she handles handfuls of gold and she only looks and gives back and never steals. She addressed Valia in a conceited, dull, and boorish way and waited to see what Valia would say. Since all Valia would do was quietly attempt to blend into the wall, Marya Ivanovna would get all black with anger that she couldn't really yell, and she would start crouching down and moaning, apparently from the weight of being entrusted with millions of rubles. Valia would try even harder to disappear into the dirty wall even harder, and she would turn her eyes upward. The ceiling was an ancient shade of yellow. Marya Ivanovna was crouching down and moving in on Valia, and the old parquet boards would pop out of their grooves due to the crouching and the lack of proper maintenance. That's how it went. And when Valia had men visitors, Marya Ivanovna would start moaning in her own room and then she would tumble out into the hallway and sit down on the communal chair to eavesdrop. Even if there was a movie on the television or she had company herself, she would abandon everything in favor of Valia and her love sobs behind the thin and dirty wall. The way Marya Ivanovna would tumble out, it was like somebody was holding her in the room, and she tumbled out following a struggle, distended and patient about the time she was going to spend sitting by Valia's love door in front of everybody.

So then Valia started getting pains in the back of her head. Whenever she got stressed out about Marya Ivanovna, a hot stream of pain would rise from her neck into the back of her head. It got worse every time. At the same time, her hands would get cold and pale till they were blue. Valia would think, "I know she is going through menopause, and I know she's been to prison where they did god knows what with her, and I know she is stupid and that she has fat in her head instead of brains, and I know that her husband is impotent even if he does have six fingers, and I know that she has nothing and she's never been entrusted with any millions of rubles and that even her daughter is a checkout clerk and her son-in-law is the night manager of a vegetable store and they haven't even provided for the granddaughter's future except for vegetables, and the granddaughter has a gift for track and field which they've stomped all over with the crouching and the moaning. Then why do I care? I shouldn't pay any attention to her, I should treat her like a flea or a bug." But she couldn't do it. She didn't know how to answer Marya Ivanovna, how to bark at her good. She was exhausted by wine and love. Then she started imagining Marya Ivanovna getting into various kinds of calamities. She imagined somebody kicking her in the ass. She imagined her crawling around in blood looking for her eyeglasses. She imagined her being hanged in a prison yard to the disturbing accompaniment of a drum and her large intestine falling out and being buried separately and her being taken down and resuscitated and being given brandy and forced to get up and bury her own intestine, and then her getting hanged again.

This helped her feel a little better. But Valia's life stopped. Even the wine stopped. Warts grew on Valia's face. They hung in a cluster off her left eye and also grew on her lip and her chin.

Marya Ivanovna cooled off. One day she was watching Valia peel potatoes, and her eyeglasses were glistening cheerfully, and suddenly she felt a pang in her heart and, simply and a little crudely, she handed Valia two robust, healthy, cheerful little pancakes.

Valia took the pancakes to her room, put them on the table, and sat gritting her teeth.

And when everyone lay down to go to sleep that night, everything became quiet and peaceful. Suddenly, Marya Ivanovna was awakened by a sense of danger. She looked and saw that the curtain on the window was moving. She thought, "What could that be?" She went up to the window, and a blue hand reached out for her from the folds of the curtain. Marya Ivanovna tried to jump back, but the hand grabbed her by her puffy throat and started choking her. Marya Ivanovna started wheezing and wiggling her fingers, and she tried to jerk away but the hand was gripping her tighter and tighter, and funeral lights floated by in front of her eyes.

When Ivan Petrovich woke up that morning, there was no breakfast, no one screaming, no one crouching. He went in and saw that Marya Ivanovna was lying there dead with the imprint of a blue hand on her throat.

They ran to Valia's room, but she had vanished, and the only thing left was a nightie crumpled up on the bed.

They picked up the nightie, and it turned to dust in their hands.

They Froze

This is about retards. I had to make some money to buy a pair of jeans. I said to my mother, "You drink all your money with your lovers, and meanwhile I have nothing to wear. I'm gonna go to work."

My mother said, "Go, who is stopping you?"

I got a job as a janitor in a theater. The only pain is we have to dump the water out outside. The superintendent keeps saying, "Girls, try to get it closer to the garbage, otherwise it's gonna ice over and everyone's gonna be falling down."

But who wants to go catching a cold? We are all heated up, and we are naked under our uniform coats—and we are supposed to run all the way to the garbage! So, of course, everyone dumps it out right by the door—they just open the door, swing the bucket, and throw the water as far as they can. And then I notice there is a retard hanging around the theater. His name is Uncle Leo. That really gets on my nerves. Uncle Leo. I have a guy named Leo, and here's this retard named Leo. And the thing is, the retard is tall, too, practically the same height as my guy, which is totally disgusting. It makes me crazy, anyway, when they name a retarded individual Leo or Andrei. I get this sense that they've wasted a name. Better to call them Vasia or Kolia.

So I guess I disliked him from the very beginning, and I couldn't hide it because I didn't even notice how it happened.

Everyone gives their empty bottles to this retard. And I just figure that he's got a place here and everyone tolerates him because the theater is in an old church. Actually, it's more like there is a bell tower and some other little building left from a church and they've gradually grown into the theater building. Oh, and another thing: they were staging "The Bandits," and they put a cross outside to dry. They leaned it against the wall of the little building. It was a decent size cross, about as tall as a man. And the dumpster is right across from it, so I run by with the garbage three times a day. Then one day I look—what in the world?—god's face is changing! Maybe it's the light—the way it's falling because in the winter dusk turns to dark faster—or maybe it's just I don't know what! And there was a puddle right there, so I couldn't go up close to it because I was just wearing slippers with no socks. So I went right up to the puddle and looked, and it looked like everything was all right: the cross standing there, the papier-mâché god painted black. His stomach had cracked, so the laborers nailed on a plank, painted it over, and put it out to dry. But you could still tell that there was cotton coming out of the muscles where the cracks were and that the hands had two or three nails in them to make sure they didn't fall off. The thing I couldn't understand was why they didn't paint the nails, because this way they just shone there like new. And there were nails in the stomach, too. Couldn't they have made a new god? Because this one was going to slide right off the cross after a couple of shows. The audience would love that. So I was standing there at the edge of the puddle, and then I looked over and saw the retard was standing just down from me and looking at me. He was all covered with snow like a statue. I thought, I wonder what his life is like: what he does at home, what he eats, what he feels…And then he started swaying like someone had hit him and he was going to fall now, but he didn't fall but wandered off somewhere. But anyway.

Anyway, I would be taking out the garbage, and it would be slippery, and it would be snowing, and there would be steam coming off the ground from all our water and snow falling from the sky—a regular hell—with god drying against the wall. And then once I happened to look and saw—I saw!—how his face changed. It changed every time! That could drive you mad! It was like it moved out of the snowy mass, out of the dusk, straight at me. I'm not crazy. He didn't even have much of a face, seeing as it was all pained over with black—he just had some rough bulges, the nose, the mouth, a few dents to make it look like something on stage. It didn't even have to look like anything up close. And then suddenly it wasn't even like it was some face just for the sake of having a face: it was some face! Maybe it was the snow that was making the air move and seem alive and make shadows or something. I couldn't tell what it was. And then I thought that either he was looking at me special, in which case it was some kind of miracle, or I was still basically normal and not crazy, in which case it was a misunderstanding that would be easily explainable. At this point I walked right into the puddle in my slippers—the heck with it. The puddle was hot, being wash-bucket water from the whole theater that we'd dumped there ourselves, and when I stepped out of the puddle and into the snow, my feet froze right away, but I could finally get close enough to the cross, walk right up to it. And then I got it— it was the snow. Which is pretty much what I'd figured—that it was something natural that had just fallen and flashed in such a way as to make a face like that show up. The thing was that snow had gotten into all the cracks, which made everything stick out so horribly, making it look like the eyes were closed and had bags and wrinkles around them and stuff...Which made it look like he was, like, already—dying...Damned bastards. I tried to rub it away, but I was wearing this slippery rubber glove that made a sound from the friction that made me shiver. I can't stand those kinds of sounds. Then I pulled off my glove and used my hand to clean his eyes, his cheeks, his mouth, and his beard. I turned to go back, and I saw the retard was hanging around again. He is so tall, so long, that Uncle Leeeo. He's got a huge nose, eyes that bug out like boiled eggs, and wrinkles that hang down like on the god's face, and he is so gross that I wouldn't touch him with my bare hand even if he were all covered with snow. He always has an expression on his face that's real conceited and mean. He only ever looks pleased if he is sitting around with the laborers in their room, where it's warm and there is a television and people and hot tea.

But when he is hanging around by himself, he's got an expression like god forbid. He looks like he is real important, when in fact he is just a retard. He can't even talk. Everyone gives him their empty bottles. He is slow and retarded from birth. I wonder what kind of dreams he has. I've tried saying hello to him, and he doesn't even react. He can't tell people apart; he only recognizes motion here and there. But if you call him by his name, he'll turn and start moaning like he's about to die and drag himself to the call. I've seen it. The way he moans, it's like something inside him is collapsing and breaking and all the pieces are scraping against one another. And then I saw him staring at me real mean again, mean like I'd been stealing his empties. I spat demonstratively and walked on. I was thinking, either I'm imagining things or the retard really hates me. But how can he hate me if he doesn't know anything and can't tell people apart— why me then? To think of it—he's only tolerated here out of charity, and now he is acting like he is somebody. Then I finished cleaning and went to dump out the water and saw that Uncle Leo was still hanging around like he was stuck. He could at least have been sitting at the laborers' when it was storming outside and our water was steam- ing—instead, he was just squelching through all this like a pestle. I opened the door, swung the bucket, and splashed all the water out. Of course, I didn't run to the dumpster like the superintendent said—I just did what all our girls did. And then the retard started howling something awful! He grabbed a stone and sent it flying for my head. I crouched down, and the stone whistled above my head and smashed right into the second set of glass doors. And the retard howled even louder, puckered his lips, and stuck his eyes out at me. And even before he did that, I was already losing it, because the stone had whistled right over my head and now I had broken glass behind me and a crazed retard coming at me from the front. "Mama, help me," I thought. Somehow, I managed to grab my bucket and run away. I didn't tell the superintendent anything. Naturally, the retard didn't either. I didn't say anything because I was only going to work a month and make my seventy r. and take off. And the next day I wore a hat, so he wouldn't be able to smash my head in.

Then I was getting some water, and I heard the superintendent rep- rimanding somebody. I moved my hat off my ears to listen. Somebody was answering her in a slow booming voice that sounded like it was coming from a precipice, but at the same time it sounded solicitous, the way we all sound when we talk to the boss. I could even hear what they were saying: "I already promised, Flora Mikhailovna: it won't happen again."

It sounded like a subterranean force of nature was asking our Flora for forgiveness. And then Flora: squeak-squeak-squeak, squeak- squeak-squeak about something. But you can understand her, too, because she is always having to deal either with drunk laborers or with no-show janitors.

I got the water, which was real hot, and threw some detergent in it and even worked up some foam so Flora wouldn't start squealing that we didn't use detergent. I was carrying it real careful so I wouldn't spill the boiling hot water on my feet, thinking that I would just sneak by while Flora was yelling at whoever that was so she wouldn't notice me and make me do the stairs. And then, of course, who came out but

NINA SADUR

our shapely Flora, looking quite pissed, followed by some screw-off droning on and making excuses. Flora saw me and waved to me to wait a minute, which meant that I would be doing the stairs. And then she said, "Look, you keep promising, and it keeps happening."

And then there came the retard again with his mean hangface, looking like his wrinkles were pulling him down. And I was waiting to see who would come out behind him that she was yelling at. And then Flora looked at the retard with a totally regular look, like she'd just been looking at me, and said to no one but him, "Make sure this is the last time, Leo!"

And Leo opened his mouth and howled, "Of course it was the last time, Flora Mikhailovna." And then he made some kind of loose gesture and said, "I'm your favorite baby after all, Flora Mikhailovna, and here you are yelling at me."

And Flora said, "Fine, here, take the key and go to work."

And the retard reached out with his imprecise, limp hand and took a whole set of keys—not a single key but a whole bunch—and stuck his pouty lips out. "Don't yell at me any more. I'm your little Leo."

"All right, all right, Leo, go work," said Flora and turned to me. "All right, now you. You'll wash the stairs—"

But I—I—I dropped the bucket and started backing up those very stairs and collapsed onto the steps and let out such a scream of fear! That meant he worked there and he had papers and he could talk!

I locked myself in my room and kept crying all the time for some reason. I didn't even notice how the night went by. I was sitting there, and then suddenly it got all light. I looked out the window, and the sky was there, a real blue blue like a miracle, like spring, because it's never like that in the winter. I was standing by the window and thinking about how my eyes hurt to look at it. I was going to step away when a wave of really warm air engulfed me, and I even had trouble standing for a minute. And then there was another wave, even warmer, and then another. It was like a sea of warm air at high tide, and it was getting lighter and lighter.

The whole room filled up with sun and light, and it got hot.

In the next room, my mother was getting ready for a date, and her footsteps sounded like everything that was happening to us was a lie and we would never see what really happens to us.

My mother has footsteps that are light and cheerful. I've never had footsteps like that. And as she was clicking about in her heels in her room, I was sitting there and watching more and more light pour into the room, like somebody was trying to see how much would fit. At first it was nice and warm, but then it kept getting hotter and over-heating.

The heat got into the corners of my room. Then my room started getting burning-hot while my mother's footsteps, light as the wind, kept clicking away on the other side of the wall, all inexperienced and naïve.

And if I had moved, I would have burned myself, and if I had changed positions, then the heat would have bitten into me.

And as soon as I thought that, I heard a little ring and a buzz—it was the glass breaking—and the most important heat rolled into the room from the sky or some place, the most deadly heat rolled into the room, and that very minute, I jumped up, screamed, and ran for my mother. "Mommy, Mommy, what was that? I could have burned! Mommy!"

"Take some aspirin and keep your head clear!" said my mother and went off to her date, the skinny little thing: click, click, click.

The Witch's Tears

The boards in the old sidewalk squeaked softly, as though they were breathing.

They still had those kinds of sidewalks —wooden ones—in Ordynsk. She was told to go down Sibirskaya Street first, to the news-stand, then left and down Burlinskaya to private houses, and then the left one was the witch's.

The girl had fifteen rubles and his photo ready. The photo was from before he met her, when he was just a baby soldier still with his deli-cate curls, with a light smile on his puffy lips.

She'd been told the witch's address by a friend—in confidence, of course. Galia had told her it was best to go late at night and have the money with you.

The sidewalk ended suddenly, and the girl stepped onto the ground. She could barely make out the outlines of a newsstand up ahead. When she reached it, the girl turned left down a street of wooden houses that were drowning in a black thicket of maple and bird-cherry trees. She walked down the dark street, past a row of houses that were guardedly silent—she'd heard a lot of Tatars lived here. They don't let their beautiful daughters marry Russian men.

Blood had been shed here recently…

The girl thought that she'd never be able to find the green house in the dark, but then right away she found it and knew that it was the green house, even though it was black like the rest of the street.

She knocked. Then she knocked again. And again.

Somebody sighed. Then she started knocking nonstop, shaking with all her body but pressing the strap of the flat white purse with fifteen rubles and his photo in it to her left shoulder.

There was a shed in the yard. There was a pig living in the shed, and it sighed.

"It's probably bewitched," thought the girl when she heard the pig oink. "The witch probably isn't home; she's probably out visiting somebody," she figured when no one opened the door.

But when she had finally given up and was ready to leave, the door softly opened a crack, and the smell of fried onions washed over her, and in the dim light escaping through the crack she saw the witch.

The witch asked nothing—just looked her over and turned her back to her and went back into the room, leaving the door as it was—half-open.

There was nothing for Nadia to do but go in uninvited. Using her purse to cover her heart, she stepped over the threshold, and the door immediately shut behind her with a loud bang, like it was angry.

"Must be the wind," thought Nadia, who felt less scared once she saw it was just a regular room. She walked into the middle of the room to the table covered with a pretty fresh tablecloth and stopped. She was looking around for the old lady.

There was a rug hanging on the wall, and on it there were two deer fighting. As Nadia stared at them, she realized she was holding something in her hands that started trembling, became warm, took some fearful breaths, and sprung out, flying up right by her face.

"My purse!" screamed Nadia, cautiously reaching for the white dove into which the fun-loving witch had transformed her purse.

She heard a laugh behind her back and laughed herself: the dove was really pretty, with prominent fragile wings and a curly crest on its round little head.

"Sit down, girl," said the witch, pointing to a Viennese chair by the window.

She sat down and looked at the witch, who turned out to be just an old woman in a strange linen dress that was very light and very sad and had big pockets on its long skirt, which fell in tired and sorry folds.

Meanwhile, the dove was walking up and down the table with no fear of them.

Only then did Nadia notice that on the dove's chest was a little pulsating and contracting heart that looked real (in fact, it was real, Nadia was sure). And what she thought most suspicious (though it's unclear why, since it didn't even scare her) was a small dark red spot in the middle of the heart. The spot looked solid and prominent, like a stone in a medallion. When light from the lamp fell on it, it radiated thin rays in response.

The witch started pacing the room, considering something, looking like she didn't notice Nadia. And the girl forced herself to take her enchanted stare off the dove and look at the witch. In addition to this dress, which had for some reason surprised Nadia, she had on little white socks and a pair of cheap—plastic—but cheerfully light sandals with wide straps. The witch's face was pale, very old, and somehow flat, as though it were painted on. Her whole being—tall and thin and very flat—seemed like a cardboard cutout.

The witch paced the room deliberately, not making a sound and not looking at Nadia or asking her anything.

Nadia, who suddenly felt shy, was also quiet. She was watching the old lady fearfully and obediently.

Suddenly, the yellow curtain on the window moved. The window wasn't closed—just covered by the curtain.

"It's quite possible that the curtain was moved by the wind," thought the girl, but she scrunched up anyway.

Behind the curtain, something was stirring, moving, pushing, and whining.

It was flowers. Heavy bunches of foamy-white, damp flowers were pushing against the curtain and babbling pathetically. They were pushing the curtain away with their stubborn little foreheads and starting to climb in through the window.

"Out! Out!" the witch screamed, stomping her feet and waving her arms until the flowers, squeaking, made themselves scarce.

These weren't flowers at all; they were light, round little baby heads.

To keep herself from dying of fear, the girl squeezed her knees together, pushed them down with her fists, and stuck her chin up high. She thought, "I am here to give it to him, to Vitka, my soldier. I should just say it and give her the money right away—just do it, just do it..."

She turned to the witch and opened her mouth.

"Hush, hush," the witch waved her away with her hand.

The hand was big, pale, and covered with freckles.

And then something horrible happened. Nadia knew that it was happening, and she knew where—on the table. And she knew that if she looked, her heart would break, she wouldn't be able to take it, but she couldn't not look—which is how it always is in life: the thing that's going to kill you attracts you. And her eyes, her crazed, wandering eyes, were pulled to the circle of light on the tablecloth. The dove—it was standing there frozen with its head cocked to the side. Its curly white crest looked like it was made out of plaster or soapy foam, like when you are a child and you are washing your hair, and after you soap it up, you stand in front of the window making it into strange old-fashioned hairdos...Its eyes were glazed over. The dove was asleep, oblivious to what was happening, not knowing, not sensing that its own beak was growing, getting longer and bending and reaching for the little golden heart, frozen in frightful anticipation.

"I'm not going to look, I'm not going to look," the girl mumbled, as her eyes bugged out. She was struggling, but she knew what was going to happen now. And she knew why.

The beak felt for the heart and found it and lightly pierced the dark red droplet and drank it. It wasn't a stone; it was blood in a thin coating of film, which the beak ripped through and drank the droplet, leaving only an empty hollow, like when you take a stone out of a ring. And then the heart shivered and froze, and the dove, which had killed itself, fell onto the table with its wings spread out and its beak, meek as before, half-open.

The girl was no longer certain that she was doing the right thing, and she felt weak all over like after an illness. But she was firm in her resolve.

"I don't care," she said stubbornly. "I want trouble for him. He lied to me—he didn't marry me—and I killed my baby. Give him trouble."

"Get up," said the witch, and the girl stood up.

"You are going to do as I say. If you say even one word, it won't work. Give me the picture."

The girl picked her white purse up off the table, took out the picture, glancing at it quickly: he was real young in it, a clear-eyed little soldier.

"Are your intentions pure?" asked the witch.

And she was about to say that they were when she realized that she was supposed to be quiet and that the witch was asking on purpose, trying to trip her up like in a children's game. So she didn't say anything—let her think that she had impure intentions and not just pain and despair. She stood there handing the witch the picture of his face, and the witch took it and even looked at it, and then threw it into a pot that was all black and covered with soot, and threw some kind of grass in after it and poured in water, and then suddenly there was a weak little blue fire under the pot and suffocating steam coming from nowhere. The witch looked in the pot, muttered something, moved her hands over it, and started yawning, which meant, as Nadia had been told, that she'd summoned the evil spirits. And a little cloud appeared beside her, and there was a little person standing in the cloud and waving his arms and looking around all funny. It was him!

It all ended when the witch stopped yawning and moved her hand over the pot for the last time and everything disappeared. She took the pot into the kitchen, came back, and sat across from Nadia, looking through her, looking pale and like she was about to fall asleep. She was rocking in her chair, thinking. Did she send him trouble already? Could she go now? But the girl was quiet, remembering that she wasn't allowed to talk.

"You are going to go to the river now. You'll walk backwards, without looking. You'll walk until I say 'Stop.' Then you'll take the stocking off your left leg and a hair off your left temple, and then he'll have trouble—"

She stood up and went outside, and the witch followed her. She walked backward toward the river, without looking, walking and looking at the witch, who was coming at her, staring at her with an empty stare. She was doing everything to give him trouble! It was so scary! They walked down the Tatar street, where blood was shed, where they don't let their daughters marry Russians...One streetlight was on and the next one was off, on then off, on then off...the witch was coming at her, and she was walking backward, like she'd said, just like she told her, but it was like the witch was after her and she was escaping. The street ended, and she felt a fresh breeze off the river at her back. It started to smell like water, mud, and black oil. There was the sound of a ship's horn somewhere. There was sand under her feet. Could she look up? She wouldn't say anything—just look. There were stars above, blinking, looking at her making trouble for her beloved. Oh, how he loved her, how tender he was, how passionate—the words he would whisper to her...And now she was making trouble for him...But how he tormented her! What was she supposed to do? Now she was going to stop and take the stocking off her left leg...Vitka's heart was going to start aching, he was going to suffer and start withering, and then wither and die. He'd cheated on her. No more. But when was she supposed to stop? The stars in the sky were shivering, raising a ruckus—what were they trying to tell her? It was going to be soon, soon...It was all his fault. The pain she had to go through because of him, the fear! It wasn't going to be long now. That would be the end of him. The end. Of him...the end. She'd have no one to pine away over, no one to curse. The world would be empty. It would always be night...

It wasn't too late yet. She should stop. She should say something. Or else she'd have no one to pine away over.

There was water under her feet now—oh, she should stop...The water was cold. She wanted to go home and drink warm milk with honey and go to sleep, soaking her pillow with tears. The water was squeezing her legs together now, her stomach, it was cold against her chest. She liked sleeping at home in bed with her cat Murka, and seeing geraniums in the window at sunrise through her sleepy eyelids...Then in the morning she would go to work and then to the movies with the girls.

The water was at her throat already...

No one should ever kill anyone!

"Granny, I..." and then air bubbles.

"Oh, Marekyare! Oh, Marekyare!" the voices on the ship were screaming. Cheerful lights were going by. The people on the ship couldn't see that there was an old woman in white standing on the shore, her face turned upward, her arms hanging limp by her sides. Then she plodded home. She turned on the light in the empty room, tidied up, put the chairs where they belonged, and sat down by the window. She waited. There was a moan at the window, and a wet ghost flew in wearing a soaked undershirt, dripping water.

The ghost fell to her knees and stretched her pale arms toward the old woman. "You killed me! You killed me instead of him! Make trouble! Make trouble for him, too, then!"

"Go away. Your place is there now, on the river. You'll be a river light. You'll fly over the beacons, see the ships off, scare the buoy keepers. That's your place now. That's your freedom."

The ghost crawled around at the old woman's feet, begging for trouble.

"Go away. Who wants trouble for their beloved?"

The ghost flew away. The old woman wiped the floor dry. She sat down by the window again, but she wasn't waiting. She was crying. She felt bad for the poor girl—so young. But the little soldier was sleeping peacefully. He didn't know anything. And no one was going to hurt him now.

Kindness is easy, light, and open; it has no fear—only joy. But when suffering turns to evil and evil is awakened, no one can tell what kind of torment it can bring, guided only by pain and injustice.

Books from Cleis Press

FICTION

Another Love by Erzsébet Galgóczi.
ISBN: 0-939416-52-2 24.95 cloth;
ISBN: 0-939416-51-4 8.95 paper.

Cosmopolis: Urban Stories by Women edited by Ines Rieder.
ISBN: 0-939416-36-0 24.95 cloth;
ISBN: 0-939416-37-9 9.95 paper.

Dirty Weekend: A Novel of Revenge by Helen Zahavi.
ISBN: 0-939416-85-9 10.95 paper.

A Forbidden Passion by Cristina Peri Rossi.
ISBN: 0-939416-64-0 24.95 cloth;
ISBN: 0-939416-68-9 9.95 paper.

Half a Revolution: Contemporary Fiction by Russian Women edited and translated by Masha Gessen.
ISBN: 1-57344-007-8 $29.95 cloth;
ISBN: 1-57344-006-X $12.95 paper.

In the Garden of Dead Cars by Sybil Claiborne.
ISBN: 0-939416-65-4 24.95 cloth;
ISBN: 0-939416-66-2 9.95 paper.

Night Train To Mother by Ronit Lentin.
ISBN: 0-939416-29-8 24.95 cloth;
ISBN: 0-939416-28-X 9.95 paper.

The One You Call Sister: New Women's Fiction edited by Paula Martinac.
ISBN: 0-939416-30-1 24.95 cloth;
ISBN: 0-939416031-X 9.95 paper.

Only Lawyers Dancing by Jan McKemmish.
ISBN: 0-939416-70-0 24.95 cloth;
ISBN: 0-939416-69-7 9.95 paper.

Unholy Alliances: New Women's Fiction edited by Louise Rafkin.
ISBN: 0-939416-14-X 21.95 cloth;
ISBN: 0-939416-15-8 9.95 paper.

The Wall by Marlen Haushofer.
ISBN: 0-939416-53-0 24.95 cloth;
ISBN: 0-939416-54-9 paper.

We Came All The Way from Cuba So You Could Dress Like This?: Stories by Achy Obejas.
ISBN: 0-939416-92-1 24.95 cloth;
ISBN: 0-939416-93-X 10.95 paper.

LATIN AMERICA

Beyond the Border: A New Age in Latin American Women's Fiction edited by Nora Erro-Peralta and Caridad Silva-Núñez.
ISBN: 0-939416-42-5 24.95 cloth;
ISBN: 0-939416-43-3 12.95 paper.

The Little School: Tales of Disappearance and Survival in Argentina by Alicia Partnoy.
ISBN: 0-939416-08-5 21.95 cloth;
ISBN: 0-939416-07-7 9.95 paper.

Revenge of the Apple by Alicia Partnoy.
ISBN: 0-939416-62-X 24.95 cloth;
ISBN: 0-939416-63-8 8.95 paper.

You Can't Drown the Fire: Latin American Women Writing in Exile edited by Alicia Partnoy.
ISBN: 0-939416-16-6 24.95 cloth;
ISBN: 0-939416-17-4 9.95 paper.

LESBIAN STUDIES

Boomer: Railroad Memoirs by Linda Niemann.
ISBN: 0-939416-55-7 12.95 paper.

The Case of the Good-For-Nothing Girlfriend by Mabel Maney.
ISBN: 0-939416-90-5 24.95 cloth;
ISBN: 0-939416-91-3 10.95 paper.

The Case of the Not-So-Nice Nurse by Mabel Maney.
ISBN: 0-939416-75-1 24.95 cloth;
ISBN: 0-939416-76-X 9.95 paper.

Dagger: On Butch Women edited by Roxxie, Lily Burana, Linnea Due.
ISBN: 0-939416-81-6 29.95 cloth;
ISBN: 0-939416-82-4 14.95 paper.

Daughters of Darkness: Lesbian Vampire Stories edited by Pam Keesey.
ISBN: 0-939416-77-8 24.95 cloth;
ISBN: 0-939416-78-6 9.95 paper.

Different Daughters: A Book by Mothers of Lesbians edited by Louise Rafkin.
ISBN: 0-939416-12-3 21.95 cloth;
ISBN: 0-939416-13-1 9.95 paper.

Different Mothers: Sons & Daughters of Lesbians Talk About Their Lives edited by Louise Rafkin.
ISBN: 0-939416-40-9 24.95 cloth;
ISBN: 0-939416-41-7 9.95 paper.

Dyke Strippers: Lesbian Cartoonists A to Z edited by Roz Warren.
ISBN: 1-57344-009-4 29.95 cloth;
ISBN: 1-57344-008-6 16.95 paper.

Girlfriend Number One: Lesbian Life in the 90s edited by Robin Stevens.
ISBN: 0-939416-79-4 29.95 cloth;
ISBN: 0-939416-8 12.95 paper.

Hothead Paisan: Homicidal Lesbian Terrorist by Diane DiMassa.
ISBN: 0-939416-73-5 14.95 paper.

A Lesbian Love Advisor by Celeste West.
ISBN: 0-939416-27-1 24.95 cloth;
ISBN: 0-939416-26-3 9.95 paper.

Long Way Home: The Odyssey of a Lesbian Mother and Her Children by Jeanne Jullion.
ISBN: 0-939416-05-0 8.95 paper.

More Serious Pleasure: Lesbian Erotic Stories and Poetry edited by the Sheba Collective.
ISBN: 0-939416-48-4 24.95 cloth;
ISBN: 0-939416-47-6 9.95 paper.

The Night Audrey's Vibrator Spoke: A Stonewall Riots Collection by Andrea Natalie.
ISBN: 0-939416-64-6 8.95 paper.

Queer and Pleasant Danger: Writing Out My Life by Louise Rafkin.
ISBN: 0-939416-60-3 24.95 cloth;
ISBN: 0-939416-61-1 9.95 paper.

Rubyfruit Mountain: A Stonewall Riots Collection by Andrea Natalie.
ISBN: 0-939416-74-3 9.95 paper.

Serious Pleasure: Lesbian Erotic Stories and Poetry edited by the Sheba Collective.
ISBN: 0-939416-46-8 24.95 cloth;
ISBN: 0-939416-45-X 9.95 paper.

SEXUAL POLITICS

Good Sex: Real Stories from Real People, second edition, by Julia Hutton.
ISBN: 1-57344-001-9 29.95 cloth;
ISBN: 1-57344-000-0 14.95 paper.

The Good Vibrations Guide to Sex: How to Have Safe, Fun Sex in the '90s by Cathy Winks and Anne Semans.
ISBN: 0-939416-83-2 29.95;
ISBN: 0-939416-84-0 14.95 paper.

Madonnarama: Essays on Sex and Popular Culture edited by Lisa Frank and Paul Smith.
ISBN: 0-939416-72-7 24.95 cloth;
ISBN: 0-939416-71-9 9.95 paper.

Public Sex: The Culture of Radical Sex by Pat Califia.
ISBN: 0-939416-88-3 29.95 cloth;
ISBN: 0-939416-89-1 12.95 paper.

Sex Work: Writings by Women in the Sex Industry edited by Frédérique Delacoste and Priscilla Alexander.
ISBN: 0-939416-10-7 24.95 cloth;
ISBN: 0-939416-11-5 16.95 paper.

Susie Bright's Sexual Reality: A Virtual Sex World Reader by Susie Bright.
ISBN: 0-939416-58-1 24.95 cloth;
ISBN: 0-939416-59-X 9.95 paper.

Susie Bright's Sexwise by Susie Bright.
ISBN: 1-57344-003-5 24.95 cloth;
ISBN: 1-57344-002-7 10.95 paper.

Susie Sexpert's Lesbian Sex World by Susie Bright.
ISBN: 0-939416-34-4 24.95 cloth;
ISBN: 0-939416-35-2 9.95 paper.

REFERENCE

Putting Out: The Essential Publishing Resource Guide For Gay and Lesbian Writers, third edition, by Edisol W. Dotson.
ISBN: 0-939416-86-7 29.95 cloth;
ISBN: 0-939416-87-5 12.95 paper.

POLITICS OF HEALTH

The Absence of the Dead Is Their Way of Appearing by Mary Winfrey Trautmann.
ISBN: 0-939416-04-2 8.95 paper.

AIDS: The Women edited by Ines Rieder and Patricia Ruppelt.
ISBN: 0-939416-20-4 24.95 cloth;
ISBN: 0-939416-21-2 9.95 paper

Don't: A Woman's Word by Elly Danica.
ISBN: 0-939416-23-9 21.95 cloth;
ISBN: 0-939416-22-0 8.95 paper

1 in 3: Women with Cancer Confront an Epidemic edited by Judith Brady.
ISBN: 0-939416-50-6 24.95 cloth;
ISBN: 0-939416-49-2 10.95 paper.

Voices in the Night: Women Speaking About Incest edited by Toni A. H. McNaron and Yarrow Morgan.
ISBN: 0-939416-02-6 9.95 paper.

With the Power of Each Breath: A Disabled Women's Anthology edited by Susan Browne, Debra Connors and Nanci Stern.
ISBN: 0-939416-09-3 24.95 cloth;
ISBN: 0-939416-06-9 10.95 paper.

Woman-Centered Pregnancy and Birth by the Federation of Feminist Women's Health Centers.
ISBN: 0-939416-03-4 11.95 paper.

AUTOBIOGRAPHY, BIOGRAPHY, LETTERS

Peggy Deery: An Irish Family at War by Nell McCafferty.
ISBN: 0-939416-38-7 24.95 cloth;
ISBN: 0-939416-39-5 9.95 paper.

The Shape of Red: Insider/Outsider Reflections by Ruth Hubbard and Margaret Randall.
ISBN: 0-939416-19-0 24.95 cloth;
ISBN: 0-939416-18-2 9.95 paper.

Women & Honor: Some Notes on Lying by Adrienne Rich.
ISBN: 0-939416-44-1 3.95 paper.

ANIMAL RIGHTS

And a Deer's Ear, Eagle's Song and Bear's Grace: Relationships Between Animals and Women edited by Theresa Corrigan and Stephanie T. Hoppe.
ISBN: 0-939416-38-7 24.95 cloth;
ISBN: 0-939416-39-5 9.95 paper.

With a Fly's Eye, Whale's Wit and Woman's Heart: Relationships Between Animals and Women edited by Theresa Corrigan and Stephanie T. Hoppe.
ISBN: 0-939416-24-7 24.95 cloth;
ISBN: 0-939416-25-5 9.95 paper.